R

Mack Bolan had long accepted he was living on borrowed time

Over countless missions he had gambled against the odds, and as time went by he realized those odds were becoming slimmer with every mission he accepted.

Stepping as he did into the killing grounds, facing enemies intent on turning Bolan's world into a savage hell on earth, he saw himself not as some indestructible automaton, but a normal guy doing extraordinary things by simply refusing to give in to savage man. The rules devised for civilized existence were being trampled into the dust by the hyenas walking around on two legs.

Mack Bolan did what he could to bring some kind of sanity to the evils perpetrated by the spoilers.

Other titles available in this series:

Shock Tactic	A Dying Evil
Showdown	Deep Treachery
Precision Kill	War Load
Jungle Law	Sworn Enemies
Dead Center	Dark Truth
Tooth and Claw	Breakaway
Thermal Strike	Blood and Sand
Day of the Vulture	Caged
Flames of Wrath	Sleepers
High Aggression	Strike and Retrieve
Code of Bushido	Age of War
Terror Spin	Line of Control
Judgment in Stone	Breached
Rage for Justice	Retaliation
Rebels and Hostiles	Pressure Point
Ultimate Game	Silent Running
Blood Feud	Stolen Arrows
Renegade Force	Zero Option
Retribution	Predator Paradise
Initiation	Circle of Deception
Cloud of Death	Devil's Bargain
Termination Point	False Front
Hellfire Strike	Lethal Tribute
Code of Conflict	Season of Slaughter
Vengeance	Point of Betrayal
Executive Action	Ballistic Force
Killsport	Renegade
Conflagration	Survival Reflex
Storm Front	Path to War
War Season	Blood Dynasty
Evil Alliance	Ultimate Stakes
Scorched Earth	State of Evil
Deception	Force Lines
Destiny's Hour	Contagion Option
Power of the Lance	Hellfire Code

Don Pendleton's Mack Bolan®

War Drums

A GOLD EAGLE BOOK FROM

W RLDWIDE®

TORONTO • NEW YORK • LONDON
AMSTERDAM • PARIS • SYDNEY • HAMBURG
STOCKHOLM • ATHENS • TOKYO • MILAN
MADRID • WARSAW • BUDAPEST • AUCKLAND

First edition July 2007

ISBN-13: 978-0-373-61518-6
ISBN-10:   0-373-61518-3

Special thanks and acknowledgment to
Mike Linaker for his contribution to this work.

WAR DRUMS

All ambitions are lawful except those
which climb upward on the miseries or
credulities of mankind.
> —Joseph Conrad,
> 1857–1924

Jackals in human form are quick to cash in on
the misery of their fellow man. I do what I can
whenever I can to even the odds.
> —Mack Bolan

PROLOGUE

London, England

He never saw his killer. At the last moment he heard a faint click as someone eased off a safety. Before that, nothing. Whoever had come to end his life was good. That he had got this close meant he was better than good. And the sudden realization that he was about to die brought a rush of emotions and an overwhelming sadness that unrealized dreams would now never be. In the final moment he did make an attempt to pull out his own weapon, but the very act of reaching for it became his last. The bullet that blew apart his skull impacted a scant second before the second one followed. He felt only a solid blow that completely took away all of his senses in the ferocity of its effect on his brain and the functions it had controlled. There was no sound. No time to think about what had happened. Just that stunning blow that wiped his life away in an instant. The second bullet cored its way through and blew out his left eye. His body lurched forward, then dropped to the ground in the fluid slackness that comes only with death. There was no grace in his demise, simply the collapsing of a lifeless corpse that had only seconds before been a living, breathing man.

The body lay for almost twenty minutes before it was spotted by an employee of one of the restaurants the alley ran behind. Stepping outside for a cigarette the kitchen assistant almost tripped over the corpse. He recoiled at the sight of the body and the pooling, drying blood that had edged out from beneath the head. He stood for a few seconds, simply staring, uncertain what to do now that he found himself confronted by the corpse of someone who had been the victim of a violent death. He turned and went back inside to let others know what he had found, then made his way to a telephone to inform the police.

TWENTY MINUTES LATER THE crime scene team showed up. The metropolitan police cruiser that arrived earlier had cordoned off the area, holding back onlookers so the crime scene was untouched. With practiced efficiency the CS team marked possible relevant evidence, took photographs and checked the vicinity. When they were satisfied, they had the body removed, the contents of the victim's pockets tagged and bagged and sent to the CS lab. In due course fingerprints were taken and fed into NAFIS, the UK cousin to the American AFIS system. It was, due to the current security conditions, connected to the U.S. database and it was able to identify the dead man. According to the criminal database the deceased was one Harry Vincent. NAFIS threw up a rap sheet that showed Vincent to have been arrested twice in the U.S. for suspected arms trafficking, but insufficient evidence had meant he was never charged. He had done time in prison for minor criminal acts. His background read like a familiar story of early criminal activity that continued into adult life. Certain questions arose that the UK police needed answers to. The main one concerned the seeming ability of a known criminal to be able to move back and forth, through customs, without his past raising a flag.

Before the police could continue their investigation, matters were taken from their hands in the form of agents from the London field office of the CIA stepping in with a claim for Harry Vincent. Protests were stepped on harshly by orders from the higher-ups in Scotland Yard, who had received their instructions from MI-5, acting on calls originating in Langley, Virginia. Everything referring to Harry Vincent was confiscated by the CIA. Their was a brief flurry of protest that ran all the way up to the top and back. At each level, those in control were given the stern warning to stand down. This was not a request, it was a top-priority command. Those who had identified Harry Vincent were told to forget about him. They found their computer access blocked, all references to Harry Vincent deleted. The phrases "need to know" and "in the national interest" were trotted out. That didn't settle too well with the police department, but in the era of cooperation and national-international security, any tardiness was frowned on when it came to interfering with due process. The CIA team did its work with cool efficiency, whisking away Harry Vincent, his belongings and all the data gathered by the police. By the end of the day it was as if Vincent had never existed.

In truth he never had.

Only those at the uppermost level knew that Harry Vincent was simply the cover identity created by the CIA's Deep Cover section for one of their agents. His fingerprints, fed into NAFIS, then AFIS, had set of alarm bells at Langley. Langley had informed the London field office, issuing a removal authorization that entitled the team to acquire Vincent and all relevant data. The body was driven directly to a small airstrip used by the CIA and put on a plane that would finally deliver Harry Vincent to Langley, Virginia.

CHAPTER ONE

Stony Man Farm, Virginia

Two days later Hal Brognola, director of the Sensitive Operations Group, based at Stony Man Farm, received an urgent summons that took him directly to the White House where he was ushered in to see the President of the United States. The big Fed was sequestered with the Man for almost two hours. When he left, with a briefcase holding a "need to know" file, he returned to Stony Man. During the helicopter flight, he sent an e-mail directive requesting an immediate mission briefing. On touchdown he went directly to the office he used while at the farm and made four copies of the file, then headed to the War Room.

Those in attendance were Barbara Price, mission controller, and Aaron Kurtzman, the facility's cybernetics chief. The third person he had requested was missing.

"Where is he?" Brognola growled as he sat, opened his briefcase and slapped the presidential files on the conference table.

"He's on his way," Price said. Concentrating on her own

paperwork, he maintained a calm manner, hoping that her emotions didn't betray her.

Brognola sorted the files, muttering to himself, and failed to hear the door open and close behind him.

"Time on this is scarce," Brognola said sharply.

"I'm all ears, Hal."

Brognola glanced up to see Mack Bolan facing him across the table, a slight smile on his face. The big Fed loosened his crumpled tie and opened the top button on his shirt. He noticed that Bolan looked cool and relaxed in clean, casual clothing, his hair still holding the damp shine from a recent shower.

"By the look of you, I'm being too easy. Not interrupting your free time am I?"

Bolan sat. "Not right now. R and R is over."

If he hadn't been so immersed in his paperwork Brognola might have noticed the sudden rush of color that invaded Price's cheeks. It was only Kurtzman who picked up on it and chose to ignore it, sliding out a computer keyboard from the table, busying himself logging on. For the briefest moment Price's eyes caught Bolan's and they exchanged a fleeting smile. Then the soldier turned his steady gaze on Brognola.

"So what have you got, Hal?"

Brognola slid the a copy of the file to each person in the room and sat back while they read and digested the data inside. He allowed them the time they needed before clearing his throat to open the discussion.

"Comments?"

"Why us?" Price asked. "I mean, the President has lifted the case from the CIA and pushed it our way."

"Plain and simple. The President wants Stony Man to handle this. He had a visit from the CIA special ops director, and from what he told me the U.S. is in a fix over this Iranian deal.

Intel has Iran's hard-liners pushing for their own nuclear capability in defiance of UN rulings. They're doing their damnedest to refine weapon's grade plutonium and intelligence sources say they have some underground development work on the technical side."

"Hardly a threat in the short term," Price said.

"No one is expecting them to suddenly have fleets of ICBMs targeting New York," Brognola replied. "But the very thought of Iran having any kind of nuke is sending shivers all across the Middle East, especially in the direction of Israel."

"Those hard-liners have been laying it down pretty fierce," Aaron Kurtzman pointed out. "They blame Israel for every problem in the region. I understand the rhetoric involved in politics. It's all to do with psyching out the enemy, but in an area like the Middle East it's very easy to start the fires."

"If Israel gets pushed too far she might use one of her own surgical strikes against Iran," Bolan said. "Preemptive. It wouldn't be the first time."

"Exactly. If that happens, we could end up with one hell of a conflict. But there's more to it. The President has intel that points to Chinese involvement, behind-the-scenes courting of Ayatollah Muhar Razihra. He's the man behind the belligerent criticism of Israel and the West. The Chinese are promoting themselves as the emerging political and market successor to the U.S. They have their eye on the future *and* Iran's oil reserves. Iran as a superpower, wielding the strength of nuclear capability in the region means they'll have clout. Beijing hasn't been slow at seeing the benefits of wooing the Iranians. The country is oil rich. And oil is as important to China as it is to us. The Chinese are willing to work at this over the long term."

"What about the rest of the region?" Bolan asked.

"Unrest. Negative feelings where it comes to Iran becoming nuclear. That's another of the President's concerns. We all understand the uncertainty in the region in general. All it needs is one country suddenly having a big stick they can use it to intimidate other countries."

"What about Iran's moderates?" Price asked. "Isn't there a calming influence?"

Kurtzman nodded. "Sure. There are government members who want to stay out of the nuclear club. They see the problems on the horizon. Right now they seem to be shouted down at every turn and the problem is they don't have enough backing from the military or the religious community, which Razihra does."

"Aaron, put up those images I sent you," Brognola said.

Kurtzman tapped his keyboard and one of the wall screens lit up.

"The guy on the right in the black robes is Ayatollah Razihra. He's the big gun in the pro-nuke debate. His direct opponent is Nuri Masood, a government minister who argues against the program. That's him in the middle. On the left is Dr. Shahan Baresh. He works under Masood, and he's a skilled negotiator who does all the Iranian dealings with the UN and other groups trying to ease the tension. He spends a great deal of his time out of the country in meetings, seminars, doing his best to promote a better image for Iran."

"I've heard about Razihra," Price said. "He's not the kind of man you'd want standing against you."

"I imagine this is only part of the picture, Hal," Bolan said.

"Oh, yes." Brognola tapped the file in front of him. "The CIA had a man infiltrated into a group that has been supplying the Iran Secret Service with conventional weapons and technical data on the construction and deployment of nuclear weaponry. This sweet bunch has even been negotiating with them to purchase this information and hardware. If the Iranians get their hands on this data, it gives them a jump-start on their development program. If they aren't already up and running.

"The CIA director had initiated the covert operation himself, choosing his own agent and keeping it close to his chest after getting the go from the Man. It appeared to be running pretty smoothly until a few days ago when the undercover agent was assassinated in London. Professional hit. Two shots to the back of the head. The agent was working under the name Harry Vincent. When Scotland Yard put the name through their system it went all the way to Langley and was red-flagged in the director's office. The numbers clicked in and Vincent's body was appropriated by the CIA's London field office and flown back to CIA headquarters. The director did his best to keep the details under wraps, but the killing made him suspicious and he went straight to the President. He suspected he had a leak within the Agency. The President took over the covert operation and told the director he'd take care of it."

"He didn't mention us?" Price asked.

"How could he?" Kurtzman asked. "We don't exist."

"Exactly," Brognola agreed. "The President hinted the military would look into the matter and told the director it would be dealt with. I guess the director would have been relieved to have it taken off his hands. He's going to have enough explaining to do over the Agency leak."

"So we pick up the slack again," Price commented.

"It's what we do best," Brognola said. "The director handed over all the intel his agent had gathered. His real name, by the way, was Carl Marchesse. Thirty-four years old. Native New Yorker. Joined the Agency when he was twenty-two and worked his way up through the ranks. Seems he showed a flair for undercover work early on. Worked a number of assignments that gained him a lot of brownie points. Five years ago he was recruited into a special ops section, specializing in the really down and dirty covert operations. He did well. When the Iranian operation was set up around five months ago, Marchesse was the man the director chose. He disappeared for a couple of months and when he resurfaced he was Harry Vincent. According to the director, he infiltrated the group suspected of providing the Iranians with weapons and data on nuclear weapons. The group's headed by a Russian named Anatoly Nevski."

"If a double agent in the CIA ordered his murder," Bolan said, "all that intel is most likely in his hands, as well."

"Unfortunately that's probably true. Aaron, second file, please."

"The gaunt-looking guy is Dr. Gregori Malinski, a Russian nuclear physicist. After the Soviet Union collapsed he was more or less out of a job. He moved around and started to sell his knowledge on the open market to whoever would pay. Marchesse's intel told us the Iranians had him working big-time on their nuke development. But he dropped out of sight some days ago. Nevski had brokered Malinski's contract with Razihra and his military backers. From what Marchesse managed to pick up the Iranians are less than pleased about Gregori's jumping ship. It could be he left them at a critical stage in the development. If the Iranians had people clever enough to develop their own nuclear weapons they wouldn't have needed to buy Malinski."

"This is an old photo," Kurtzman said. "The girl is Malinski's estranged daughter, Sashia. She's management in an international travel agency. Hops around all over the place. Right now she's based in Paris. It might be that Malinski got in touch. It's a long shot, but it could happen. It would be helpful for us if he did. But not so much for Razihra."

"And this is because…?" Bolan asked.

"Malinski knows the location of the Iranian base where the nuclear development is taking place," Brognola said. "Also, he's just one of the equations in the picture."

"I get the feeling you're about to tell me what I'm about to let myself in for."

"That's my guy."

Kurtzman brought up more pictures. "This next batch show the members of the Russian syndicate Marchesse infiltrated. I mentioned Anatoly Nevski. He's the lean guy with the blond crew cut. He might look like California basketball player but don't be fooled by his good looks. He's the top man. Not exactly Russian *mafiya*, but no Mother Theresa, either. It isn't difficult to categorize him," Kurtzman said. He pushed at a thick file across the table for Bolan to scan. "Courtesy of your buddy Commander Valentine Seminov, Moscow OCD. His attached note says he would be most appreciative if you could 'take the piece of scum down.' Do that and he will forever be in your debt. Nevski is no more than a connected street thug. Background is pure Moscow underworld. Worked his way through the ranks. From street hustler, pimp, pusher to present day global arms dealer.

"When the Soviet regime collapsed, Nevski was in the front of local crime. Anything is fair game for the man. Stolen cars. Drugs. He was, and still is, one of Russia's promoters of the white-slave trade, snatching young women off the streets to put them into prostitution and porn. He trades them across Europe, the Middle East and here in the States."

"Sounds like a sweet guy," Price said.

"Nevski has a unique business procedure," Kurtzman went on. "If he takes a liking to your business, he makes a single, time-limited offer. If you say no he sends in his people and you get a bullet to the back of the head. Deal settled. No sentiment. No reasoning."

Bolan was leafing through the file. "How did he segue into the arms business?"

"He saw the opportunities when the Soviet military machine started to fall apart. He nurtured contacts, wiped out a couple of smaller dealers and took their place. No hassle. He surrounded himself with plenty of muscle and firepower, and within twelve months he was one of the major players. He added industrial espionage and technical expertise to his catalog."

"Which brings us back to the good Dr. Malinski," Brognola said.

"Nevski looks for what the client wants, makes them a good offer because money is never a problem in this market," Kurtzman said. "He sets up the whole package and delivers."

"A nuclear physicist to jump-start your missile program," Bolan added.

"Exactly."

"But Malinski going AWOL has spoiled his customer satisfaction record."

Kurtzman nodded. "Damn right. It isn't going to make him popular with Ayatollah Razihra. Nevski will do anything to stay on Razihra's good side. The word is Nevski is in very deep with the Ayatollah. This is more than just a one-off contract. Nevski is with Razihra for the long term. He's realized the profit margin that staying with the guy will bring. So he's in there pitching. Anything Razihra wants Razihra gets."

"So he quickly gets rid of the CIA mole as soon as he's been exposed," Brognola said. "We were right it being a professional hit."

Kurtzman tapped in another image. "The scowly guy is Nevski's second in command. Lem Kirov, all round bad guy. Unstable and very violent. Next up is Claude Stratton. Brit-

ish. He's a fixer, paymaster, dealer, for any number of dissi-
dent groups floating around Europe and the UK. He does a
lot of transactions for ex-Saddam Hussein loyalists, like these
three charmers—Ahmer Musak, Omar Jafir, Ibrahim Hassan.
They appear to have access to some of the money Hussein
stashed away. They're using it to help Razihra and keep things
hot in the region. They were all colonels in the Iraqi military.
Now they're being feted by militant Jordanians. They're holed
up in the desert at some training camp, along with some of
Razihra's hard-liners, led by Yamir Kerim. Marchesse knew
that a consignment of weapons was shipped out to this camp.
He never got the chance to find out what it was for."

"Educated guess?" Bolan asked and answered the question
himself. "Israel?"

"Borders Jordan. And we know Razihra is anti-Israel. It's
one of his main political rants," Kurtzman said. "And why
would weapons be delivered to Jordan if they were intended
for Iran? Too far to risk transporting all that way. Could be
part of Razihra's aim. He doesn't hide the fact he wants Israel destabilized. To be frank, his ideal would be Israel up in
smoke."

"If Razihra's group has its way, it will boost its standing
within the radicals across Iran," Brognola said "It would
strengthen their cause. A victory over the current administration isn't what Iran needs. It could make for an isolationist
condition that would back them up against the wall. It could
happen if Razihra plays to fundamentalist emotions. The man
in the street already sees the West and Israel as the brokers of
everything going wrong in the region. If Razihra gets his
hands on the reins we can kiss goodbye to any negotiations.
And that feeling could spread beyond Iran's borders."

"According to the intelligence progress reports, Iranian nuclear development is still on a low learning curve," Bolan stated.

"For now. Getting his hands on U.S. data and hardware is going help Razihra make a big jump in nuclear development," Brognola said.

"It won't get him a warehouse full of nukes. Having the instructions isn't the end of the R and D. His teams will still have to build the devices," Bolan said.

"That's why Razihra is buying the components. Nevski has been orchestrating the search. It was Marchesse's job to find out who was in the running and stop them," the big fed told them.

"Any leads?"

"Thin. Mainly what we have already gone over. He managed to pass along a few pointers to the director. You have his last one in your file."

"London?" Bolan queried.

"Yes. Activity appears to be fairly strong right now, according to security readouts. London's at the crossroads for international dealing, the jumping-off place for Europe and the Middle East. It's a financial hub, as well. You've been there before. You know the situation Wide-ranging cultural mix. Large urban sprawl. Easy place to hide. And Claude Stratton is based in London."

"I'll make it my starting point."

"There's an Air Force plane on standby," Brognola informed him. "I'll make the arrangements. Tell Barb what you need and it'll make the flight with you."

"Backup data to be forwarded?"

"As long as we can maintain contact, you'll receive it ASAP. Aaron will check out your communication gear before you leave."

"Fine."

"You need any local backup?" Brognola asked.

"I'll call if I do."

"Any local interference, just dial the number."

"Time to move out."

"Striker, stay sharp. Don't trust anyone. We don't know how deep this CIA connection to the opposition goes."

"Trust is for little children and old ladies," Bolan said. "I'm not expecting to meet many of either in the field."

"This could turn into one hell of a mess, Striker," Brognola said. "We don't want to be caught with our pants down if it blows up. Too much is at stake—future relations with less aggressive Middle East countries. Then there's Afghanistan watching what's going on. India and Pakistan edging around each other. If it comes out that U.S. technology has been assisting the Iranians, denying our complicity is going to be one hell of a job. And don't forget the Israelis. If they suffer any damage, they'll hit back hard and fast. Do what you have to. Find the players. Shut down the supply of U.S. data being fed to the Iranians. Take down Nevski's organization. See who and what's behind this Jordanian connection. You won't have any interference from U.S. security agencies. If you do, refer them to me and I'll field them to the Man. He's told me you have absolute authority to get what you want."

"Knowing that is going to make it so much easier out there," Bolan said dryly.

"Sad to see such blatant cynicism," Kurtzman said.

Bolan pushed to his feet. "I'll see you in thirty, Aaron. Just make sure my cell phone is fully charged."

"Give me your details and I'll make sure your flight is on standby," Price said. She knew Bolan would be moving out within a short time. Going back into the hell grounds to take on yet more faceless enemies in his continuing struggle.

As he stepped by her, the soldier briefly laid a big hand on her shoulder, then he was crossing the War Room, going out through the door and she knew the mission had started.

CHAPTER TWO

London, England

Claude Stratton lived in a mews apartment in Chelsea, a double garage taking up the lower floor, with the living quarters above. Sitting in his car across the street from the enclosed courtyard, Mack Bolan judged the place to be prohibitively expensive. For someone like Stratton it would be pocket change. Bolan read the profile Stony Man had provided during his flight to the UK. It had detailed Stratton's business ventures, his connections with various dubious organizations. Despite that, the man had never been convicted of any crime due to the fact Stratton was a clever man. His wealth allowed him the privilege of hiring the best lawyers available and their legal machinations kept him free and clear. Stratton was able to continue in business and stay one step ahead of prosecution.

This was Bolan's second day tailing the man, and during that time Stratton had done little to arouse suspicion. From what he had seen, Stratton lived a solitary life in London. He made few contacts during the time Bolan had been watching him, visiting exclusive stores, dining alone. If he was involved in anything big at the present time, he appeared to be playing a waiting game.

That changed late afternoon of the second day.

Bolan could see Stratton's silver Rolls-Royce parked outside the apartment. He was debating his strategy when a dark-colored Toyota slowed and turned into the mews, pulling up behind the Rolls. A dark-haired man climbed out and pressed the bell at Stratton's door. When the door opened Bolan caught a glimpse of Claude Stratton as the visitor stepped inside and the door closed. Bolan memorized the license plate on the Toyota. He turned on the cell phone Kurtzman had provided. It had Tri-Band connections and a dedicated e-mail interface. He logged on and established a connection, wrote and sent an e-mail request for a check on the UK registration of the Toyota. He received his reply in less than ten minutes.

The vehicle was registered to a Jason Novak, UK citizen. A check on the man revealed his business as an import-export dealer. His main client base was in the Middle East, and British Intelligence was investigating the possibility that he could be in the arms business, using his legitimate trading as cover.

Bolan logged out and switched off, checked his 93-R and exited the rental. Crossing the street, he entered the mews and walked to the big Rolls-Royce. He leaned against the side of the car and braced his heels to the ground, using his body to rock the vehicle. Nothing happened until he repeated the move, using more pressure, and heard the alarm system kick in. The shrill beeping sounded loud within the confines of the courtyard. Bolan flattened against the wall to the left of Stratton's front door and waited.

The door was yanked open and Stratton stood with the car's remote in his hand. He pointed it at the Rolls and depressed the button, shutting off the alarm. As he turned to reenter the apartment Bolan stepped into view, pressing the muzzle of the Beretta against Stratton's spine and urging him forward. As soon as they were inside, Bolan pushed the door shut behind him, locking the dead bolt.

"What the hell is this?" Stratton demanded. He had a soft face, and his loose double chin quivered with indignation. Bolan didn't miss the cold gleam in his eyes.

"Just a home visit," Bolan said, and pushed the 93-R hard into Stratton's soft flesh. "Keep quiet and let's get back upstairs."

Stratton had the sense to do what he was told and preceded Bolan up the stairs. If he had been planning any tricks, Bolan was ahead of him. As they reached the head of the stairs, the soldier edged around him and scanned the room that spread out to his left. Well appointed, with furnishings that had to have cost a small fortune, the living room had a wide window that overlooked the courtyard. Stratton's visitor, Jason Novak, was standing at the window. His lean features paled when he saw Bolan and the weapon he was carrying.

"Claude, what the hell is going—?"

"Novak, keep the hands where I can see them," Bolan ordered. He was running his free hand over Stratton as he spoke, checking the man for weapons and finding he was clean. "Stratton, sit over there. Do it now."

Bolan turned his attention back to Novak. "What's on the table today, Novak? Autorifles? RPGs? Electronic technology? You cut your deal yet?"

Novak didn't respond, but the expression on his face told Bolan he had touched a nerve.

"Don't tell this bastard a thing," Stratton said.

Bolan raised a hand in Novak's direction. "Take the jacket off."

"What?"

"The coat. On the floor."

Novak shrugged out of his jacket and dropped it on the carpet. A bolstered handgun rode his left hip, butt forward.

"Two fingers. Left hand. Take it out. Place it on the coffee table and join your pal." Bolan picked up the revolver, a 5-shot, .44-caliber Charter Arms Bulldog. He flipped out the cylinder and let the bullets drop to the carpet. "This has to be illegal, Novak. UK has a no handgun policy for civilians."

"So what's that in your hand, Yank? A stick of candy?"

"I admit to bending the rules."

Bolan had seen the sheets of paper spread over the surface of the coffee table. He scooped them up and checked them out. One was a list of ordnance, covering a wide spectrum of weapons from handguns to autorifles, machine guns and even explosives. There were details of a port of destination in Jordan. The other sheet that caught his eye was a letter of introduction, which had been signed by Stratton. The final item was an airline ticket and hotel reservation—again the destination was Jordan.

"You guys are making this too easy for me," Bolan said.

"I don't know who you are," Stratton said, sounding extremely nervous. He wasn't used to being threatened. "But you should understand this is something you don't want to get into."

"Uh-huh," Bolan said, "it's something you should have *got* out of. Now it's too late."

"Too late? What is this crap?" Stratton asked, his attempt at bluffing failed. He tried another tack. "You realize who I am?"

Bolan shook his head. "I only heard about you recently. From what I read I haven't missed a deal. You run errands for bottom-end terrorists. We'd call you a gofer in the States. Somebody calls you, fetch. Have I got it right?"

Stratton's plump face reddened at the insult. "You bastard. I don't run errands for anyone. *They* come to me. I…" He closed his mouth before he said too much.

"Okay, you got the drop on us," Novak said. "So who the hell are you? A cop? Not British. American? Some agency? You can't be CIA."

"Why not?" Bolan asked.

Because I have some kind of Agency protection. Was that what Novak meant?

"I…"

"Jesus, Novak, shut your bloody mouth," Stratton snapped. "Is this a rip-off?"

Bolan smiled. "You mean, a shakedown? I don't think so, Stratton." He folded the papers from the coffee table and slid them into a pocket inside his leather jacket.

That action forced Novak's hand. He lunged forward, ignoring the weapon in Bolan's hand, and cleared the coffee table in a desperate dive. One foot hit the top of the table, and he used it to propel himself at Bolan. In the fleeting moment before Novak made contact, Bolan saw Stratton move, too, pushing to his feet and turning toward an antique roll-top desk against one wall. He lost eye contact as Novak slammed into him, driving Bolan backward. They hit the room's end wall, the soldier feeling the hard impact.

Novak clawed at Bolan's throat, fingers attempting to gain a hold. He failed to divert his adversary's gun hand, and it cost him when the solid bulk of the 93-R slammed down across the side of his skull. The blow dazed him, and Bolan struck again, aware that Stratton was still in the game. Novak gasped, shaking his suddenly bloody head and slackened his grip on Bolan's throat. The soldier immediately slammed his left hand under Novak's chin, the heel impacting hard. Novak gagged, head arcing back, and Bolan swung the Beretta one more time, steel crunching against the other man's jaw. The blow spun Novak to one side and as he slumped to the carpet Bolan swiveled to face Stratton, and met the guy as he turned from the desk, his right fist gripping a SIG-Sauer P-226. The muzzle was already arcing in Bolan's direction, Stratton's flushed face taut with rage. The Executioner didn't hesitate, his finger stroking the 93-R's trigger. The pistol fired a suppressed 3-round burst into Stratton's chest. He fell back against the desk, eyes widening in total shock, sliding to the floor, facedown, the P-226 spilling from his limp fingers.

CHAPTER THREE

Bolan stood in the silence, shaking his head at the sudden change in the situation. Soft to hard in a matter of seconds. No way could these events be predetermined.

He stripped off Novak's belt and used it to secure the man's hands behind his back. He lifted the unconscious man onto the leather couch, then bent over Stratton and took his belt. Kneeling in front of Novak, he bound the man's ankles together.

Bolan took out his cell phone and made contacted Stony Man. The connection was smooth and fast in spite of various cutouts and Bolan asked for Brognola. When the big Fed came on the line, Bolan explained the situation and made his request.

"You sure on this, Striker?" Brognola asked, then caught himself. "I know you wouldn't be asking if you weren't."

"I need Stratton's body removed and Novak in secure—and I mean secure—isolation. We remove Stratton's Rolls from outside his place and have it hidden in a secure garage. Make it look like he's gone on a trip. Novak's car, as well. It might be less suspicious if his car is removed ASAP. It might give me some lead time. And Stratton's phone needs monitoring for any incoming calls."

"Give me his number and Aaron can access it and keep 24/7 surveillance. Anything else?"

"Not at the moment."

"I'll arrange the removals."

"Novak's flight isn't until tomorrow afternoon. I'll lay low until then. I also need a UK passport in Novak's name with my photo and details on it. A suggestion—have the removal team arrive late the evening. Less chance of anyone getting suspicious, or seeing it isn't Stratton driving away. As soon as it's done, I can leave and get back to the air base."

"Stay close, Striker, I'll call back with details."

BOLAN LOCATED THE SMALL, expensively fitted kitchen and made himself a mug of coffee. He took it back to the living room and waited for Novak to regain consciousness. The man eventually roused, groaning at the pain in his head. Blood had run heavily down his face and soaked the front of his shirt. He struggled against the bonds at his wrists and ankles. He finally raised his head and stared across the room at Bolan.

"What's your game?"

Bolan remained silent. He let it stretch, waiting until Novak looked around the room and saw Stratton's corpse.

"Jesus, is he dead?"

"He's dead. You can be next, Novak."

The man shook his head. "If you wanted that, I'd already be dead. You want something. So we have a trade-off coming."

"You can still end up like the deceased Mr. Stratton. Let's be clear, Novak. If I can get what I want, fine. If not, I can go with what I have."

"And what's that?" Novak's voice held a trace of a sneer.

"Your inventory. Your flight ticket and the reservation at Le Meridien Hotel in Aqaba, Jordan."

"Maybe I don't know what the hell you're talking about."

"Then we don't have anything to discuss," Bolan said, and reached for the Beretta on the coffee table. "Like I said, it makes no difference to me. Two dead is just as acceptable. Actually it would make my life easier."

BY THE TIME THE CLEANUP team arrived it was dark. Bolan had received an advance call and was there to let the four men into the apartment. They worked quickly and efficiently. Within twenty minutes Stratton's body had been taken outside and placed in the trunk of Novak's car. One of the men took the keys, slid behind the wheel and drove off. Novak, hands cuffed and mouth gagged, was taken out of the building and placed in the rear of the Rolls. All this was done with the minimum of fuss and at chosen moments so as not to alert anyone in the other apartments. There was only one of them that showed any light in a window, and close observation by the cleanup team ensured no one was watching. After the Rolls had driven out of the mews, the remaining member of the team handed Bolan a package.

"I believed this is what you've been waiting for, Cooper," he said, using Bolan's cover name.

"Thanks."

They were standing in the gloom of the apartment, all the lights turned off following Stratton's supposed departure.

"Novak?" Bolan asked.

"Don't worry about him. Where he's going they don't have guest telephones. He'll be out of circulation big-time until we get the word. Could be useful. We've been dying to get our hands on that character for some time. This gives us the opportunity to talk to him without his legal team breathing down our necks."

"If you get anything that might be of use to me, I'd appreciate the information."

"We know where to pass it along." The man pointed at the laptop. "Likewise, anything we can use."

"I'll give my people the word to download the contents soon as they can."

The apartment had offered up nothing else in the way of information. Bolan made and the cleanup man slipped out of the apartment, pulling the door shut behind them. They stayed out of the security light and left the quiet mews. Bolan crossed to his rental car, the cleanup man already out of sight on the far side of the street. He started the vehicle and swung it around, his destination the military airfield where he had landed in the UK.

Military Airbase, Oxford, UK

"DOWNLOAD COMPLETE," KURTZMAN said over the com link. "We'll go to work on the files and give you anything useful."

"Once I get to Jordan I might be out of touch for a while. There's no way of knowing how this is going to play out."

"Take it easy, big guy."

Brognola came on the line. "The package you asked for?" He was referring to the passport Bolan had requested.

"Looks good. I don't know how far it's going to get me," Bolan said. "If someone over there already knows Novak…"

"This is not a good idea," Barbara Price said over the multilink. "You're going to walk in blind."

"It's a chance I'll have to take," Bolan said. "I don't have much more to go on, so I have to take what I've got."

"Just watch yourself, Striker. Backup's here. Just remember that."

BOLAN, DRESSED CASUALLY AND carrying a small flight bag, arrived at Heathrow Airport well ahead of his flight time. He checked in and went to the departure lounge, bought himself a light snack and a coffee, and took a seat. He used the time to go over what he had already learned from his encounter with Stratton and Novak.

Prior to the arrival of the cleanup team, Novak had given Bolan what he wanted. The destination and time of a shipment that would complete his transaction with the group based in Jordan. Novak had finally accepted his delicate position in relation to staying alive. Stratton's unexpected death had shaken the man, and Bolan's cool demeanor had convinced him his continuing existence was dependant on cooperation.

Armed with that and the documents he had found Bolan was going to step into the viper's nest willingly. It wouldn't be the first time. He knew he was putting himself at risk, but there was no way he could control all aspects of any mission. A degree of calculated risk was there, and Bolan had to chance it. There was no other way of moving forward.

At the back of his mind lingered the suggestion of some kind of Agency involvement. And that was something that would keep the Executioner looking over his shoulder.

CHAPTER FOUR

Aqaba, Jordan

Bolan's flight touched down in Jordan just after noon. He hailed a taxi and headed to Le Meridien Hotel, where a room had been booked for Novak. Bolan checked in, went to his room and settled down to wait. When he had collected his key card, there had been a message waiting for Mr. Novak. It had informed him that he would be contacted and to wait at the hotel until then. There wasn't much Bolan could do until that contact was made. Nothing happened during the rest of the day, and after a meal, he turned in and slept.

BOLAN SAUNTERED OUT OF the bathroom of his hotel room, towelling his hair dry after a cooling shower. He dressed in black, lightweight clothing and lace-up boots, then crossed to look out the second-story window. The sun was already up over the busy city.

Because of the high security in Jordan, Bolan had been forced to enter the country without the benefit of weapons. He hadn't been happy with that idea, but he had been left with little choice. Somehow he was going to have to get his hands on some weapons.

As he considered his options, there was a light tap on his door.

"Who is it?"

"Clean towels, sir."

When Bolan cautiously opened the door he was confronted by a lean man in a creased, cream linen suit. The man held a well-used Browning Hi-Power pistol, and was pointing it directly at Bolan.

"Please step back, Mr. Novak," the man said politely. "I would hate to have to shoot you out here."

Bolan retreated. The man knew his business. He stayed far enough away from Bolan to avoid being jumped while keeping the 9 mm gun on target. However much he might have disliked the situation Bolan wasn't reckless enough to try to take the gun away from the man just yet. Not until he had gained some information at least.

The man followed Bolan inside, pushing the door shut with the heel of one worn and scuffed brown shoe. The cuffs of his pants were grubby around their frayed edges, and the overlong legs dragged on the floor when he stood still.

"Am I supposed to be expecting you?" Bolan asked. "Or is this just some local custom?"

The man's wrinkled brown face creased into a semblance of a smile. "You had a message waiting when you arrived?"

Bolan nodded. "It said to wait, so I waited." He turned and indicated his breakfast cart that had arrived minutes earlier. "You mind if I finish my coffee before it goes cold?"

The man gestured with the Browning, then went and sat on the other side of the room, the gun still trained on Bolan.

"You want any?"

The man shook his head. His black hair was worn thick and

long, and kept sliding over his left eye. He brushed it back with a flick of his hand.

Bolan drank his coffee. "You know who *I* am."

"Forgive me. I am Salim."

"And your job is to…?"

Salim smiled. "I am your escort."

"Why the gun?"

"To maintain mutual trust and ensure your good heath."

"You speak good English."

"Thank you. For an Englishman you have a very good American accent."

Bolan didn't miss a beat. "That's what happens when you spend too much time over there. I do a lot of business with the Yanks. Goes down better if they understand what I'm saying."

"I need to see your passport and a certain letter."

Bolan handed over the items and watched the man study them. Finally satisfied, Salim pushed them into a pocket.

"Time to go," he said.

Bolan pulled on his jacket. They left the room and made their way out of the hotel lobby without incident. Once outside, Salim guided Bolan to a black Audi. A solidly built man sat at the wheel. All Bolan saw were wide, powerful shoulders and a shaved head set on a thick neck.

"In the back," Salim said. He followed Bolan inside, then spoke in rapid Arabic to the driver. The Audi swung around and out of the hotel parking area, merging with the traffic.

"Are we doing business, Salim? Or are we just going to tour the city?"

"Enjoy, Mr. Novak. This is a beautiful city. Look at the architecture. The sea."

"I can do that on the travel channel."

"True, but not with all the ingredients. Television is a false medium. Not real. Like you, Mr. Novak. It only pretends to be what is is."

In that instant Bolan knew his claim to be Jason Novak hadn't been believed. He was ready to make a move when Salim suddenly lashed out with the Browning Hi-Power, striking him across the skull.

BOLAN AWOKE IN A SHADED room that held the stale odors of casual existence in the dusty shadows and a scent of danger that heightened his awareness.

He sat up, leaned against the wall at his back and took a look around. Shabby furniture occupied a shabby room. Sunlight permeated the thin blinds drawn across the windows. He was facing the door and as he focused his eyes, pushing back the dull ache from where Salim had struck him, he saw the man watching him. Salim said something and a second figure materialized from the far side of the room. The driver. On his feet he was tall, his dark features held an expression that suggested he was more than ready to inflict harm on Bolan.

"Tell me where Novak is. And refrain from maintaining this deception. I *know* you are not Novak. Your false identity was spotted at the airport. Whatever your intention, it has failed."

"It got you out in the open."

"Much good that will do."

"The game isn't over yet, Salim."

"If I shoot you now, it will most certainly be over."

Bolan ignored that. "I'd guess you need to know why I took Novak's place."

Salim stepped forward. "And you are going to tell me." It wasn't a question. "I am also still curious about Novak himself. Is he dead?"

"I'm sure you'd like that to be true. Novak dead means he

can't talk about you and your people. Sorry, but he's very much alive. The people who have him are very good at getting what they want. He'll tell them everything in time."

Salim closed in on Bolan, raising the pistol in his hand. "Death comes quickly in this country. Life can be cheap."

"But not from you, Salim. You need *my* secrets. Kill me, and you'll never find out what I've learned about your organization."

"Nothing. You know nothing." The words were spit out in an angry moment. He didn't believe Bolan. Salim was eager to inflict harm, but something held him back and the soldier figured he had his orders. His threats *were* threats and little more.

"Your employers believe that? Razihra? Yamir Kerim? Anatoly Nevski? Hard men to keep happy I'd say."

Bolan was deliberately goading Salim, using names he hoped would get a reaction. And they did. Salim failed to conceal his surprise. The man was nervous. Excitable. He turned and said something to his helper. The big man came forward, his large hands forming even larger fists.

"You *will* tell me all you know," Salim said. "I need to understand."

Bolan pushed slowly to his feet, watching the advancing figure. The man was slow, his movements heavy. No fast mover, Bolan realized. He'd work on that. The man depended on his strength, not his speed.

Salim was urging on his man now, his Arabic racing out in a continuous stream. The guy reached behind him and produced a broad knife. He cut the air with it to show Bolan what was coming.

"Yusef is very skilled with the blade," Salim said. "He can cut you and you will still live. Save yourself the pain and give me what I need."

Yusef leaned forward, the gleaming steel blade threatening Bolan.

"It is not too late."

Bolan ignored Salim's taunt. He stayed where he was a second longer, then spun hard and went low, driving a clenched fist into Yusef's groin, catching him unprotected. Bolan's fist went in deep, drawing a high yell from the guy. While Yusef's attention was centered on his pain, his stride faltered and Bolan reached out, grabbing the wrist of the knife hand. His grip secured, the Executioner turned his back on the guy, twisting the arm and bringing it across his shoulder so that when he applied unrelenting pressure against the natural bend of the arm, bone snapped.

The knife slipped from loose fingers. Keeping hold of the wrist, Bolan turned, staring directly into the face of the moaning assailant, then launched a crippling punch that crunched the side of Yusef's jaw with force enough to fracture the bone. The guy went down on his knees, lost in his new world of pain, blood dribbling from a slack mouth where teeth had dug into his cheek. Bolan slammed a brutal, sledgehammer blow to the back of Yusef's neck and he flopped to the floor and lay still.

Salim had moved up behind Yusef, not wanting to miss what was supposed to happen to the American. When Yusef went down, Salim was left exposed. Before he could recover, Bolan was on him. He closed his left hand over the barrel of the pistol, twisted hard. Salim's trigger finger, caught in the guard, snapped like a twig. He howled in pain and didn't stop until Bolan backhanded him across the side of the face, the blow stunning the man. Salim started to transfer his pistol to his other hand and Bolan kicked his feet from under him, dropping him to the dirty floor. He bent and took the pistol from Salim.

Bolan stepped close, running skilled hands over the man as he checked for more weapons. He found a couple of filled magazines for the Browning and little else except for some coins and crumpled banknotes. He found his passport and the Novak letter, which he retrieved. He slipped the Browning mags into his pocket. Taking hold of Salim's coat Bolan pulled him across the room and swung him into a sagging cane chair. He raised the man's head and stared into his pain-dulled eyes.

"Is this the way it works, Salim?"

The man in the chair clutched his broken finger and shook his head. Up close his brown face was a mass of fine wrinkles, his slack jaw unshaved and he was sweating heavily.

"Maybe I should break the rest of your fingers. Just to show you *I* don't play games." The man shrank away Bolan. "Your choice," the Executioner said. "Personally, I don't care if I have to break both your legs, as well."

"You are a cruel man."

Bolan found it hard to hold back a smile. "That from the guy who just tried to have a knife stuck in me? What was that, a local greeting?"

"That was business. Nothing personal."

"Wrong there, friend. When someone comes at me with a knife, it gets very personal." Bolan straightened, regarding the man silently, waiting.

"What do you expect of me? Should I tell you who wants you dead?"

"It would be a start. Right now all I want to know is where they are."

"You expect me to take you to them?"

"Why not?"

"You expect me to betray them? That will never happen."

"Wrong answer. I'm not happy with that and you are getting closer to having something else broken. Maybe I'll just shoot you now and get it over with."

Salim's eyes widened and the man sweated even more. He regarded the tall, cold-eyed American closely. The man had a look about him that indicated he meant what he said. He handled the pistol with authority, and it was plain to see he had killed before.

Salim, in fact, had a long acquaintance with violence. It had been his business for many years. In that time he had come up against many men of violence, and he had dispatched many of them. Always in the line of work. Never with any personal animosity. His killing trade was just that—his trade. He worked quickly and efficiently, mostly with his knife because it was that weapon he had mastered at an early age. He had killed his first victim when he was fifteen and ever since it had been the way he had earned his livelihood. Salim had an excellent reputation among his people. In some quarters he was feared. Others envied him his skill and his discretion. Yet here he was another man's prisoner. The man he had been paid to capture. It was, above everything else, humiliating. To have been overpowered and wounded by an American. If the story got out, Salim would lose much of his status.

"So if you will kill me, do it. There is nothing I can tell you."

Bolan backed away, turning to peer through the window. The narrow, sunlight street below had little traffic. Between the houses he could see the glittering water, boats bobbing gently. Here, away from the tourist hotels and the busy shops, life went on its slow-paced way. Just as it probably had for a thousand years. Change here was slow to the extreme. It didn't stop the shadow people from plying their back street trade in arms dealing. Weapons were always in demand, and the enterprise was thriving. The merchandise was no longer the usual crates of Kalashnikovs and RPGs. The stakes were far higher.

Nuclear stakes.

"If they know I'm not Novak, they must be concerned," Bolan said. "Worried I might be close to discovering something about them. Like the location of the desert camp."

Bolan watched Salim's eyes as he spoke. Though he tried not to Salim made an involuntary movement with his head when Bolan mentioned the camp.

"There is nothing to say," Salim muttered, avoiding looking directly at the big American.

"I'll be sure to let your employers know you helped me find them. Yamir Kerim especially."

Salim became instantly alert, eyes wide with alarm. "You cannot do this…"

"You haven't told me anything. Yet. But you will."

Bolan let his words hang in the silence that followed. He could almost sense Salim's mind working overtime, assessing and debating which way to go. He was caught in a dead end. No matter which way he turned, he was facing threats. Bolan on one side, Kerim on the other.

"Why should this happen to me? I only offer my services as a business. Not to become involved like this." His voice had taken on a whining tone as he tried to worm his way into Bolan's sympathy. "I am just a poor man struggling to make a living."

"About now might be a good time to consider a change of occupation."

Salim stared at the American. When he looked deep into the hard blue eyes he saw no consideration. Only the steady gaze of a man who knew his own mind.

"What do you want from me? If I offer you information, how do I know you will not betray me?"

"I don't go back on my word. All I want is to find the camp. Give that to me and I'll let you go."

"Why should I trust you?"

Bolan leaned in close, his blue eyes looking directly into Salim's.

"I never lie. If I give my word, I don't go back on it."

Salim knew instinctively that the American was telling the truth. There was no guile in his voice. It was that of an honest man, which was something of a novelty in Salim's world. He lived in the shadows, surrounded by lies and cheating. Truth and honesty were items in short supply, so to be confronted by such things left him briefly at a loss for words.

"You tell the truth? What guarantee do I have?"

"How about I let you live."

Salim recalled how easily this man had broken Yusef's arm. The easy way of violence was in him.

"What do you want?"

"Get me to the camp. I need to go there. If you don't I'll kill you here. Now."

"If I do this, you will set me free?"

"As I said, you walk away. No strings."

Salim sighed. He had little choice. If he gave this American what he wanted, at least he would have his life. He would need to have his injuries attended to, collect his money from his apartment and take the first coach heading up country. He could always find work. His expertise was always in demand. After that…

"Do I need to explain what will happen if you betray me?" Bolan asked. "Just remember one thing. I'm very good at finding people."

CHAPTER FIVE

Bolan hired a high-end Range Rover from a Jordanian rental company. The vehicle was fitted with satellite navigation, had climate control and a digital communications setup. Bolan, carrying a couple of cameras he had picked up from a local store, said he was scouting locations for a movie.

"Do you think they believed you?" Salim asked as he accompanied Bolan from the rental office.

"They believed the money I handed over."

"Only an American would say such a thing," Salim said.

"You didn't take on your contract for money?"

Salim shrugged. "Perhaps it came into the picture a little."

The rental assistant showed them around the gleaming vehicle. "It is very new, Mr. Cooper." He was fussing over the Range Rover, rubbing a smudge with his sleeve. "Only a few hundred miles on the clock."

"We'll take good care of it," Bolan said. "We are just going for a short trip."

"The tank is full. You have spare cans of petrol and water in the rear. You understand how to operate the satellite navigation?"

"America is a big country, too," Bolan said. "We use them all the time."

"Then have a good trip and be safe."

They climbed in and Bolan fired up the powerful engine. He eased away from the rental lot onto the smooth tarmac of the highway.

"Head north for now," Salim said. He was hunched in his seat, keeping his head low, cradling his broken finger. Bolan had allowed him to go to a local drugstore to purchase a bandage to bind it. Coming out, Bolan had spotted rack of long-billed baseball caps and bought one.

"Are you expecting to be recognized?"

"If you expect the worst, it isn't so much of a surprise when it comes."

Salim was left to figure that one out.

THEY STAYED WITH THE HIGHWAY for an hour before Salim directed Bolan off-road. The flat Jordanian desert stretched out on all sides, wide and dusty, with little vegetation. The afternoon was hot. What wind there was blew gritty dust across the parched land. It hissed along the Range Rover's sides and peppered the windows. According to Salim they were moving in a northeasterly direction. Bolan activated the sat-nav and the screen flickered into life. The readout pinpointed their position and when Bolan ran a check he found they *were* on a northeasterly setting.

"You did not believe me," Salim said. "I do not need machines to tell me where I am."

"I guess not," Bolan said.

Salim fell silent. He kept looking in Bolan's direction, but said nothing. The only time he spoke was to direct Bolan's line of travel.

When it became dark Bolan slowed. The sat-nav would

keep him on course but he didn't want to risk hitting some unseen pothole or deep depression. After a couple of hours, the moon rose and bathed the landscape in a cold light. Bolan finally stopped. He was ready for a break after almost five hours driving. Beside him Salim sat up, staring around.

"Why have we stopped? Is someone out there?"

"I need a break, is all," Bolan said, taking the key from the ignition.

He opened his door and climbed out, working the stiffness from his body. The desert spoke in its eternal whisper. The movement of the wind stirred the sand, rattling the sparse and dry grass. In truth the desert was never silent. It had a voice all its own and it was the same voice that had spoken for a thousand years. Bolan moved away from the Range Rover, feeling the still warm wind tug at his clothing. He felt Salim at his side, the man gazing out across the empty place.

"What do you hear?" Bolan asked.

"It is the song of the desert," Salim said. "The sound that draws men to this place. They say it can bewitch a man. Make him follow the sound until he is lost. Did you know, American, that the desert is a woman? She has the power to lure men into her heart and turn them mad with her song. Do you believe that?"

"I believe a man could get himself lost out here. And be lonely. Put those together and a man could start to hear things. Maybe see what wasn't there."

"You see. I was right. The desert is a cruel mistress."

Bolan understood the man's feel for the desolate space. At the same time beautiful and indifferent, it had the timeless appeal of all great empty places. With no distractions, barely any sound, the desert could cast its hypnotic spell and isolate a man. Cut off from the reality of normal existence it would be easy to start imagining things. Bolan pushed the thoughts from his mind and focused on the present, where he needed to stay alert. He smiled to himself. Maybe he had been letting Salim's desert get to him. An all too easy condition to submit to. But not one he could afford to give in to.

His mission in Jordan wasn't to admire his surroundings, but to locate the isolated camp being used by Razihra's group. He had a job to do. It was his priority. His focus had to be on that and nothing else.

Bolan turned to see that Salim was inside the vehicle, leaning back in the seat, his head resting against the window. The man was a strange one. Hard to figure, except in the respect that Bolan didn't trust him fully. Salim had already changed sides once. Why wouldn't he do it again if the opportunity presented itself? Bolan considered that and figured he had it just right. The man had no loyalty, except to himself. He was of that breed who worked one against the other. Salim would never tread the middle ground. Both sides of the street were fair game. He could only be bought for what was the current rate. If the pay went up in the opposite camp, Salim would choose to step over the line. Bolan had no doubts on that.

He climbed back inside the Range Rover, taking the rear seat so he could watch Salim. The man made no signs he had heard Bolan return to the vehicle. He was either a heavy sleeper, or a good actor. Bolan went with the second option and played along. He settled in the corner of the seat, making a play of taking out the Browning and cocking it. Now he sat with the pistol resting in his lap, the muzzle pointing at the back of Salim's seat.

THEY MOVED OUT AS SOON as it was light. Bolan had dozed lightly, always conscious of Salim's presence. The man had stirred a number of times during the night, perhaps in sleep, or to test Bolan's response. Each time the man moved the soldier had responded by making sure the Browning could be seen. Eventually, Salim had slept soundly.

Bolan splashed water from a canteen on his face and drank a little. He allowed Salim the same privilege, but the man only swallowed a little of the water before resuming his seat. He seemed to have lapsed into a sullen mood, speaking only when he needed to offer directions, and Bolan had little he wanted to say to the man.

Midmorning Salim indicated they should stop. Bolan guided the Rover into a low, dry wadi and switched off the engine.

"Are we near?"

"Close enough that we should leave the vehicle here and walk."

"How long?"

"Maybe two hours."

"We'd better fill those canteens in back," Bolan said.

He climbed out of the vehicle and followed Salim to the rear, then stood back, the Browning in his hand. Salim stared at the weapon.

"What is this? Suddenly you need to keep a gun on me?"

"You never know who might be waiting over the next rise. I'm just being cautious."

"Then you should watch me in case I poison your water."

"I will."

They moved out, Salim in the lead, stopped to fill the canteens hanging from his shoulders. Bolan, his baseball cap pulled low to cover his face, walked a few paces behind. The Browning was tucked into his belt.

The first hour went by quickly. After that their pace slowed and even Salim seemed affected by the heat. He trudged to a near stop until Bolan caught up and prodded him.

"Yes, yes. You do not have to push me. Am I a camel?"

"A camel would be better company."

"Ha, ha." The exclamation was harsh, the derogatory meaning clear.

"Just keep moving, Salim."

"And what if I refuse to go farther? What then? Could you find this place without me?"

Bolan's silence made Salim turn. He saw the big man looking at the sky, his right hand resting on the pistol in his belt. Despite his curiosity Salim still managed to persist in his question.

"What now? Have you not heard my words? That you will never find the camp without me?"

"I have a feeling your time as a guide could be over. My guess is I don't need to be shown where the camp is. I think they just sent us an invitation. And a ride."

Salim followed Bolan's gaze and saw the dark shape coming at them from the empty sky. A shape that rapidly formed into the outline of a helicopter.

Salim picked up the distinctive beat of the rotors. The sound grew in volume as the aircraft swept toward them, the rotors stirring up great clouds of dusty sand that peppered them with its gritty hardness. The helicopter made a firm landing. Bolan recognized it as a Westland Lynx. By its faded, dun color it was an ex-military aircraft, much used but still serviceable. The side hatch slid open and armed figures jumped out, covering Bolan and Salim. A lean figure dressed in khaki shirt and pants, and wearing a checkered kaffiyeh, came forward, raising a hand in Salim's direction.

"*Salaam aleikum,* my brother. I see you have brought our guest safely this far." The man turned to Bolan. "Novak? You have changed greatly since the last time we met. I am Yamir Kerim. Do you not recognize me?" Kerim was smiling as he spoke, amusing himself at revealing Bolan's ploy. He looked at the pistol in Bolan's belt and reached out and took it. "You will not be needing this. I would not want you to come into our camp armed. It would be looked on as an insult. You understand that some of the men are not as worldly wise as we. They live by the old rules of hospitality, you understand."

"We wouldn't want to upset them then. Would we, Mr. Kerim."

Kerim's face hardened. He heard the coldness in Bolan's words. Saw the contempt in the blue eyes. "Your arrogance defines you as an American. Only one of your kind would dare to try and walk into *my* camp and then insult me as if I was nothing but an ignorant *Arab*. Isn't that how you see us? All of us from this region? Dirty, ignorant Arabs? You class us all as one type. Perhaps, American, you need a lesson in the geography of where you are."

"And you're the man to teach me?"

"Perhaps I am." Kerim nodded in agreement. "Yes, perhaps I am."

CHAPTER SIX

The flight was short and, as far as Bolan was concerned, one of the roughest he had ever experienced. Kerim's men had manhandled him to the helicopter. He had been thrown inside, the men using their boots to force him to the deck. Bolan hadn't fought back. That would have resulted in far worse injuries than those he did receive. During the flight, he was dragged upright and subjected to a beating that left him bruised and bloody. The assault only stopped when the helicopter made its landing and Bolan was hauled outside. He was dragged by a couple of the men as they followed Kerim to the largest of the tents that formed the camp. He was pulled inside and thrown to the sand floor.

Kerim stood in front of a wooden desk, arms folded, waiting for Bolan to climb to his feet. Salim stood to one side, trying to appear relaxed. His eyes told a different story. Even in his dazed condition Bolan realized things had moved a little faster than even Salim had expected.

"So," Kerim began. "We know at least that you are not Novak. So who are you? Or should I be asking, what are you? Obviously some kind of undercover operative working for…?"

"This could be a long day," Bolan said.

"He would not tell me his real name," Salim said eagerly.

Kerim shook his head. "His name doesn't matter. The important thing is that we have him. Oh, I forgot, American, an old friend is here to see you, too."

Someone moved out of the shadows at the far end of the tent and into the light. Bolan saw Yusef, Salim's driver. His broken arm was encased in a plaster cast. His face was badly swollen and bruised where Bolan had hit him. It explained how they had known he was coming.

"Forgive Yusef if he does not express much pleasure at seeing you," Kerim said. "He is still in great pain. Though he says little, he does hold a grudge."

Bolan remained silent. He realized he wasn't going to gain very much by getting into a vocal trade-off with Kerim. His prime concern now was to get himself out of their hands and make his attempt to destroy their nuclear cache before it could be moved on. To antagonize his captors was to invite the threat of an early death. Bolan had no plans for that to happen, so it was time to tread lightly until he could make his break.

"Contrary to what you might believe, we are not stupid. Since your involvement with our affairs suggests you work for one of the American agencies, it is important to us that we learn about *you*. Agreed?"

Bolan remained silent.

Yusef leaned forward and spoke softly into Kerim's ear. Kerim raised a hand and nodded. "Yusef asks if he may be included in your interrogation. I understand his motive. He wants to hurt you. Tell me, should I accede to his wishes?"

"His risk."

Kerim smiled. He turned and spoke to Yusef. The big man lunged at Bolan, his good arm flailing as he lashed out. Bolan attempted to step back but the armed men behind blocked his movement and the heavy blow rocked his head, knocking him to the ground. Yusef went after him, slamming his powerful fist into Bolan's side. The blows came hard and on a regular basis, sending shock waves of pain through Bolan. He could hear Yusef's ragged breathing as the man expressed his rage through the assault.

Kerim finally put a stop to it, the guard's intervening to push Yusef back. Bolan stayed on his knees, sucking in breath through clenched teeth. He could taste the blood in his mouth from where Yusef's first blow had cut his lip. A command from Kerim and the guards hauled Bolan upright and back to where he had been standing before Yusef's attack.

"So, Yusef is at risk? Yes?"

"He won't do that again."

Kerim seemed to find this amusing. "You are extremely confident, American. Or very naive. You are aware of your position here? *I* am in control. You are the captive. Yet you prefer to see it differently by giving me ultimatums."

"It kind of makes you wonder."

The man's face lost all of its humor. "Enough of this. Time to give me the answers I require. As in, who do you work for? How much information have you gained concerning our operation? Believe me, you should be advised to tell me what you have sooner rather than later. Holding out will only prolong your suffering. I am indifferent to that. In the end we will only kill you, so believe me when I say this place is where you end your days. There is no going back from here."

Just behind Kerim, the impatient Yusef was making an effort to hold himself back. From the expression on his bruised face he wasn't doing a very good job. His free hand was clenching and unclenching. Bolan knew he couldn't take the kind of punishment the man handed out indefinitely. Yusef's interrogation technique was crude, but effective. If he was allowed free rein he would eventually beat Bolan to death. A simple fact. Inescapable but true. Kerim wanted answers. If he kept Yusef on the interrogation, he might lose Bolan altogether. The soldier had nothing to tell the man, but Kerim had no way of knowing that. He would keep Bolan alive for as long as he thought necessary.

Kerim noticed Bolan's glance in Yusef's direction. He made up his mind and flicked a hand to motion Yusef forward, speaking to him quietly. Yusef nodded and moved in Bolan's direction.

"Keep him away from me," Bolan said.

"Or?"

"Or you're going to need a new dog to bark for you."

Kerim translated Bolan's words for Yusef, which galvanized the big man into action. He came at Bolan in a rush, his uncoordinated lunge avoidable. The Executioner didn't step away this time. He waited, tensed, and as Yusef loomed large, he struck.

His first blow was a savage strike at Yusef's throat, the crushing jab collapsing the man's cartilage and windpipe. Yusef came to a sudden halt, gasping as he vainly attempted to inhale through his ruined airway. He was still trying when Bolan's second blow landed, coming up from his waist, the upturned heel of his right hand impacting with Yusef's nose, driving bone shards into his brain. A gush of blood from the shattered nose spread out across Yusef's face as he toppled back, dying even as he fell. His body curved in a single spasm before he lay spread-eagled at Kerim's feet.

Bolan stepped back, his gaze fixed on Kerim's face. For an instant there was a gleam of respect in the man's eyes. He recovered quickly, snapping his fingers at the two guards.

"Enough of this. Take him away. Put him with the other prisoner and they can convince each other it will be best they cooperate. I will talk to him later."

Kerim's dismissal was complete. He turned away to deal with other matters as the armed guards escorted Bolan from the tent.

Walking just in front of the guards Bolan took the opportunity to look around the camp. Tents and parked vehicles. The helicopters on the slight rise beyond the main area. A couple of stone buildings, one, just beyond a low stone wall, well guarded. He was taken away from the tents to a single stone building with barred windows and a heavy wooden door. The door was opened and Bolan pushed inside. A filthy passage led down to another door, which was barred from the outside. While one man covered Bolan with his rifle the other freed the door and held it open. The muzzle of an AK forced the big American in through the door. He was given a final push, sending him to his knees in the middle of the cell. Behind him the door was slammed shut and the bolts rammed home.

Bolan heard a slight movement on the far side of the cell. He glanced up and realized he wasn't alone.

CHAPTER SEVEN

Bolan pushed to his feet and checked out his cell partner.

The man was of medium height, with wide shoulders and lean hips. He was clad in torn, stained black clothing that was covered by a loose robe. His neat black beard framed a light brown face that had undergone recent hard treatment. Bruises and bloody cuts marked his flesh and his hooked nose was badly swollen. Dried blood crusted his mouth. He regarded Bolan with a fierce stare. His dark eyes held an undiminished gleam that his rough treatment hadn't dimmed.

"Do you speak English?" Bolan asked. "I ask because my Arabic is not good."

"Of course I speak English," the other replied in a tone that suggested he was talking to a child. "Do you think I am just another desert savage?"

"No, I was hoping to make conversation with a fellow warrior." Bolan had recognized the configuration of the man's dress. The black garb and flowing robes, the Jalabiyya, of a Bedouin. His head was covered by the traditional Arab kaffiyeh, the black cloth held in place by the double-corded agal.

The man's interest brought him closer, examining Bolan's own black attire. "You are a warrior, too?"

"So I've been told, though I would never class myself in the same league as a true Bedouin."

The man straightened, staring into Bolan's eyes. His expression showed approval. His stance, though regal, wasn't from vanity. The Bedouin tribes, though much decimated, were men of enduring pride in their long and noble history. Monarchs of the desert lands, they had once been many, ruling their dusty kingdoms with a fierceness little could equal. Reduced to dwindling numbers and with many of their kind having deserted the almost barren terrain, the few who remained close to their roots upheld the nobility of their past and retained their customs.

"You are American?"

"Yes."

"They know of the Bedu in America?"

"Men of wisdom and influence know of the Bedouin. Of their history. Their great deeds."

"Good. I am Ali bin Sharif of the Rwala."

The Rwala, Bolan recalled, were one of the Bedouin tribes who wandered the dusty terrain of Syria and Jordan and the northern parts of Saudi Arabia.

"Then I am in good company," Bolan said.

"How are you called, American?"

"Cooper is my name."

Sharif spoke the name to himself, nodding as he registered the strange word.

"If they have brought you to this pigpen, Cooper, then you must be an enemy of these dogs as I am."

Bolan smiled at that. "No doubt about that, Ali bin Sharif. I *am* their enemy."

"Then we are allies."

"How did you come to be in this place?"

"Two of my fellow warriors and I stumbled across this place. We rode in asking for water and we were attacked. My friends were shot down in front of me even though we came in friendship."

The Bedouin had moved to stand and stare out through the tiny square in the wall that served as the only window in the cell. Bolan sensed he was stifled within the confines of the room, longing to be back in his wide, clean desert.

"If we stay, they are going to kill us," Sharif said as he turned, reluctantly, from the window. "I know this. They took great delight in telling me I would die when they poison me with the weapon they plan to use against the Israelis."

Bolan tensed. "Tell me what you have heard, bin Sharif. It is important that I know."

"Did you see the stone building standing on its own? Just beyond the wall?"

When he had arrived Bolan had made a silent appraisal of the camp's layout. Recon was important when it came time to effect an escape. something always at the forefront of Bolan's mind whenever he found himself disadvantaged. Thinking ahead and formulating an escape route could make the difference between staying free—or failing completely.

"Look beyond the window," Sharif said. "At the eastern edge of the camp. Do you see the wall?"

Bolan nodded. "And the square stone building thirty feet out?"

"Yes. In there they store weapons. Guns and ammunition. Explosives. And the weapon they will kill the Jews with. Those Iraqi dogs who yapped at Hussein's heels showed me. They delivered it here for the Iranians to use. They said it would make me scream like a child as I died. Ha, they must not be aware I am Rwala, of the Bedu."

"What did this weapon look like? Liquid? Was it gas in cylinders?"

"In round glass balls. Big enough to fill my palm. Inside was a green-colored liquid. One of those Fedayeen laughed in my face when he told me one drop would spread all across my body and eat me alive."

A reactive bioagent that became active when it made contact with living tissue. Bolan had heard about the varying strains of biological weapons, created in labs by men to use against other men. Another of the vile products of the endless search man immersed himself in to destroy his own kind. He wondered briefly where the Iranians had gotten hold of this particular strain. Not that it mattered right now. The where could come later.

"Did they say where it would be used in Israel?"

He shook his head. "If they send it into Israel it will set this whole region alight. Iraq. Iran. Why cannot these fools be satisfied with what they have? When will they be content? Only when we are all fighting each other? Or dead and the desert is rid of us all?"

"Ali, we can stand around day discussing the worst. Or we can get out of this place and stop what these men are planning."

The Bedouin thought about it for only a moment. "You are right, Cooper. So what is your wonderful plan that will release us from this miserable dung pit?"

"The truth?"

"Always."

"I have no plan."

Sharif smiled, stroking his dark beard and said, "Then we must do it anyway."

"Do they feed you?"

Sharif laughed. "If you can call it food. I believe it is the slop that even the camp dogs refuse to eat. But they say I must eat to keep up my strength. So that when they use their chemical I will be strong and resist better."

"That suggests they're not sure of its power. They need to test it."

"Is that good?"

"It means they may not have worked out how to use it. So there might not be a date for attacking Israel. It gives us an edge."

Sharif frowned. "An edge?"

"Time to destroy the cache."

Sharif grunted, deep in his own thoughts. "If we could break free and gather my brothers, we could return and attack this place."

"My own thoughts exactly."

"You have seen the helicopters they possess. They would track us."

"The Bedu aren't afraid of helicopters," Bolan said.

Sharif slapped him on the shoulder. "Of course not. If you believe that then I am not the only mad one in this cell."

They waited. According to Sharif, midday was when his food was delivered. Bolan's watch showed they weren't far from that time.

He sank down on his heels, his back to the wall, and let his body relax, conserving his energy. He still hurt from the punishment he had received from Yusef. The only good thing to come from his recent confrontation with Kerim was being locked up with Sharif. Kerim deciding to delay his interrogation might yet prove to be Bolan's way out of his current situation. While his body rested, his mind was busy, evaluating the information he had gathered since becoming fully involved in the convoluted twists of the mission. There was a repeated strain of deceit embedded within the relationships he had come in contact with. Mistrust permeated every strand. No one was comfortable with the next in line. It loosened the secrecy that should have knit the whole thing together, allowing Bolan to extract information with less effort than he might have expected. It also meant those involved were acutely nervous and liable to hit out unexpectedly. Sudden violence was chosen as the swiftest way of resolving problems. Bolan was always aware of that during mission time so he never took anything for granted. There were still times when even his keen awareness failed him. He had only to look around the cell to confirm that.

"Cooper."

Bolan glanced across at Sharif. The Bedouin nodded in the direction of the cell door. He picked up the soft whisper of footsteps moving in the direction of the cell, a murmur of voices.

"We have a choice. Die of poisoning from the execrable food they are bringing, or the cleaner death from a bullet."

Pushing to his feet Bolan lounged against the rough wall, head down and he remained in that position as the door was unbolted and pushed wide. Sunlight streamed into the cell, bright, with swirling dust motes in the hot shafts. Then the fall of light was partially blocked by a man carrying an AK-47. He paused to check the position of the two prisoners, then stepped aside to let a second man enter. This one carried two wooden bowls of steaming food. He bent and placed them on the floor.

Sharif began to berate the two guards in wild, explosive Arabic. Bolan didn't know what he was saying, but the tone and phrasing suggested he was delving deep into his knowledge of his language's obscenities. The unexpected outburst delivered in a ringing volume, caught the guards by surprise, if only for a fraction of time. In those scant seconds each man turned his startled gaze on the ranting Bedouin.

With only the briefest reprieve Bolan moved, powering

himself away from the wall to launch a blistering strike at the guard with the rifle. His sweeping kick drove the toe of his combat boot into the guy's groin, producing a shocked grunt. The guard began to double over, tears welling from his bugging eyes. Bolan slammed his bunched right fist into the exposed throat, feeling flesh and bone cave in under the unrestrained power of the strike. The choking guard fell back against the open door, wide-open eyes seeing nothing. He offered no resistance as Bolan stepped in close, snapped an arm around his neck and yanked the guy off his feet. As they dropped, Bolan spun the helpless guard back across his knee and snapped his spine. The guard uttered a final gurgle of agony as his entire body became limp.

As Bolan took the AK-47 from the dead guard, Sharif went for the second man as he grabbed for the pistol holstered on his belt. The Bedouin moved with the speed of a striking snake, one big hand clamping over the guard's pistol, preventing him from lifting it, the other driving full-force into the man's face. The solid impact of the blow was accompanied by the sound of breaking bone as the guard's nose was crushed into a bloody pulp. Without pause Sharif hit the guard again, this time delivering a hefty punch that drove the target's lips into his teeth and snapped his head back. Sharif snatched the guard's heavy weapon from his belt and used it to hammer the guy's skull, driving him to the floor.

Following Bolan's lead, the Bedouin dragged the downed guard away from the door and deeper into the cell. Bolan crouched beside his man and checked him for additional weapons. He was going to have to be content with the AK. The 30-round magazine had a second taped to it for quick reload.

"Tell me about this gun, Cooper," Sharif said, thrusting the pistol at the American.

Bolan checked it out. It was a 9 mm Glock 17, with an extended 31-round magazine. He made sure the safety was off, then handed it back to Sharif.

"Just aim and pull the trigger," he said. "Thirty-one bullets in the mag."

"Like this one?" Sharif asked, showing Bolan a second magazine he had pulled from the guard's belt.

Bolan nodded. "When the magazine is empty the slide will lock back. Press here and the empty mag drops out. Snap in the fresh one, release here and you're ready to go again."

Sharif nodded. "I understand."

They left the cell and moved down the passage to the main door. Bolan eased it open so he could check outside. Their most likely mode of transport was one of the dusty trucks.

"See the trucks?"

"Yes."

"That's our way out. We break for them."

Sharif considered the suggestion. "But the weapon they have stored?"

"If we can get clear, we reorganize and come back."

"If we can reach my camp, there are others there who would help."

"Let's do it, Ali."

BOLAN MADE A FINAL SCAN of the camp, seeing the tented area off to the right, the parked vehicles across to the left. Between the lockup and the vehicles the ground was open, uneven, a rocky stretch that would offer little in the way of cover. It was far from ideal but there was no alternative. If he and Sharif were going to make their escape they needed a vehicle. On foot they would be an easy target if one of the helicopters came looking for them.

The only thing in their favor was the fact that being the middle of the day, the occupants of the camp had retreated to the comparative coolness of their tents. Bolan silently thanked the collective thinking that had created this siesta-like observance. Apart from an unfortunate sentry on the far perimeter and a second man standing in the shade provided by one of the helicopters, there was no sign of the camp occupants.

"Ready, Ali bin Sharif?"

The Bedouin shrugged, a fatalistic gesture that expressed his feelings. "As ready as I will ever be."

"We won't have a better opportunity. Go."

Bolan slipped out through the door, picking up the pace as he moved away from the lockup. The black-clad figure of Ali bin Sharif stayed close behind him. The ground beneath their feet offered minimal resistance and they made little sound as they made their dash for freedom. Bolan made frequent checks on the two sentries, hoping neither glanced in their direction.

They traversed a low rise of ground, skirting one of the tents, dust rising from their passing, over the top of the rise and along the final stretch, closing in on the parked vehicles.

As always, it was the unexpected that posed a challenge as Bolan angled in on the truck he had chosen. A lean figure in khaki pants and shirt, wearing a long-billed baseball cap, stirred from his resting place in the rear of the truck. As he sat up, the man saw the approaching figures, mouthed a few words and fumbled for the AK-47 resting across his lap. He leveled the weapon and opened fire. His instincts were sharper than his aim—the stream of 7.62 mm slugs pounded the ground yards away from his targets.

Bolan came to a dead stop, raising his own AK. He targeted the shooter who had raised himself to a kneeling position, finger stroking the trigger, sending a single shot into the guy. It cored deep into his chest, spinning him sideways. He struggled to stay upright but a second shot from Bolan's rifle laid him flat.

"Get him out of there," Bolan called to Sharif as he climbed behind the wheel.

The Bedouin dragged the body out of the rear of the truck, commandeering the man's rifle and scrambled into the passenger seat next to Bolan. The engine burst into life as the soldier pressed the button. He worked the stiff gears, released the handbrake and floored the gas pedal. The truck lurched forward, dust billowing as Bolan swung it away from the camp and headed for the desert beyond.

"Any suggestions on our direction?" Bolan yelled above the howl of the engine.

Sharif pointed. "To the north for now. That way."

The crackle of autofire rose over the engine noise. Slugs snapped through the air, some clanging sharply against the metal sides of the truck.

"I think we have upset them," Sharif shouted, his face creased in a smile.

Bolan concentrated on driving. The truck had little in the way of sophisticated suspension. Every bump and ripple in the ground was transmitted through the vehicle's framework. Bolan had to fight the shuddering wheel as they bounced and lurched across the uneven terrain. His arms and shoulders began to ache. There was nothing else he could do but keep going, using whatever cover he could find. He gave up that maneuver when he became aware of the rising dust trail they were creating. It hung in the hot air long after they had passed.

"If they get those helicopters into the air, we will be spotted easily," Sharif said.

"Tell me about it."

Minutes later Sharif twisted in his seat, searching the sky behind them.

"I see one," he said.

"Has he picked us up yet?"

The Bedouin studied the distant aircraft. "I think he is turning this way, Cooper."

"If he starts firing, we abandon this vehicle. Understand?"

Sharif nodded. "I understand."

CHAPTER EIGHT

"I want them dead. No questions. No excuses. Track them down and kill them. That American has caused us too much already. I can't afford to have him running around wreaking more havoc."

Kerim's tone warned his men he was in no mood for compromise. They retreated from the tent, checking weapons and communication equipment, heading for the remaining truck to take up pursuit. One of the helicopters had already taken to the air.

"Do you think they will catch them?" Salim asked.

Kerim caught the light taunt in the other man's tone. "Yes, they will, because if they fail, they will know not to return. Do not underestimate us, Salim. My brothers do not play the fool's game."

"The thought was not on my mind, Kerim. Forgive me, my friend."

Kerim shrugged off the apology. He turned back to his deliberations, mulling over the charts spread across the table. There was so much to deal with. The upset caused by the American had left Kerim with a bad feeling. Not of defeat, more of a sense of being made to look weak within his own camp, the secret place that the Jordanians had promised him would be safe. Now even that sanctity had been broken and one man—*one man*—had already killed three of his loyal fighters.

The sting of embarrassment made him lose his concentration. He found he could barely make any sense of the information spread out before him. Kerim concealed his bitterness, not wanting to exhibit it in front Salim. He was aware that Salim had drawn his own conclusions from the incident. Like it or not, Kerim had been made to look foolish. He couldn't trust that Salim would keep the matter to himself. The man had a loose mouth. Though he had proved useful during negotiations, acting as a go-between, the man had always struck Kerim as slightly untrustworthy. Salim had a way about him that indicated he was forever on the look out for himself. There was that slyness about him that Kerim had always found disagreeable. And knowing his greed when it came to money, Kerim didn't doubt he would be prepared to offer what he knew about the incident at the camp.

Loyalty wasn't a word Salim understood, apart from loyalty to himself. He wouldn't hesitate to let Razihra know what had happened if the chance came up. One mistake could ruin Kerim's future, maybe even threaten his life. Failure, in any form, was frowned upon and the camp fiasco wouldn't be seen in a favorable light. It would matter little to Razihra that Kerim had been strongly instrumental in setting up the camp by making a deal with the Fedayeen and their Jordanian sympathizers. He had also helped to broker the deal with the Russians to obtain the consignment of bio weapons. Kerim, not Salim—nor even Razihra—had done any of that. Their contribution had been to supply the cash, then sit back in safety and let someone else do the work. There was a bitter irony for Kerim when he thought about Ayatollah Razihra gathering all the praise if the operation was a success. He knew without a doubt that Razihra would claim it all as his own work. That realization had become apparent to Kerim quite some time ago.

Kerim glanced across the tent at Salim's back. The man was lighting a cigarette, his actions slow and deliberate as he sat gazing out through the open tent flap. So calm and all-knowing. Kerim felt his anger rise. Why should his word have so much influence? Enough that it could destroy all that Kerim cherished. There was no one with as much loyalty to the Ayatollah's cause. No one. And it could all be wiped away by idle gossip. Salim's whispered words would be carefully chosen so as to lay full blame on Kerim. The reprisal would be swift and without mercy. Kerim had no doubts as to that. He had seen it happen to others under Razihra's command.

Without turning his head Salim said, "It would be a pity if my bringing the American here came to nothing. At great personal risk. Would you not agree, Kerim? A chance to find out who had sent him and what he might already have learned. Now we may never know." Salim paused, letting his words hang in the silence. "I am sure the Ayatollah wouldn't be pleased if he was to hear of this. Of course I am only thinking of you, Kerim. The Ayatollah holds you in great esteem. My own small part in this is insignificant against your position of great authority."

Kerim had been waiting for that. The thinly veiled threat of exposure to Razihra. No doubt, if told by Salim, the error would be exaggerated out of all proportion. And once primed with this, Razihra would do his own search for what had happened. Kerim saw this as nothing more than a threat against his very life. If he waited, Salim would reach out the hand of friendship, pledging to help Kerim bury the matter. However there would be certain matters to be dealt with and money would need to change hands.

So it comes down to one life against another, Kerim thought. If Salim speaks with the Ayatollah, I am finished. It will be as if he had pulled the trigger himself.

His life was under threat. When that happened was not a man allowed to defend himself against the perpetrator? Kerim turned and picked up the AK-47 that was resting against the leg of the table. He raised it, turning the muzzle in Salim's direction as he snapped back the bolt to arm the weapon. Salim heard the sound, pushing up off his chair and turning. He stared at the black muzzle, eyes suddenly glistening with unconcealed terror.

"Kerim? What is this…?"

"Self-preservation," Kerim said, and pulled the trigger.

The burst hit Salim in the chest, throwing him backward. As he fell, Kerim followed his body, still firing, the muzzle rising up to Salim's throat and head. Kerim kept firing until the AK fell silent, its magazine exhausted.

Armed men crowded the tent opening, staring down at the bloody, lacerated form at their feet. The savage volley had reduced Salim's head and upper torso to a bloody wreck.

"Get that thing out of here and bury him," Kerim shouted, seizing the moment. "He spoke treason against Ayatollah Razihra. He wanted *us* to turn against him. To betray our brothers and the cause. This I will not stand from any man. Now drag the dog out of here and bury him with no marker. Let him lie in a traitor's grave."

One man pushed to the front, confronting Kerim.

"They have spotted the truck," he said.

THE HELICOPTER MADE A LONG, low sweep, approaching the truck from the side. Bolan threw a swift glance in its direction and spotted the stubby pod attached to the lower fuselage.

Missiles.

"Ali," he yelled, "missile incoming."

The Bedouin followed his gaze and saw what the American meant. There was a sudden whoosh of sound as the slim missile erupted from the pod. It began an erratic flight that looked as if it might terminate at the truck. Bolan swerved violently, the missile slipping by and exploding yards ahead.

Not a heat-seeker, Bolan realized.

The helicopter zoomed in behind the truck, the pilot realizing his error. His second shot was fired at minimum range.

"Jump!" Bolan yelled.

They exited the truck together, hurling themselves clear of the vehicle and hit the duty ground, rolling and staying low.

The missile impacted against the rear of the truck. The explosion threw up a mass of sand and rock, tearing the vehicle apart in a searing flash of fire. Smoke followed, billowing thick and acrid. The explosion sent out shock waves in a rippling effect that battered at Bolan and Sharif, shoving them farther across the ground. They were lost in the dust and the rain of debris that dropped back to earth.

THE LYNX HELICOPTER SURGED closer, rotor wash swirling the dust and smoke in eccentric spirals. The pilot stayed high until the explosion faded, then dropped to a position where the scene below could be examined. The truck was a blazing wreck, torn apart by the missile, blackened and skeletal, tires smoldering and sending out black, bitter fumes.

"Where are they?" The question came over the pilot's headset from the door gunner.

"I don't know," he said. "Maybe the missile blew them into little pieces."

The gunner grunted. "I'm sure I saw them jump clear just before it struck."

Easing the helicopter down, the pilot cut the power, reaching for the AK on the deck at his feet: "We had better make sure. If we go back and say we *think* they're dead, Kerim will make it hard for us."

The gunner's sigh was audible over the headset. "I know."

They exited the helicopter and walked to view the wrecked truck.

"They went out on the far side," the gunner said, checking his AK again, nervous and hoping it didn't show.

The thick smoke from the wrecked truck had laid an opaque curtain across the immediate area, denying them a clear view beyond the vehicle.

"The blast could still have hit them. Knocked them unconscious."

It was a hope, one the pilot was depending on.

In the midst of the swirling smoke Sharif was slapping at his scorched robe, trying to put out the smoldering fire. In any other situation it might have offered a moment of light relief, but Bolan had picked up the sound of the descending helicopter and knew for certain that the attack was far from over.

"Ali, the chopper is coming in for landing. They're still looking for us."

The Bedouin snatched up his assault rifle, checking the action to make sure it hadn't been clogged with dust. "Then I hope they find us."

"Go around that way," Bolan said. "I'm taking the rear of the truck."

He moved out quickly, conscious of the helicopter engine winding down now that it was on the ground. He used the smoke as an effective shield, hiding his movements until he was able to determine he was well clear of the demolished truck. As the smoke began to thin out, Bolan moved forward, seeking his targets, and in a few seconds when the hot breeze dispersed the smoke he saw one of two figures turning in his direction, registering Bolan's presence. The man tried to gain target acquisition, but the Executioner took a swift two-step to one side, crouching slightly as he brought his AK in line, finger already pressuring the light trigger. The assault rifle jacked out its deadly fire, and the other man shuddered as the 7.62 mm slugs struck him in the chest. He fell back, making an attempt to push to his feet. Bolan cut him down with a second burst that ripped into his left side, shattering ribs and spinning the man facedown into the bloody sand.

More autofire caught Bolan's attention. It came from the area Sharif would have been approaching. Bolan sprinted around the wrecked truck, eyes searching for the Bedouin. He spotted him moments later. The man was bending over his downed target, taking the man's weapon from him and removing the magazine. He glanced up at Bolan's approach.

"These are not fighters," he said. "Any Bedu child would defeat these idiots."

"I'll take your word for it, Ali." Bolan glanced at the helicopter. "Could you guide us to your camp from the air?"

"You can fly this thing?"

"I'm no ace, but I can make it stay in the air."

Sharif grinned and said dryly, "Then, indeed, Cooper, we will take your Western magic carpet."

Telling himself he would have to buy Jack Grimaldi a drink, in fact a couple of drinks for the flying instructions he had given, Bolan settled in the pilot's seat and went through the routine of adjusting the controls, boosting the idling power up to speed. He watched the instrument panel. His takeoff was steady, with only a little side slipping as he worked the controls.

"One thing about the desert," Sharif said. "At least there are no tall buildings in the way."

Bolan wasn't sure whether he was making a joke or passing a genuine comment. He closed his mind to Sharif's muttering and concentrated on getting the chopper on an even keel.

"So which way do we go?"

"Toward those hills," Sharif said.

Bolan's handling of the helicopter settled down within a few minutes. His confidence grew, familiarity allowing him to keep the aircraft on an even keel and maintain height and speed. He promised himself an intensive refresher course once he returned to Stony Man and got Grimaldi on his own. Even Sharif relaxed, ceasing to grip the frame of the seat so tightly. He began to scan the terrain below. Some minutes into the flight he leaned to peer through the side canopy.

"We are being tracked, Cooper. It looks like one of the trucks from the camp."

Bolan took a look. He could clearly see the vehicle following them. The configuration of the truck matched that of the ones at the camp.

"How far before we reach your people, Ali?"

"Less than an hour."

"We need to deal with that truck. I'm not going to risk leading it right into your camp."

"Then send a missile. Like the one that hit our truck."

Bolan checked the missile configuration. The readout told him the pod was empty. "No more missiles, Ali."

"Can you fly this machine lower? Close enough to bring the machine gun back there into range?"

"Just make sure you use the harness. I'd hate to lose you now."

Sharif clamped a strong hand on Bolan's shoulder as he clambered out of his seat. "I have faith in you, my friend."

"And put the headset on so I can talk to you."

While Sharif made his way through to the cabin section Bolan pulled on the pilot's headset. He began to maneuver the helicopter in a wide circle, intending to come up on the truck's rear, at the same time losing some height.

"Cooper? Do you hear me?"

"Ali, you don't have to shout. That microphone is sensitive."

Sharif lowered his voice. "Is that better? Good. I am ready. The machine gun is loaded and also ready."

Bolan leveled off behind the truck. The driver had anticipated what Bolan was intended and had started to swing the truck, removing it from a direct line of travel. The soldier heard the door-mounted machine gun as Sharif fired a test burst. His volley fell well short. His second was better, still off target, but closer.

"Can you not keep this machine steady?" Sharif yelled into the headset.

Bolan settled the controls and managed to hold the chopper on a smooth line. This time Sharif managed to lay down a burst that tore at the truck's rear body section. Even Bolan saw the debris that flew out from the damaged area.

"Steady enough for you, Ali?"

All he received was a flow of what he took to be Bedouin curses. Then the machine gun crackled again.

The line of slugs hammered the truck cab and the vehicle swerved. Sharif then hit it with an even longer burst that punctured the driver's door and window and blew out the windshield from inside the cab. Sharif's final volley sent slugs through the hood into the engine and it began to die.

In the same space of time someone opened up from the canvas-topped rear of the truck, a stuttering volley from a lighter SMG. The moment he heard the clatter of shots Bolan banked the chopper away, but not before he heard the metallic clang and ping of bullets striking somewhere along the helicopter's fuselage. As the chopper pulled up and away, the truck lurched to a jerky stop.

"Cooper? Did I hear bullets hit us?" Sharif's tone was urgent over the headset.

"I think so, Ali. You'd better come up front and strap yourself in."

By the time Sharif strapped himself into the co-pilot's seat Bolan had the helicopter back on track. He had already become aware of a slight, irregular beat to the sound of the engine. Adjusting the power he coaxed the aircraft along, keeping the helicopter at a lower altitude than before.

"Is this bad, Cooper?"

"I'd be happier without it."

"Will we reach my camp?"

Bolan smiled. "Time will tell, Ali."

CHAPTER NINE

The helicopter quit on Bolan just as night started to spread across the desert. He had been aware of the increasingly uneven sound from the engine and discovered that power was reducing. He tried to compensate but it made no difference.

"Looks like we get to walk the rest of the way," was his only comment on the situation.

"Then it is providential I know how to reach the camp," Sharif said.

Bolan took the Lynx down. Before he and Sharif left the aircraft, Bolan ripped out the wiring from beneath the control panel and did the same after he had raised the engine cover. Disabling the machine would reduce its use against Bolan and the Bedouin.

"Perhaps one day we will come back and salvage what we can," Sharif mused. "The Bedu are the best traders in the area."

He led the way into the dusk, sure of his path, walking steadily without pause. Bolan followed, making frequent checks on their back trail. It was almost 8:00 p.m. by Bolan's watch when Sharif signaled for him to halt. Bolan joined him and they looked down a long, sandy slope to where a small camp had been set up around a well.

"Your people?"

"Welcome to my camp, Cooper," Sharif said, and made his way down the slope, calling out as they neared the camp.

Bolan saw the erected tents. A short way off tethered camels grumbled softly to themselves. Glowing cook fires glowed in the shadows and robed figures, alerted by Sharif's voice moved out to meet him.

There was much conversation, hands slapping Sharif across the shoulders once he had been recognized. Bolan stood to one side, waiting to be invited into the camp. The Bedouin were a proud people who clung to the customs of their past, and he had no intention of offending them.

Eventually Sharif himself turned and gestured to the American. "I welcome you to join us, my friend. Welcome to the home of the Rwala."

It was obvious that the Bedouin had regaled his brothers about Bolan and what he had done. The members of the group clustered around the tall American, greeting him in their own tongue and parting to allow him to pass. Sharif watched him, nodding his approval as Bolan acknowledged his invitation with small bows of his head, to the delight of the Bedouin tribesmen.

"Tell your brothers I am honored to be invited into their company."

"Tell them yourself, Cooper," Sharif said. "They all understand some English."

Bolan repeated his gratitude. It was greeted with a chorus of approval, his words translated for those who had difficulty understanding. With Sharif at his side and slightly behind, Bolan was escorted into the camp. A rug was spread before one of the tents and Bolan was invited to sit. While the majority of the group sat in a semicircle around him, others brought utensils and placed them in the warm sand. Bolan watched as coffee was prepared in smooth worn copper pots over a small fire of red-hot glowing embers. The rich brew, spiced with cardamom, was served in small ceramic cups.

Bedouin custom decreed the first cup be tasted by the host, to satisfy the guest he wasn't being offered anything suspect. When Sharif had done this, he indicated that Bolan himself pour the next cup and taste it. On the third filling Bolan was allowed to drink the full cup. Bolan raised his cup to his hosts before he drank. Rich and spicy, the coffee burned its way down into Bolan's empty stomach.

At his side Sharif spoke quietly. "They greet you as a brother warrior. The coffee is their way of acceptance."

"I have been told the Bedouin are great warriors," Bolan said to the assembled group. "Now I see that their hospitality is as justly praised."

Bolan's words were well received. There was much talk then, some of it directed at Bolan. He kept his replies short and respectful.

"Now they will bring food, Cooper. What is ours is yours. We apologize it is not a sumptuous as we would like to offer you, but as you may see, this is a small group. We were on a hunt for food when my brothers and I stumbled into the hands of those dogs."

Bolan had observed the way the Bedouin settled themselves to eat. Left leg tucked beneath them and the right raised so the arm could rest on it. He adopted the same position as his hosts, and remembered the custom he had read somewhere that the Bedouin ate with three fingers of the right hand *only*.

The food when it arrived on a circular flat dish consisted of a deep layer of rice cooked in *samn,* a form of clarified butter. It was accompanied by roast mutton. Around the edge of the dish was a sprinkling of pine nuts. There was also cooked bread made of flour, dates and *samn*. The dish was placed centrally and Bolan felt all eyes on him. As the guest he was given the first choice from the communal dish. He obliged, taking rice and mutton in his fingers, tasting the spiced food and nodding in appreciation. Once Bolan had made the first move it was open for the gathering to join in. Bolan ate along with the Bedouin, listening to their conversation, sometimes in Arabic, while English was also used as a gesture of respect to their American guest. He joined in when a question was put to him. The Bedouin were excellent hosts, making Bolan feel at home in their midst. When the meal was over and more coffee was passed around, the business became serious.

"I have explained to them about the camp where we were captive," Sharif said. "About our murdered brothers and the terrible weapon those criminals intend to release on the Israelis."

Bolan was aware of the silence that had fallen as Sharif spoke.

"I have to go back, Ali. One of the reasons I came here was to destroy whatever the Iranians and their Fedayeen allies have stored. Now that I've learned about the chemical, it is even more important I stop them."

Sharif nodded. "This I understand. And what I said before I will honor. I will go with you."

"And I," called one of the gathered Bedouins.

His offer was picked up by the others.

"We have a duty also to avenge our slain brothers," said another.

"It is Bedu tradition that those who are wronged must be avenged. It has always been this way. We would be betraying our own if we did nothing," Sharif explained. "You understand this?"

Bolan nodded. He understood only too well.

"We will leave in the morning. Tonight we rest. Will you share my tent, Cooper?"

"Thank you, Ali."

THEY ROSE EARLY, THE BEDOUIN leaving Bolan as they said their morning prayer. Breakfast was dates and Bedouin coffee, following which the camp was broken up and packed on two camels. The Bedouin then prepared their weapons, checking and loading the assault rifles they carried. Bolan noticed they were all armed with AK-47s. Sharif explained that the weapon was the common denominator in the region. It was readily available wherever they traveled and could be purchased easily. The Soviet Union military complex, if it was remembered for little else, had sustained a legacy that would survive forever. Some of the men carried handguns and they all, to a man, wore sheathed knives.

Sharif was leading Bolan across to the camel herd when the American paused, looking in the direction of the slope that had brought them into the camp. There had been a single Bedouin on sentry duty since first light. The man had gone.

"Ali, has the guard been relieved from the ridge?"

"Of course not…" Sharif said. He followed the line of Bolan's gaze, stared at the empty spot, and was immediately galvanized into action, shouting orders to the others.

Bolan had already picked up the rising throb of an approaching vehicle. "They found us."

The truck appeared above the rim and swooped in toward the Bedouin. The crackle of a machine gun sounded, flat and brittle, sending a line of hot slugs that chewed at the sandy ground then hit a couple of the tethered camels. Blood sprayed the air as the animals staggered, bellowing in pain as they fell. The action galvanized the tribesmen into movement, some turning to reach for their weapons, others running in shocked panic. The firing continued as the truck sped down the sandy slope, the heavy burst ripping into flesh. Two men went down, spinning in stunned agony, disbelief in minds unable to grasp the reality of what was happening.

Sharif stumbled as he neared the cover of the trees, his anger making him turn to see what had happened. On his knees he fumbled with the AK-47, his dark eyes fixing on Bolan.

"You see what these dogs are doing to my people? This will be slaughter."

Bolan was watching the circling truck, his unwavering gaze fixed on the vehicle. "Maybe not," he said quietly.

"What are you thinking, Cooper?" Sharif asked. "To attack that truck?"

Bolan's next act gave Sharif his answer as the tall American moved quickly around the stand of palms, taking cover by the thick trunk of the last in line. He leaned around the palm, settling the AK-47 as he tracked in on the moving truck. He made no indication he had noticed when Sharif joined him, watching in silence as Bolan studied his intended target.

The armed truck spun wildly as the driver worked the gears. The machine gun opened up again, the barrel sweeping back and forth, raking the area with further blistering bursts. The weapon was swung out at an angle, flexible on its universal mount, allowing the gunner plenty of latitude when it came to widening his field of fire. There was a cold efficiency as he targeted more of the Bedouin's camels. The helpless animals were cut down ruthlessly.

Sharif sighed in despair. The camel was a prized possession within the Bedouin tribes. They allowed the roving tribes to move whenever and wherever they wanted, providing them with far-ranging freedom and independence. Killing them was a direct insult to the Bedouin, showing contempt for them and their age-old traditions.

A half-strangled scream of defiance came as one of the tribesmen ran into view, shaking a clenched fist at the attackers. The robed figure took a stance, raising the assault rifle he carried to his shoulder and opening fire. It was a pointless exercise. The man fired without aiming, allowing his anger to dictate his actions rather than employing cool logic to the situation. All he did was waste his ammunition and present himself as an easy target for the truck's gunner. There was a chill finality in the way the gunner eased his weapon around, lining up on the Bedouin. The machine gun crackled briefly, directing a white-hot stream of 7.62 mm slugs into the Arab. His body jerked awkwardly as the bullets hammered into him and tore open his yielding flesh.

Bolan fired, taking his cue from the slowing truck as the driver watched the gunner's handiwork. The AK's 7.62 mm slugs hit the windshield, shattering the glass. The driver threw his hands up at his pierced face, screaming as keen shards penetrated his eyes. The out-of-control truck made a sudden turn, spilling men from the rear. Bolan raked the hood, sending slugs into the engine compartment, and the vehicle stalled as the power was cut.

The dazed men were hastily climbing to their feet, reaching for dropped weapons.

"Let's go," Bolan snapped.

Sharif realized Bolan's intention, and though he responded quickly he was steps behind the big American as Bolan ran toward the truck, the AK tracking and firing. His first burst took down two of the strike team, knocking them off their feet in bloody disarray. Others returned fire as they found themselves caught by the autofire from the rest of the Bedouin. Bolan kept moving forward. There were enemies to deal with and there was no other way than to maintain the advantage.

One of the attackers got behind the machine gun and swiveled it around to track Bolan's advancing figure. The moment the Executioner saw the weapon move he dropped to a crouch, bringing him below the immediate trajectory of the muzzle.

Before the gunner could realign his weapon Bolan opened
fire, burning off a volley that clipped the edge of the truck before locating its human target. The would-be gunner was
thrown back, bloody debris exploding from his chest. Bolan
angled away from the truck, coming in from the side and
caught the next man as he dropped from the vehicle. The
warrior's burst hit the guy in mid-jump, knocking him sideways and dropping him bloody and squirming into the sand.

Sharif gave a warning yell as a second man pushed to his
feet from the bed of the truck, clutching a hand grenade. He
had pulled the pin when Sharif fired, his burst rippling across
the man's chest. As he fell he dropped the activated grenade.
Seconds later the truck was the center of the explosion. The
grenade set off stored ammunition and extra fuel cans, and the
vehicle vanished in a burst of shivering fire and smoke.

Bolan had a split second to drop to the ground as the truck
blew. He buried himself in the sand, hoping that Sharif had
done the same. He felt the slap of flying debris across his
prone form and sensed the wash of heat from the explosion.
Something hard and sharp scored a searing line across the
back of his left shoulder. As the heat died away the rumble of
the blast began to fade, leaving Bolan with diminished hearing. He shook his head against the effects of the explosion,
pushing to his feet, sleeving stinging smoke from his watering eyes.

He was on the periphery of the blast area. Burning chunks
of wreckage were strewed around the former camp. One of
the Arabs was slapping at a smoldering robe. Within the blast
circle scorched bodies lay on the blackened sand. One man
was still on his feet, stumbling blindly, clothing and flesh still
burning, blood soaking through his clothing. Sensing Bolan,
the man turned in his direction, pained eyes pleading from the
grisly, burned-raw face, his lower jaw blown away. He raised

an arm in Bolan's direction, not realizing he had lost the limb below the elbow. The sound that issued from his heat-scorched throat was less than human. Bolan raised the AK and laid a short volley into the torso, a mercy burst that ended the man's suffering.

"It speaks well of a man that he treats his enemy with compassion," Sharif said from where he stood at Bolan's side.

"No man deserves to suffer that way."

Sharif considered the American's words. "Some of my people might question that. Perhaps we are not as civilized as you might expect us to be, Cooper. Remember we are only a tribe of roving Bedu. What do we know of compassion and justice?"

Bolan glanced at the Arab. He had noted the sardonic tone in Sharif's voice, and he knew the man was teasing him, seeking to clarify the American's opinion.

"Small in number, perhaps, Ali. But the reputation of the Bedouin is known throughout the world. And that isn't a small reputation. The Bedouin are known for their courage, compassion and their sense of honor."

Sharif nodded slowly. His brown features quickly became a mask of quiet pride.

"The camp where those dogs came from? It is still your wish to go back?"

"Yes, Ali, this's still my wish."

Sharif nodded. "Today you have fought with us as a true Bedu. So as a brother of the Rwala, your wish is ours." The Bedouin looked into Bolan's face. "Have we not found a common enemy, Cooper?"

Bolan indicated the burning hulk of the truck. "What does that tell you, Ali? They came to slaughter your people, simply because you stood against them. Because you and I know they are planning to attack across the border into Israel. They will release their poison on women and children. They want to create fear and distrust that will spread all across the Middle East. Turn brothers against each other and soak the desert with blood."

Sharif considered the American's words. "True, I have no great love for the Israelis. But they have stayed within their borders and the Bedu have had little dealings with them. Even so, these damned Iranians and their Fedayeen have set up camp on the land of the Bedouin and they chase *us* away if we venture near. And now—" he gestured dramatically with his arm "—they have dared to strike at us at our own well.

"The Bedu are few now. Our times of ruling the great desert lands are well past. But what we have left we guard with our lives. Our pride is all we have, Cooper, so we will go with you to this place and we will show these foreigners it does not pay to camp on Bedu land without permission."

CHAPTER TEN

The dead and wounded were tended to. It was decided that they would be returned to the main encampment in the far desert. The survivors would have to share camels because of the loss of a number of animals during the attack. Sharif and twelve of the Bedouin would accompany Bolan for the strike against the Iranian-Fedayeen camp. Apart from their weapons and ammunition they took little with them except for water skins and a little rice and bread.

One of the Bedouin had cleaned the bullet sear on Bolan's back, smearing it with cool ointment then covering it. Before the group moved off in the direction of the main camp, they presented Bolan with a black Bedouin robe and a headdress.

"Your Western clothes will not be good enough. These Bedu robes will protect you from the desert," Sharif said as he helped Bolan put on the clothing. "And Allah the compassionate will do the rest."

SHIMMERING HEAT WAVES DANCED across the silent desert. To Bolan it was a featureless landscape with little to show one mile from the next. His Bedouin companions rode with the confidence of a people in total accord with the hostile terrain.

Bolan's Bedouin companions had instructed him how to sit on the curved, padded saddle on his camel, showing him the way to hook his right leg around the high saddle horn and tuck his foot beneath his left knee. It helped support him as the plodding camel created a swaying motion. Bolan was aware they were watching him as they set out. He adjusted to the motion after a time. Once he had mastered the art of sitting on the saddle, he found it to be more comfortable than he had imagined. Sharif showed him how to handle the reins, patiently advising the American and nodding in satisfaction at Bolan's ability to take the advice on board and put it into practice.

"You see, it is not difficult. Even for an American," he said loud enough for the others to hear, and eliciting a round of amiable laughter.

"You are as good a teacher as you are a warrior," Bolan returned.

"This one has also been listening to Ali's words, as well," one of the Bedu said. "His praise slides off the tongue like honey from a bee."

There was more laughter from the group and the Bedouin rode their camels around Bolan, bowing and saluting him with great affection. Later, as they strung out again, moving silently across the desert, Sharif moved his camel alongside.

"You have become one of them. What you did back at the camp will be long remembered. The Bedu respect courage and loyalty and above all they honor friendship, Cooper. You will always be welcome in the camps of the Bedu."

"Thank you, Ali. I will treasure that above all else."

TOWARD NOON OF THE following day they came within sight of the camp. Sharif had brought them to a place where they could sit concealed by sweeping sand slopes and ridges. A hot desert breeze sifted fine sand across their path, drifting in fine clouds, and they pulled the folds of their keffiyahs over their mouths to protect themselves.

"Cooper, come with me," Sharif said, dismounting.

Bolan followed him and they climbed to the top of the steep ridge, going prone and looking across the open stretch of sand that led up to the campsite.

Sharif produced a battered pair of binoculars. The outer casing showed extreme wear and the original leather carrying strap had been replaced by a hand-braided cord.

"These are English glasses. My family acquired them from a British officer during the Second World War. Since then they have been passed down through the generations of my family."

The Bedouin raised the glasses and focused on the distant camp.

"Three vehicles. The helicopter. I see much activity, Cooper."

Sharif handed the binoculars to Bolan. The magnification was impressive. As he brought the camp into sharp relief, Bolan saw armed figures taking down the tents and loading equipment onto trucks. Even as he watched he saw a third truck move up to park near the stone building housing the weapons cache.

"Looks like they're moving out," Bolan said, "and taking the weapons with them."

"Then we have little time to wait," Sharif said. "We must strike now."

Bolan had the same feeling. If they allowed Kerim to leave, it would prove difficult to deal with the group banded together to protect their cache of weapons. Kerim would also have his armed helicopter as his main deterrent. Machine guns and missiles would present a deadly threat to Bolan and his mounted allies.

As they returned to the other Bedouins were waiting Bolan saw their main chance lay in a fast strike. Sweeping in out of the desert they might gain the advantage and inflict heavy casualties before the terrorist group could retaliate. It was a calculated risk, which was accepted by Sharif's Bedouins when the suggestion was put to them. In battle there was no such thing as a cut-and-dried victory. Any plan, no matter how carefully set out, could change during its execution. Mack Bolan, better than any of them, could agree to that. He only had to recall the times when intended soft probes of an enemy had turned hard, more often than not when a small change kicked in the warning alarm. Simple things, incidental to the big picture, but happening at the wrong time in the wrong place. Risk came with the job, Bolan knew, and this time would be no different.

"Did you see the ridge that curves in around the east side of the camp?" Sharif asked. "If we ride behind this ridge, we can bring ourselves close to the camp before we show ourselves."

"I saw the ridge and had the same thought. But remember, Ali, they have automatic weapons, too. And they're not about to stand by when we hit them."

"If Allah decrees some of us must die, then it is written and will be so," one of the Bedouin said.

"Then it will be my honor to fight beside you," Bolan said.

Sharif placed a hand on Bolan's shoulder. "My friend if you had darker skin I would believe I had just listened to a Bedu speaking."

Weapons were given a final check and spare magazines placed for easy availability. Bolan's own check was done automatically, his mind on something else.

The bioweapon.

Conventional weapons were one thing. The very presence of the bioweapon notched up the threat rating. It needed erasing fully. Bolan could only see a single, reliable way to achieve that.

Fire. The cleansing power that would consume and nullify the terrible weapon.

Bolan's first thought was fuel. There had to be some kind of fuel dump within the camp. Gas for the vehicles and the helicopter.

And with that thought Bolan's thinking progressed to the helicopter itself, which was armed with a missile pod that would offer a sound means of destroying the weapons cache.

"Ali, I need time to reach the helicopter. Get it in the air."

"Why?" Sharif asked, not up to speed.

"When they chased us earlier with the other helicopter, how did they destroy the truck?"

"Of course. A missile. You will do the same to the weapons store?"

"That's the idea."

Sharif turned to his men and rapidly explained what Bolan had outlined to him. A round of agreement followed, and the Bedouin turned to their camels and mounted up. Sharif waited until Bolan had settled on his own mount, then led the group along the base of the curving sandy ridge until they were near its end. They gathered for a final moment before Sharif edged his camel alongside Bolan's.

"We will do this, my friend."

CHAPTER ELEVEN

The Bedouin coaxed their camels into a gallop, emitting loud cries as they rounded the cover of the ridge and raced in the direction of the camp. There was a short break of inactivity before Kerim's men froze, not quite realizing what was happening. They sprang into action as the Bedouin opened fire, the startlingly loud crackle of their AKs defining the moment. Return fire followed as the Bedouin closed in on the camp's defenders. Bolan saw two of Kerim's men go down during the initial assault, and as the defenders rushed to protect the perimeter their answering fire brought one camel crashing to the ground, spilling its rider onto the sand. The Bedouin scrambled behind the downed animal and used it as a shield while he kept firing. A second Bedouin was toppled from his saddle by a bullet that lodged in his chest. Neither side faltered.

"Let's go, Ali," Bolan said, and kicked his camel into a run, angling away from the main fight.

Sharif fell in at his side and they directed their mounts toward their objective. Bolan had already seen two armed figures stationed close to the helicopter. He transferred the AK to his left hand, laying back in the saddle as Sharif had shown him, and felt the camel increase its stride.

Swinging his mount away from Bolan, Sharif gripped his saddle with both legs, leaving his hands free for his weapon. He saw a pair of Kerim's men moving forward to intercept them and leaned to one side, lowering the AK's muzzle. He triggered a burst that struck the sand only feet from his target, causing the gunner to sidestep. Adjusting his aim, Sharif fired a second time. His slugs caught the guard midchest, spinning him off his feet and dropping him to the ground. Sharif hit him with a final burst as his camel closed in on the landing pad. He didn't hear the next shots, coming from the second man, only felt the solid impact as slugs tore into his side. He lost his grip and fell from the saddle. Sharif hit the ground with stunning force, his momentum sliding him for yards before he rolled to a stop.

Bolan saw the first terrorist fall, then registered Sharif tumbling awkwardly from the saddle. Before he could fire himself, his camel slammed into the second man, throwing him across the sand. The guard scrambled to his knees, spitting sand from his mouth, his rifle still in his hands, searching for a target. He had little opportunity as Bolan turned his own AK loose, the assault rifle jacking out its shots and driving the man to the blood-spattered sand. Bolan slid to the ground and crossed to where Sharif was sitting up. His hand clasped against his bleeding side.

"Let me take a look, Ali."

The Bedouin pushed his hand aside. "Now is not the time, Cooper. Take that helicopter and do what we came here for. Go. Go now."

Bolan opened the hatch and climbed into the pilot's seat. He ran a swift check, then started to wind up the Lynx's power plant. While it built speed Bolan checked the weapons array, activating the firing controls. His readout told him he had six HE missiles. They would be adequate for what he intended. Over his head the rotors were spinning with increased velocity. Bolan took a breath and forced himself to go through the instructions Grimaldi had implanted during their training sessions.

The chopper eased off the ground. Bolan didn't waste time, turning and throttling back so he wouldn't overshoot his intended target. The chopper slid forward and the soldier could see the weapon store ahead. He reminded himself not to get too close. There was other ordnance in there as well as the bio-weapon. A hit from one of the missiles was liable to set that off that, as well.

Bolan felt something whine off the side of the helicopter. He was under fire. He could imagine Kerim's rage when he realized what was about to happen. His precious cache of bio-weaponry was about to go up in smoke, terminating his operation against Israel. The chopper took a few more hits. One shattered the side window behind Bolan. He felt shards of Plexiglas spray across the interior.

He checked weapons control and fired the first missile. The white trail angled down toward the store. It struck a foot short, but there was still enough force for the outer wall to be demolished. Bolan adjusted his trajectory, hit the button again and this time made a direct hit. The stone building vanished in the blast, sending splintered stone and sand into the air. The truck he had seen close by the structure was caught in the backlash from the explosion, the blast turning it on its side before a spread of fire washed over it. A secondary blast followed as the munitions and explosives stored within the cache detonated. Bolan laid down a third and fourth missile, reducing the building and the immediate area into a blackened crater that sent flame and smoke into the clean desert air. A hard rain of debris began to fall back to earth.

Aware he was still under small-arms fire Bolan swung the chopper away from the camp, then turned so he could survey the scene below. The main battle looked to have petered out, with Sharif's Bedouin having overcome the camp's main force. He could see the Bedouin riders crisscrossing the area, still firing at stragglers. Then he picked up one of the trucks moving away from the camp, armed figures leaning out from the rear and firing at the Bedouin. Bolan turned the helicopter and swung in behind the truck as it picked up speed, a thick trail of dust in its wake. The moment the men in the rear realized he was locked on, they began to fire up at the helicopter. Bolan came in low, directly behind the vehicle, ignoring the frenzied fire, and took his shot. The missile struck and the truck was lifted off the ground by the impact of the HE blast. It turned over onto its roof, spinning and toppling, trailing a tail of flame and smoke. Debris, mechanical and human, was strewed in its wake before it came to a stop, black smoke rising into the air.

Bolan swung around and took the helicopter back to the campsite, putting it down and climbing out. He had spotted a SIG-Sauer P-226 in a clip beside the pilot's seat. The weapon held a full mag. Bolan tucked it behind his belt before he exited the aircraft, his AK cradled in his arms. He made his way to where he had last seen Ali bin Sharif and found the Bedouin being carried by two of his men. They placed him on a makeshift mattress. Sharif waved his arm across the campsite.

"Today we have shown the Bedu are not to be trifled with, Cooper."

"Yes, Ali, we did. You will have a great story to tell your grandchildren."

"And of the American warrior who rode and fought with us. Do not forget that, Cooper."

"Now let me look at your wound," Bolan said.

Sharif had caught a couple of 7.62 mm slugs in the right side. The bullets had gone in deep enough to require surgery. All Bolan could do in the meantime was pad the wounds and bind them tight to prevent too much blood loss.

"Ali, stay still. I'm going to get help."

Bolan crossed to the helicopter and worked on the radio. It took him a while but he eventually picked up the Jordanian MilNet. He had to do some fast talking when he was put in contact with an English-speaking officer. The prases "terrorist incursion" into Jordanian territory, "possible attacks on Israeli soil" and the need to send in a biohazard cleanup team seemed to push the right buttons. Bolan also made his contact aware there were wounded Bedouin needing urgent assistance. His final request was for the Jordanians to make contact with the U.S. He gave a code name that would alert Stony Man, via the President, then went back to help the Bedouin tend their casualties.

Two were dead. Apart from Sharif, three others had sustained wounds. The campsite was searched for anything that would to comfort the injured until help arrived.

There were no survivors from Kerim's force, and Kerim himself was among the dead. The Bedouin had exacted their own form of justice, and the dead bore mute evidence of that. Bolan made no comment. This was Bedouin land and they had taken summary justice against those who had invaded their territory and attacked without provocation. For himself he was content the bioweapon had been neutralized. The Jordanian biohazard team would check the area and make sure of that.

Sitting in the scant shade provided by the bullet-scarred helicopter Bolan thought ahead. He had succeeded here, but his mission was far from over. The destruction of the camp and its potential threat had been removed, but the Iran nuclear problem was still up and running. He needed to follow through and to get himself on the trail of the stolen data that could lead him to the supplier and, ultimately, the Iranian facility.

IT MIGHT HAVE GONE HARDER than it did for Bolan if his Stony Man contact hadn't cleared a way. The arrival of the Jordanian security team, accompanied by a biohazard squad, resulted in Bolan being put under armed guard. The captain in charge, a slim, handsome Jordanian in immaculate uniform and traditional headdress, eyed the tall American with obvious suspicion. He had Bolan searched, and debated whether to put him in restraints. Something about the American's manner told him Bolan wouldn't cause any problems, so the captain left him under armed guard. To his credit the captain had the wounded, including Sharif, placed in one of the helicopters that had flown him in and ordered they be flown to the nearest hospital for immediate treatment. Bolan was allowed to speak to Sharif before he was airlifted away.

The captain's surveying the scene proved to him that what had been reported was accurate. The camp was certainly not an official site. And the presence of weapons lying beside the bodies added to the initial effect. The captain spoke with the Bedouin, who related what had happened. In the meantime the biohazard team had sealed off the area where the weapons cache had existed. They began a thorough examination of the crater and the debris.

Bolan watched the activity with interest, hoping his story had been accepted. He had little control over events here now and would have to remain an observer. The Jordanians worked with quiet efficiency, checking bodies, feeding data into the laptops they carried, and all the time the young captain oversees the proceedings. From his expression Bolan could sense he was working things out in his own mind, only breaking off from his assessment when his cell phone rang a number of times and he took the calls.

Some time later the captain made his way across to where Bolan stood. Dismissing the armed guard, the captain looked Bolan up and down, taking in the Bedouin garb.

"I have to say it suits you, Mr. Cooper. Your Bedouin friends obviously hold you in high regard." His English was impeccable.

"They are good people. I owe them a great deal."

The captain looked around. "Well, you have certainly had a busy time here one way and another."

"I guess you could say that."

"My name is Hassan, Captain Aleer Hassan." He held out a hand to Bolan. "That call I took confirms everything you told me, though it's unusual to have an American operation in the country. You seem to have friends in high places. So, a little late, but welcome to Jordan."

He led Bolan across to where a small field table had been erected in the shade of one of the helicopters. Laptops were being used to collate information.

"Fingerprint and facial evidence from a number of the dead have been scanned into the data banks. We have identified three people so far. These two are former Fedayeen from Saddam Hussein's Republican Guard units. This one, unfortunately, is a Jordanian national known for his extreme views, especially concerning the Israelis. We have yet to identify the others, but from what we have learned so far it would appear your earlier information holds true."

"Anything on the bioweapon?"

"The biohazard team is reviewing what they found. They should have something for us very soon."

"What now, Captain?"

"I will arrange for you to be taken to Aqaba. It seems you will have an aircraft waiting for you. But first there is someone who needs to talk with you. It has to do with what has happened here. It seems you have far reaching influence." Hassan smiled. "I could wish for such power. It would make my job so much easier."

One of the biohazard team met them as they walked across the camp site. He still wore his bright orange protective suit but had removed the helmet and gloves. He had a printout in his hand.

"Captain Hassan, we have our results." The man stared at Bolan, reluctant to say more.

"It's fine, Mahun. Mr. Cooper is clear to be included. Now, what have you found?"

"The missiles destroyed almost everything, but we were lucky and found a small glass fragment that still held trace evidence. We put it through the analysis program and it came up with this." He waved the printout. The paper was covered with technical data that might as well have been an ancient language to Bolan and Hassan.

"In English, please," Hassan said.

Mahun nodded. "Yes. In essence what we found was a sample of a powerful virus. It is known to us, stored on our database of bioweapons. It's of Soviet origin. Something they developed quite a long time ago. ZK386 is its designation, and it's an extremely virulent strain that the Soviets found to be very unstable. If it had been released into the civilian population there would have been many thousands of deaths. In its unstable form the virus was found to be self-sustaining. If it drifted, it could have infected a far greater area. Bioweapons have no regard for territorial borders, shall we say."

"Has the virus been destroyed?" Bolan asked.

"Your missiles saw to that. We will, however, monitor the

crater until we are completely satisfied." Mahun turned to leave, paused and turned back. "We are in your debt, Mr. Cooper. There is no doubt the effects of the weapon could have easily have drifted into our country. Thank you for preventing that."

Before he was airlifted out Bolan met with the Bedouin to offer his thanks as they prepared to return to their distant camp. The last he saw of them was the single line of camels and riders fading into the distance of the Jordanian desert.

"They are a part of our history," Hassan said. "Still fiercely independent."

"I hope they're allowed to stay that way," Bolan said.

"It would be a struggle to make them change." Hassan smiled. "Then why should they?"

"It isn't always left to the ones it concerns."

"True." Hassan gave Bolan a crisp salute before he turned and returned to his teams.

Bolan climbed on board the Royal Jordanian Air Force helicopter and settled in his seat. The aircraft rose into the air, swinging around as the pilot set course for the distant city of Aqaba. Bolan's question on flight time got him a satisfactory answer—just under two hours. He settled back in the seat, closing his eyes, letting sleep take over.

CHAPTER TWELVE

Aqaba glittered in the soft night. The city was dotted with lights, the sky overhead bright with stars. Bolan emerged from the shower, feeling a degree better than when he had entered the hotel. His robed appearance had caused something of a stir, but Bolan had ignored that and strolled to the reception desk.

"Messages?" he had asked the clerk.

"Yes, Mr. Novak." The clerk handed over an envelope. He inspected Bolan from head to foot. "Are you all right, sir? Do you need anything?"

"Only a shower and a pot of strong coffee."

"I will have the coffee sent to your room." The young man's face was still full of concern.

"Camel ride went a little haywire," Bolan said lightly. "We didn't get along to well."

"I am sorry, sir."

"Not as much as the camel is," Bolan said, and turned away.

HE OPENED THE NOTE IN his room and read, "Call me," followed by a telephone number. Bolan picked up the room phone and punched in the digits. The cell was answered immediately. A man's voice.

"Do I call you Novak or Cooper?"

"At the desk I'm Novak. Hey, I hope we're not going to start throwing silly passwords at each other."

The other man chuckled. "Is it a problem?"

"Could be. I don't have one."

"I need to see you."

"Give me half an hour to shower and change."

"I'll have a friend with me."

The phone went dead.

Twenty minutes later Bolan had showered and shaved, taking care around the bruises and abrasions on his face. When he'd stripped, he had noticed the bruises on his torso. They were sore but not bad enough to slow him down. Out of the bathroom he dressed and had another cup of the coffee that had arrived a few minutes earlier.

He opened his bag and took out his cell phone, plugged in the charger and connected to the wall socket. The SIG-Sauer P-226 he had picked up at the camp went into the drawer of the bedside cabinet.

WHEN BOLAN ANSWERED THE knock at his door, two men stood in the corridor. The lead figure was a tall, fit-looking man with tanned skin and thick black hair. His name was Ben Sharon. He was with Mossad and had worked on a number of occasions with Phoenix Force. Bolan had met him a few months earlier on a covert mission involving David McCarter. Sharon held out a hand and took Bolan's.

"Cooper," he said. His knowledge of Bolan's current cover name revealed he was up to speed. "This is Major Afif Mushar, Dairat al Mukhabarat."

Jordanian General Intelligence Department—the GID.

The agency was responsible for protecting the country's security. The GID handled various aspects of intelligence work—information gathering, counterespionage, protecting the country against terrorism. Because of the alliance between the Israeli and Jordanian governments, cooperation had also been extended to cover the workings of the GID and Mossad. It was, in essence, mutual protection and survival.

Mushar was small in stature, but carried himself with confidence. Even in casual civilian clothing he looked as if he were wearing a uniform. He took Bolan's hand and shook it strongly.

"Good to make your acquaintance," he said.

Bolan closed the door once they were inside his room.

"I take it this isn't just a social call?"

Sharon laughed. "I wish I could recall the last time I made a social call. It tends to be all business these days."

"And this is no different?"

Mushar placed his slim attaché case on the bed and opened it. He removed a black folder, then spread out surveillance photographs.

"Mossad and GID have been monitoring the movement of a cell under the command of this man, Ayatollah Razihra, an Iranian. It's a name you have heard recently, I believe?"

"Among others," Bolan said. "Razihra seems to be the top guy. A man by the name of Kerim was in charge of the camp. He had two of Hussein's ex-Fedayeen loyalists along for the ride. There is a third guy on the loose somewhere and some pro-Iran Jordanians."

"Yes. Unfortunately there is a faction within the country sympathetic to Razihra's cause." Mushar glanced at Sharon. "It would appear Mr. Cooper has picked up information rather quickly."

"It's his way of working," Sharon said. "At least it shows

our intel gathering has been along the right track. Razihra's main supplier of weapons is this Anatoly Nevski. He's Russian born, but moves to wherever the market is buoyant. Our intel suggests Nevski has been moving consignments around the Middle East. He's no beginner and is happy to lay out big money to get what he wants and to get protection. It seems to be working, too."

"We have data on the guy. I guess you heard what I found at the camp?"

Mushar nodded. "I will be honest, Mr. Cooper. That came as a shock to us. We had no idea that was Razihra's intention. My country owes you a debt of gratitude for destroying that cache."

"Your biohazard people identified the virus as of Russian origin."

"Yes. They have a database on many bioweapons. The ZK386 is one even the Russians hoped would never be brought into play."

"Unstable, I recall your man saying."

"Exactly. The Russians couldn't truly control it. Somewhere during its development the strain overrode every protocol and became self-replicating. It was locked away and no further work done on it, which means there was never an antidote developed for it."

"In my book we owe you more than just a vote of thanks, Cooper. A hell of a lot more," Sharon said.

"Is the general line of thinking that Nevski handled this for Razihra?"

"He's the only one we know of who could pull off something like that," Mushar said. "Nevski has ex-military contacts, people who have access to all kinds of military hardware. He also offers technicians to back up weapon development for his clients. Cooper, have you heard the name? Gregori Malinski?"

"Part of my initial briefing. He's a nuclear physicist who believed to have sold his expertise to the Iranians. But it appears he's gone AWOL."

"Nevski was the middleman. He contracted Malinski to work for Razihra."

Bolan was standing at the window, looking down on the city. "If Malinski has gone into hiding, the Iranians will want him back. He'll also know the location of the research facility. Now there's a guy I'd like to link up with."

"You're going to make an attempt to pull the plug on the nuke research?"

Bolan nodded.

A cell phone rang and Mushar pulled one from his pocket. He listened intently, a thin smile showing at what was obviously good news. When he finished the call he glanced across at Bolan and Sharon.

"We have Razihra's safehouse located and under observation."

"This has been our priority for the past week," Sharon explained. "We knew the group had a location in the city somewhere, but we couldn't pin it down until we started picking up cell phone calls from Lem Kirov. Something about a delivery. It was pure luck one of our listening stations locked on to the cell. We checked out the number and found it belonged to Kirov. Traced it back and located his call list. The man has been careless with his calls. He's either convinced he's untouchable, or he doesn't understand a cell phone call can leave a trail. One of the numbers he called on a regular basis turned out to be located here in Aqaba."

"The signal never moved, suggesting it was in a permanent location," Mushariff said. He held up his own phone. "That was the call we have been waiting for. Our people have the address, and they have identified our suspects. We have at least two of the pro-Iranian locals going in and out. And within the last hour Jafir, one of the Fedayeen exiles, was photographed at a window."

"No evacuation of the house?" Bolan asked. "They're all still there?"

Mushar frowned. "Yes. I don't understand..."

"I think Cooper is saying the occupants in the house haven't heard what happened at the camp," Sharon said. "If someone had got through during the attack, the cell would have broken cover and scattered."

"Taking any information with them," Bolan said.

"Of course," Mushar said. "It means we have a chance of taking them unaware." He glanced at his watch. "We have a few hours before full light. I suggest we go in then. I will contact my teams and have them make sure the house is surrounded. If anything happens in the meantime, at least we can prevent their making a run for it."

"I'd like Cooper to come along," Sharon said. "He may find information there that might help his own mission."

"He's earned the right," Mushar said. "Welcome aboard."

Iran

RAZIHRA WAITED UNTIL HIS GUEST was seated before he took his own place. He smoothed his black robe, then quietly made his welcome. The chosen language was French, one that was familiar to both parties.

"I hope the accommodation is to your liking, Fu Chen?"

The slim, expensively dressed Chinese smiled. Razihra had noticed in the early days of their relationship that Chen's eyes maintained an icy distance, even when he was offering a smile. "As expected, you have provided us with the most comfortable quarters, my friend."

"Although your stay will be brief, I felt we needed to make you as comfortable as possible."

The door to the high-ceilinged, airy room opened and a wheeled cart was brought in bearing tea, coffee and bowls of fruit. They engaged in small talk while the refreshments were served. Only when they were alone again did the conversation move to more important matters.

"In a few days the information will be in your hands," Fu Chen said. "I have a courier waiting for when the ship docks. The data will allow you to overcome the difficulties you have been experiencing and hopefully advance development."

Razihra nodded his acceptance.

"Our research has been lacking this data. Without it we would have been forced to delay our program."

Fu Chen raised his cup in the Ayatollah's direction. "Our gift to your beloved country from the People's Republic."

"One we accept with gratitude, especially as it comes from the Americans themselves. A little ironic seeing that they are the most vociferous in denying us the right to create our own destiny."

"An irony that does not go unnoticed," Fu Chen added. "The Americans make a great fuss over their superiority, yet it is one of their own who has been the broker in this transaction."

Razihra sighed. "We must be successful in this endeavor. A great deal depends on it. If we allow the Americans and their allies to force their policies on the region, we will suffocate beneath a great black cloud of repression. The Americans want our natural wealth. If we allow them to walk over us, they will strip away all we have."

Fu Chen leaned forward. "They covet your oil above all else. It is needed to perpetuate their war machine. It is why they court Masood. You and I both know he is in their hands. The Americans will connive to draw him into their camp, and if that happens he will negotiate away the oil concessions and they will become just another U.S. possession."

"It is no secret that Nuri Masood favors the Americans." This came from Reza Khammere, sitting to Razihra's left. He was a big man, powerful beneath his linen suit, dark, with glittering eyes that seemed able to see deep inside a man's soul. "And he has the majority of the cabinet on his side, the moderates, modernizers who have visions of Iran becoming another Saudi. Oil rich, with the elite driving around in great American cars while the rest of the country falls behind."

"Reza speaks the truth," Razihra said. "His security people listen and watch, and they are aware what is happening."

"Then we are placed in the position where we must act," Khammere said. "If we do not, Iran will degenerate into a godless place where the people see only the blasphemous ideology of the Americans and their Israeli lapdogs."

"Masood is too comfortable with the American way of doing business," Fu Chen confirmed. "He lacks the fire to stand against them. If he ever possessed the will to fight that feeling has long since died. He prefers to sit back, nodding in agreement with his American advisers."

"And our nuclear weapons?" Khammere questioned.

Razihra did nothing to hide his contempt. "He will give in under the guidance of his American friends. I have no doubt they will persuade him to quash the program. He never truly wanted it, and he believes that renouncing it will increase our standing in the region."

Fu Chen leaned back, expressing an audible sigh. "Ending the research would not be advisable. To stop now would set Iran back years. Fall behind and you will be left in the cold, a country without the strength of arms to back your policies."

"The Americans favor Iran as a nonnuclear power. It suits their purpose. A weak Iran poses only a small threat to them."

"Then we must commit to whatever requirements are needed to continue development," Khammere said. "We know that Dr. Baresh will attend the conference with the American, Cameron Gordeno, in a few days. Baresh carries Masood's words on dismissing the nuclear proposals."

"Baresh is a skilled negotiator," Razihra agreed. "He could convince the Americans Iran is ready to acquiesce. They would be prepared to be more generous if that was assured."

"Masood depends on Baresh," Khammere said. "If he was removed it would disrupt the discussions. He would be a hard man to replace. Masood has no one who could step in."

Khammere let his words hang. It was Fu Chen who added his thoughts to the moment.

"There is much in what Reza says. A prolonged delay in negotiations would cause difficulties for Masood and the Americans, but it would benefit our cause. Dare I say it might help to sway opinions?"

"Reza, I will leave the matter in your capable hands," Razihra said. "Instruct Nevski to prepare his man to deal with Baresh."

Khammere nodded. "It will be done." He excused himself and left the room.

"A capable man?" Fu Chen asked.

"Extremely."

Fu Chen helped himself to a glass of cool water, drinking slowly. Razihra sensed the man was deliberating over something.

"I would have regrets if Masood became too insular," the Chinese said. "I respect your views on maintaining Iran's secular stance. However there is a need to remain viable as a nation and the natural resources you possess could benefit the country immensely."

Razihra smiled at Fu Chen's reticence. "I understand exactly what you are saying, Fu Chen. There is a popular move to gain closer ties with our Asian brethren, which is why your assistance and advice have been so well sought. Our futures are linked in many ways. Culturally, spiritually and from a desire to rid ourselves of American domination. Let us not be coy, Fu Chen. We unite to destabilize a common enemy. A simple fact, but one that holds much credence in both our regions of the world. Even I am not naive enough to deny there is a Chinese agenda. That part of your cooperation that has eyes for Iran's oil. I am not offended. In truth, Fu Chen, I would prefer our oil to go to your country at a loss, than to America for a fortune."

Fu Chen inclined his head slightly. "I bow to your forthright openness, Razihra. Perhaps I was taking Chinese diplomacy too far. I should have realized that you have understanding far beyond your projected image."

Razihra nodded. "The general consensus is that a man who wears religious garb is nothing but a spokesman for his god. He has no awareness of the real world and is of no consequence where financial or business matters are concerned."

"I would not insult you by even harboring such thoughts."

In truth Fu Chen had more than thoughts where Muhar Razihra was concerned. Razihra had his own secrets, but Fu Chen's people had uncovered them. Their extensive probe into the man's personal life had exposed his financial status, kept healthy by the carefully hidden Swiss bank accounts held under assumed names. Razihra had been funding those accounts over a number of years, and he was a wealthy man. The retreat in the Alborz mountains, paid for by Razihra's followers, was another cleverly maintained facade. The retreat was supposed to be for Razihra's spiritual refreshment. Very little of what went on within the walls ever left the estate. Fu Chen had visited on a number of occasions, and even he had been surprised at the people who came and went. As well as his political and religious guests, Razihra entertained any number of military advisers, people from disparate regimes and those who could only be described as having distinctly dubious and suspect backgrounds.

A frequent and always well-feted guest was the Russian, Anatoly Nevski. It paid to watch and listen, Chen realized. He soon became aware of Anatoly Nevski's position in the hierarchy. The Russian and Razihra did a great deal of business. As well as his armament and technology, Nevski provided a people service. It was Nevski who had recruited Gregori Malinski. The ex-Soviet nuclear expert had become Razihra's top man at the isolated Wadi Hattat facility.

Fu Chen's train of thought was interrupted by Khammere's sudden return. The man tapped once on the door, then entered the room and crossed to Razihra's side. He bent and spoke quietly to the Ayatollah. Whatever he said had a disturbing effect. He dismissed Khammere with a curt gesture, then stood and crossed the room to stand at one of the large windows, staring out across the expansive grounds. Khammere waited to one side, impassive. Fu Chen allowed Razihra some time before he spoke.

"Bad news, my friend?"

"It appears Dr. Malinski has deserted us. There were suspicions that have now been confirmed. Malinski took a leave of absence from Wadi Hattat to secure dental treatment in Tehran and has disappeared. The security man who accompanied him is nowhere to be found." Razihra turned to face the Chinese. "What would you deduce from that, Fu Chen?"

"That we may have a setback. An unfortunate one, but I'm sure you will find a way around it."

"Replacing Malinski is not going to be a simple matter. His scientific input was the mainstay of our development work. As clever as our people are, they fall extremely short of his skills. If he has decided to leave, I have a feeling he will have left behind a few surprises for our people to work out."

"Why would he suddenly turn against what he was doing?"

"That is hard to determine. A better offer? That I doubt. Since he has been at Wadi Hattat, he has had little contact with outside influences. Perhaps a crisis of conscience. He decided he did not like what he was doing. To be honest, Fu Chen, I see little profit in guessing games. I would rather we were more productive. I want him back. We need to get into that mind of his and extract his secrets." He turned to the waiting Khammere. "Nevski provided me with that Russian. Let him know what has happened and tell him I want him and his people to look into this. Locate Malinski and get him back to Wadi Hattat. We cannot afford to let this interfere with what we're doing."

Khammere's cell phone rang. He answered it, listening, the blood draining from his face as he did. Finishing the call, he seemed reluctant to face Razihra.

"What is it this time? Reza, I do not shoot the messenger."

"The camp in Jordan has been attacked. Many casualties, including Kerim. And the ZK386 has been destroyed."

Razihra caught Fu Chen's eyes. "What were you saying about working around problems?"

"Should I warn Messina?" Khammere asked. "He may not have heard what happened at the camp."

"Do that, Reza. Right away."

When he and Fu Chen were alone again, Razihra sat, considering his options.

"If Nevski was able to obtain the ZK386 for you once, he may be able to do so again," the Chinese said. "The strike against Israel could still be carried out. And they might locate Malinski and bring him back."

"I hope you are correct, Fu Chen, I really do," Razihra said.

CHAPTER THIRTEEN

Aqaba, Jordan

"I still think something is wrong," Messina said. "It is the longest time they have been out of touch."

"Kerim told us he might decide to close communication from time to time to avoid any monitoring picking up transmissions."

Messina was unconvinced. "Rahim, you always seem to have a convenient answer to everything."

Rahim shrugged. "It's part of my charm. I can't help being optimistic. That's what all the ladies say."

"You see," Messina went on. "He always has to have the final word."

The third man in the room, Nussein, was slightly older than the others. He put down the newspaper he was reading. "Why don't one of you do something useful and make some tea? Just listening to you makes me thirsty."

Rahim crossed to the sink and turned on the faucet. Nothing happened. "It's dry. No water."

"It was working earlier," Messina said. He stood, checking out the room, feeding his rising suspicion. "Did anyone turn out the light?" He was looking at the ceiling light.

Rahim was near the switch. He flicked it on and off. No one said anything, but Messina reached down to pick up his AK-47. He worked the bolt, cocking the weapon and eased off the safety. He crossed to the blind covering the window that looked out onto the dusty square fronting the building.

And saw a couple of armed figures moving into position.

"We are surrounded. Jordanian security. Rahim, warn the others."

Rahim left the room and they could hear him running up the stairs.

"Who?" Nussein asked. "Have we been betrayed?"

"I was right. Something has happened at the camp. That is why we have lost contact."

"It can—"

Nussein's words were lost as something crashed through the window, disturbing the cane blind and dropping to the floor. It was a metal canister. Smoke started to issue from it, spiraling into the room.

Angry shouts came from the upper floor. Seconds later glass shattered and someone opened up with an automatic weapon.

There was little time for anything else as the main door shuddered under a solid impact. Wood creaked. The blow was repeated and panels splintered. A third blow and the door flew open, allowing the entry of armed figures in protective combat gear and gas masks. In the brief moment of silence before autofire erupted Messilna heard a commotion at the rear of the house.

The crackle of gunfire drowned everything except the screams of the wounded and dying. The cloying smoke reduced visibility, and Messilna found himself struggling to see much farther than the muzzle end of the AK. He was firing at the advancing figures, aware that he had hit at least one of them. His anger at being discovered evaporated in the desire to survive and take down as many of the enemy as he could. He turned and fired, blinking his eyes against the thickening smoke, which impaired his breathing.

The chaotic rattle of gunfire stung his ears. Something hit the floor at his feet, and his sweeping glance showed the bloodied form of Nussein, chest and throat punctured and torn. Then he was backing up as the intruders pushed deeper into the house, pounding up the stairs and setting off more autofire. He felt the wall at his back. His weapon clicked empty. Messina turned it and used it to club the figures pressing in on him. Someone caught hold of his shoulder and jerked him around. The cold muzzle of a pistol was rammed against the back of his skull.

Messina was preparing to drop his weapon when the pistol was fired, a second shot following the first a second later. The impact of the double-tap rapped his head against the wall. Messina felt only a stunning force before the smells and the noise went away and he slumped to his knees, resting against the wall before dropping facedown on the floor. Above where he lay the wall was spattered with blood and brain and bone fragments.

THE ASSAULT WAS OVER IN minutes. There were no survivors from the house. They all resisted violently, refusing to quit even after they were overwhelmed. At the body count later, eight were identified, including the remaining Fedayeen, Jafir. One member of the Jordanian team died and two were wounded. The short struggle had been intense and extremely violent.

Once the house was secured, Bolan, alongside Ben Sharon, checked out the contents. There were a couple of expensive laptops, cell phones, one of which later turned out to be the one that had led them to the house. There were computer printouts, and in one of the rooms they discovered a cache of weapons and ammunition. As well as AKs and handguns, they found a couple of boxes of hand grenades, blocks of C-4 plastique, fuses and electronic detonators. In one corner were a half dozen Russian-made rocket launchers and a supply of the missiles that went with the weapons.

"I'd say these guys meant business," Bolan said, examining one of the autopistols. "Most of this stuff looks pretty new. If Nevski provided all this, he has a line to a good supplier."

"Our intel suggested he has a contact in the Russian military, someone who can get his hands on prime ordnance and none of that ex-Afghanistan cast-off crap."

"Perhaps if it's the same source that got him his ZK386 virus?" Bolan asked.

"We might be able to trace this back to source through serial numbers," Sharon said. "Mossad has a link with Russian security. I'm certain they'll be interested in any information we can pass their way."

"If you need a good contact in Moscow, try Commander Valentine Seminov," Bolan suggested. "Organized Crime Department. I've worked with him before. He's a good man."

"I'll remember that."

Mushar joined them. He appeared well satisfied with the result of the raid. "I think we will gain much information from all the material we found."

"You mind of I do some looking?" Bolan asked. "I might get something I can use."

"I'm arranging to have it taken back to GID headquarters. You are welcome to come along and go through it."

A COUPLE OF HOURS LATER Bolan and Sharon were ensconced in an office at GID headquarters. Mushar kept them supplied with batches of the written material found at the house, though much of it was unreadable, being written in Arabic. The Jordanian brought in a slim, attractive female operative who made swift translations for Bolan who made quick notes on any relevant sections. They worked well into the afternoon, with only a couple of coffee breaks. By the time they had gone through all the paperwork they had a reasonable breakdown of the cell's intentions.

Mushar had been moving back and forth within the department, checking the progress of his own teams of investigators as they broke down cell phone calls and dug into the data on the laptops.

He came into the office toward the end of the afternoon, sheets of paper in his hands, the expression on his face telling Bolan he had something important to tell them.

"I believe this is what you may have been looking for," Mushar said. It was the transcript of a cell phone discussion between Ayatollah Razihra and Anatoly Nevski. "As neither of them speaks the other's language, the conversation was in English."

Bolan read the printed paper. The two-way conversation was brief and references to individuals sparse, but it didn't take a semantics expert to be able to grasp the subject matter and who was being discussed. When he had read the transcript a couple of times Bolan handed the sheet to Sharon. The Israeli scanned the text.

"So Malinski has disappeared. When Razihra hears about what's happened here, he's going to be really happy."

"I'll be broken up about that," Bolan said. "It means they'll step up the hunt for Malinski. What he's doing for their nuclear program is going to be affected. And they're going to be worried he might give away the location of their research facility."

"What's your next move?" Sharon asked.

"To reach Malinski before Nevski's people. Paris looks to be the main chance. It's where Malinski's daughter is. He might make contact with her. If he does, I want to be there." Bolan reached for a sheet of paper and noted some details. He handed the paper to Mushar. "This is what I picked up from the real Novak. Location of the arms shipment he was coming here to oversee. He finally decided to tell me about it before he was taken into custody in London."

Mushar smiled. "We'll be there. Jordan has had enough of bombings and violence over the past few years. We haven't forgotten the chemical bomb threat we prevented. If that had been used, thousands could have died. Similarly if the one just stopped had been activated. At least that one was prevented, thanks to you, Mr. Cooper." He held up the paper. "This consignment will be seized, I can promise you that."

Sharon stood. He put out his hand. "Good luck in Paris, or wherever you find yourself. Someday we'll meet and have time for a long talk. Or am I just hoping?"

"One day, Ben. One day."

"*Shalom,* my friend."

CHAPTER FOURTEEN

Paris, France

Gregori Malinski had trained in the Soviet Union as a nuclear physicist. His potential had been noted during his days at the state school, and he'd been recruited directly from the Moscow State Technical College before his twenty-first birthday. From then he was trained, directed and indoctrinated by the state machine. In his midtwenties he met and married Vashti Petrovski. They had one child, a daughter they named Sashia.

In 1988 Vashti Malinski became ill with cancer and due to the impoverished condition of the medical services she wasn't given the correct treatment in time. She died, wasting away in front of her husband's eyes, in 1990. A widower with a teenage daughter to raise, Gregori Malinski had looked at his life and found it wanting.

The once mighty Soviet Union, after all those years, was crumbling. A malaise had swept over the country. It was a time of massive change, culminating in the collapse of Communist ideology in 1991. The Soviet Union was no more and there was a mad scramble for position and power, for men of entrepreneurial skills to seize the moment and make their fortunes. For Malinski the new world looked little better than the old one. Cast out by the system that had cloaked him in its stultifying grip since his school days, Gregori Malinski was abandoned. He was a nuclear technician, with skills in mathematics, electronics and quantum physics. He understood the intricacies of the atom and the neutron. He could look at a highly complex mathematical problem and solved it without missing a breath.

He was a highly educated, innovative physicist, but less than a year after the Soviet collapse he was reduced to working in the offices of a computer repair shop. The work was mind-numbing for a man of his skill but it at least paid him a wage. It helped pay the rent of the small apartment he had rented after his state house had been taken from him because he no longer worked for the old department.

Sashia had long ago moved away from Moscow. An attractive, intelligent girl, she had viewed the way things were going and decided to leave. After vain attempts at persuading her father to leave with her—at that time he still believed he would be reinstated in his old job—Sashia had moved on, weary of the constant arguments and the tension it created between them. She took a job in Vienna working for an international tourist company. She rose swiftly up the promotion ladder, being offered a managerial position after two years that took her to Paris, Berlin and a year in New York, before a long-term posting to London. She'd managed to persuade her father to visit her once and was shocked at his changed appearance. The handsome man she had adored had become gray, bespectacled and slightly stooped. She recalled the phrase "old before his time." It fitted him totally. With the outward aging had developed a bitter disillusionment. He felt cheated, robbed of his dignity and forced to work in a dismal world of broken machines.

After the London visit Sashia didn't see her father for more than three years. They corresponded for a time, then even that stopped. It came to the point where she lost touch with him completely, and though it left her saddened she accepted it because she couldn't do a thing to change it. She carried on with her own life, becoming even more successful, traveling the world in an executive position for her company.

She was currently in Paris, on a six-month secondment, living in a suite at the Paris Hilton Hotel, when she received the telephone call that was to change her life. It took a few moments before she realized who was on the other end of the line.

"Father?"

"*Da.*" There was a hesitation. "Sashi," he said, which was his pet name for her, "it is so good to hear your voice." Now he was using English, though with a strong Russian accent.

"What do you want?" She spoke a little harshly, unable to control how she felt.

"Is that a proper greeting for your father?" he chided.

"Don't do this. After years of silence you still treat me like a teenager? I run my own life now. I have a responsible position in an international company. People take orders from *me*. You've pretty much ignored me and left me to survive on my own."

"And you have, Sashi. Wonderfully. I have kept track of your progress. From a distance, yes, because I did not want my life to interfere with yours."

"I have no idea what you are talking about."

"My life has changed, too, Sashi. Depending on your perspective, maybe not for the best. But I did what I had to, in order, as you put it, to survive. But it has not turned out so well. Now it might be about to involve you."

A sense of unease crept up on Sashia. What was her estranged father trying to say?

"I don't understand. Why are you telling me this?"

"Sashi, there are people looking for me. Not very nice people. They might try to locate me through you."

"But I have no idea where you are. I haven't for the past few years."

"They do not know that. And they will not believe you even if you said so." Her father's voice became weary with the burden he was carrying. "They could use you to force me into the open."

"God, what have you done? Who are these people?"

"You don't want to know. Just listen to me, Sashi. Leave wherever you are. Tell no one where you are going. Find somewhere no one knows you. Don't make contact with any of your friends. Or the authorities. These people have high connections. Do not trust anyone. Just drop everything and go."

"You can't expect me to simply walk out on my life on a whim."

Her father's voice sharpened as he spoke. "Listen to me, Sashia Malinski. Do as I say and go if you want to live. Now write down this telephone number but only use it if there is no other way out."

He read out a number sequence and she wrote it down. Before she could say anything more, the line went dead. Sashia stared at the receiver, her mind racing. She juggled the facts, trying to make sense of the conversation. She was still holding the receiver when she heard the tap on her room door. The sound startled her and she almost dropped the phone. She took a breath, replaced the receiver and crossed the room. The tapping came again.

"Yes?"

"Your dry-cleaning, Mlle Malinski."

Sashia recognized the voice of the young woman from the hotel's laundry service. She opened the door and accepted the freshly cleaned clothing. The young woman stared at her for a moment.

"Are you not well?" she asked.

"I'm sorry?"

"You look very pale."

Sashia thought quickly. "Oh, I had a very late business meeting last night and didn't sleep too well. My own fault. Thank you for your concern, Mirelle."

"You are welcome."

Sashia closed the door and leaned against it. Her father's call had affected her more than she had realized. She went to the bathroom and peered at herself in the vanity mirror. He usually healthy face had taken on a gray pallor. Shock? Caused by what? Her father's reappearance, or the suggestion she might be in danger? Sashia decided it was probably a combination of both.

She sat in one of the comfortable leather armchairs and gazed out through the window. It afforded a wide panorama of the city, which was something she normally enjoyed seeing. Now her eyes saw nothing except a distant blur. She was trying to work out what to do. Take heed of the warning from her father? Ignore it? Tell someone and ask for help? But she had been told not to trust anyone.

Wait, Sashia, she thought. Think about this. For the moment assume that it's true. You cannot involve anyone. No friends, or colleagues, because that would draw them into the spotlight, too. The police? Father said these people have connections. A slow smile curved her lips. Sashia, you are on your own again. Just like before. You survived then, you can do it again. Deal with it yourself.

She folded the strip of paper with the telephone number and tucked it inside her wallet. She stood up and made preparations to go out. She needed time to think this through.

Changing into slacks and a roll-neck sweater, she pulled on a pair of leather half-boots and a tan leather jacket. Making sure she had her cell phone and her wallet zipped inside the jacket she made her way downstairs and out of the hotel. The air was fresh and cool. Sashia closed the jacket's zip and turned up the collar, turning and headed out along the boulevard in the direction of the Seine. It would take her at least ten minutes to reach the river. Halfway there she felt the first spots of fine rain. Pausing, she pulled a folded wool cap from an inside pocket of the jacket and slid it over her thick, short cut black hair, then continued.

When she reached the embankment she stood for a while watching the slow-moving river. To her left she could see the see the quay where the Bateaux Mouche boats moored. She had spent time on them herself, enjoying a many course meal as the boat cruised the river. The floating restaurants were a well-known Parisian feature.

Always before, she recalled, she had been in good company for the Bateaux Mouche. Not like now because she was alone. The thought made her shiver. Very alone. A brittle laugh emerged and she scolded herself for being foolish. She was simply reacting to her own thoughts, her father's words working away in the background and throwing up shadowy threats. She didn't dismiss them completely but conversely she refused to be intimidated by them.

She found herself approaching one of the many bridges that spanned the river and walked across it, emerging on the Left Bank. She was near Montmarte and within the area of the Place du Terte. In the evenings the area attracted local artists who worked on their paintings while the crowds wandered around viewing them. It was one of Sashia's favorite places. Glancing at her watch she realized it was already late afternoon. If she whiled away an hour or so the artists would start to gather. She located a bistro and chose a table beneath the extended awning, out of the rain. A young waiter came out, smiling and flicking at imaginary crumbs on the table, asking what she wanted.

"Coffee with cream, please," she said in French.

He nodded attentively. "Right away."

Three cups later Sashia was finding it hard to totally relax. She realized she was checking out every new arrival, even people across the street if they lingered for more than a couple of minutes. She felt ridiculous that the unease refused to go away. In the end she left money on the table and, walking quickly, wended her way through the pedestrians, not even sure just where she going. Before she realized it, she had cleared the Place du Terte and was walking along a quiet street. Overhead, the clouds were gathering, the rain increasing, making the sidewalk slick. She paused to establish exactly where she was and in the silence she heard the soft murmur of a car engine. Turning slowly she detected the front of an automobile, a black SUV, nosing out from a side street. There was something about the way the vehicle seemed to creep along, rain glistening on the black hood, peppering the windshield.

Just beyond her was a steep rise of stone steps that would take her to a higher street level. She made for the steps, comforting herself with the notion that at least a car wouldn't be unable to follow her—if it *was* following her. She hurried up the steps, gripping the central metal rail.

She heard the sound of footsteps behind her, moving quickly, closing in. Sashia pushed herself harder, admitting to being a more than a little scared. She also accepted she could be wrong and the person behind was just in a hurry to get out of the rain. She looked up to see that she was only halfway up the steps. Breath caught in her throat as she heard a grunt of sound behind her.

A hand clutched at her jacket, fingers failing to get a grip as she pulled away. Swinging her head around to see who was there, she caught a blurred glimpse of a man in a long dark coat, his wet face turned to glare up at her. Then he reached out again and snatched at her coat, jerking her to a stop. Sashia gave a half-strangled cry of alarm, kicking out instinctively, the sole of her boot hitting the man in the stomach. He lurched back, almost falling, but stayed upright by retaining his grip on her coat. He snapped something out in an angry voice—in Russian.

Hearing her native tongue galvanized Sashia into action and she tore free of the man's grip, hurling herself up the steps, feet slipping on the wet stone. She fell forward, felt strong hands catch her and drag her upright. Almost crying out with fright, she looked up into another strange face. Startlingly blue eyes met hers and without reason she felt a surge of hope. Then this newcomer gently moved her aside and went down to meet her first attacker. The Russian exploded with rage, lunging at the tall, dark-clad figure, swearing loudly. The newcomer stood his ground and Sashia caught a glimpse of his sweeping move, followed by a solid sound, a second, meatier blow, and the Russian went down on his knees, head hanging.

"Let's get out of here," Mack Bolan said, taking her arm and guiding her toward the top of the steps.

A warning sound reached his ears. The scrape of shoe leather on the worn steps, the hard breathing as someone closed in on Bolan and the woman. He pushed her ahead of him, turning about and saw a second man lunging at him. The guy had a hard-boned Slavic face, his bald head glistening from the rain. Out the corner of his eye Bolan saw the one he had put down slowly haul himself up behind his partner.

"She comes with me," the new man said. His English had a strong Russian accent. "Let her go."

Bolan blocked his way, saw the instinctive move toward a weapon concealed under the guy's leather topcoat. Rain-misted light reflected from the blade of a knife. The man held it ready to cut, moving up the next step to bring himself closer to Bolan before he made his strike. It delayed his move, and Bolan used that fraction to his own advantage. He laid his left hand on the central rail, then swung his right leg up in a savage kick that smashed the hand holding the knife. The guy grunted in pain, the knife spinning from his numbed fingers.

"She goes with—" the guy yelled, powering up the last step to throw himself at Bolan.

Bolan bent at the knees, his right fist driving forward to connect with the guy's face. Bone cracked under the blow. The Russian gagged, dazed, his coordination gone. Unfocused eyes stared at Bolan. Blood was pouring down from his crushed nose. The Executioner raised his foot and planted it against the guy's chest, shoving him backward. The Russian fell, arms flailing, and collided with his partner before the man could get out of the way. The entangled pair were propelled down the long flight of steps.

Bolan followed Sashia, catching up with her just as she reached the top of the steps. He ignored her frightened expression, grabbing her arm and hurrying her along the sidewalk.

He had no way of knowing how many more there might be, and right now he wasn't all that keen to find out. Counting numbers wasn't his immediate priority.

Keeping Sashia Malinski alive was.

CHAPTER FIFTEEN

Sashia allowed herself to be moved along the rainswept street to a dark-colored Citroën parked at the curb. The stranger helped her inside, then walked around and got behind the wheel. His movements were deliberate, precise, without undue haste. The car eased away from the curb and Sashia sank back in the passenger seat, feeling a wave of nausea sweep over her. Reaction to the fear and the unexpected attack against her. She turned to look at her rescuer, wondering sho he was.

Let's get out of here.

The accent had been American. No doubt about that. But what did it signify? In terms of her safety, not a great deal. She watched him as he drove, noting his dark hair, his taut profile. Aware of her scrutiny, he turned to give her a quick glance, streetlight briefly illuminating his face. And he smiled.

"You're safe enough now, but I need to keep it that way."

"Who are you?"

"Matt Cooper," Mack Bolan said and left it at that.

"And who is Matt Cooper?"

"A friend."

Sashia considered that. "True you saved me from that man back there, for which I thank you. But who was he? All I know is that he was Russian." She hesitated, then went on. "Is this to do with my father?"

"Gregori Malinski. Nuclear physicist who worked for the Soviets before the fall. It seems that for the past few years he has been hiring out his expertise to whoever was willing to pay him. His current clients are the Iranians. He's been helping them in their attempt to develop their own nuclear capability."

He delivered the information in a neutral manner, making no inferences, nor seeing to judge. The facts were a shock to Sashia. Her lack of contact with her father had left her in a vacuum where his work was concerned. She recalled what he had said about the pattern of his life changing. Not for the best, he had added. To learn just exactly what he had been doing left her slightly numb.

"Until today I hadn't spoken with my father for a number of years. We had lost contact. When the Soviet Union broke up, it left him out in the cold. Without his secure government position he lost everything, including his self-respect. He became bitter at the way the government abandoned him. We parted on…on less than pleasant terms. I moved on and built my life. Then today I received a telephone call from him, telling me he was in some kind of trouble and that people might be searching for me in an attempt to find him."

"It looks like they found you," Bolan said.

"Why? What has he done that is so wrong?"

Bolan swung the car over one of the river bridges and cut along the road that ran parallel on the far side. They cut into the underpass, the tunnel lights going by in bright flashes.

"I think he's had a crisis of conscience. Maybe he realized that what he was doing wasn't the way to salvation. So he walked out on the people he was working for. From what I've

learned, he's left them high and dry. His work had reached a
critical point and without him to reach a conclusion, nothing
is going to come of it. His employers want him back. Otherwise they're going to lose their advantage."

"Mr. Cooper, are you with the American government?
Some kind of agent?"

"Some kind of something," he said, "just about covers it."

"Why are the American's interested in…" She paused. "Of
course. America doesn't want the Iranians having their own
nuclear weapons. It would only add to their current difficulties in the Middle East. So you need to stop whatever they're
doing." Her face paled. "You want to find my father and prevent him from going back. My God, you want to kill him."

"No. I want to find him and get him to safety. But I also
need to find out from him what I need to do to neutralize what
the Iranians have."

Sashia leaned back hard in the seat. Her thoughts were in
a confused state. She didn't know what to think. What to believe. Since her father's call her life had taken a strange turn
from what she knew as normal. The man on the steps. Now
this American, Cooper. It was a time of confusion. What and
who should she believe?

"I can understand your feelings," Bolan said. "Out of the
blue I tell you a story and you're supposed to take it in and
agree. On the other hand, you say your father phoned after a
long break and warned you of possible trouble. Then that
Russian on the steps—and me." He let the words sink in.
"Sashia, if you still feel uncomfortable, I can stop and let you
out whenever you want. I won't force you to stay. But I'll offer
one comment that might help you decide."

"What's that?"

"We're being tailed."

Sashia glanced in the sideview mirror and saw a dark vehicle close behind. She couldn't be absolutely certain, but it did look like the vehicle she had spotted just before the episode on the steps. A longer look and she realized she had been right. The black SUV.

Bolan trod hard on the accelerator, sending the Citroën surging forward. Behind them the tail car did the same. Sashia hadn't missed that.

"I think you could be right, Mr. Cooper."

"Make sure your seat belt is secure," Bolan warned and pushed the gas pedal to the floor, feeling the Citroën pour on the speed. He concentrated on keeping the speeding car stable, weaving in and out of the thin traffic. He heard the slight squeal as the tires protested, but the French car remained under control.

"They are doing the same," Sashia told him. "I can't believe this is happening. Are you a good driver?"

"I think we're about to find out," he said.

They erupted from the underpass in a cloud of spray, the rain having increased while they were under cover. He hung a long, sweeping right, the rear of the car edging out a little, cut between two other vehicles, then spun the wheel hard and made a risky turn that took them up a narrow street off the main route. Buildings flashed by as Bolan exercised every driving skill he possessed. Sashia clung to her seat, hypnotized by the close buildings blurring past the windows. The vehicle's engine was powerfully quiet, which meant she could hear every sound from the tortured tires.

"Do you actually know where we are?" she asked.

"Paris?" was the dry reply.

She left it at that. The ride seemed to last for a lifetime. Sashia folded her arms tight across her chest, wondering just how all this would end. She wasn't sure of anything any longer. When she eventually risked a glance behind, she realized the SUV was no longer in sight.

The Citroën began to slow. Bolan finally pulled over and parked between a large Suburban and a delivery truck.

"We'll pick up a taxi," Bolan said.

Sashia followed him in a daze, staying close to him as he led her along the sidewalk, through a narrow side street until they emerged on a wide boulevard. Bolan flagged down a taxi, gave the driver an address and they climbed in. Beside her the big American seemed relaxed, but Sashia was aware of his alert manner even as they were being driven through the streets. Minutes later they were out of the taxi and walking into the lobby of a quiet hotel. Bolan took his key from the desk and they walked up two flights to his room. Inside he secured the door and switched on the lights.

"So is this how you normally pick up girls?" Sashia asked.

Bolan unzipped his leather jacket and took it off, and for the first time Sashia saw that he was wearing a shoulder-holstered handgun. Seeing the weapon brought home what had happened earlier and she felt the rush of nausea rise again.

Bolan had seen her go pale and moved to support her. He eased her into a seat, standing over her, his expression showing his concern.

"Drink?"

She nodded and Bolan crossed to a cabinet and opened it. He returned with a tumbler, passing it to her hand. Sashia took a sip, feeling the warm flush as mellow brandy slid down her throat.

"I guess I'm not as tough as I thought I was," she said.

"It hasn't exactly been a normal evening."

"Something like that." Sashia drained the glass and held it out for a refill. Before Bolan made any comment she said, "Yes, I need it."

Bolan poured her more brandy. She took it, this time gripping the tumbler and leaning back in the comfortable seat.

Bolan took another seat and allowed her to relax. He was aware of her agitated condition. She needed time to work things out in her own mind. He waited until she was ready to speak.

"How did you find me?" she asked.

"It wasn't difficult."

Sashia smiled quickly. "Proved by those Russians? What you are saying is, no one can hide forever these days."

"Technology works both ways," Bolan said. "Depends how it's used."

"How did you know where I was?"

"My people located you from your company, and I tracked you to the hotel you were using. I spotted you as you were leaving, followed in my car, then on foot. I thought perhaps you had arranged to meet with your father. I stayed back because I didn't want to scare him off. When you picked up your tail, I figured it was time to make myself known."

"I'm glad you did."

"My pleasure."

"So where do we go from here?"

"We try to find your father before Anatoly Nevski's people do."

"Be honest, Cooper. Do you think they will harm him?"

"Truth? I don't know. It depends how they view him now. If they consider him a risk they might decide to cut their losses and just do what they can to prevent him from betraying them. The last thing they need is the location of their facility being exposed. On the other hand, they could be on a retrieval hunt to take him back and force him to carry on with his work."

"Force him? You mean, torture him? Please, no."

"If they get their hands on you, they have the bargaining chip they need."

Sashia shook her head. "This is becoming a nightmare.

Whichever way it goes, my father and I are going to be the losers."

"Not if I can prevent it."

"Can you?"

"If we can find your father before anyone else does."

"But I have no idea where he might be. Remember what I told you? We haven't had any contact for a number of years. The last time I saw him was during a visit he made to London. The telephone call I had today is the first time I have even spoken to him since then."

"Did he write to you at all?"

"A few times after the London visit. Then even the letters stopped."

"Where did the letters come from? Postmarks. Can you remember?"

"I…they were a few years ago." Sashia thought for a moment, her forehead creasing in concentration. "I'd forgotten." She looked across at Bolan. "Some came from here. Paris."

"So he may be back in the city. You also said there were letters from elsewhere?"

"Yes. Somewhere in the UK. I can't recall the location but the letters are back at my hotel. I still carry them with me wherever I go. They have been my only connection to my father over the years."

Sashia placed her glass on the small table beside her chair and unzipped her jacket. She took out her slim wallet, opening it with fingers that were starting to tremble. Bolan watched her remove a folded strip of paper. She smoothed it out, staring at the figures written in her neat hand.

"With everything that has happened, I'd forgotten about this. A telephone number. My father gave it me when he called. For me to use if things became too difficult."

She stared at the numbers as if they held the secret of life itself, fixated on the slender link to her father.

"Can I see?" Bolan asked, and held out a hand.

She passed him the paper and Bolan read the number. It meant little to him. He reached inside his jacket and took out the cell phone, tapping the key that would speed-dial Stony Man Farm. He eventually got through to Aaron Kurtzman and asked for a rundown on the telephone number.

"See if you can get me anything on this cell phone number. Most recent call we know about was this evening to a hotel in Paris. I'm going to have the number called. See if you can get a lock on it."

"Okay. Let me establish a network trace, then make your call. Remember this is a cell phone. It's not as easy to get a location as a landline. But not impossible." Bolan could hear Kurtzman talk to someone in the Computer Room. Then he was back. "Akira has made a connection. He's bringing up the call details now. Paris Hilton. Suite 401. Call put through to Sashia Malinski at 6:34 p.m. Paris time."

"That's the one. Caller's number?"

The number Kurtzman quoted was the same as the one Sashia's father had given her.

"I'm going to get her to call it now. See if you can find out where the other phone is located."

"We'll do our best, Striker. This isn't as easy as it sounds."

"I'll check after Sashia makes her call."

"Ask her to stay on the line as long as she can."

Bolan ended the call. He picked up the room phone and handed it Sashia. "Call your father. If he does answer, try to find out where he is. Keep him talking if you can. The longer he's on the line, the better chance we have of getting a location."

Sashia took the phone and tapped in the number her father had given her. From the expression on her face Bolan understood she was waiting for it to be answered. It took a long time. When the call was picked up relief washed across her taut features and she relaxed a little. Her gaze settled on Bolan and she nodded.

"Poppa, this is Sashia…"

CHAPTER SIXTEEN

"Well?" Kirov asked. "Do you have them?"

"Of course," the technician said.

"So where are they?" Lem Kirov wasn't known for his patience. He demanded instant answers to his question and soon became irritated if he didn't receive satisfaction.

"This equipment works at its own speed," the man replied, unaffected by Kirov's attitude. He wasn't a fool. He knew his job and did it well, and there was no one within Nevski's organization who could better him. "It doesn't run faster for anyone."

"I need results," Kirov yelled. "Now."

The technician ignored him and returned to his electronic equipment, tapping in keyboard instructions. Behind him Kirov paced back and forth, muttering in a low voice.

Nevski came into the communications room, aware of the tension immediately. One look at Kirov and he understood. His second in command, as good as he was, had never fully controlled his emotions. He allowed situations to get to him, especially if he thought things weren't being handled efficiently. Nevski also knew his technician. The younger man was second-to-none with his electronic surveillance and tracking devices. Nevski paid him very well for his skills and his ability to pluck data out of thin air.

"Karel? How's it going?"

"Working on the triangulation now. We started as soon as the cell phone was activated. It was fortunate we had Malinski's number. At least it gave us somewhere to go. The problem is that the signal's weak, but I'll do what I can."

"What about the woman?"

"I am tracing the call back from the connection to the cell. Hers is a landline, so it won't be so hard to locate. We already know it's here in Paris. Tracing *that* call is not such an effort."

Nevski heard Kirov's grunt of annoyance. He straightened from leaning over Karel's seat. "Lem, if you can't wait, why don't you find a couple of tracker dogs. Maybe you'll have a better result."

"All this electronic shit and we still can't find them," Kirov snapped. "How much longer?"

"Are the cars standing by?"

"Yes. Ready to go unless the drivers have died of boredom."

Nevski smiled. "That's what I love about you, Lem Kirov. Never without a touch of humor to lighten the darkest day."

"I have the woman's location," Karel said. "A hotel on Rue Victor Masse."

Kirov reached out and snatched the paper from Karel. "About time."

Nevski laid a hand on Karel's shoulder. "Keep trying for the cell phone."

Kirov was already speaking to the waiting cars, giving them the location of the hotel. "It's certain she's with the American. We know it was him on the steps when Boris tried to snatch the woman. Just remember who that bastard is. If he gets in the way, kill him. But we need the woman alive for the present. Now go."

"Feeling better?" Nevski asked.

"I'll feel better once we have that bitch tied up in a locked room."

TWO BLACK SUVs, LIGHTS dimmed, pulled to a halt across the street from Bolan's hotel. In the time it took them to cross Paris and locate the address, information had come through from Karel. He had accessed the hotel's computer and found the room occupied by a Matt Cooper.

"As long as they are still there, you have an opportunity to take the woman," Kirov said over his cell phone. "Make sure you don't screw up. We can't afford to lose her now."

"No problem," the crew chief said. He cut the connection and turned to his five-man team. "Let's do this."

They exited the car, turning their collars up against the rain. The crew chief, Duchev, paused beside the second car, speaking to the three men inside. His instructions were simple. They were to keep a check on the hotel entrance and rear exit. The trio climbed out, one watching the front door, while other two crossed the street and moved down the narrow alley that ran along the side of the building.

Duchev led his team into the hotel. The lobby was quiet, and no one occupied the front desk at the time they entered. The team moved quickly to the stairs and made its way up to the third floor and the softly lit corridor that took them to the door of the room the American occupied. At a nod from Duchev, the team produced their weapons. They were armed with 9 mm Glocks. Duchev signaled his men to cover both sides of the door, stepping forward himself to kick it open.

Three rooms down the corridor a door opened and a middle-aged woman stepped out. She saw the armed men clustered outside one of the rooms, her face registering the scene, her mind raced through every dramatic scenario possible, and she began to scream in utter terror.

CHAPTER SEVENTEEN

Bolan heard the shrill outburst, followed by muffled voices directly outside the room. His hand went directly for the holstered Beretta, easing it out, his finger flicking the selector switch to 3-round-burst mode.

"What…?" he heard Sashia say a fraction before he took the phone from her and dropped it back on its cradle, caught her arm and hauled her across the room until they were alongside the bed.

"On the floor," he snapped.

The door was smashed in by a hard kick, tearing away the lock and splintering the wooden panel.

Still beside the bed, Bolan snapped off the room light.

The first man through the door was left in shadow, his weapon arcing back and forth.

Bolan raised the Beretta and triggered a burst that punched the intruder in the chest. He fell back against the door frame, his handgun discharging into the wall over the bed. Other figures jostled together in brief panic as the first man went down. Bolan didn't give them time to regroup. He fired again, seeing one man spin away from the open door, clutching a shattered shoulder.

"On your feet. Stay close."

Sashia did what he told her and followed as Bolan moved across the room, the Beretta tracking ahead. He pressed against the inner wall, picking up the murmur of voices in the corridor. Crouching, he snatched up the Glock dropped by the first man down. Still low, he peered around the frame. The right corridor, dead-ending some doors down, was empty. Angling around he picked up the hunched form of the shoulder-hit man crawling away to his left. Farther back were more men, all armed, ready to take up the assault again.

"When I say go, run out the door and to the right. The door at the end of the corridor is an emergency exit. Just hit the bar."

He didn't wait for her answer. Bolan raised the Glock and shot out the corridor's ceiling light, dropping the area into shadow. Then he leaned out farther and fired at the armed men, pushing them back.

"Now—go," he snapped, and felt Sashia brush by him.

He heard one of the armed intruders cursing, saw him run forward, raising his weapon. Bolan shot him in the body and saw the dark shape stumble and drop to his knees, starting to fall forward. Bolan fired again, two shots that blew the guy's skull apart. One of the other men double-fisted his weapon, tracking Bolan as he moved down the corridor. He began to fire, his shots spaced out, but he failed to make a hit as Bolan turned and crouched below the trajectory, his own weapons returning fire. The corridor echoed to the sudden thunder of gunfire as more guns let loose, plaster gouged from walls as bullet struck.

Cold air blew into the corridor as Sashia shouldered the emergency door open and stumbled onto the metal walkway outside. Bolan took that as his own moment to clear the corridor, emptying the Glock at the distant figure before he kicked the door shut, dropping the pistol at his feet. Shots thudded against the solid bulk of the door. Bolan saw that Sashia was already descending the rain-slick fire-escape steps to the alley below. He took a moment to set the Beretta to single-shot mode, then followed the woman.

They descended the steps as swiftly as safety allowed, the wet metal slippery under their feet. Bolan kept an eye on the door they had just exited, expecting pursuit at any moment. When it came, it was from a different location. He was warned by Sashia's sudden cry a moment before she threw herself sideways, pulling him with her. They slammed against the side wall a fraction before the crash of a single gunshot. The bullet whined off the metal rail of the fire escape.

"Stay back," Bolan said.

They remained flat against the wall and their action drew the shooter from his spot, the muzzle of his pistol searching the shadows. Bolan could make out the dark figure, hazed by the rain, and dropped the muzzle of the 93-R, waiting his moment.

Behind and above them the emergency door swung open, the armed survivor from the corridor stepping out.

Bolan locked on his target in the alley and fired twice, seeing the man stiffen under the impact of the 9 mm slugs, then he twisted, tracking in on the figure above even as the man was searching for his own target. Bolan took a moment to settle his aim and fire. The slug from the Beretta angled in beneath the guy's jaw and cored its way to erupt through the top of his skull.

"Let's keep moving," Bolan said. "We don't know how many more there might be."

He kept his Beretta ready as they descended to street level, moving past the huddled form of the man Bolan had put down. The rain had increased to a heavy downpour, aiding their concealment as they moved to the mouth of the alley. Bolan held Sashia back as he checked out the street. He knew it wouldn't be long before the shooting attracted attention and eventually the local police. They had a slim period of grace before that happened.

He felt Sashia tense under his guiding hand, picked up the drawn breath, and over her shoulder he saw light glint off the metal of a raised handgun. The waiting man was partly concealed by a side door, holding back until Sashia passed before he dealt with Bolan. There was no time for finesse. Bolan placed his palm flat against Sashia's back, pushing hard. She was propelled forward, beyond the waiting gunman's place of concealment. Still walking forward himself, Bolan spun, closing on the hidden man, and was on him even as the guy assimilated what was happening. The target's gun swung toward Bolan. He batted it aside with his forearm, hearing the heavy sound as the pistol fired. Bolan caught the guy's collar, jerking him off balance and slamming him face-first against the brick wall. The guy gave a groan, but still resisted, his gun hand rising as he tried to target Bolan again. Distant shouts from the top of the fire escape reached Bolan's ears. Someone started shooting, the bullets way off target, but to Bolan they indicated his time was running away faster than he had anticipated. His captive gunman made another attempt at lining up his weapon. Bolan pushed the muzzle of the Beretta against the side of his skull and curtailed any further attempts with a single 9 mm round. As the man dropped, Bolan raised his 93-R and placed a couple of shots at the distant figures on the fire escape, turning quickly to join up with Sashia.

"Come on," he said, taking Sashia's hand and leading her from the alley. He had already slipped the Beretta back into its holster, zipping up his leather jacket. He could feel Sashia trying to move faster, her fear encouraging her to get away from the scene quickly. He pulled the woman closer to him as they walked in the opposite direction of the hotel. Not hurrying, simply two figures caught in the rain and staying close as they moved away. "Just walk. If we run it will only attract attention."

"What if they…?"

"By the time they get out of the hotel we'll be out of sight among the other pedestrians. In a while the area around the hotel will be swarming with cops. And spectators. Those people know that. All they'll want to do is get to their vehicles and get out of here."

Bolan hadn't failed to notice the pair of dark-colored SUVs, identical in model, standing nose-to-nose on the opposite side of the street. There was something about them that caught his attention, and after a second he realized what it was. They were the same model as the vehicle that had followed him through the streets after he had picked up Sashia earlier. If they did belong to the Nevski group Bolan had to compliment the man on his organization. They had tracked him and Sashia to *his* hotel, homing in like guided missiles. That would suggest sophisticated electronic equipment. He didn't doubt the Russian being able to afford such hardware. Nevski was in a lucrative business.

They reached the corner of the street, where it intersected with the main thoroughfare, pausing beneath the shelter of an awning. Bolan had picked up the wail of police sirens, and in the distance he saw the strobing blue light of one as it sped in their direction. They stayed where they were, close together.

Bolan put his arms around Sashia and pulled her closer. He could feel her trembling. Reaction was setting in. He wasn't surprised after what she had gone through only a short time earlier. She offered little resistance, pressing her cold face against his as the police cruiser sped to the intersection, sliding as it took the corner and continued on toward the hotel.

Now they could hear more sirens as other vehicles approached from multiple directions. Bolan waited until the way was clear, then slipped his arm around Sashia's waist and took her across the street. They continued walking for the next few minutes, merging with other pedestrians, Bolan leading them farther away from the scene of the shooting until he spotted the signs for a Métro station. Inside the concourse Bolan purchased tickets and they went down the steps, following the signs until they emerged on the platform. They were both wet and chilled. They stood waiting for the first train. No one paid them much attention. The few others waiting were in a similar situation, caught out in the rain and interested only in getting home.

"Where are we going?" Sashia asked, her voice sounding frail. She edged closer to his comforting presence, seeming to want to hide herself in his bulk.

"Right now, away from here. Somewhere we can catch our breath."

"Translated as it 'isn't over yet.'"

"Not until we get your father to a safe place."

"I'm beginning to wonder if there are any safe places left. We can't go back to my hotel. Or yours. Once the police read your passport, they'll be looking for you."

Bolan put an arm around her slim shoulders. "Looks like it's all over for us then. You want to jump onto the live rail first? Or shall we hold hands and do it together?"

She stared up into his face, frowning. Then she caught the gleam in his eyes and saw the slight smile edging his lips. "That was not funny, Cooper."

He shook his head. "Not funny—Matt. I thought it was a pretty good effort under the circumstances."

"Okay, I was feeling sorry for myself."

"Hey, it's allowed."

The sound of an approaching train reached them. They waited and stepped on board as soon as the doors opened. They found empty seats in an almost deserted carriage. Despite the space, Sashia still wanted to sit close to Bolan, resting her head on his shoulder. They took the Métro to the end of their particular line, emerging in some distant suburb. Bolan spotted a café across the street and they made their way inside. At least it was warm. There were only a couple of tables occupied. Bolan chose a booth where he could watch the door.

"Here," he said, handing Sashia money. "Go order us some food and coffee. And while you're there, find out exactly where we are."

Watching her cross to the counter Bolan took out his cell phone. He called Stony Man via the satellite link and spoke first to Kurtzman.

"Hey, Striker, what happened?"

"The opposition interrupted us," Bolan said. He gave a rundown on the incident, adding, "Did you have any luck with tracking Malinski's cell?"

"I could take exception to 'any luck,' Striker. This is no geek's radio shack here."

Bolan grinned at Kurtzman's feigned indignation. Just hearing the man's gruff tones made his situation seem less grim.

"It's been a rough evening," he said. "So I guess we have the location?"

"The boy wonder," Kurtzman said, referring to Akira Tokaido, "has pinned it down. Under my scrutiny, of course. Gregori Malinski is in the remote and lonely northeast of Scotland. Give the boy a little more time and he'll probably be able to come up with details of what the guy had for his evening meal."

"You're a wonder to behold, Bear."

"You okay, Striker?"

"Let's say I've been in worse situations." Bolan was watching Sashia return to the table carrying two generous mugs of steaming coffee. "Is the head honcho around?"

"On his way. Listen, is there anything else we can do for you?"

Bolan detailed how Nevski had managed to track Sashia through her father's cell to the hotel telephone.

"Sounds like they have some pretty hard-edged stuff available themselves. If money is no object, it's out there. Hate to say this, but they might have been able to trace Malinski's cell, too."

"That's what worries me. So I need to get to him ASAP."

Brognola came on the line. His voice sounded tired, but that was nothing new. The Sensitive Operations Group's director was very seldom off duty when there were missions rolling. His philosophy was simple. If his people were putting themselves on the line, he felt he had no right to be sitting back with his feet up.

"Sounds like Paris is no picnic, Striker."

"Something like that. I need some backup fast. Like a car to pick me and Sashia up and get us back to my Air Force ride. Tell them we're going to the UK. Those strings you handle need some urgent pulling, Hal."

"You got it. Anything else?"

"Is Phoenix Force on stand down?"

"Yeah. No mission for them right now. You need backup?"

"Only the British connection."

"He'll be waiting when you get there."

Sashia had been writing on a paper napkin. She slid it across to Bolan so he could read what she had written. He quoted the location to Brognola. There was a brief pause before the big Fed spoke again.

"Hang tight there. I need to make some calls. Striker, this thing coming together for you?"

"In a weird, tangled way. But right now I'm going to have a meal with a beautiful young woman and sit back while you work your own kind of magic. Got it?"

"Oh, yeah," Brognola said, and hung up.

CHAPTER EIGHTEEN

Kirov's grip on the phone threatened to shatter the casing. His knuckles showed white, and his face was suffused with rage. He had listened to the report from the lone survivor of the abortive hotel raid in a stunned silence. He snapped the cover shut and stood for a moment, trying to control his anger.

"Most of the team dead. Lipov barely walked clear before the police arrived. He had to abandon both vehicles. One man and a fucking woman and they wipe out our people."

"This American should be leading our people, not shooting them," Nevski observed quietly from where he was sitting.

Kirov turned to stare at him. "Perhaps I should take out an advertisement in *France-Soir* and ask him to contact us."

"Lem, what we should be doing is making sure we can locate Malinski. With all respect for the dead, they were being well paid to find the woman and get rid of the American. They did neither. We have more pressing matters to concentrate on. If we fail to produce Malinski, our impetuous employer, Razihra, will be dispatching his own death squad. They will be coming after *us*. Bear that in mind, please. He's isn't noted for his patience. Right now he isn't in the best of moods. Losing Malinski was bad enough. Having the camp in Jordan and the sleeper cell wiped out hasn't helped. And losing the nerve gas, too." Nevski shook his head. "Some people just can't help being losers. So we'd better come up with the goods, or lose a paying client."

"I'm glad you reminded me about that," someone said from the other side of the room. The speaker leaned out from the deep armchair he was seated in. He smiled in Kirov's direction. "You want Malinski? Let Cooper lead the way. He's got the woman with him. It's more likely she'll draw her old man out into the open. Family ties? Works every time."

Nevski considered the advice. It was sensible, he thought. Sashia Malinski, now she had contact with her father, would continue to search for him. And most likely find him.

"You think we should step back? Just stay on their trail and let the woman lead us to Malinski?"

"For what it's worth," the man said.

"Make sure we maintain that trace on the woman's cell phone. If we can keep that, we'll be able to follow at a discreet distance until she makes contact with Malinski. Then we can take them all."

Kirov nodded. He turned to leave, deliberately ignoring the man in the armchair.

"Now I've gone and done it," the man said. "Upset our friend. I'll have to watch my back from now on."

He didn't appear to be overly concerned.

His name was Victor Capstone. Born in the UK, he had joined the army at seventeen and had served for eight years before being accepted into the SAS, where his specialty had been team sniper. Capstone found he had an affinity with the discipline required for the role. One of his instructors had made the comment that he had a better relationship with his rifle than he did with women. The remark, intended for an officer, had been overheard by Capstone himself. He hadn't taken offense because it actually confirmed his own feelings about his skills. He served for five years with the SAS, undertaking a number of covert missions that took him to trouble spots in Europe, Asia and the Middle East.

At thirty, Capstone found the SAS was stifling him. He enjoyed the buzz of the missions, but there was a lot of stand-down time and a number of hits were called off due to political pressure. Disenchantment set in and as soon as he was able Capstone put in his papers and left the service. He didn't leave behind his profession. It wasn't long before he was contacted through unofficial channels and undertook covert missions, often for vaguely remote clients, though on a number of contracts he knew without a doubt that he was doing government work.

His reputation grew quickly, and his avowed credo of never asking questions about a hit meant there were never any moral barriers to overcome. Capstone accepted a contract, took the money and completed his assignment. It was as simple as that. There were no gray areas as far as Capstone was concerned. Pay his price, and Capstone would take out the Pope. The identity of the victim meant nothing to him. Man, woman, child, Victor Capstone saw them as little more than a target. He held the same indifference as the metal bullet he fired. Sight, aim, fire. Once he pulled the trigger and the bullet left the barrel, his job was over. He stayed up to the moment the bullet struck and the target started down. He left the scene after that, moving on, his mind concentrated on his escape route. He built his reputation on being thorough, totally dedicated and detached from the target.

Right now he was on an extended contract for Anatoly Nevski. The Russian had put a number of hits Capstone's way. The first had been the termination of the CIS plant within

Nevski's organization. The man they had known as Harry Vincent had been taken down in London. Capstone had made the hit at an arranged meet designed to lure Vincent into a trap. It had worked nicely. Capstone completed his assignment and was back in Paris by the evening of the same day, where he waited to carry out the next part of his contract for Nevski.

SINCE THE LONDON HIT matters had accelerated at an unexpected and down-turned rate. The man they had come to know as Cooper had taken out Nevski's paymaster in London. Novak, the dealer arranging a shipment of ordnance for Nevski, had vanished after Cooper had shown up in Jordan. The American had posed as Jason Novak and might have made further progress if Ayatollah Razihra's CIA informer hadn't warned them. Taken hostage at the isolated camp in Jordan, the man had effected an escape, later returning with a band of rebel Bedouin, and had succeeded in destroying the camp. The group, headed by Kerim, had been wiped out. The greatest loss was the consignment of ZK386. It had taken a great deal of organization and a greater deal of money for Nevski to get his hands on the virus. Bringing it from Russia had involved many people and to find out it had been destroyed had left the Russian angry and a little embarrassed. To add to the insult, the American had joined forces with the Jordanians and Mossad, mounting an attack on Razihra's cell in Amman.

As if all that wasn't enough, Gregori Malinski, the physicist Nevski had contracted to work on Razihra's nuclear program had upped and gone AWOL. Desperate to maintain his credibility with Razihra, Nevski had mounted a hunt for the errant Russian. Yet once again the elusive Cooper had shown up, snatching Malinski's daughter from under the noses—and the guns—of Nevski's men. The pursuit was still on. Anatoly Nevski, never having suffered setbacks of this scale before, needed to show Razihra he was still in control, so his next action had to go to plan.

Which brought Victor Capstone center stage. As the door closed behind Kirov, he stood and helped himself to a drink from the supply Nevski always kept available. He held up a tumbler holding mellow bourbon, gently swirling it around the glass.

"I'm not one to interfere in another man's business," he said, "but keep an eye on Lem. One day his lack of control is going to let him down. He gets too emotional."

"I know. But he is a good man none the less. I appreciate what you say, Victor, and I will do as you suggest. Now, what about this hit on Baresh?"

"I'm ready, Mr. Nevski," Capstone stated. "Just give me the word and Dr. Baresh is history."

"We know he's already in Paris for the meeting with the members of the antinuclear lobby at the end of the week. Razihra doesn't want him to make those meetings."

"He won't, Mr. Nevski. I promise you that."

Nevski didn't need to broach the subject again. He accepted that Dr. Shahan Baresh would die within the next day or so. At least he would be able to confirm that to Ayatollah Razihra. It would at least reduce the heat over the Malinski affair and give his teams some leeway while they continued their pursuit of the Russian and his daughter.

BACK IN THE ROOM HE had been assigned in Nevski's large house, Victor Capstone stood at the window watching the armed guard patrol the expansive grounds. The house lay some six miles out of the city, on a landscape of green and timbered land, at a slightly higher elevation than Paris itself. The view was magnificent at night, with myriad lights bathing the city in a misty glow. On this particular day the mist of rain sweeping in across the broad landscape hid Paris.

Capstone didn't mind that. The last thing he needed was distraction. He was thinking about what lay ahead. His hit against Baresh. Now that he had the go-ahead, his whole being would be concentrated on the kill. This was where Victor Capstone came into his own. He turned from the window and crossed to the project board that stood on a large easel. Pinned to the green baize surface were photographs of Baresh, the phalanx of armed bodyguards who accompanied him wherever he went, the armored Bentley he traveled in. The heavy, plated vehicle, with its sophisticated protection, was flown with Baresh on any visit he made, no matter where.

There were more photographs, taken by Capstone himself, showing the official building where the meeting would take place. Capstone was a skilled photographer, always taking his own surveillance shots. He had also added a series taken from the firing point he had chosen. The images were spaced out on the board, and he had spent a couple of days simply studying them until he decided on the exact position.

Easier to obtain had been the exact timing of Baresh's arrival at the meeting place. Ayatollah Razihra had furnished that. Once he had the time Capstone was able to backtrack and decide on his own timetable. That was as important as Baresh's. Capstone needed to be in place well in advance, equipped with his rifle, a full clip, his escape route clear.

The assassin turned to check his equipment. He handled his weapon himself. No one was allowed near it. He wasn't being petty. The weapon was the tool of his trade. If anything failed to work as it should, the hit might be compromised. That was something Capstone refused to even consider. In his profession mistakes weren't tolerated. There were already too many variables. Missing the intended target would be the worst thing he could do. Killing the target was the whole purpose of the exercise. A designated target left alive threw the whole deal out the window. The intentions of the party paying for the hit would be wiped out. In some circumstances *not* eliminating the target could mean death for the instigator. Cause and effect. Neutralizing the outcome. Capstone tried not to get into that part. He hated politics. The whole concept left itself wide open to corruption and double-dealing. It was too complicated for him. So Capstone stayed with what he knew: the cool feel of gunmetal, the familiar texture of the hand grip and the faint smell of oil, load weights, muzzle velocity and wind driftage, the honed pull of a fine trigger. He relished trapping the image of his target in the sights, holding the moment as he drew down on the unsuspecting individual, then easing back on the trigger and watching the target's head explode in a fan of skin and bone and hair. By the time the target hit the ground he/she would be dead. Just a limp body hitting the ground, unfeeling and uncaring...

He picked up the closed case that held his rifle, placed it on the table and opened it. The Barrett M-82 A-1-M nestled in the cutout foam layer, protected by the cushion. Below the rifle, in a similar cutout, was the D-830 2.5-10x Optics scope. Capstone lifted the rifle and ran his gaze over the smooth, sculpted lines. A work of art in his eyes, the LRSR rifle was more than just an instrument that delivered instant death. Constructed from the finest materials and perfectly balanced, it lay in his hands like any crafted musical instrument, just waiting for his skill to make it sing.

Weighing in at 32 pounds, with a 29-inch barrel, the rifle operated on a dual-chamber muzzle brake and recoil pad. The design reduced recoil to a minimum, enabling the shooter to maintain his sighting. The action was utilized as a means to both eject the spent cartridge, feed in the next load and cock the striker for the next shot. A magazine holding ten of the .50-caliber BMG rounds was available, but Capstone only ever utilized the 5-round alternative. He loaded his own bullets, weighing and calibrating each cartridge to maintain consistency. If a cartridge veered from the fixed specification by a fraction, he discarded it, refusing to lower his standards. He knew that a less than perfect load could make all the difference over a long shot. When the time came to fire, he had to know he had eliminated every possible problem that might affect the outcome. His need for perfection extended to the D-830 scope that could be fitted to the rifle via a Picatinny rail.

Capstone knew the rifle and its capabilities with an intimacy bordering on the sensual. Like a man who knew his lover's innermost desires and was capable of arousing them with the lightest of touches, Victor Capstone held that closeness with the weapon of his trade. Its feel and smell. The smoothness of its inner workings and the deadly power that lay dormant until his touch set it off.

He had spent long hours in isolated places firing the weapon, setting and resetting the calibrations until his body and mind ached from the effort of constantly rechecking the precise calculations. When he was finally satisfied, he knew he could hit any target with his first shot. It wasn't a grandiose claim, simply a statement of fact. Important because in his position he had little chance for a second shot. No one stood around waiting if an assassin missed. The slim window of opportunity was one that closed swiftly. Shooter and weapon had to work as one, each complementing the other, and within that framework Capstone was a craftsman.

Ayatollah Razihra had expressed his wish that the Iranian negotiator be neutralized, removed from the scene so that the ongoing round of talks be stalled. It was an integral part of Razihra's operation. Get rid of Shahan Baresh, then Nuri Masood. Add confusion to the internal struggle going on within the Iranian administration. Capstone didn't personally give a damn whether the scheme worked out in Razihra's favor or not. He was simply doing what he was being paid for. He never allowed himself to become bound up in political maneuvering. He saw enough of it to understand it was a dirty, self-perpetuating monster. Friends became enemies at will. The accepted policy of one week became the outlawed conspiracy of the next. Capstone was one who benefited from the constant change. His expertise was always in demand. From where he stood he realized there was little chance he would ever join the ranks of the unemployed.

Which suited him well.

CHAPTER NINETEEN

RAF Lossiemouth, Northeast Scotland

"Do you think Nevski's people can find my father up here?"

"They located you in Paris. They found my hotel. That's the best answer I can give you, Sashia."

"I suppose."

She stared out the side window of the USAF Gulfstream C-20F as it taxied along the runway following landing at the RAF field. Lossiemouth was an important UK base. Stationed there were squadrons of strategic swing-wing Tornado GR-4 strike aircraft. The station also maintained helicopter search-and-rescue units that served the North Sea area. The rain had followed them all the way from France and even now, as the jet rolled along the strip, rain was sheeting in from the coast.

Bolan had noticed the woman's mood changing as the flight had progressed. She was looking nervous, restless despite the comfort of the reclining seats. The soldier tried to figure what the problem was. Meeting her father again after such a prolonged separation? Or a deepening concern for his overall safety? In truth it could have been both. He could understand it. Her ordered world had been overturned in the space of a few hours. Violence and sudden death had been thrust into her life. She was being attacked by faceless enemies, and she most certainly wasn't fully sure of what was behind it all, and just as uncertain how it might eventually turn out.

He reached to touch her arm and as gentle as his touch was, she seemed startled.

"What?"

"Hey, easy. I just wanted to see if you were okay."

She took a breath, lowering her gaze for a moment. Bolan noticed the slight flush that colored her cheeks. "I'm sorry, Matt. It's not your fault. I'm not looking forward to this. Not the meeting with my father, even though it isn't the way I expected our reunion to turn out. It's just this whole business. It's like I'm watching a movie. Car chases. Guns. People being shot. It's not real, but it is."

"You'll get through it. I'm here to keep you safe."

The Gulfstream came to a gentle stop, the engines winding down.

"Time to go," Bolan said.

They moved to the open hatch and waited until the steps had been lowered. The pilot appeared from up front.

"Thanks for the ride," Bolan said.

"No problem, Mr. Cooper. We're here on standby until you need us."

As they stepped onto the tarmac an unmarked dark blue RAF 4x4 came speeding in their direction. It didn't slow until the last minute, then executed a controlled turn that brought it close to the steps of the plane. Bolan knew who was behind the wheel. No one else he knew could drive in such an apparently reckless fashion and be able to stop like that.

The driver's window powered down and a familiar face leaned forward.

"How's that for service, Yank?"

David McCarter, the leader of Phoenix Force, grinned at Bolan. His lean face was tanned, his hair ready for a trim. He looked for all the world to be a reckless, gung-ho, adrenaline junkie. In truth he was, plus being one of the finest commandos Bolan had ever fought alongside. Since his promotion to the top of the Phoenix Force ladder, McCarter's brash exuberance had been toned down by his new responsibilities. He had matured into an excellent leader. But the old McCarter was still alive and kicking, and broke through sometimes. Only when the situation called for it and never to the point where it put his men, or the current mission, in jeopardy.

"Hello, Ray," Bolan greeted his friend. "It's been a while."

Ray Travis was the cover name McCarter had been allocated for this alliance with his Stony Man partner.

"Yeah. Well, there I was taking it easy. Then they told me this Yank needed some help. And you know how I feel about bailing out our Colonial buddies, so here I am."

McCarter was out of the vehicle now, opening the rear door for Sashia.

"This must be the fair Miss Malinski. Ray Travis. Sorry we couldn't come up with better weather for you."

Sashia smiled at his banter. "It's not a problem, Mr. Travis."

She climbed in and McCarter closed the door. He grinned at Bolan. "Round the other side, chum, and *you* can open your own bloody door."

The second Bolan was inside McCarter booted the vehicle into motion, moving swiftly through the gears as he headed in the direction of the base's living quarters.

"We've been assigned rooms in the officers' block," he said. "Since I got here I've been checking things out locally. Had a word with base, and we've established a link so you can talk direct to the 'old man.'" The Brit put the emphasis on old man, meaning Brognola. The remark wasn't meant as any kind of slight against the head of the Special Operations Group. McCarter, as they all did, held Hal Brognola in great esteem. The big Fed worked hard to maintain the group, and even harder to protect and serve his teams. His efforts were always 101 percent. On more than one occasion he'd put himself on the line to justify mission extremes, fending off any criticism of his methods. He often explained to the President that the SOG's mandate was to handle those events standard agencies either could not, or would not, deal with. Brognola never compromised, never backed away from a fight. It earned him the undying respect of his people.

They reached the officers' quarters and McCarter took them inside. They were housed on the upper floor. He led them into the room where the communications system had been set up. Bolan checked it out. The RAF had given them the use of some sophisticated electronics.

"This should be fine."

Sashia had slumped down in a chair, her eyes drooping. Bolan glanced at McCarter. The Briton nodded. "She'll be okay with some rest."

Bolan sat and made contact with Stony Man via the online satellite link. He'd slipped on a set of headphones to keep the conversation one-sided.

"Hey, Barb, we've just arrived at RAF Lossiemouth."

"Is David there?"

"Waiting and ready to tear the Scottish Highlands apart. I want to move on this fast. Nevski and his crew aren't going to be sitting back twiddling their thumbs, either, so Ray and I are going to move out shortly."

"The woman?"

"She's pretty well tapped out. We'll leave her here. The RAF will keep an eye on her. She'll be safe enough with a whole fighter base to protect her. What I need to know is whether the Bear has managed to pin down Malinski's cell."

"He's managed to get it to within a pretty tight area. You're lucky his phone is a Tri-Band, satellite-linked model. It helped when it came to capturing the signal from the provider."

"Can you send us the coordinates?"

"Akira is going to download the data over the Internet link you have there. If you log in on your computer, it should download in next few minutes."

"Any other information I should know about?"

"There wasn't much on the laptop you took from Novak. Most of what we got just confirms names we already have."

"Can't pick a winner every time."

"We haven't had much luck isolating this supposed CIA insider who's been information dealing with Razihra and Nevski. The director has been working his own covert investigation, but he has a lot of CIA personnel to check through. Hunt has been running checks, as well. He's going at it from another angle to see if he can come up with any operatives suddenly striking it rich. Nothing so far. Carmen is using every contact she has in the FBI, but she has to play it carefully so she doesn't make too many people curious."

"Someone tipped off the opposition. The go-between, Salim, knew I was a fake from day one. It was more than just having known the real Novak. And I haven't forgotten the reaction I got from Novak himself when I got the drop on him and Stratton. He practically advertised he knew I wasn't from a U.S. agency."

"Maybe he'll spill while he's in deep lockup."

"Maybe? I'm starting to twitch when I hear that word."

"You guys be careful. Hey, you got everything you need?"

"You packed enough stuff in that Gulfstream to equip me for the next decade."

"Well, I know you follow the Boy Scout motto."

Bolan checked the computer and saw the data had arrived. "Information has come through. Time to move out. I'll update you as soon as we have anything."

He cut the connection. McCarter was already printing off a hard copy. He scanned the page, then passed it to Bolan. Crossing the room the Phoenix Force leader studied a large-scale map pinned to the wall.

"Coordinates put him in this general area," he said, using a marker pen to draw a rough circle. "Some territory to cover."

"Malinski is a physicist, Ray. He's no outdoorsman, so he'll stay close to inhabited areas. I'd be surprised if he was living in a tent."

"What is it about this bloody place that drew him back? Look at it. Remote. Out of the loop when it comes to most things. What's the attraction?"

"That has me wondering, too. I understand Malinski wants to be off the beaten track. He's trying to stay low profile, but why this particular spot?"

"I think I can answer that."

Bolan turned and saw Sashia sitting up.

"I couldn't understand why Father wanted to come here. It didn't make sense until now. I was thinking about those letters I received from him. Trying to remember if they could help."

"And?"

"I started trying to recall the postmarks. Lossiemouth didn't mean a thing. Then it clicked. Craigimore. That was one of the postmarks. Craigimore on the Moray Firth."

McCarter checked the wall map, then stabbed a finger at a point farther along the coast. "It's there. Bloody hell, I thought we were in a lonely place here at Lossiemouth, but Craigimore is strictly for the birds."

Bolan tapped the name into a search site and it eventually

flashed up. There wasn't a great deal of information regarding Craigimore. Some old newspaper articles said it was a small village that had once served the Scottish fishing industry when it existed. That had run out of steam years ago, leaving the village to slowly wither as many people moved elsewhere. Bolan scrolled through the text seeing little that might attract someone like Gregori Malinski. He was about to log out when Sashia, leaning over his shoulder, pointed at the screen.

"There. Next paragraph."

Bolan looked again and saw what had caught Sashia's attention. It was a few words highlighting a separate page: Craigimore Research Facility Closed Down.

Bolan hit the search button and the new page was loaded and displayed.

The short article from a few years back described the operation of a dedicated research program looking at the possibility of converting nuclear waste into a stable fusion fuel capable of powering automobiles. The research had been highly controversial within the oil conglomerates. They saw it as a threat to their tight grip on the fuel industry and did everything to stall the development once a small breakthrough occurred. Though it was never admitted, the project was deliberately denied adequate funding, pressure was applied from outside sources and the project finally abandoned. The research team was disbanded. The research complex was left empty. No one in the Craigimore area had any use for it.

"I wonder if Father was happy doing that work?" Sashia asked, more to herself than to Bolan and McCarter.

"It might explain why he came back. Better memories than he's been making lately maybe," Bolan said.

"Gives us a starting point," McCarter added.

BOLAN AND MCCARTER WERE able to arm themselves from the equipment Barbara Price had sent along in the Gulfstream. The crew from the Air Force plane were being looked after by their RAF counterparts, leaving the Stony Man pair to choose their weapons.

"We'll look a right pair of idiots if we go storming in on Malinski and find him sitting with his feet up, drinking tea and reading the *Times,*" McCarter observed.

"I'll risk it," Bolan said.

McCarter grinned. "Wouldn't be the first time."

They wore dark, outdoor clothing and sturdy walking boots, which fit the terrain. Bolan's leather jacket hid his shoulder rig, bearing his Beretta 93-R. McCarter carried his favored weapon, the Browning Hi-Power. They had a backpack to carry a pair of mini-uzis and extra magazines for their weapons. Bolan picked up digital transceivers. He checked the power supplies and handed one to McCarter.

"Wouldn't want you to feel lonely if we get separated."

"I knew you still cared, Striker."

They took the 4x4 back to the officers' quarters. McCarter stayed behind the wheel while he went inside to speak to Sashia. Earlier she had protested when Bolan had told her she was going to have to stay behind, but she realized the sense in his resonating.

"If things get rough out there I can't have you at risk. If we find your father, we'll bring him back here. I doubt even Anatoly Nevski would consider taking on the RAF."

"You're right." As Bolan turned to leave, Sashia reached out to grip his sleeve, leaning across to kiss him. "For helping. Thank you, Matt Cooper."

THE DRIVE TOOK JUST OVER two hours. The weather hadn't improved. When McCarter braked on the road overlooking the small town of Craigimore, rain was sweeping in across the headland and heavy clouds hung low in the gray sky.

"Scotland isn't always like this," McCarter muttered. "Only when *I* visit."

Bolan was peering through the windshield, using binoculars. Something had attracted his attention. He studied the landscape a little longer, then lowered the glasses and reached behind him for the backpack, pulling it to him.

"Let's roll, David."

McCarter started the 4x4, heading down the long slope in the road that would eventually bring them into the hamlet of Craigimore. Something in Bolan's tone warned McCarter not to expect the peace and quiet to last for much longer.

CHAPTER TWENTY

Craigmore

The Bell JetRanger swung in over the rain-swept vista of
Craigimore, turning almost lazily as it lost height and touched
down on the wide sweep of grass that lay just beyond the town
square. As soon as it landed, the side hatch slid open and dis-
gorged five dark-clad, armed men. They fanned out across the
grass, waiting until Lem Kirov joined them. He adjusted the
microphone of his lightweight com set.

"Try the hotel first," he ordered two of the men. "Oleg, you
take Beeker and try the bar over there."

The two pairs moved at his order, heads down as they
made for their objectives.

Kirov raised his hand and drew the remaining man close.
He pointed in the direction of the opposite end of town.

"Check it out."

Kirov watched his team move into action, then returned to
the comparative comfort of the helicopter, using the com set
to keep in contact with his men.

He settled in a seat behind the pilot's seat.

"I can understand why Malinski would want to come here. This place is dead."

"This is where he used to work?" the pilot asked.

"There was some kind of research facility outside town. Malinski worked at it until it was closed through lack of funding."

Kirov thought back to the moment when Karel made his discovery concerning Gregori Malinski's movements over the past few years. How he had jumped from job to job following his dismissal from the Soviet-era service developing nuclear weaponry. His disillusionment with the new government in Russia had soured him, and free enterprise had led him to offering his services to anyone willing to pay. He took small contracts, then spent time at the Craigimore research facility until it was forced into liquidation. It was in the year or so after that when Anatoly Nevski found the man and encouraged him to sell his expertise to interested parties.

Three deals later and Malinski, now a relatively wealthy man, had showed signs of slowing down. His work, always meticulous, took longer and longer. His qualifications made him the ideal candidate for the Razihra contract. When he heard the money offer, he had taken it, but even Nevski had noticed his attitude wasn't as sharp as it had been. He mentioned it to Kirov, and they had decided to keep a close watch on Malinski.

With the contract well under way and Malinski having been relocated to the remote facility as he moved into the critical phase of the development, it had become difficult to watch him. When it became known that he had performed a vanishing act, Kirov wasn't entirely surprised. He was angry because it left the Nevski organisation in a bind. Razihra made it clear he held them responsible, and Razihra wasn't someone you crossed. So Karel, Nevski's in-house cyber-genius, was let loose on the electronic hunt. It took him time, but the joy of cyberspace meant that somewhere, sometime, Malinski had left a fingerprint, a tiny scrap of detail that led the searcher further, deeper, until he came across press reports detailing the closure of the Craigimore research project. There were articles in a number of newspapers, some in learned journals. And in one were photographs of the researchers, showing the thin-faced Russian himself, in a group shot with others from the aborted project. There was another that featured Malinski in one of Craigimore's pubs, enjoying a drink with the locals. This information, coupled with the trace on Malinski's cell phone had given his location as somewhere in the general area, and offered Nevski's team a target. A hastily arranged flight from France, and a pickup by helicopter, had brought Kirov and his strike team to the isolated community of Craigimore where their intention was to locate and snatch Gregori Malinski.

THEY ROLLED IN FROM THE south, following the narrow, winding road that swept them past the outlying houses, taking the final bend in the road that brought them in sight of the helicopter. McCarter hit the brakes and swung the slowing 4x4 to the side of the road, almost into the thick hedge flanking it.

"There's something you don't see every day in a place like this," the Briton said.

Bolan had the binoculars in his hands again, scanning the area, then the helicopter. He focused in on the aircraft, bringing it into sharp relief. The side hatch was open and hunched over in a seat behind the pilot was Lem Kirov. There was no mistaking the man's hard, uncompromising features.

"Malinski is a popular guy," he commented. "Nevski's intel is as good as ours."

He swung the binoculars back and forth, pausing as he saw

two armed men making their way in the direction of the main street.

"David, it's time to move out.

CRAIGIMORE HAD ONLY ONE hotel, a two-hundred-year-old building constructed from local granite that had withstood wind and weather. It was solid and functional. The tourists who passed through kept it going. Craigimore House was never going to be fashionably popular, but no one wanted it that way. The locals liked the hotel as it was. *Change for change's sake will ne'er profit a man,* was a well-known saying in the area.

Kirov's men walked into the lobby of the hotel and demanded to be told of Gregori Malinski's whereabouts. The question was emphasized when one of the men showed the autoweapon he carried under his coat.

"Kindly remove yourselves from these premises," the manager said. Peter McCloud wasn't a man who scared easily. It wasn't in his nature to accept any kind of deviation from the norm, no matter what the circumstances, and the hard-faced men who strode into the hotel gave that distinct impression. "Do you not hear me?"

Per Yakov glanced at the man. He held McCloud's steady gaze for a few solid seconds. When he moved his action was lightning-fast and utterly ruthless. He leaned across the desk, took hold of McCloud's dark hair and yanked down hard, slamming McCloud face-first onto the surface of the reception desk. The desk was constructed from solid oak, smooth and glossy from being polished countless times.

"I ask the question. You answer. We know he's in this fucking village. Maybe here in hotel. *Where?*"

McCloud, bleeding from his mouth and nose, stared up at him. He was too stunned from the blow to speak. Yakov pushed him away.

Petrov threw open his coat and took out his handgun. He strode across the lobby and caught the arm of one of the hotel's female staff, swinging her around to face him. She was wide-eyed with fear. Petrov lashed out with a large, open hand and struck her across the side of the face. The blow sent her crashing against the reception desk. Petrov caught a handful of her thick hair and yanked her head back.

"Understand your position. Tell me what we need to know and you may live. Refuse and you *will* die. Gregori Malinski?"

The young woman, eyes brimming with tears, nodded. "He is staying here," she said. "Room 18. The second floor."

"Show me." Petrov dragged her upright, viciously punching her shoulder and pushing her toward the stairs. "Keep these idiots quiet."

Yakov nodded. He moved to where he could observe the front entrance and also cover the lobby. The muzzle of his submachine gun covered the few people in front of him. "Move before I tell you and I will shoot."

His com set hissed briefly. It was Kirov's voice that came through.

"Well?"

"He's here at the hotel. Petrov is going to find him now."

"About time we had something go right. As soon as you have him bring him to the helicopter so we can get out of this damn place. I'll inform the others." There was a pause. "Yakov. Just don't lose him."

With what had been happening to them over the recent past Yakov declined to make any comment. His attention was taken by movement behind him. It was McCloud, moving slowly from behind the desk. Blood was streaming down his face, soaking the once white front of his shirt. His actions, slow and deliberate, unsettled Yakov.

"Stay where you are," he said.

McCloud appeared not to have even heard what was being said to him. He reached the end of the desk and moved around it to step into full view. It was only as he did that Yakov saw the over-under configuration hunting shotgun in his hands. The totally unexpected action caught Yakov unprepared and his reaction was equally slow. He yanked his auto weapon around, finger tightening on the trigger. The tilted muzzles of the shotgun showed black and menacing in the instant before McCloud emptied both barrels into Yakov's exposed body. At such close range the effect was devastating. The searing twin bursts ripped into him midchest, shredding clothing, flesh and bone, the impact actually taking his feet off the lobby floor as he was driven backward, trailing a bloody mélange of glistening viscera. The SMG went off in the split second after McCloud fired. The 9 mm burst hit the hotelier in the upper chest, spinning him and dumping him on the floor.

PETROV WAS PUSHING THE woman ahead of him, along the corridor in the direction of Malinski's room, when the double blast of the shotgun reached him, followed by a burst from an autoweapon.

"What the hell is going on?" he demanded.

There was no reply from Yakov, but Kirov had picked up the sound over his own com set.

"Petrov? What was that?"

"I don't know, but it came from the lobby downstairs. I'm close to Malinski's room."

"Stay on that."

"Go," Petrov said to the hesitant woman. "No reason we need to worry."

CHAPTER TWENTY-ONE

Gregori Malinski heard the distant boom of the shotgun. This was wrong. First the helicopter landing across the way from the hotel. Men exiting and spreading out across the village, two of them heading in the direction of the hotel.

He panicked then, because without having to be told, he knew they were coming for him. His hideaway had been discovered and if he allowed himself to be captured, his life would be over. His defection from Razihra's isolated research facility, so good at the time, was turning into a nightmare.

Malinski's initial escape from Wadi Hattat had been engineered in part by the exposure of one of the young Iranian technicians as an undercover operative from a group opposed to what was being done at the facility. Malinski had been under the impression the man was part of the facility's security detail, and his eventual challenging of the man had revealed some surprising facts.

Tariq Kemal was a diagnostic technician. He worked in the same section of the facility as Malinski. A quiet, lean young man, he maintained an unobtrusive presence, carrying out his work efficiently. Like the majority of Iranians on the project, he appeared totally dedicated to the program. Yet there was something in his manner when he was alone with Malinski that intrigued the Russian. He began to observe Kemal and over a period of time he realized the young technician was taking a greater interest in Malinski himself, rather than his work. At first it suggested Kemal was part of the security contingent based within the facility, which gave Malinski cause to tread carefully.

He knew of the existence of the Iranian Ministry of Intelligence and Security. The MOIS had a fearsome reputation, and it wasn't wise to arouse their interest. To Malinski, who had lived under the threat of the KGB during his time within the Soviet Union, being watched and monitored was nothing new. Gregori Malinski had escaped that shadowy past with the breakup of the Soviet empire and during his contact with Western living had enjoyed the comparative freedom of coming and going when and where he wanted. Since his contract with Nevski and his employment by Ayatollah Razihra, he was spending the greater part of his time at the desert facility. The technical labs, the equipment, were superb. No expense had been spared to ensure the technicians had everything they needed. Despite all that Malinski felt smothered, hemmed in, and knew he was in a closed community. He was one of a very few non-Iranians, which meant a fairly isolated existence. It got to him after long months entombed in the concrete environment, with few breaks in Tehran being allowed. Malinski was aware his discomfort was obvious and it was his discomfort, coupled with the intense interest from Kemal that created the illusion he was being studied.

It came to a head late one night when Malinski, at the end of a long shift, barely able to keep his eyes open, made a simple mistake that deleted the piece of calculation he had been working on. As it vanished from his monitor, Malinski slammed his hand down on his desktop and vented his anger in a string of verbal curses, then swung his chair away from his workstation and came face-to-face with Tariq Kemal. Seeing the young man, standing silently watching, caught Malinski off guard. In his agitated state he pushed to his feet, thrusting a long finger at Kemal.

"Isn't it enough that I work myself into the ground for you damned people? Every time I turn around I see you watching me like some overzealous spy. Am I a child not to be trusted? Do you think I am going to mess up, so your precious Ayatollah Razihra has ordered you to peer over my shoulder in case I delay his chance at becoming Iran's first nuclear cleric? You want to know something? I don't even know why I am here in this godless place, helping that madman achieve his weapons. I have had enough of building machines of death."

Malinski felt his pulse racing. He was acting way out of character. He knew that and immediately wondered why he had reacted so strongly to Kemal's presence.

Kemal made no response. He and Malinski were the only ones present, so in the empty lab no one else had overheard the Russian's outburst. After a moment the young Iranian reached out and laid his hands on Malinski's shoulders, easing him back into his seat. Then he slid his hands into the pockets of his white lab coat and observed Malinski for a moment.

"I understand your frustration, Dr. Malinski. However let me assure you I am not watching you in the way you seem to believe. Yes, I have been observing you, but for very different reason." Kemal paused, weighing what he was going to say next. Even Malinski sensed he was debating whether to trust him. "I know I am taking a risk here, but I have to use this opportunity. My reason for watching you is that I have sensed your disillusionment building over the past weeks. You want to get away from here. I want you to leave because if you do and they lose your input, the program here at Wadi Hattat will stall. And any delay will help our cause."

"Cause? What cause, Tariq?" Malinski's weary brain was finding it hard to grasp the meaning behind Kemal's words.

"I infiltrated this place to learn exactly what they are doing. The degree of development. The group I am involved with only want to put a stop to this…this terrible research. Razihra's ambition is going to put Iran on a race to disaster. The Americans and the Israelis don't want a Middle East nuclear threat. Nor do many of the Iranians themselves, but we are outnumbered by the ones in power who do want this to happen. They have much of the military behind them. They have people in positions of power able to put down groups like ours. Control of the media means they have the upper hand so we cannot even get our message out to the masses."

"So you deliberately came to work here to sabotage the nuclear research?"

"Yes."

"You are a brave young man."

"Or a foolish one."

"When I was your age I might have exhibited the same righteous fervor."

"Fervor has no age limit, Dr. Malinski."

"Tariq, I came here of my own free will. I'm being paid a great deal of money to help Razihra realize his dream. I can't deny that. Nor can I deny this isn't the first time I have sold my knowledge on the open market. Tell, me, how does that place me on the list of ethical degenerates?"

"I admire you too much to even think about judging you."

"What is there to admire?"

"Your intelligence. The knowledge you use so easily. I have seen you solve the most testing mathematical problem with the stroke of a key. Explain a nuclear theory as if you were debating the recipe for an egg omelet. It's genius at work, Doctor."

"Nuclear calculus likened to an omelet." For the first in a long time Malinski smiled, liking the analogy. "If nothing else, Tariq, you have given me a moment of light in the darkness. I thank you for that, my young friend."

Malinski gazed around the lab. His work. His life. But now something he had little pleasure in being involved with. The responsibility had become too much to shoulder any longer, and Kemal's words had exposed what he had been partly suppressing—that he really wanted to be out of it. Away from this place. The word "free" skittered around the edge of his conscious thought, but he doubted he would ever really be totally free of what he had done over the years. His crime was that he hadn't considered the implications of his work. He had always been a death merchant, creating machines that were for one thing, and one thing only. Nuclear annihilation. That shadow would follow him around for a long time. Yet if he *was* to escape from his present, making it his past, there had to be a moment of separation.

And now seemed to be as good as any other.

"Tariq, if you truly want to help me, tell me how I can get away from this place."

"Let me think about how we can do this thing. Dr. Malinski, I will work this out, and you will be able to go where you want and leave the memory of Wadi Hattat behind."

The change in his attitudes to what he was involved in had forced him to take a long and detailed look at his life. What he had become and how he had allowed his self-held ideals to drift away. A reaffirmation of his principles made him look deeply at the nightmare scenario he was working to develop and he found his perceptions had altered and the very notion of helping to construct yet more devices of unimaginable horror had overwhelmed him. The gleaming, sterile research lab deep in the secret Iranian complex, silent save for the subdued hum of electronic equipment, took on a sinister aspect. What he had once looked upon as his own private enclave now became his prison. The place he was tied to like a man in an isolated cell.

He wasn't entirely alone. There were the assistants who did his bidding, who followed his every lead in the intricate and time-consuming procedures. Compared to Malinski they were novices, understanding little of the complexities of nuclear physics. As well as creating Razihra's nuclear weapons Malinski's contract called for him to instruct these people so they could carry on the work. It was difficult.

The Iranian scientists were eager enough to learn, but their nuclear background was nowhere near as sophisticated as Malinski's. It added to his burden, and their clamoring for more information became tiresome. They were, he realized, devoted followers of Ayatollah Razihra, and their demanding attitudes, coupled with the almost fanatical eagerness to create destructive weaponry had been the germ that propagated his own doubts. There was something almost repellant in the way they gloried over what they were doing, in the fervent adulation of Razihra and his relentless desire to be able to wave his nuclear capability in the faces of those he deemed unworthy.

Alone in his quarters, unable to sleep, Malinski had spent an evening going through his few personal belongings. Over the recent years his constant moving had forced him to abandon much, until he had only a few items left. A few letters and faded photographs of his daughter, Sashia, his Sashi. How many years had passed since he had seen her? Too many. He missed her more with every passing day, knowing the situation was his own fault. Pride more than anything had kept him

from making contact. All he had were the letters they had exchanged many months ago. He had learned of her success, her
rise to a strong position in the company and that she was now
based in Paris. Staring at the old photograph of her he had experienced a great longing to be with her in that wonderful city.
Instead he was deep in the Iranian desert, helping to build in-
fernal machines of destruction.

He didn't even attempt to fool himself. Razihra wanted the
nuclear capability because the man was little short of a war-
monger. He carried an abiding hatred of the West and wanted
to be able to brandish his missiles at them. He wanted nothing less than the destruction of the Israeli nation. And Malinski, who had met the man on number of occasions, had seen
the gleam in his eyes that had little to do with religion and
more to do with a zealot's blind devotion to his desires. Something made Malinski think of Sashia at that moment. And he
was suddenly made aware that what he was doing for Razihra
could affect her. Missiles had no conscience. They were
guided by men who decided the point of impact, the trajectory that would send a nuclear missile on a journey of total
destruction. Innocent lives would be put under threat of annihilation. Total and indiscriminate annihilation.

His Sashi was one of those innocents, and he, Gregori Malinski, was helping to create more of those weapons. Something he created might one day be launched in the direction
of some city where she was working, maybe living, and in a
blinding white burst of terrible energy she would be burned
in an instant.

Those thoughts remained with him over the next few
days, growing stronger, and the work he was doing turned
sour before his eyes. His concentration weakened, and if
he hadn't maintained an outward veneer of normality his
attitude might have betrayed him. He had made his deci-

sion to walk away from the project, well aware that in doing so he would put himself at risk. At that moment in his life Malinski cared little for his personal safety. He wanted out and he was prepared to risk everything to achieve it.

He worked at his computer station, quietly creating a program that would effectively shut out anyone attempting to access his work-in-progress. He could have quite simply deleted everything he had already developed, but that would have aroused suspicion immediately. His plan was simple in the extreme. He was going to leave the research facility, get himself clear and then use a remote access on his laptop that would lock his coworkers out of his data. As added insurance he altered mathematical equations and tolerances within the mass of his research. Not by great degrees that would be spotted immediately, but by subtle bending of the figures. If his work *was* accessed by the people in the facility, after he had departed, they wouldn't be able to reach satisfactory conclusions based on his altered material. If they continued to extrapolate, all they would do would be to move further and further away from a satisfactory end result. The final calculations would become a meaningless jumble of unrelated figures.

Malinski was no slouch when it came to programming. His quiet manner hid a mind that could acquit itself in any number of devious ways. Securing and altering his data had been something Malinski had done many times in the past. Security had been paramount when he had worked in the Soviet era. They had been paranoid when it came to safeguarding their secrets, and it had been instilled into anyone working for the state to maintain the highest levels of security. It became second nature, and Malinski had achieved what was required of him and had taken it to the next level. Now he worked his ingenious subroutines into his data, ensuring that when he left the facility he could trigger the lockdown from a distance. His laptop contained everything he had worked on down to the last decimal point. Once he had his fail-safe hidden away he moved to the next phase of his escape plan.

Simplicity.

Nothing too complex. He declared once again his desire to leave Wadi Hattat, informed Kemal what he had done to prevent his research being taken over and between them they devised the means by which he would effect this disappearance.

Malinski worked the deception it into his routine over a few days, feigning an increasingly painful toothache. He kept up the subterfuge, letting the pain distract him from his work, constantly apologizing for his tardiness until the project director himself visited him at his workstation.

"Dr. Malinski, I have been informed you are in some degree of pain."

"I feel bad about it, Director. Trying to ignore it does little to help. I'm finding it difficult to concentrate on some of these intricate calculations."

"We are at a critical stage, yes?"

Malinski tapped his monitor screen with the pencil in his hand. "Certainly. Once I have this section complete, our data can be applied to the material from the Americans, and we will have reached the next level. Which is why I feel I need to be fully able to concentrate."

The director nodded. "We are well within our development schedule, Dr. Malinski. I have no objection to you seeking medical help. There are excellent dental surgeons in Tehran. If you will make yourself available, I will arrange for you to be flown there in the morning. Have your problem seen to, recuperate for a day or so, then return."

"I am most grateful for your concern, Director."

"Think nothing of it. After all, we cannot afford to have our top physicist unable to give his best."

Malinski had smiled, holding a hand to his cheek as if in pain. Back at his workstation he had continued his data input, scrupulously coordinating the connection between his lab computer and his personal laptop, checking a number of times until he was satisfied he would be able to initiate his lockdown code.

He held a staff meeting the evening before his departure, assigning each member to his or her own individual tasks. When they had gone off duty he had switched his own computer to deep standby mode, clicking off the monitor so that to all appearances his machine was idle. He had given strict instructions that his machine be left untouched, emphasizing that it contained highly sensitive data at the most critical stage and that nothing should be accessed in case codes were disturbed and possibly lost. He knew that the Iranians he worked with had a rigid sense of duty and would follow his instructions to the letter. As an additional safeguard he detailed Kemal as to what he had set up and asked the Iranian to keep a close watch on his computer until he was able to access it from a safe distance. It was all he could do until he was clear.

Malinski spent a restless night, worrying that his subterfuge might be exposed. He presented himself the following morning with a small traveling bag that contained a few clothes and his laptop. After a few words with the director he was escorted by the security guards out of the facility to the helicopter pad. One of the security men accompanied him on the trip, sitting behind the Russian. Malinski did not breath easy until the aircraft had left the ground, turning before setting course for Tehran. It was a four-hour flight. Malinski settled in his seat, clutching his travel bag to him and concentrating on how he was going to get out of Iran once he reached the city.

It proved to be easier than he had imagined.

Kemal had furnished him with a telephone number, and Malinski called this number from one of the pay phones in his hotel the following morning when his guard was at his daily prayers. He found himself speaking to the man Kemal had put him in contact with.

Amir Fayed proved to be a man of his word. He told Malinski he would have him out of Tehran within twenty-four hours. The only question he had was the destination Malinski had chosen for himself. While Fayed made the arrangements, the Russian arranged an appointment with the dentist he had been advised to use. In his room that afternoon Malinski activated his laptop, making a connection with his distant computer in the facility via the Internet. Once his computer recognized his code, Malinski sent the coded message that would initiate the lockdown sequence. He received an acknowledgment with a few minutes.

On the morning of his appointment Malinski and his security man took a taxi to the dentist. There were three other men in the elevator taking them up the floor where the dentist had his practice. Before the elevator had risen more than a few feet the security guard was overpowered by two of the men. No one knew what happened to the guard. He was never seen or heard from again and by the time his disappearance became noticed it was too late. Malinski and the third man exited at the next floor and calmly took the stairs back to street level. There they climbed into a waiting car and were driven away. Malinski was delivered to an address in the city where he came face-to-face with Amir Fayed.

Two days later he was in Paris where he lost himself in the city he knew well. In comparative safety he allowed himself to relax, despite knowing that once his flight to freedom was discovered Ayatollah Razihra's people would come looking for him. They would check his stored data, find it had been locked and they were unable to get to it. Once that happened they would do all in their power to find him and return him to the research facility. The work he had developed for them was too valuable to abandon. If they did that, it would set their program back years and Razihra wouldn't tolerate such a condition. As well as sending out his own people, he would demand the assistance of Anatoly Nevski and his men. Nevski had brought Malinski into the program. His knowledge of Malinski would be invaluable in a recovery mission. Nevski would do it out of loyalty to his client and for his own reputation. They would go to any lengths to get him back and would use anyone who meant anything to Malinski.

Such as his daughter, Sashia.

The mere thought of her being dragged into the affair made him sick. He had realized he needed to contact her, to let her know she might be in danger. In his darkest moments Malinski feared for her, his mind conjuring up images of the terrible things his pursuers could do if they believed she knew where he was. He decided to leave Paris before he made contact, deny her any knowledge of where he was…

CHAPTER TWENTY-TWO

"We have company," Petrov said into his throat mike.

"Locals?"

"Only if they dress like us and carry automatic weapons."

"The man Cooper?"

"Maybe. Only there are two of them."

"Where?"

"Moving in from the south end of town. Kirov, they have done this kind of thing before."

"Your point?"

"These men are not local poachers. They could make this hard for us."

"Just think about the money you are earning."

"I am. And wondering how I might manage to spend it from the grave."

"Look at it as an exercise for your combat skills."

"Kirov?"

"Yes?"

"Is it safe and comfortable inside that chopper?"

Petrov cut off, leaving Kirov without someone to shout at.

GREGORI MALINSKI HEARD A voice in the corridor outside his room, urgent, demanding, and most certainly not a Scottish brogue. For a moment he froze, panic seizing him, blind terror that held him motionless. Then he broke the paralysis, turning to snatch up his coat. He crossed the room and pushed open the window, ignoring the cold rain that burst into the room. Malinski stepped out onto the metal fire escape stairs that ran down the outside wall. He had requested this specific room in case a hasty retreat was required, making the excuse he had a phobia. As the hotel had few guests, it was no problem getting what he wanted. Since his break away from the desert facility, survival had become his overriding concern. He shrugged into the coat as he descended the metal steps, missing his footing once and almost falling. He grasped the rail at the side to steady himself. The falling rain stung his face, chilling his flesh.

"*Gregori Malinski,*" a voice called. "You cannot hide from us."

Malinski didn't respond. He stepped from the fire escape and ran, angling in the direction of the village main street. He had no idea where he was going. There was nothing except a single thought in his mind: to get away from the men who had come after him.

Nothing else mattered right now. If he failed to outrun them and they captured him, his future would turn bleaker than it seemed to be at the present.

He emerged from the side of the hotel and started across the street until he came to a stop partway across, unsure of his next move. Leaving the village behind presented its own problems. Beyond the straggle of houses and stores the rugged Scottish terrain lay open, hostile, with nothing for him. Malinski still saw it as his only option. He wouldn't remain in the village and expose the inhabitants to danger. They had done nothing to deserve being placed in the firing line of his troubles. His return to the village had rekindled old friendships. People had remembered him and showed their remembrance by making him welcome. And here he was paying back them back by drawing Anatoly Nevski's men of violence into their community.

Malinski decided that shouldn't be allowed to happen and acted with it in mind. Pulling his coat around him, he cut across the street, intending to vacate the village.

"HE'S MOVING NORTH, OUT of the village," Petrov said into his com set. "Pursue him."

He turned from the open window, his face suffused with rage. He could hardly believe Malinski had slipped from of his hands so easily. If the man made it out of the village and eluded them in the wild countryside, Kirov wasn't going to be happy. The man was a hard taskmaster at the best of times. It they failed to capture Gregori Malinski, he was going to be in a killing mood. Petrov left the room, ignoring the young woman who had brought him to Malinski's room. He ran the length of the corridor and started down the stairs leading to the lobby. He had his gun on track, conscious of hearing the gunfire earlier.

Before he reached the bottom he spotted Yakov's bloody corpse on the floor. The shotgun blast had cut him virtually in two. It had been a long time since Petrov had seen such an extreme wound. He checked out the lobby as he moved from the stairs. It was deserted save for Yakov and the man who had been behind the desk. He was on his back, yards from Yakov, his chest bloody, an over-under shotgun on the carpet close by.

Petrov headed for the door, eager to get after Malinski.

The main doors swung open and a tall figure stepped inside.

MCCARTER CUT ACROSS THE street, drawn by the sound of the shotgun blast. The Briton caught sight of Bolan moving in from farther along the street, so it was up to McCarter to check out the disturbance.

He was still some distance from the building when a tall, rangy figure emerged from the alley at the side of the hotel, paused partway across the street, then turned and headed north.

Bolan waved McCarter, then changed direction and went after the running man.

McCarter reached the closed doors, shouldered them open and burst inside, scanning the lobby. A couple of bodies were sprawled on the floor. A third man, weapon up and tracking, was striding across the lobby. He spotted McCarter and brought his weapon into target acquisition.

The Briton swerved to one side, behind a pillar, as the gun went off. Plaster blew out from the pillar, peppering the side of his face.

Gripping his Browning two-handed, McCarter leaned out from the far side of the pillar and returned fire. He took a moment to settle his aim, then triggered three fast shots that took Petrov in the chest, knocking him back against the desk. The Russian stared across at McCarter as the Briton rounded the pillar. Biting back the pain Petrov dragged his sagging pistol into position again.

McCarter didn't hesitate and put two 9 mm slugs into Petrov's head. The force slapped him back and he twisted, slithering along the side of the desk before he fell to the floor.

It went very quiet for a moment until the woman Petrov had forced upstairs appeared, hugging the wall as she moved down the stairs. When she saw McCarter she raised a hand.

"Please, no more."

"I'm not with them, love. Anyone else up there?"

She shook her head. "There…there were only the two of

them." She pulled her horrified gaze from Yakov's bloody corpse. When she recognized the hotel manager she gave a soft cry. "Is he dead?"

McCarter had turned to leave. "I don't know. Check him out then call for help. You have a number for the RAF base at Lossiemouth?"

"I'm sure we have."

"Then call it. Tell them what happened. Say Cooper needs medical assistance and quickly."

McCarter heard the distant crackle of gunfire and ran out of the hotel.

THE RUNNING MAN WAS Malinski. Bolan recognized him from the file photographs he had seen at the original Stony Man briefing. He raced after the Russian.

He had only gone a few yards when two armed figures burst from cover, between him and Malinski. He heard one of them shout. Malinski faltered, throwing a look over his shoulder, then ran on. One of the men took a shooter's stance and raised his pistol, firing quickly. The slug hit Malinski in the left leg. He staggered, falling forward as his weakened leg went from beneath him, and pitched facedown on the wet street.

Bolan, still running, closed the distance and the two men became aware of his presence. One turned to face Bolan and caught a pair of 9 mm slugs in his body. He gave a grunt of pain as the slugs shattered ribs, stumbling and dropping to his knees. The second shooter, the one who had put Malinski down, swiveled at his hip, bringing his pistol around for a wild shot. Bolan caught him with a single head shot that blew a bloody fountain from his cracked skull. Out of the corner of his eye Bolan saw his first target haul his own weapon up from his side. He turned and put two shots into the guy's head that dropped him to the ground.

McCARTER WITNESSED THE SHOOTING, saw the two men go
down under Bolan's gun. As he hurried to join the Executioner, he saw a third man step out from behind a telephone
booth, his weapon starting to rise. The guy hadn't seen Mc-
Carter, so the Phoenix Force leader skidded to a stop, brought
up the Browning. It was a fair distance, but he knew his weapon. The Briton thrust it forward, gripped in both hands and
pulled the trigger, and kept firing repeatedly until the pistol
jacked out the final round. The target fell back, his upper
body riddled by McCarter's shots. He crashed against the
side of the telephone booth, the impact splintering one of the
glass panels before he toppled to the ground. McCarter ejected
the empty magazine and snapped in a fresh one as he closed
in on the scene.

"You okay, Mack?"

Bolan nodded. He looked from the dead man to McCarter.
"I owe you one there."

"Too bloody right you do," McCarter grinned.

They both moved to where Gregori Malinski lay clutching
his bloody leg. The left side of his face was scraped and bloody
from his fall. He looked up at them, concern on his face.

"Who are you?" His tone implied he was expecting the worst.

"For certain we're not the bloody Red Cross, chum," Mc-
Carter said.

"Let's get you under cover, Dr. Malinski," Bolan said.

"I called in for help," McCarter said as they hoisted the
Russian to his feet. "Don't be surprised if you see the whole
of the RAF descend on us."

Bolan smiled. "Right now nothing is liable to surprise me."

They headed back toward the hotel.

"Please tell me who you are," Malinski said. "You won't
take me back to that damn desert, will you?"

"Be a damn sight warmer than this place," McCarter observed.

"Dr. Malinski, the only concern you have coming up is explaining how you got into this to your daughter," Bolan said.

Despite his pain Malinski's face ghosted a thin smile. "Sashia? She is here?"

"Not far away. You'll be seeing her soon enough."

KIROV TRIED TO SUPPRESS HIS rage at the end result of the skirmish. Even while he held his temper in check he ordered the pilot to take off. As the Bell rose and swept away from the village the Russian was trying to figure out what he was going to say to Nevski. He wasn't looking forward to it.

A MEDICAL TEAM WAS WAITING when the RAF helicopter touched down. Malinski was helped inside and taken directly to a treatment room to have the bullet removed from his leg. Peter McCloud, the hotel manager, had been ferried out, too, and the helicopter took off immediately to fly him to the nearest large hospital for major surgery. Bolan and McCarter found Sashia waiting in her room.

"Is he all right?"

"He took a bullet in his leg," Bolan explained. "They have him over at the base medical center right now. He'll be fine once they take the bullet out."

Sashia stared at him, eyes brimming with tears. "I told myself I would never let this happen. That there was too much distance between us and I could never forgive him. But—"

"But now you just want to be with him. To tell him all that doesn't matter and you're glad he's still alive. Something like that," Bolan suggested.

"Yes, Cooper, something like that. In the end it comes down to the simple facts. He's my father. I love him and I want to be near him. Just like when I was a child." She raised her head. "Does that sound silly?"

"Silly?" McCarter said. "Good God, girl, it's the only thing that does matter. Now let's get down to the canteen and I'll rustle up some mugs of tea. Best thing out for an emotional moment like this. Any more of this maudlin stuff and I'll burst into tears myself."

Sashia laughed and glanced at Bolan. He shrugged. "Don't look at me. He's always telling me mugs of tea and bacon sandwiches were responsible for Hitler's defeat in World War II. What do I know?"

EARLY EVENING SAW BOLAN, McCarter and Sashia being ushered into the room where Gregori Malinski had been settled following the operation to remove the bullet from his leg. An RAF military policeman stood guard outside the door.

"You don't think those people would try to do anything here, do you?" Sashia asked when she saw the guard.

"It's a precaution until we can have your father moved to a secure location," Bolan said.

She paused in midstride, a stricken expression crossing her face. "You're not talking about some kind of prison?"

"No. Sashia, you father hasn't strictly broken any laws as far as I can tell. He isn't on any Wanted lists, except the one posted by Ayatollah Razihra and Anatoly Nevski. Right now we have to keep him away from them. My people can arrange for him to go somewhere safe. I've already spoken to them. A plane will come and fetch you both, if you want to go with him. It will take you out of the reach of the people who hired your father and you will be well protected."

"Yes, I want to go with him. Cooper, can you promise he'll be safe? That those men won't find him?" She looked him in the eyes and spoke again before Bolan could answer. "I'm sorry. I shouldn't put you in such a position. I understand you want me to feel secure in the knowledge that my father can forget what happened and start living his life again free and clear. But I realize total security is hard to achieve. We are bound by the smallness of this world we live in. I accept what you say. My father will be well protected, but there are no guarantees."

"Now that's what I like," McCarter said. "Not just beautiful. She's smart, as well."

"Thank you, Ray. Thank you both. Father and I owe you our lives. It won't be forgotten."

"Sashia," Bolan said, "before we go in. I need some information from your father. One way we can help end this so you both can be really safe is for me to learn as much as I can about Wadi Hattat. Ray and I have to get to that place and put it out of action for good. And deal with the people operating it. Your father worked there and he managed to get away. He had help. Now we need that help. To get us inside Wadi Hattat."

"Go inside? But that's impossible."

"Listen love," McCarter said, "I should have added after beautiful and smart, that *we* are good-looking, but bloody crazy. Let's just leave it at that."

"Cooper?"

"It has to be done, Sashia. Our only link to that place is Gregori Malinski. His information could be the key that opens Wadi Hattat for us. So I need your help to get him to tell us what he knows."

Malinski was still a little groggy from the anesthetic but he was alert enough to recognize his daughter. Bolan and McCarter stood to one side while the reunion took place. For a few minutes Malinski and his daughter concentrated on each other. Finally the Russian raised a hand and beckoned Bolan and McCarter across to the bed.

"Sashi has been telling me how you helped her in Paris, Mr. Cooper. It would seem I am in your debt twofold. What can I say? I do not deserve what you have done. A misguided man who has put at risk the one thing that should never be placed in such a position." He touched a hand to Sashia's cheek. Then he turned his head to study Bolan. "She tells me you want to go to Iran and get inside Wadi Hattat."

Bolan nodded. "We have no choice if we want to put a stop to what goes on there."

"It would be suicide. You would go to your deaths."

"Not without a bloody fight," McCarter said.

"You are brave men and I owe you so much. But…" Malinski shook his head.

"Father, do this one thing for me and make it right," Sashia said. "Give Cooper the information so he can end this madness."

"Wadi Hattat is not somewhere you can just walk into. It is a fortress. And if you did get inside, what would you do?"

"Destroy what you've been working on," Bolan said. "You know they have been using stolen American technology to advance the project. I need to neutralize that. Put back the Iranian development so the diplomacy has a chance. If the nuclear program is delayed, it might allow the talking to go on."

Malinski stared at him as if he was confronting total naïveté. "It is madness to even think about going there." Malinski looked from Bolan to McCarter. "How can I be a party to sending these men to that place? It would be a crime."

"Any more of a crime than the Iranians are committing? Trying to create a region where every country mistrusts its neighbor? A condition where they just add more nuclear weapons to those already in place. Father, you should know more than anyone there are enough stockpiled weapons than the world will ever need. Technology has already given us the ability to wipe ourselves out a hundred times over."

Malinski looked at her with an embarrassed expression. "I understand only to well that I am one who has been helping to do that. First back home for the Soviets, then to whoever would pay me. If there is guilt to be apportioned I would be first in line. Why do you think I left Wadi Hattat? It occurred to me that with all I knew, my contribution to science has been to create machines of death. I used my ability to threaten the lives of the human race. I won't leave much of a legacy." He reached out to touch Sashia's cheek. "That day, the one that decided me, I had been thinking of you, Sashi. Thinking that it might be one of the bombs I built that killed you, and I knew it had to stop."

"Then help these two men. Show them how to find the facility. Tell them how to get inside. Where to look."

"If we can get inside, Dr. Malinski, our mission is to destroy that place. But we need help to get there."

Malinski gripped his daughter's hand. "I am doing the correct thing, yes? Very well, Mr. Cooper. You need to find a man named Amir Fayed. He may be able to help you to get inside the facility. He was my contact in Tehran. He got me out of the country. I was given a telephone number by Tariq Kemal inside the facility. It put me in touch with this man Fayed and he organized my flight out of Iran. Fayed and Kemal are part of a resistance group working against Razihra and his desire to create Iran's nuclear capability. Kemal works inside the research center, gathering information. He is a very courageous young man."

"If we can convince Fayed what we intend doing, maybe he can get us inside Wadi Hattat," McCarter said.

"I'll need whatever you can tell me about the interior layout."

"Anything."

"Did you have access to the material they were bringing in from outside? Especially the hardware from America."

Malinski nodded. "Oh, yes. It was part of my work to re-appraise those items and make them compatible to the schematics for the project we were developing."

"So you had to be able to get to them?"

"All the time." Malinski glanced at his daughter. "Now you see what a fraud I have become."

"No," Sashia said. She gripped his hand. "I don't care about that. It is past. Now you can help to stop it."

"Dr. Malinski, could you draw me a diagram directing me to the section where they stored the stolen technology?"

"It was within my own lab," Malinski said. "In a secure cabinet. I will put it all down. At least it will be something I can do to make amends. Wait. What about Tariq Kemal? He helped me get out of the facility. He knows where I worked. Even the location of the technology. He will be able to guide you."

"If he's around," Bolan said. "I have to work on the assumption he might not be. Since you left, they might have discovered his involvement and removed him."

"Removed?" Malinski's face paled. "My God, you mean they might have killed him? Because he helped me?"

"Doctor," McCarter said, "these are not nice people. They have a simple rule for dealing with anyone who steps out of line. Look how they went after Sashia. Don't give yourself any hang-ups over what they might do."

"We all survive in our own different ways," Bolan said. "That diagram could be what helps keep *me* alive once I get inside that place."

McCarter produced paper and a pen. He handed them to Malinski and the Russian began to work, bending over the paper like a schoolboy at an exam.

"That is how he used to work at home," Sashia said. She glanced at Bolan. "You know, since we first met in Paris all you have done is to protect me. Now you have done the same for my father and brought him back to me. How can I repay you for that?"

Standing just behind Sashia, McCarter's expression was a priceless study that Bolan chose to ignore.

"Your father is doing just that right now," he told her.

She touched his face. "That is all you ask?"

"Promise me you'll keep him out of trouble. Do that and we're quits."

"Then I promise." She raised up and kissed him on the cheek. "You have my word, Cooper."

"Call me Matt."

CHAPTER TWENTY-THREE

Mehrabad International Airport
Tehran, Iran

The Iranian customs official examined passports and documentation closely, peering up at Bolan and McCarter, then back to the photographs. He had already signaled the MOIS agent hovering nearby and the security man joined him at the desk. The MOIS official was young and smartly dressed, a pleasant expression on his face.

"You are here for what purpose?"

McCarter tapped the cameras draped from his shoulders. "To take pictures."

"Of what?"

"The country. People. Landmarks." The Briton grinned amiably. "Don't worry, chum, we had our instructions when we applied for our visas. We ask permission first and don't go where we've been warned off. Fair enough. All we want are nice pictures for the magazine."

"And you?"

Bolan smiled easily. "He does the camera work, I write the text."

"This magazine you work for?" The man held up a printed sheet introducing Bolan and McCarter. "I have not heard of it."

"First issue due out in two months," Bolan said. "New publication. We aim to give *National Geographic* a run for its money."

The MOIS agent checked the address text on the letterhead,

"Perhaps I should call your office and verify you are genuine?"

"Why not?" Bolan said.

"Hey, if you get through," McCarter butted in, "ask them where my bloody expenses are from the Tokyo assignment."

"You didn't get them yet?" Bolan asked. "My check came last week."

"Bloody great," McCarter mumbled, moving aside, his voice dropping to a continuous monologue.

"Sorry about that," Bolan apologized. "He gets a little cranky when this happens." He leaned forward. "Truth is, he has two ex-wives to pay off each month."

The MOIS agent glanced sideways at the still mumbling McCarter, then turned back to Bolan.

"So, you are Mr. Cooper?" he asked.

Bolan nodded. "He's Ray Travis. Great with a camera but lousy at relationships."

The security agent had busied himself working the keyboard of the computer set up behind the desk. He tapped in the Web site address from the letterhead and the site flashed on the monitor, allowing the man to check out the data.

GlobalScan International magazine, due to be launched in approximately eight weeks, listed Cooper and Travis as one of the assigned roving teams covering the globe and gathering material for a forthcoming edition. Personal photographs accompanied the biographies of the listed names.

In reality the magazine existed only on the Stony Man covert background site. Created and developed by the SOG's in-house team, it offered solid cover for Stony Man operatives who needed it in the field. Stored profiles of Bolan and Mc-Carter had been inserted into the staff listing. It was a neat, well-developed piece of subterfuge. If the MOIS man had called the telephone number listed he would have been routed to Stony Man, where one of the personnel would have answered any queries as a member of *GlobalSpan International* at the "New York" offices. Statistics and assignments were updated at regular intervals to give the impression work was actually going on at the magazines offices.

The MOIS agent checked passports and documents again. "They work you hard," he said. "Japan. China. Europe."

"Too bloody right they work us hard," McCarter said, warming to his part again. "From here we fly off to New Zealand. I haven't slept at home for weeks."

For a moment the MOIS man allowed a thin smile to show. "I can see why he has *two* former wives."

"Right now he's working on making it three."

"Enjoy your stay in Iran."

The agent handed the documentation across to the customs official who stamped the passports and slid them across the desk. Bolan picked them up and turned to McCarter.

"Quit grumbling and let's go find a cab."

McCarter, still into his role, snatched up his bag and slouched his way out of the terminal and into the bright glare of the day.

"How long do I need to keep playing this arsehole?" he griped.

"You're *still* acting?" Bolan said. "Sorry."

"Very droll, all-American boy," McCarter said.

"Let's keep it going at least until we're in a cab and out of sight. We might still be under observation."

"I give an award-worthy performance and you think it didn't fool them?"

"I'm sure you did."

"This could end up as a really fun trip," McCarter said. "Or the biggest letdown since the *Titanic* sank."

"I'll go for your first thought, minus the fun part."

"Well I suppose I was being a little casual there. Then again it all depends what you define as fun, Mack, me old mate."

A shining dark-blue Mercedes with a Taxi sign on its roof swung into view and cruised to a stop in front of them. The driver stepped out and came around the vehicle to take their bags. He was a handsome man in his early forties, black hair hinting at gray. As he picked up their bags he caught Mc-Carter's eye, pausing for a moment before he turned and took them to the rear of the Mercedes. He opened the trunk and placed the bags inside. Back at the rear door he opened it and gestured for Bolan and McCarter to get in. As they settled, the driver returned to sit behind the wheel, starting the car and moving off. No one spoke until the Mercedes was on the main highway heading in the direction of Tehran.

Bolan broke the silence.

"Okay, what's going on?"

The driver's eyes filled the rearview mirror, flicking between Bolan and McCarter. "American, you are Cooper? And he is Travis?"

"Yeah. You're…"

"Amir Fayed," McCarter said. "I know him. Last time I saw him was in London. He was Iranian Security looking for the same people we were."

"Is this right, Fayed?"

The Iranian nodded. "Then I *was* in security. Now I am working against Razihra and what he is creating."

"Back then you'd taken a bullet," McCarter said.

"And you had a different name."

"Well, it isn't why we're here today," McCarter replied. "And it's a damn sight deadlier than a fake bloody name."

Fayed glanced at Bolan through the mirror. "Your English friend I think he is always impatient?"

"You haven't got that wrong, Fayed. But what he says is correct. Our problem is out there somewhere in the desert where no one can see what Ayatollah Razihra is doing. We know he's developing nuclear capability. He's also using stolen American technology to jump the research gap."

"And you wish to stop him because…?" Fayed smiled. "Ah, I know. You are concerned for the Iranian people? You are on a mercy mission. Or is it because the U.S.A. wishes to save face by not having its secrets exposed as part of the Muslim plot to overthrow democracy? I'm sure that if I looked deep enough the word 'oil' would rise to the surface. Am I wrong, Mr. Cooper."

"That's your reasoning, Fayed," Bolan said. "I wouldn't insult you by denying the possibility in your words. We live in a world that runs hand in hand, despite political and religious differences. We all have our agendas. But it doesn't wipe out a need for good men to fight against what they see as evil. I'm here because Razihra represents a threat that could move far beyond Iran's borders. There are many countries out there all watching what Iran is going to do, and some of those countries are feeling vulnerable and nervous. If we reach critical mass this whole region could get dragged in. We can all guess how that might develop. If it does it could spread a long way. Suck in bigger players. The Middle East has gone through hard times over the past few years. It needs a time to stabilize. To establish itself, not plunge into more conflict. Razihra wants the chaos. His rhetoric is for intolerance, not parity. The man is looking for a fight, and he'll drag your country into it regardless of how the majority feels. From what I've seen and heard about your resistance, it's there because you don't want what Razihra does."

"And American interests?"

Now it was Bolan's turn to smile. "I won't deny that we want to protect our interests, too."

"At least I am spared the duplicitous words of a politician," Fayed said.

"You've never been more correct," McCarter said.

"When we were in London and we made our bargain, you gave me what you promised. It was one of the first times I trusted a Westerner."

"We're not all bad," McCarter told him.

"You were very insistent I contact my superiors and persuade them we should cooperate."

"If I recall, we were on thin ice for a time," the Briton stated.

"Very thin," the Iranian said. "But my people agreed and we all profited from the association."

"So what changed?"

"Many things, Travis. Months after our mission there were big changes in Iran. Politics and religion. Religion and the military. New alliances within the country and most of them bad. Ayatollah Razihra came into prominence and began to incite the masses. He preached aggressive attitudes, catered to the basest emotions, mixing it with religious bigotry and promising to make Iran so powerful no one would dare oppose us. Nuri Masood, the defense minister, is shouted down every time he makes a speech. His life is under threat from Razihra's followers, yet he still stands by what he believes."

"He sounds like an honest man," Bolan said.

"For a Muslim fanatic?"

"We both know that isn't true. Fayed, all your people aren't extremists. The same as we accept there are extremists in my country. Let's not get into that game."

"If it helps, I understand there are some crazy buggers in the UK," McCarter said. "I have an uncle in—"

"Travis, never mind your uncle."

"He is correct, though, Cooper," Fayed said. "We judge all by the behavior of a few. It is wrong but emotions become the driver of our actions in some instances, and incidents are built up into major events."

"It gets hard to know who you can deal with," Bolan said, "who you can trust."

"Betrayal is commonplace these days in my country," Fayed said. "It is difficult to know your friends from your enemies. As Razihra's power has increased, his allies are more vigilant than ever. They are constantly seeking out those believed to be unsympathetic to Razihra. It is his way of dealing with any kind of opposition."

"Amir, when we talked in London you mentioned you had a family here," McCarter said.

The expression in the Iranian's eyes was unmistakable. "I sent them away. The moment I realized the coming threat, I arranged for them to go to friends in Turkey. It became unsafe for them here."

"Must have been hard for you."

"They understood. Remaining here they would have been used to draw me into the open. At least this way I have only myself to worry about."

CHAPTER TWENTY-FOUR

Fayed drove to the outskirts of Tehran. He turned along a narrow street, sure of his way, and pulled the Mercedes into a shaded courtyard. He led Bolan and McCarter to an apartment on the upper floor of the house. Once inside the he showed them into a room that had a wide panoramic view of the city.

"Please be seated. I will bring coffee."

McCarter flopped down on a wide couch, stretching his long legs out. "Take the weight off your feet, mate. Learn to relax. You'll live longer."

Seated across from him, Bolan smiled. "Is that the secret of life? Just relax?"

"Works for me every time."

Fayed appeared, carrying a tray holding a coffeepot and small cups. He placed the tray on a low table and took a seat next to Bolan. He poured coffee and passed it around.

"To your continued good health, my friends."

The coffee was hot, dark and very strong.

"You will enjoy Iranian coffee. It is very special."

"Amir, can you get us into Wadi Hattat?" Bolan asked.

"Travis, your friend is extremely single-minded. The facility is very secure. Do you really believe you can get to the stolen hardware even if you did get inside?"

"Yes. Gregori Malinski drew me a schematic of the interior. The level I need to reach and the location of his lab," Bolan said. "And I have this." He reached into his pocket and took out a small microchip, placing it on the table. "These will tell us where the contraband is being stored."

Fayed picked up the chip and examined it. His eyes returned to Bolan. "Tell me what this does."

"Each manufactured component has one of these embedded within the circuit-board configuration. With a tracking device the chip can be located from the pulse it gives out. The U.S. has been using this identification responder for only a few months. Before the integration of these chips there was no way stolen components could be relocated."

"Very clever," Fayed said. "You have one of these trackers?"

McCarter opened his camera case and took out what looked like an exposure meter. "It's built into this."

"All this technology is strange to me. We have little that could match such creations." Fayed looked from Bolan to McCarter and jabbed a finger at the Briton. "Do you actually have a real name?"

McCarter grinned. "Of course I do. One day I might tell you. But right now it's Wadi Hattat that's important and what we can do to shut it down."

"You really want to do this?"

"We *have* to do it." Bolan said.

"Wadi Hattat is a restricted area," Fayed said. "It has been for almost two years. It is in a very large desert, and it is easy for someone to vanish. And who out here would question such a thing?" He indicated a topographical map pinned to the wall. "You see how isolated the area is."

Bolan turned his attention to the wall map. Fayed had been

speaking the truth. The location was completely isolated. No habitation for miles around. Whatever was going on inside Wadi Hattat it was well protected. He spent a few minutes going over the map, finally admitting to himself that getting inside wasn't going to be easy.

"Fayed, this all started for us when an American undercover agent, working inside Anatoly Nevski's organization, was assassinated in London. He had passed along enough information to create suspicion about what was going on. It wasn't difficult to pull the threads together and make us aware of Razihra's intentions. The man died because he'd got too close. We owe him enough to try to finish the job."

Fayed nodded. "I accept that. My concern is only that getting inside Wadi Hattat is not going to be a simple task."

"Your inside man got Malinski out. Maybe we can turn it around this time. With his help and yours, we should be able to get inside."

"If you are willing to try, I will do everything I can to help. And Tariq will help when you get inside."

"Let's hope so. I still have my Malinski guide," Bolan said. "So tell me all you know about Wadi Hattat."

The oasis at Wadi Hattat had been a favorite during the trade days, Fayed explained, when camel trains moved across the desert. They carried goods back and forth. Spices, silk cloth, every kind of merchandise. As time passed, the ancient trade routes withered and were lost beneath the ever-shifting desert sands. War and revolution did away with the need for the oasis, and it became little more than a water hole for infrequent travelers crossing the silent wilderness. It faded into obscurity, and few outsiders became aware of a modern-day interest by certain departments of the current Iranian government. They needed an isolated base, far away from prying eyes, a location they could manage in the secretive way they desired. Over a period of months the construction of the research facility at Wadi Hattat went unnoticed. When it was complete and operating, the vast area that surrounded it became a death trap for any unwary individual who set foot within its unmarked boundaries, and the deadly work that went on there was known only to a few.

"Is there no other way of doing this?" Fayed studied Bolan closely.

"It has to be brought down from inside," Bolan said. "It's where they keep all their data, the research modules they are designing. It all has to be destroyed, Fayed. If we achieve that, it puts Razihra back to where he was. With nothing. We know he has to store everything here, away from the people in government who oppose his plans. He needs the power a nuclear capability would give him. Take that away and he's reduced to just another voice. One without anything to back him up. It will weaken his credibility and his strength."

"There used to be a small village at Wadi Hattat. In the 1960s a military base was established. It was said to be a training center, but there was a research lab for nerve and biological weapons. In the end the testing failed, people died and the military abandoned the place. Wadi Hattat stood empty until Razihra's people took it over. Much of the facility is below ground. Better protection from the weather and easier to contain experiments if there was an escape."

"Hell of a history," McCarter said. "Bioweapons, and now they're going nuclear. These people don't give up do, they?"

Fayed smiled. "We could discuss the morals and ethics of numerous countries in that context, my friends. Yes?"

Bolan raised a hand. "Can't argue that point. Let's stay focused on why we're here now. Fayed, your group wants to end Razihra's nuclear ambitions. Travis and I need to deal with the contraband hardware. Looks to me we both have close intentions."

"Exactly," Fayed said.

"Razihra has been trying to step up his power base in Iran," Bolan said. "He tied in with some of Hussein's ex-Fedayeen in Jordan, working on a plan to strike at Israel as part of the overall campaign. If Israel hits back, it gives more strength to Razihra's argument about Iran needed its own nuclear weapons. We stopped that. Then Gregori Malinski breaks away from Wadi Hattat, and Nevski sends his team out to find him. That didn't happen, either."

"Malinski locked his computer to prevent his nuke calculations being used," McCarter said. "That must have pissed off Razihra big-time. But I'm sure he'll find someone clever enough to break through Malinski's blocks and get at the data. It isn't going to happen overnight so the program is going to stay on hold for a while."

"That gives us a chance to make our strike," Bolan said. "The sooner the better."

Fayed understood the explanations. With his Israeli attack thwarted and Malinski gone, the Ayatollah was left with his nuclear ambitions his remaining asset. He would protect that to the last man. Fayed wasn't as cold-bloodedly determined as Razihra, but he could understand the man's relentless drive to gain success with his project. If he let that slip away from him, Ayatollah Razihra would have little left to satisfy his military backers.

"My group were able to obtain a layout of the place. We only got hold of it a few days ago," Fayed said. He stood and crossed to a desk in the corner of the room. He opened a drawer and took out a large, thick envelope from which he removed a folded paper. "Would you clear the table, please."

Fayed opened and spread the paper sheet across the table.

It was a faded, but legible diagram of Wadi Hattat, showing the old village underlaid with a schematic of the research facility.

"Entrances to the base are through these village houses. Air vent ducts and exhausts are also concealed within old structures. At a glance Wadi Hattat looks as it has for years. Just an abandoned desert settlement." He stabbed at a section. "This is the actual watering hole, fed from an underground source that has been alive for hundreds of years."

"Has anything been added recently?" Bolan asked.

"Our scouts have seen a landing pad for the helicopters that ferry personnel and goods into the base. There are also a number of vehicles hidden beneath camouflage netting. Oh, there is an antenna concealed within the trees around the water holes. It supports a satellite dish, too."

"Communications," McCarter said. "Bet he has some kind of sat com uplink working off it. We need to take that out. Cut his contact."

"Fayed, how many of your people have enough combat experience to do this with us?" Bolan asked.

"Ten, twelve. That many I can organize quickly. We also have a helicopter to take us out to Wadi Hattat."

"Travis and I will need weapons and equipment. We couldn't bring anything in with us."

"No problem."

"We'll need two groups," Bolan said. "One will plant explosives to take out the choppers and ground vehicles. They'll need to deal with the communications aerial, as well. The other group will head the initial strike against the facility."

"Fayed, can you include a couple of men who know explosives? Do that and I'll handle that part of the assault," McCarter said.

"I can do that."

They spent more time going over Fayed's schematic and the diagram Malinski had drawn for Bolan. Each man memorized the details.

Later that day Fayed's people began to assemble. They came singly, some in pairs, until the full complement was there, in a cellar beneath the house. He revealed the cache of weapons, and the group armed themselves with Kalashnikov AK-47s. There were handguns, and McCarter was delighted to find a 9 mm Browning Hi-Power. A sealed container held blocks of plastic explosive that McCarter took and fashioned into brick-size units. Fayed produced a box with detonators and compact transmitters. McCarter was able to prepare the components into packs they could distribute at chosen targets and set off by a remote handheld unit. He questioned the pack of batteries Fayed supplied.

"There will be no problem. These are fresh. I change them regularly to make certain they are sound."

McCarter fitted each detonator with batteries and ran power checks, satisfying himself that the supply was stable. He did the same with the handheld unit, a simple black handset that had power-check, activate and detonate buttons. He wanted to be sure they would work when needed. He knew of failures before, when someone had omitted to check the equipment thoroughly. A flat battery could prove fatal. When he packed away the prepared explosives, the Briton was confident they would perform as required. All he and his team had to do was to place the packs and set them off. It sounded easy, but McCarter knew they would need to deal with sentries first. Razihra wouldn't trust to luck, even in a desolate location such as Wadi Hattat. He would have the area patrolled. This was confirmed some time later by a text message from Tariq Kemal. Fayed's inside man told them that the regular patrol consisted of four armed sentries who watched over the exterior of the facility and the helicopter-motor pool.

The Briton sat back from the table, feeling the need for a cigarette. He had tried to cut out his craving for tobacco, but there were times when he still needed a smoke. Now was one of those times. The pack of Player's was a little crumpled when he pulled it from his shirt pocket. McCarter took out a cigarette and lit up. The taste of the rich tobacco soothed him. He picked up a soft footfall nearby and sensed Bolan's closeness.

"We're as ready as we can be," McCarter said.

"Fayed is organizing transport."

McCarter nodded. "This could be a busy trip, Mack."

"Oh, yes." Bolan paused for a heartbeat. "Glad you were able to come along, David."

"For something like this—how could I stay away?"

CHAPTER TWENTY-FIVE

The chopper was a well-worn old Huey. It needed a fresh paint job and there were cracks in the side windows. The engine, though, had been lovingly maintained. It was the quietest helicopter power plant Bolan had heard, excepting *Dragon Slayer,* Stony Man's one-off combat chopper.

Bolan was in the seat next to the pilot, Fayed himself. The Iranian turned out to be an excellent flyer. He flew through the Iranian night with a sure hand on the controls and unerring accuracy.

Behind them the rest of the Iranian team occupied the passenger space along with their equipment. McCarter was in the middle of the ten-man team.

"We touch down in another twenty minutes," Fayed announced. "Just over twelve miles from Wadi Hattat."

Bolan checked his watch, making a swift calculation. "We walk in and get there just before it gets light. We'll need time to deal with any guards and plant the charges. As soon as that's done, we choose our moment to go."

Fayed nodded. He called over his shoulder and one of the Iranians moved to stand behind his seat. "Tell them we will land soon. Make sure they have checked weapons and equipment."

The man, Anwar, acknowledged his instructions. "I will tell them."

FAYED PUT THE HUEY DOWN lightly, cutting the power and shutting off everything. Bolan loosened his seat belt and pushed to his feet, picking up his backpack and weapons. He made his way aft, tagging on to the line of Iranians as they filed to the open side door. He jumped down into the soft, still warm sand. A faint breeze, with a cool edge to it, was soughing in over the low sand hills, disturbing dry grasses and rattling the brittle, scant foliage.

Bolan and McCarter helped unroll the camouflage nets Fayed had brought along. They covered the chopper to hide it from any overhead spotting, pegging the edges of the netting to hold it down.

For a time there was little noise other than the group strapping on backpacks and adjusting the body harnesses holding extra ammunition and grenades. McCarter and the three Iranians with him, chosen for their explosives knowledge, stood a little apart. They spent some extra time making sure the explosive packs they carried between them were secure. McCarter moved from man to man, making certain all the ordnance was safe, patting each man on the shoulder as he completed his checks, talking to them in a low, reassuring tone.

Bolan made his own checks, ensuring that his backpack was secured in place. He had one of McCarter's explosive packs inside the backpack. It would be placed inside the cabinet that held the stolen hardware once he located it. As well as an AK-47, Bolan had a sheathed Tanto combat knife on his belt and a holstered 9 mm SIG-Sauer P-226 pistol he had chosen from Fayed's arsenal. He had extra magazines for his weapons and carried a number of fragmentation and stun grenades clipped to his combat harness. In pockets of his blacksuit he had the chip tracker unit and his Tri-Band cell phone. He was as ready for what was to come as he ever could be.

"Okay, boss man," McCarter said when Bolan joined him. "We're all set here. I hope you're not going to hurt our feelings by asking us to walk way behind in case one of us goes boom?"

"Never crossed my mind."

"I'm sure."

Fayed called out they were all ready. "Let's go then," Bolan said.

They strung out in single file, Fayed in the lead. Within a few minutes they had achieved a steady pace, knowing they had a long trek ahead of them and not wanting to force the march. The steady, ground covering walk would help them reach Wadi Hattat without wearing down their strength. They would need it for the struggle that would come once they engaged Razihra's force.

CHAPTER TWENTY-SIX

Dawn was fast approaching by the time they took up their position on the dusty perimeter of Wadi Hattat. While the main group rechecked equipment and weapons, Fayed took Bolan and McCarter to a spot where they could observe the site.

"There is what used to be the old village," Fayed pointed out. "Many of the houses are still standing, but they are not inhabited. The lights you see are for the guards."

Scanning the area, Bolan had to admit that at a distance the place did look like a deserted settlement. A closer look revealed that there was no movement of any kind within any of the weather-beaten stone buildings. Some of them were in a state of collapse, their walls having been reduced to dusty shambles.

"That has nothing to do with a village," he said, indicating a metal structure within the half-demolished walls of one derelict hut.

"It is one of the outlets for air and fume ducts coming from below. There are others located around the site," Fayed said. "It was how the military originally built the place so no one would suspect what they were doing in their laboratories.

That supply and exhaust system has become useful to Razihra's people."

McCarter had been checking out the area and had spotted the helipad, which housed two aircraft beneath camouflage nets. He could make out the shape of the nearby fuel dump. A large number of metal drums holding fuel for the choppers and the cluster of wheeled vehicles, also under netting, was somewhat closer to the village.

"Got my job sorted," he said. "Helipad, fuel and the motor pool. I'll go talk to my team. Let me know when you need us to move out."

Fayed had taken out a cell phone. "I will send a text message to Tariq. Let him know we are in position."

Bolan let him concentrate on the text. He and Fayed had discussed strategy on the flight. If Tariq Kemal could create a distraction within the facility just prior to the attack, it might give them a slight advantage. Fayed had agreed that he would try to contact the inside man.

"I have sent the message," Fayed said. "Let us hope he receives it and can help."

"If not, we still go in," Bolan said.

He wasn't averse to making a direct strike against the facility, but he also acknowledged that a helping hand would also be welcome.

When twenty minutes passed without any kind of response both Bolan and Fayed were ready to move. McCarter and his team would move out and hit their designated targets and that would be the moment for Bolan to launch the frontal attack on the facility itself.

He was about to give the go when Fayed's cell buzzed gently. The Iranian checked the message, a smile crossing his face.

"He got the message. He will cause a short-circuit in one of the labs. The facility will be in darkness until the power is reconnected, in about thirty minutes. It might not give us long but it is better than nothing. Yes?"

Bolan nodded.

"Tariq will try to connect with you inside."

"We'll go on his signal," Bolan said.

He turned and beckoned for McCarter to join him. "It's a go. Get your team in position and watch for the village to black out. Soon as it does, you set off the charges."

"How long?"

"Approximately thirty minutes," Bolan stated.

Bolan watched the Briton move out, staying low as he rejoined his group. Following the power cut, the detonations as McCarter's team blew the helicopters and the transport would be the final proof the strike against Wadi Hattat was under way.

Mack Bolan rechecked his handgun and the AK-47. It never paid to become too complacent. As he settled down to wait. Bolan's calmness reached out to touch those around him and he nodded in acknowledgment as he caught the eyes of the Iranians. His silent reassurance settled them.

Bolan thought ahead to what he needed to do once he got inside the facility. The route to Malinski's lab was imprinted on his memory. The tracking device was secure in a pocket. Once he managed to locate the lab where the stolen devices were held he would plant his explosive pack and get out. In theory it all sounded direct and straightforward. Bolan had been on enough of these kinds of exercises to know in reality it didn't always pan out that way. Human and technical snags could foul up an operation in a split second. Even with those thoughts on his mind he remained optimistic, willing to face whatever came his way, and more than capable of standing up to them.

Fayed slid down into the sand, nodding at Bolan. "Everyone is in position."

Bolan nodded. "Now we wait."

MCCARTER'S TEAM SETTLED IN the shadows below a crumbling stone wall, the Briton peering over the top to acquaint himself with the area. He picked out two of the armed guards immediately. The pair was moving away from McCarter's position, angling in the direction of the helicopter resting on the pad. A third man was stationed at the pad itself. He moved forward to greet the approaching pair and McCarter could hear their muted talk as they congregated in a loose group. The fourth guard was on the far side of the perimeter, well away from where the Phoenix Force leader was situated.

Next to McCarter the three Iranians watched the sentries. Anwar, the English speaker, touched McCarter's shoulder.

"How will we do this?"

McCarter sank down out of sight, his back to the wall. "Give me a minute, chum, and maybe I'll come up with a brilliant piece of strategy. If I don't, we'll just have to up and shoot the buggers."

Anwar was still having problems with the Briton's vague sense of humor. "Travis?"

McCarter glanced at the man's solemn expression. "I didn't mean that. We stay with the plan. Wait for them to separate then deal with them one by one."

That appeared to satisfy Anwar, and he settled himself to wait as McCarter was doing. Thankfully, aware of the time slipping away, they didn't have to wait for long as two of the guards separated and went in different directions, leaving one man guarding the helicopters.

"Time to go, Anwar," McCarter said. "I'll take the bloke by the choppers and plant the explosives on them and in the fuel dump. Same needs doing with the vehicles, and someone has to place a pack at the base of the antenna tower. On second thought, we need two packs there. Make sure the bloody thing comes down."

Anwar spoke with his men. Between them they came to an agreement.

"They will deal with the vehicles," Anwar said. "I will go for the antenna."

McCarter nodded and passed out the explosive packs. He had gone over how to place them and activate the detonation receiver.

"Make sure the guards don't spot you. If they do this mission is over before it starts. Make them understand, Anwar. If the guards get too close, deal with them fast. We don't have any space, or time, left for mistakes."

Anwar gave his instructions to the Iranians. They glanced at McCarter and nodded.

"Let's get this rolling," the Briton said. "As soon as the packs are set get back here so I can detonate."

The four men went their different ways, each concentrating on his particular part of the incursion into enemy territory.

McCarter saw Anwar vanish, then took his own course for the helipad. There was too much open ground leading up to the pad, eliminating any form of direct approach for the former SAS commando. He was going to have to make a circuitous approach. The Briton made use of natural cover until it ran out and he was forced to cut around to the far side of the helipad. He had the aircraft between himself and the single guard.

A rising breeze drifted dusty sand across the area. McCarter felt its gritty touch against his face. The breeze strengthened, dust rising and for a few seconds the guard was hidden by it. McCarter saw his chance and pushed to a crouch, moving quickly beneath the tail of the closer helicopter. He snaked his Gerber blade from its leg sheath, bringing his right hand up as he closed in on the unsuspecting guard.

McCarter slammed the heel of his boot into the back of one knee and as the guard slipped to one side the Briton clamped his left hand over the guy's mouth, pulling his head back. The Gerber arced around the guard's neck, making a deep incision that followed back to terminate beneath the right ear. Blood began to pump from the severed arteries and the opened windpipe turned the guard's cry into a wet gurgle. McCarter held his grip as the guy began to go down, first to his knees, then a slow, erratic slide to the ground. He held on to the guard while his spasms went from frantic to no more than final shudders.

Moving the man's weapons aside, McCarter took out the first explosive pack and positioned it. He saw the red light come on as he activated the unit. He repeated the operation at the second chopper, then cut away in the direction of the fuel storage area where he placed his final pack in among the drums.

Turning, he retraced his steps to his original position and arrived seconds before Anwar. The Iranian nodded as he slumped down beside McCarter. The front of his jacket was red with blood.

"It is not mine," he said.

"You all right?"

Anwar frowned as a recent memory flashed in front of his eyes. "There was a guard at the antenna. I used my knife but he fought to the last moment. All the time he was staring into my eyes. It was his expression. Accusing me..."

McCarter laid a hand on the Iranian's shoulder. "It's never easy taking another man's life. You die a little yourself every time you do it. The day you don't feel it is the day you walk away from it."

A frantic scrabbling in the sand made McCarter whirl, his Browning in his hand. He saw the two other Iranian returning.

"Everything is set," one of them said to Anwar. The Iranian translated for McCarter.

The Briton took out the compact device that would set off the packs. He extended the short aerial and switched the power to active. Now they had to wait until the village lights went out. McCarter glanced at his watch.

"Come on, come on," he said to no one in particular.

Then the security lights dimmed and there was no more time for waiting.

McCarter pressed the button. He felt the ground tremble as the multiple explosions shattered the dawn calm. He watched with quiet pleasure as the targeted sites went up, throwing sand and debris into the air. The rippling detonations followed one another in a measured pattern, spiraling streaks of fire lancing across the area. Debris blew in all directions. McCarter saw one of the helicopters lift off the ground as the force of the explosion tore it apart. A larger fireball rose from the fuel dump. Fire burned, smoke billowed and the rising sun was obscured for long seconds before the pall drifted.

"You reckon we did it?" McCarter asked.

Anwar regarded him with a puzzled look on his face. "Didn't you just see? Of course we have done it."

"Anwar, my friend, I was making a joke."

"I see. I have been told about the very strange humor of the British."

"So what do you think of it?"

"Very strange."

McCarter checked his AK. "Time to move out. I have a feeling it's about to get bloody noisy around here."

BOLAN SAW THE LIGHTS IN the empty village go out. Even in the predawn it was easy to see the illumination disappear.

Seconds later the crackle of explosions shattered the stillness. There was a series of detonations as the various packages went off. Flame lit up the area. The group of palms near the water hole swayed and toppled, taking down the tall antenna holding the sat com dish. A heavier sound came from the fuel store, a greasy boil of fire rising into the clean air. From the landing pads the still shapes of the helicopters erupted into shattered chunks of aluminum and plastic, and the parked ground vehicles blew one after another as the planted explosive were detonated. As the explosions faded and debris thudded back to earth, the rattle of autofire reached Bolan's ears.

The battle for Wadi Hattat had begun.

"Let's go," Bolan said, pushing to his feet.

He led the way toward the entrance to the facility, with Fayed and the rest of the group close behind.

They crossed the open stretch of ground, their target building in clear sight. A machine gun opened up, concealed behind a low concrete abutment, the slugs raking the ground ahead and to the right. The firing ceased for a few seconds as the shooter adjusted his aim.

That had *not* been in the intel.

"Scatter," Bolan yelled. "Spread out."

Fayed repeated the call for those who didn't understand English, and the Iranians did as they were ordered.

The machine gun fired again, a long burst that threw a heavy volley across the line of advancing men. One Iranian stumbled, fell, but the others kept moving, returning fire.

Bolan plucked a high-explosive grenade from his harness and pulled the pin. He was to one side of the machine gun's line of fire, so he was able to get in close enough to lob the deadly sphere. His aim was on track. The grenade dropped behind the concrete and exploded with a vicious crack. The machine gun fell silent and as the smoke cleared the tattered body of one of the gunners could be seen hanging over the abutment.

Bolan closed in on the site, his AK jacking out slugs at gunners who seeped from the shadows behind the abutment. He saw one man flung back as the AK's fire caught him, then Fayed's men were rushing in fast, firing at anything moving near the entrance to the facility. The fighting intensified from that moment.

THE SOLDIER COULD HEAR the autofire coming from the farthest perimeter of the village, closer to where McCarter and his team would have been moving in to rejoin the main group. But he had no time to worry about his Stony Man partner. The struggle at the entrance had erupted into a savage, close-quarter battle and he was suddenly in the thick of it himself.

Bolan flattened against the closest wall, his AK searching for targets and finding them. The uniformed guards had erupted en masse from the portal leading into the facility, spreading out as they moved away from the buildings and encountering Fayed's group. There was no concealing the ferocity of the encounter as attackers and defenders clashed. For Mack Bolan the inner sanctum of the Wadi Hattat facility was the strategic goal. Whatever the outcome of the firefight, *his* objective was the location and destruction of the nuclear project.

Bolan saw his opening and went for it as the tail end of the squad emerged from the entrance. The steel door that had slid open allowed him to enter the upper level of the facility. The meticulous drawing Gregori Malinski had created, detailing interior levels and access points, was firmly fixed in Bolan's mind, and he used the mental images to guide him down the sloping ramp leading into the facility.

At the base of the ramp, according to Malinski, the way ahead would bisect into two walkways. Bolan needed the right fork. He took it and found himself at the head of concrete steps leading down to the next level.

The sound of boots on the concrete reached the soldier's ears, and he turned to see a trio of uniformed guards moving into view. In the time it took for them to register Bolan's presence he had turned his AK in their direction, tripping the trigger, hitting them hard and fast. Two went down immediately, crumpling under the sustained fire from Bolan's AK, the third, catching a slug in his shoulder, made an effort to resist. His own assault rifle crackled loudly and Bolan felt a sharp burn across the upper muscle of his left arm before he returned fire and put the guy down permanently.

It was no surprise to Bolan that he had encountered the guards. Fayed had admitted he had no definite figure on how many were stationed at the facility, so it wasn't unexpected that Bolan had encountered them so early during his infiltration. He headed for the steps. As he moved down Bolan registered the sound of the conflict outside fading. Below he picked up frenzied activity. The sound of hasty footsteps. An alarm ringing on a level below his present position.

He heard the rattle of a weapon being cocked, the scrape of clothing against the rough concrete wall below where the steps curved around a natural outcropping. A shadow fell across the steps, the outline of an armed man. Bolan pressed against the inner curve of the rock wall, so that he would see the advancing enemy first. The other man had to have been harboring similar thoughts as he suddenly ducked low, thrusting his weapon forward and making an attempt to move around Bolan.

The muzzle of an AK appeared, held at an angle, the shooter triggering a volley that spattered the rock face with steel-jacketed 7.62 mm slugs. The confines of the stepped area exploded with echoing sound, bullets bouncing off the stone, and Bolan was forced to fall into a tight crouch, feeling stone chips rattle against his shoulders. He was aware of his precarious position, exposed to anyone descending the steps. That would place him in a trap if more of the security guards appeared, with hostiles both above and below. His thoughts were transferred to the here and now when he heard voices from behind.

Bolan assessed the situation even as he registered the boot steps. Even as the numbers fell with increasing speed, Bolan formulated his next move within a couple of heartbeats. He knew he might step directly into what could be his final living action. If he miscalculated, or had read the situation wrongly, his demise might come far earlier than he might ever had anticipated.

Bolan took a long stride across the width of the steps, slamming against the far wall, his AK already tracking the man just below him. He caught a glimpse of a startled expression as the guy was caught briefly unaware. He hadn't anticipated his quarry to move into the open so brazenly, and before he was able to adjust his aim to pick up the American's moving shape, Bolan had triggered his own weapon. The AK's short burst hit the gunner chest high, the force kicking him back down the steps in pain-filled confusion. The guy was still toppling away from him as Bolan about-faced and pinpointed the guards hurrying down in his direction. The second they moved around the curve in the steps he laced them with a heavy burst that cored in chest high, tracking up to tear at the flesh of their throats.

Bolan plucked a stun grenade from his harness, primed it and tossed it down the steps. He took brief cover, turning as the grenade detonated, then continued down the steps.

At the next landing he was confronted by a pair of guards struggling to overcome the effects of the grenade. Bolan dealt

with them, the AK barking harshly in the confines of the area.
Pausing to reload, he repeated his stun grenade maneuver
with the steps dropping away in front of him, this time toss-
ing a pair of the bombs, then moving well clear of the flight.
He heard the twin detonations. About to head out, he heard
movement in the passage to his right. Someone was yelling
in Farsi, the voice loud and commanding. Armed figures appeared, weapons held in readiness. Bolan didn't hesitate. He
rounded on the advancing group and hammered them with
bursts from the AK. The lead gunners went down, delaying
those behind. Weapons opened up, the shots hitting the stone
walls around Bolan. He dropped to one knee, plucking a fragmentation grenade from his harness. He yanked out the pin,
freed the lever and rolled the bomb into the opposite passage.
The angry yells were replaced with brief cries of alarm,
quickly drowned in the blast. Bodies were hurled aside, flesh
torn and bones shattered in the grisly confusion. The Executioner raked the area with a sustained burst from his AK before turning and racing down the steps to the level below.

Here the decor was different. The rough stone had been
rendered smooth, strip lighting casting sterile illumination
across a floor coated by an antistatic, gray covering. As Bolan
came off the steps and crossed the landing, he moved through
a heavy steel door. The door itself had been swung back
against the wall, and the first thing he did was push it shut,
feeling it move easily on counterbalanced hinges despite its
weight. He worked the lever that secured it. Spying the locking bar, he used it to secure the door. There was a key pad on
the frame but he resisted using it because he had no idea what
the opening sequence was. He would have to depend on the
lock bar. Bolan turned to survey his surroundings.

The corridor he was standing in was at least ten feet wide,
the right side wall half-windowed. On the other side of the

toughened glass were partitioned work areas, white and brightly lit. The corridor stretched ahead of him for a couple of hundred feet. The layout was just as Malinkski had described it.

The corridor terminated at the far end with a door similar to the one Bolan had just secured. The area looked deserted. The soldier assumed that the lab personnel had vacated their workstations as soon as the alarms had sounded. He took out the tracking device and switched it on, holding it in front of him as he progressed along the corridor, wondering how much time he had before Razihra's security detail located him.

He had moved halfway along the corridor when a person materialized from cover behind a metal locker inside one of the lab units. He was unarmed and holding his hands out in front of him. The man opened the lab door and stepped into the corridor to confront Bolan.

"You are Cooper?"

Bolan studied the dark-haired young man. He wore a white lab coat over his shirt and pants.

"Tariq Kemal?"

"Yes. The alarms went off and someone warned us there was an attack on the surface. Of course I knew what it was so I stayed hidden when all the others left. I prayed you would find this level."

"Malinksi's directions were good."

The Iranian glanced at the tracking device in Bolan's hand. "What is that?"

"It pinpoints and identifies stolen U.S. technology. The hardware has embedded chips and this recognizes them."

"Very impressive. I can take you where the hardware is stored. But we may not have much time. I entered secure codes in the doors that access this section, but the security guards may be able to override them in time."

"Then we'd better move."

Kemal led the way down the corridor to a large lab near the far end. "This was Dr. Malinski's lab." He tapped in a code on the keypad and the door slid open.

Inside, the lab work areas were filled with electronic equipment and computers stations. On the main wall were message boards and a large blackboard holding mathematical calculations scrawled in chalk. Kemal tapped one of the monitors. "This was his. Since he left, no one has been able to access his work. Even the best technicians cannot get through his codes to open his data." Kemal led Bolan across the lab to a built-in metal storage unit. "This is where the hardware is kept."

Bolan scanned the unit with his tracker and showed Kemal the positive readout. "It's in here," he said. "Can you open it?"

Kemal nodded. "We are still assessing the technology. So the lab staff needs to be able to handle the hardware each shift."

"Open it."

Kemal tapped in a code, then released the handle, sliding the door aside on its silent runners. Inside the unit, padded shelves held a number of electronic pieces of hardware. There were guidance units, stabilizers, responders and circuit boards. Bolan ran an individual check on the items, identifying those that were U.S.-made. On their own, the items meant nothing, but once integrated into a completed device they would give the Iranians what they wanted—the nuclear technology that would enable them to manufacture their missiles and guidance units.

"Tariq, keep watch while I set this," Bolan said. He took a prepared explosive pack from his bag and placed it on one of the shelves. He moved the identified items and placed them around the pack. "I'm going to set this for five minutes. We need to be out of here by then." He set the time and activated the detonator.

Kemal nodded. "Before we leave we should destroy Malinski's computer as well."

"There's an easy way to do that." Bolan crossed to the computer and yanked out the cables. He picked up the tower box and carried it to the locker, placing it on the shelf above the explosive pack. He slid the door shut. "Lock it again."

Kemal tapped the keypad. He stood back as Bolan used the AK's butt to smash the pad unit.

Together they exited the lab and made their way along to the far door. Bolan stood to the side as the Iranian entered the code that unlocked the heavy door.

"Stay away from the opening," Bolan said. "Now open the door."

Kemal, protected by the steel door, gripped the bar and pulled the counterbalanced door open. As it cleared the frame Bolan spotted movement on the far side and heard the click of weapons. He picked up muttered commands. Glancing at Kemal, he saw the young man silently mouth a single word. "Security."

Bolan pulled a fragmentation grenade from his harness. It was his last. He pulled the pin, let the lever pop free and held the bomb as he counted the seconds before he dropped it through the gap. The moment he let it go he placed his free hand against the door and pushed. Kemal realized his intention and added his own weight, closing the door. The thick steel muffled the explosion, but they felt the concussion from the blast buffet the door. Metallic fragments rattled against the outer shell.

"Open," Bolan commanded.

The door swung inward, smoke sucking in through the

gap. Crouching, Bolan surveyed the scene in the corridor. Three bodies were on the floor, shredded and bloody. The man closest had lost a leg and an arm, the left side of his face was gone, too. The walls of the corridor were pockmarked and spattered with bloody debris. A distance away two more uniformed guards were down, one crawling aimlessly, his face a ruined mask of pulped flesh and shattered bone. Bolan put him out of his misery with a mercy burst to the head.

"Seal that door," Bolan said as Kemal followed him through. The Iranian stood and stared at the bloody scene in front of him. His face registered his revulsion. "Close the damn door," Bolan snapped. "You think they'd grieve if it was you?"

Kemal swung the door closed and secured it. He stood aside so Bolan could disable the keypad.

"Follow me," Kemal said, and moved ahead along a featureless corridor. "At the end there will be steps we can use to reach the surface."

He moved quickly, too quickly, driven by the need to get away from the image of the dead guards. Bolan sensed the younger man's urgency, realizing that Kemal was allowing his feeling override caution.

"Tariq, slow down. Don't show yourself…"

The Iranian ignored him. He pushed on, his very body stance showing the fear driving him forward. Just as they neared the end of the corridor, where it merged into an open landing, Kemal looked back over his shoulder. His expression revealed the shock he still felt and there were tears streaming down his face.

"Tariq," Bolan yelled. "Stay back."

Armed figures stepped into view, AKs already tracking in on Kemal and Bolan. A split second before they opened fire Bolan threw himself full-length, braced against hitting the

floor, and heard the stutter of auto fire. Kemal caught the full
brunt of the multiple bursts, his body twisting under the impact of the steel-jacketed bullets. A number cored through his
body, blowing out in spurts of bloody flesh. A brief cry came
from the stricken man as he was tossed across the corridor,
slamming into the wall before he fell to the floor. He was beyond hearing as Bolan opened fire. Propped on his elbows,
the Executioner raked the guards as they moved to take him
out. His autofire caught them as they entered the corridor, ripping into yielding flesh, forcing them to their knees. Bolan
pushed to his feet, towering over the guards, and emptied the
magazine into them. As the last man went down, Bolan
checked the landing for more hostiles and saw no one. Flattened against the corridor wall he snapped in a fresh magazine, cocked the weapon and knelt briefly beside Kemal to
check his life signs. There was none.

The man had given his life for a better Iran. Bolan rested
his hand on Kemal's shoulder for a moment, offering up his
gratitude. Then he checked his watch and saw that time was
running out. The detonator's timer in the planted explosives
was near to zero. He hoped the detonation would be contained
within the lab, but he didn't intend to stay too close to see if
his theory was correct. Pushing away from the wall, he turned
to cross the landing, heading for the steps, and saw gunners
coming toward him. They opened up the instant they saw
him, Bolan having to pull aside as 7.62 mm slugs struck the
wall close by. He moved to the far side of the landing, away
from the corridor behind him, and it was that move that saved
his life.

He was about to return fire, his finger on the trigger, when
he heard the muffled explosion and Bolan felt the shock
waves. The floor under his feet moved and dust wafted from
the ceiling and walls. The explosion was still reverberating

through the level when he heard a deeper, more powerful explosion that seemed to be coming from below, and that was followed by two more heavier explosions. This time the floor did more than vibrate. It heaved upward, the concrete splitting and throwing Bolan off balance. He heard a rushing sound, a powerful roar and saw the first fingers of flame gushing from the corridor he had evacuated. It had breached the steel door. A ball of flame and debris exploded from the corridor. If Bolan hadn't been off to the side, shielded by the rock, he would have been in the direct path. He still felt the heat as the flame shot across the landing, catching the guards at the base of the steps and engulfing them, turning them into living torches, twisting and turning in agony. Part of the ceiling over Bolan's head split, and a large chunk of reinforced concrete crashed to the landing. His only avenue of escape was the steps leading down to the next level, though he doubted that would have been a wise move, as all the movement seemed to be coming from beneath his feet. He had no idea what had happened, except that it was a result of his lab explosion. He had no time left for speculation. He was hurled violently to one side as a heavier explosion pushed its force up through the floor. Falling debris rained down around him, striking his shoulders and back. Bolan tried to stay upright but his struggles were in vain. Some invisible force tossed him sideways and he was thrown bodily down the steps into sudden darkness.

CHAPTER TWENTY-SEVEN

A tight group of security guards emerged from a secondary exit at the far end of the village, meeting McCarter's team as it made its way back to the main group. The Briton and his Iranian partners cut loose with heavy fire, driving them back to the village ruins. The bright morning was tainted by smoke from the demolition areas and any quiet was long gone, lost beneath the harsh crackle of autofire and the shouts of the combatants.

McCarter, leading the attack, used his AK to good effect, taking down two of the guards during the first seconds of the clash. Around him Anwar and the other two Iranians added their firepower and the guards were caught unprepared for the ferocity of the response. They tumbled back for cover among the ruins of the old houses, bullets following, tearing into crumbling stonework and human flesh. It wasn't all one way. Once they found cover, the guards fired back, the heavy volleys crisscrossing the area. McCarter threw himself flat, waving for the others to do the same. Anwar and one Iranian dropped. The third man was just too slow and took a sustained burst in the chest that killed him as he dropped.

McCarter saw the young man go down and his anger boiled over. He plucked a grenade from his harness and yanked out the pin, letting go the lever well before he made an overarm lob that dropped the bomb directly into the guards' position. It blew before they had a chance to move. One body was thrown over the protective cover of the crumbling wall. It lay in a grotesque sprawl, left arm gone from the shoulder, blood still pumping from the torn stump and smoke rising from scorched clothing. McCarter took the lull to exchange his magazine for a fresh one before he rolled to his feet and ran to where Anwar knelt beside the shot Iranian. He looked up at the Briton, slowly shaking his head.

"We can see to him later," McCarter said gently. "Let's finish this job first, chum."

With McCarter still leading, they moved the length of the village and joined up with Fayed and the others, hitting the security guards with unrelenting force. The number of guards had reduced considerably within as few minutes, and McCarter saw that people emerging from a number of what he figured were emergency exits identified themselves as noncombatants. They wore lab coats or civilian clothing and showed no ambition to resist. As if anticipating defeat, the guards surrendered their weapons and raised their hands in a sullen capitulation.

"Round them up," McCarter said, and Fayed and his group surrounded the dazed figures.

The deep rumble of an explosion reached their ears. Bolan, McCarter thought. A number of subsequent explosions followed the first, these much more powerful. They caused the ground to shake and sections of the village buildings collapsed, sending clouds of dust billowing across the area. At one end of the village the ground caved in, exposing a crater. Flame shot out, followed by choking black smoke. Some of the lab workers became excited, pointing and calling to one another, obviously alarmed at what had happened.

"Fayed, find out what they're on about."

The man crossed to where the workers were gathered and began to question them. McCarter listened to the rumblings coming from the facility and wondered what might have happened to Bolan.

Fayed returned, his face grave. "It doesn't sound good," he said. "The workers believe that stored chemicals and fuel for the generators on the level below the labs have been set off by the first explosion. There was much volatile material down there, stored for future use when missiles were built and tested. There was also a store of high-explosive compound for warheads in conventional missiles, too."

"Bloody great. What a time to find out. Wouldn't Kemal have known about this so he could warn you?"

"His position within the laboratory was possibly not high enough for him to be cleared on such information," Fayed said. "I am sure if he had known he would have warned us."

"You're probably right."

McCarter stood and surveyed the scene in front of him. If Bolan was down there and still alive, he was going to have one hell of a time getting out. The Briton ordered that all the exits be checked and when Fayed's men returned from doing that their findings made depressing reports. None of the exits was clear. The explosions below had collapsed the inner sections and the exits were blocked with fallen, shattered concrete and steel. Smoke was still filtering through the rubble, and in some areas the concrete was too hot to touch, suggesting the possibility of fire still burning.

McCarter was still staring at the demolished site twenty minutes later when Fayed joined him. He handed the Briton a mug of hot coffee.

"We have the workers and the guards secured," he said. "My men have searched them all and have taken any weapons."

McCarter nodded. "Damn it, Fayed, we have to get him out of there."

"If he is not already dead, he soon could be. Fallen concrete. Crumbling walls. Fire and smoke. Maybe the guards got to him."

"You don't understand, Fayed. He's down there and he's bloody well still alive. If he *was* dead, I would know it."

Fayed sighed. "I understand your desire to save Cooper. But what can we do? Look, my friend. Look at all that. If Cooper is far down there, how can we possibly find him? Where is the machinery to dig our way in?"

McCarter fell silent, his mind racing through various scenarios as he tried to figure out an answer.

"Wait a bloody minute," McCarter said. "Fayed, that layout you showed us. Did you bring it with you?"

"Yes. It is in my pack." Fayed opened his backpack and pulled out the folded sheet. "Here. Tell me what you are looking for."

McCarter ignored the question as he opened the paper and spread it. He started to search the drawing, his finger moving back and forth.

"Got it," he said. "Here. The bloody ventilation system." He found the section he wanted and traced the ducting until he reached the third level. "That's the one. It goes right down to where Cooper is. If the ducting hasn't caved in he could use it to climb out."

Fayed examined the sketch, nodding in agreement. "First we must guide him to one of the vent outlets in the section."

McCarter reached for his cell phone. "Let's hope he still has his."

BOLAN HAD GAINED CONSCIOUSNESS to find he was at the base of what had been the steps. The section above him was now

a solid mass of fallen masonry. He was slumped against a
wall, partially buried beneath dusty debris. Bolan climbed to
his feet and took a look around as he checked himself out for
any severe injury. Apart from the ragged gash in his skull that
had bled down his face, he ached from head to toe. Otherwise
he seemed to be fine. He shrugged out of the combat harness
and backpack, dropping them at his feet. During his fall he
had lost his grip on the AK. He didn't bother to look for it.
He still had the holstered SIG-Sauer. He stood for a moment,
gazing around the area. He was surrounded by fallen concrete,
with an open section to his right that might once have been a
storage area. Now it was blackened and smoking. Pale dust
still drifted around him. Fluorescent lights hung at crazy an-
gles, suspended by their wiring. A number of them still
worked, throwing a pale, diffused light on Bolan's enclosure.

He moved around, the floor under his feet littered with debris, searching for a way out. After a couple minutes he decided that escape from this underground tomb was going to
be far from easy. He never once entertained the notion he
might never get out. Mack Bolan's nature was life affirming.
As long as he had breath and the ability to think and do, then
life went on. He wasn't about to give in yet.

The muffled ringing of his cell phone caught Bolan's attention. There was something incongruous about his phone ringing where he was. He pulled it out of his pocket and flipped it
open, staring at the illuminated screen. The first thing he saw
was the reception bar. It was way down the scale. The solid concrete and the earth on top of the facility was acting as a partial
block. Bolan pressed the call-receive button. There was some
interference, but he was able to make out McCarter's voice.

"I'm listening," Bolan said.

"Look..around for venting…ducts…could be your way
out…bloody long climb…but possible…"

"Okay. I'll give it a try."

"Save your...phone power..."

"Yeah."

Bolan switched off the cell and dropped it back into one of the combat suit's pockets, closing the zip.

He started moving around the debris strewed area for a vent.

"DID HE UNDERSTAND?" FAYED asked.

McCarter nodded. "If it's possible, Cooper will do it. Fayed, old mate, we could be in for a long bloody wait. And I could do with a smoke."

TWENTY MINUTES DRAGGED BY before Bolan found what he was looking for. He had been forced to push and crawl and dig through fallen concrete and earth, pushing aside debris that had seemed to have flooded the passageway. Chunks of concrete, iron rods embedded to increase the strength, were in his way and he had to move dozens of them when they blocked his progress. His clothing was torn, covered with gray dust, and his fingers and hands were raw and scraped. The gash in his skull, though it had stopped bleeding, had left him with a relentless headache. Bolan forced the pain to the darker recesses of his mind, concentrating on getting out of the silent coffin he was entombed in.

The silence had been broken a couple of times by the sound of heavy concrete falling. The disturbance came from some distance away but left Bolan with the feeling it could happen anywhere at any time. Once he heard the hiss and crackle of severed electrical cable. He picked up the brassy heat smell, too, realizing that it wasn't far away from his own position. Awareness of his vulnerability spurred him on.

He located a vent at the top of a slope of loose debris. High on a facing wall, the aluminum access panel with its horizontal louvers was three feet by two. Bolan stared up at the vent, then checked out the pile of debris he would need to scale to reach it. The shattered concrete and bent iron rods looked firm enough. Bolan knew the mass could collapse under his moving weight once he started to climb, but he also knew he had no choice. If he wanted to get to the vent, he was going to have to climb.

Bolan didn't deliberate for long. Waiting wasn't about to improve conditions. The longer he hesitated the more likely a disturbance might weaken the debris pile. He took a breath and moved to the slope, taking the first tentative steps of his climb. The broken concrete lay in overlapping shelves, each one resting on the one beneath, with loose rubble and soil in between. Bolan tried to choose his path, testing before he put his full weight on the each section, using his hands and arms to keep him steady. The textured soles of his boots helped him grip as he worked his way across the slope. He figured he had about a ten- to twelve-foot climb. No big deal in itself, but when his chances of survival were dependent on shattered chunks of loosely piled concrete, the deal became desperate.

Some way off, but not far enough, Bolan heard a deep creaking sound, followed by the crash and thump of falling concrete. The vibrations the fall created reached out and rippled through the pile Bolan was climbing. The concrete under his feet moved. The soldier made a grab for the next section and hauled himself up as his feet lost their grip.

The concrete slid away, dragging smaller sections with it and throwing dust into the air. Bolan glanced up to see that he was still a distance away from the vent. If the debris under his feet collapsed fully, he was going to go down with it. He took a look at the next substantial section, reached out with his right hand and clamped his fingers on an exposed iron rod. He used the rod to haul himself up and for a few seconds hung

there by one hand, swinging loosely. Dust swirled up around
him, stinging his eyes and filling his mouth with its acrid taste.
Bolan threw up his other hand and got a second grip on the
iron rod. He dragged himself up, muscles screaming at the effort, and pulled himself onto the surface of the concrete section.

As he lay flat across it he could feel slight movement, and
he knew he couldn't count on this momentary safe spot to remain that way for very long. It was only the wedged chunks
of concrete and the interlocking iron bars that was holding the
debris together. Bolan pushed to his feet, balancing carefully
as he checked out where he needed to go next. Once he had
the route fixed in his mind he went for it immediately, stepping from section to section and moving upward until he was
no more than three feet away from the vent.

Bolan saw that the access panel could be opened by freeing the aluminum catch along one edge and swinging it wide
on the hinged left side. He pushed the catch aside and swung
the panel open and peered into the shaft. The dusty interior
was shadowed and didn't look promising. On the other side
of the coin, it did present itself the only way out.

"Let's do it," he said to himself, and at that moment he
heard the rumble and crack of further debris falling.

This time it was close enough to disturb the mass of concrete supporting him. Bolan felt it starting to give from under
him. He grasped the edges of the duct, pushed up hard and
propelled himself into the opening. Behind him his base slithered away, dust fogging the air. A split second later more debris cascaded down from above. The rumble became a
full-throated roar as a mass of debris crashed down outside
the duct. Dust blew into the shaft, choking Bolan. He scrambled along the shaft, away from the opening just before debris spilled inside, blocking the access and plunging him into

total and utter darkness. Above his head he could hear the creak and groan of the top of the shaft as it bowed beneath the weight of more crushing debris.

Bolan only had one way to go and that was forward. He moved quickly, feeling his way along the box section of the shaft. It had been built from preformed sections, each one about twelve feet long. Where each section butted against it neighbor there was a bolted lip that formed a two-inch internal rim. Bolan counted three of these sections before he came to a dead end. He checked out base and sides, then realized that above his head was an open section. The shaft rose vertically. Bolan peered into the darkness, and after a few seconds he was able to make out a faint rectangle of pale light far above him. He crouched at the base of the vertical shaft. He could feel very faint air movement. The air was warm and carried the scorched odor of an electrical overheat. He pushed to his feet, took a breath and readied himself for what he imagined was going to be a long climb. His initial effort required that he wedge himself against the two sides of the duct, using hands and feet to lever himself up the smooth sides of the shaft until he felt the first internal ridge. That at least gave him something to grip and use to ease himself up to the next section. It was hard work, and it wasn't long before his muscles resisted. Bolan closed his mind to that, concentrating everything on his slow ascent.

He felt sweat soaking his clothing, running down his face and into his eyes. When the palms of his hands became moist he lost his grip a couple of times and slithered down a few feet, which was something he didn't need. It was just another hazard he would have to endure until he reached that distant glimmer of light.

Twenty feet up he came to another horizontal shaft, just like the one he had first entered the duct system by. He wedged himself against the opening and took time to rest. He was soaked in sweat, his body aching from the constant friction of the aluminum panels. His hands were sore from contact burns. Bolan rested for less than five minutes. He didn't want to risk any longer in case his maltreated muscles decided to cramp. He wanted to rest, but his mind demanded he carry on.

Just before he moved, he picked up sounds, an odd mix of sliding and the occasional thump. There were voices, too, indistinct, but definitely there. He wasn't imagining it, and after listening for a time he realized what it was.

Others were doing exactly what he was.

Survivors were attempting to work their way out of the wrecked facility by utilizing the duct system.

Survivors could mean lab technicians—or security guards.

The enemy at the moment. And if they met up with Bolan they wouldn't be offering him any assistance getting out of the facility. Not after what he had done to their secret establishment.

Bolan started to move again, attempting to restrict the noise of his own passage down. The cramped dimensions of the shafts were far from ideal if it came to escaping from men with guns. This was no place for pushing to his feet and running.

And there was no place to hide.

CHAPTER TWENTY-EIGHT

He reached the next level, taking notice that the light above him had strengthened. It was still a long way off and Bolan had no idea where it would bring him out, or what kind of reception he might receive. Unknown quantity or not, he had to keep moving. The beckoning light source could be his only way out, and any risk it might present had to be faced.

Bolan's head was almost level with the adjacent horizontal shaft when the head a shoulders of a man appeared. In the brief moments before the guy spotted him Bolan saw a battered, bloody, dust-streaked face. The man's skin glistened with sweat, just like Bolan's. As he pushed his shoulders through, the guy's eyes fixed on him. He stared for a moment, then pulled one arm back. Bolan heard the metallic sound as something scraped along the ducting.

The man's hand reappeared, clutching a handgun. He angled it in Bolan's direction, starting to yell.

Bolan jammed his feet hard against the side of the shaft, his own arms reaching up, fingers desperate to grab the searching gun hand and push the black muzzle away from him. The pistol went off, the slug punching a hole through the

aluminum duct behind Bolan. The gunshot hammered at
Bolan's ears, magnified by the confined space, rattling and
echoing as the Executioner and the shooter struggled to gain
the upper hand.

Bolan's opponent was hampered by his prone position,
and struggled to get his other arm free. Bolan gave him no
chance. He closed his free hand around the pistol, slamming
the guy's hand against the raised ridge of metal, hammering
it again and again until the fingers slackened. Blood was
coursing from the deep gashes Bolan's action had opened. As
the soldier snatched the pistol free, the Iranian began to panic,
raising his voice even louder as he yelled over his shoulder
to whoever was behind him. Voices answered back. The Iranian lashed out with his bloody hand, landing a blow to his
adversary's cheek. Reversing the pistol, Bolan raised it, jamming the muzzle against the guy's forehead and pulling the
trigger. The 9 mm slug cored in deep, blowing out the back
of the guy's skull in a spurt of blood and bone.

The moment he fired Bolan lowered himself a couple of
feet down the shaft. His move proved to be wise as someone
opened up with an AK. The Russian assault rifle's sound was
unmistakable, even in the confines of the ducting shaft, the
7.62 mm slugs shredding the aluminum panels. Whoever had
his finger on the trigger kept it there until the weapon was
empty. In the ensuing silence Bolan heard voices arguing.
Whatever they were saying, Bolan decided it held nothing
pleasant as far as he was concerned. He stuck his acquired
firearm inside his web belt, noting as he did its configuration.
A Glock 17.

There was more muttered conversation from the shaft just
above Bolan's head. The body of the dead Iranian was prov-
ing to be an obstacle to his opponents, preventing them from
getting through to launch a further attack. A solution became

apparent as the body began to move—in the direction of the vertical shaft. The Iranian's companions were attempting to clear the body by pushing it out of the shaft. If they succeeded, Bolan would find his own progress blocked. He worked his way to the junction, placed his hands on the dead man's shoulders and pushed the body back inside the opposing shaft. With the bullet-punctured shaft at his back Bolan had better leverage and he felt the corpse slide into the shaft. Angry voices protested. Bolan anticipated what was coming next and dropped below the level again, out of harm's way as a second round of AK fire sent 7.62 mm retaliation his way.

Bolan retrieved the Glock, eased up to the opening and fired off a half dozen shots over the body, moving his muzzle back and forth. Someone screamed in pain, kicking against the metal duct. Bolan had felt the Glock's slide lock on empty. He dropped the weapon, knowing he still had his holstered SIG-Sauer and took the momentary cessation in hostilities to climb past the junction. It was a prolonged moment, his expectation of return fire heavy on his mind. He ignored the friction burns and the bullet-torn aluminum slicing his flesh. Despite being clear of the junction he kept moving this time, working his aching body and muscles to the limit. He wanted to be out of this claustrophobic place, clear of the shrinking closeness of the shafts. At that moment he didn't care what he might find at the summit of his climb. He would have taken on any number of Razihra's armed security men as long as he could do it in the open.

Bolan pushed negative thoughts to the back of his mind, focusing his energies on maintaining his climb, hand over hand, gripping with his body against the smooth aluminum panels, telling himself that the pain from his cramped and aching muscles didn't really exist, he moved ever upward. The tattered blacksuit clung to him, rivulets of sweat oozing from every pore. It ran down his face, stinging his eyes, creeping into every cut and graze on his body. The ache in his skull from the gash intensified. Perversely the hurt and the discomfort made him fully aware that despite it all he was still alive. As long as he could feel the pain he still functioned, and while that was a reality he could beat everything else.

He didn't rationalize the passage of time. It made no difference whether he climbed for minutes, or hours, all Bolan concentrated on was reaching that rectangle of light. The higher he climbed, the stronger the light became and as he closed in on the source he saw the blessed tone of a blue sky. Faint at first, but growing stronger, was fresh air. When he finally reached the shaft end Bolan realized noted the grilled cover. If it was secured in place, he might still find himself trapped. He dismissed the thought. He refused to accept defeat now, after his long climb. He pushed his fingers through the metal grille and rested for a while, sucking clean air into his lungs, not even making any attempt to check the grille until he felt stronger. He checked the interior first. There was nothing on the inside to suggest it was bolted in place. Bolan braced himself against the shaft, back and feet pushing hard to hold himself in position. He reached up with both hands and took hold of the cover, pushing up hard. He felt the grille move, then resist. He increased his effort and felt it move along one edge, the grille clearing the rim of the box section. He took that as a good sign, put on more pressure, his powerful arm and shoulder muscles aching from the effort. The grill resisted, then the loose edge gave suddenly and lifted. Bolan refused to quit now, working on the raised side. He heard the metal creak as his consistent effort paid off. The grille broke free with a harsh sound and Bolan thrust it clear. He caught hold of the rim and dragged his weary body up out of the shaft.

He emerged onto a raised concrete that rose from the sand and stood some three feet off the ground. The moment he was clear Bolan dropped flat, drawing the SIG-Sauer, and took a look around.

Wadi Hattat was deserted. He saw a number of bodies strewed around the area from the original firefight. Faint smoke trails rose into the shimmering air from the burned-out wrecks of trucks and helicopters. Here and there, small fires still burned.

Bolan took his time scanning the area, questions crowding his mind.

Were any of Razihra's people still around? Had anyone else got out of the facility?

And where was McCarter, Fayed and the other Iranians?

The total silence worried Bolan.

He pushed to his feet and stepped to the edge of the concrete, pistol in one hand as he searched for the cell phone. The pocket it had been kept in hung in tatters. The phone was missing. Probably lying smashed at the bottom of the shaft. Sometime during his climb it had to have been torn free and he hadn't noticed. For a flash of a second he wondered if he might climb back down to recover it, and the thought brought a weary smile to his streaked and bloody face.

Not bloody likely, McCarter would have said.

Where are you, David? Bolan knew the Briton wouldn't even consider deserting him. The word "quit" wasn't even in McCarter's vocabulary.

Moments later he got his answer as to why the place was silent. He had moved back to where the main attack had taken place, and as he rounded the edge of one of the crumbling stone walls he saw the bodies.

Many of them. Men and women in the white lab coats. Those coats were in bloody tatters, the bodies riddled with bullets. And beyond them lay more bodies. Bolan recognized them soon enough. There were the survivors of Fayed's group, the Iranians who had come into Wadi Hattat with Bolan and McCarter. He moved among them, a rising anger growing as he saw that they all had their hands tied behind them, their bodies torn and bloody from multiple bullet wounds. He stood among them, the realization hitting him hard.

Fayed's men hadn't been killed in battle. They had been taken captive, bound and executed where they stood. Bolan checked the piled corpses, searching for the one body he dreaded to find.

McCarter.

The Briton wasn't among them. Nor was Fayed.

He scanned the bodies, seeing the blood soaking the tattered clothing. The shooting had been intense. The use of extreme amounts of ammunition had torn and lacerated the Iranians. There were patches of blood that hadn't yet fully dried, so the slaughter hadn't happened too long ago. Despite the blood spray Bolan recognized every face. The last time he had seen them was at the height of the attack on Wadi Hattat. Then they had been holding their own against Razihra's security force.

So what had happened to change that?

Bolan was about to move on when he heard a faint sound. He paused, checking the area. Nothing moved. The sound came again. Low, rasping, but it was someone using his cover name.

Cooper.

He turned, realizing the sound had come from the sprawled bodies. Bolan moved in among them, searching, listening, and heard the name again even as he found the one who was speaking. He knelt in the sand, sliding a body away from the barely moving form, half covered by one of the other bodies.

Bloody and torn, his face a red mask, it was Anwar, the Iranian who had been with McCarter. A quick look at the ravaged torso and chest told Bolan there was little he could do for the man. He loosened the cords that bound Anwar's wrists.

Anwar reached out a bloody hand to grasp Bolan's sleeve, his head turning from side to side, the effort costing him dearly.

"You see what they did to us? We had victory until we were betrayed and Razihra's men came and surrounded us. They came out of the desert. Better armed and with more men than we could deal with."

"Not by chance?"

"No, they knew we were here."

"Who betrayed you?"

"One of our own. I saw him on a cell phone. Minutes later Razihra's men appeared and surrounded us. Then the traitor went to them. Rafik. Remember him, Cooper. He ordered the slaughter and stood by as we were shot down."

"I'll remember him," Bolan promised. "Why are the lab workers dead?"

"On Razihra's order, Rafik said. Razihra feared others who might work against him. Like all dictators he fears betrayal. His orders were to silence the workers so they could not speak against him."

"Anwar, I don't see Fayed, or my English friend, Travis."

"They took them away. In one of the helicopters that came. I had passed out and they must have believed I was dead like the others. I heard Rafik telling Fayed they were to be taken to Razihra. Used to give him information and held as hostages. Your English would not do as he was told. His anger was a sight to see at Rafik's betrayal."

"Sounds like him."

"Rafik put a bullet through his leg to stop him. Even as he lay on the ground he cursed Rafik. A brave man your Travis. I was proud to have fought alongside him."

"His name is David McCarter, and I'm Mack Bolan."

"You tell me because I am dying?"

"I'm telling you because you are a true warrior."

"Will you save them? Fayed and McCarter?"

"Where would they take them, Anwar?"

The Iranian took time to reply. He was dying, and only his stubborn will having kept him alive for so long. But he was losing the battle, his lifeblood draining from the savage wounds inflicted by Razihra's men.

"I heard them talk about Razihra's home on the slopes of the Alborz Mountains. It is near the southern edge of the Caspian Sea. It is his retreat. His refuge. Very well defended, Mack Bolan. No one dares to go there if they are not invited."

"I'll have to change that," Bolan said.

Anwar made no reply and when Bolan looked down at him he realized the man was dead.

"I'll get them out, Anwar," he said. "You have my promise on that."

Bolan had no way of burying the bodies. His physical condition wouldn't have allowed him, even if he had the tools for the task, so he spoke a few private words over them before he salvaged an AK and sought a couple of extra magazines. He knelt at the water pool of Wadi Hattat and drank, then did what he could to clean his wounds and wash away some of the dirt on his body. He fashioned a head covering from an abandoned blanket, letting the surplus material hang down his back before he set out to walk back to the helicopter that had brought the strike group to the oasis. He was banking on the aircraft still being where Fayed had landed it. If it wasn't, he was going to have an even longer walk out of the Iranian desert.

It was full dark when he lay prone on the cooling sand, staring down at the camouflaged Chinook. Something had warned him to check out the location before he went in blind.

His senses had warned him well. Three uniformed security guards sat around a fire, enjoying their evening meal. He had no difficulty in identifying the uniforms as those of the Wadi Hattat guards. Bolan made sure he had the count correct. Three. There was an open Jeep parked to one side of the helicopter. The camouflage nets had been taken away. Was the intention to fly the chopper out of the desert? Bolan didn't have the answer to that. It made no difference. The three guards he was observing weren't going anywhere.

Their time was almost up. They didn't realize it yet, but when he went out to meet them Death would walk alongside him.

The dead at Wadi Hattat wouldn't be forgotten.

CHAPTER TWENTY-NINE

The dense forested slopes of the mountain range running almost parallel to the Caspian Sea were heavy with lush vegetation and timber. The climate was rainy and humid, promoting the dense growth. Oak and chestnut crowded the slopes, as did ash and alder trees. The ground was thick with fern and lichen. Rain slanted in across the massed greenery, dripping from the high canopy and turning the ground soft and spongy.

From where he crouched at the base of a massive oak Mack Bolan could see the distant gleam of the Caspian Sea. He wore a waterproof camou poncho over his clothing and gear. Despite the downpour he was feeling distinctly clammy. The rain actually felt warm. He tugged the bill of his baseball cap lower, covering his upper face and checked his watch. He had been on the ground for almost four hours now. His chute and pack were buried, and he had moved closer to Ayatollah Razihra's mountain retreat. The Air Force plane that had flown him in from Incirlik, Turkey, for his HALO drop would be well on its way home by now.

Bolan was back in enemy territory, alone and ready to do what he did best.

Infiltration and confrontation.

His objectives were simple enough. His decision had been made.

He wanted McCarter and Fayed free and clear, and he wanted neutralization of Razihra and his allies.

The metaphorical rulebook had been left behind for this particular mission.

He was ready for an all out Bolan Blitz.

From the Iranian desert Bolan had flown the ancient Huey, under cover of darkness, on a direct course for the Turkish border. He had been offered little choice in his destination. It was the closest friendly country in the area. He had kept the chopper low, hoping to stay beneath Iranian radar scans and whether by good luck or proactive thinking, he had achieved what he'd set out to do. The chopper, running on the last few drops of fuel, had entered Turkish airspace in the early hours and Bolan had nursed the shaky aircraft to a bumpy landing in the middle of a farmer's field. He had gotten rid of all weapons from the chopper, including his own, while still over Iranian soil. He had picked up a sat phone from one of the security guards he had left dead in the desert and the moment he touched down, watching the approach of the angry farmer, he'd made an emergency call to Stony Man, hoping the phone would hold out long enough to send his message.

It took a long few hours before help arrived in the form of a harassed U.S. Embassy official, who took one look at the battered and bloody figure in a near-shredded blacksuit, and who found it hard to believe that this Matt Cooper was to be afforded the full treatment as ordered by the President himself. The farmer, compensated for his trouble, and his young, unmarried daughter, who had been fussing over the tall American, watched Bolan leave with more than a little regret.

The farmer left, wondering what to do with the helicopter standing in the middle of his field.

Later, Bolan was airlifted to Incirlik Air Base, where the U.S. Air Force's 39th Air Base Wing was located. He was expected and went directly to the medical center for treatment and a checkup. Following his treatment, which included a number of stitches to various wounds, antibiotics to combat anything he might have picked up, the Air Force Doctor advised complete rest for at least a week. Bolan had listened, declined the offer, and left. He had a meal, then sacked out in the room allocated to him by the Air Force. He slept soundly until the next morning. By the time he was up and dressed, sitting down to a late breakfast, his backup had arrived at Incirlik. It came on board a U.S. Air Force C-17 transport and consisted of Jack Grimaldi and his combat helicopter, Dragon Slayer.

Now, clad in his familiar blacksuit and boots, a loaded combat vest zipped in place, Bolan wore the Beretta 93-R in his shoulder rig, the big Desert Eagle in a holster on his right hip. Sheathed on his left was a keen Tanto knife. Cradled in his hands was a 9mm Uzi, still a weapon Bolan favored for its feel and awesome delivery. It was a weapon he had used consistently over the years. Extra mags for each weapon were distributed around his vest and hung from pouches on his belt. He had outfitted himself with a selection of stun and fragmentation grenades. Around his waist hung a nylon pouch that held a number of small but powerful blocks of C-4 plastique, fitted with electronic detonators he could fire from a compact unit stored in one of the pockets in his vest. In a padded, zippered vest pocket was a Tri-Band cell phone he could use to call in *Dragon Slayer,* Stony Man Farm's state-of-the-art stealth combat chopper, when he was ready for extraction. Grimaldi was sitting on the ground at Diyarbakir Air Base,

Turkey, where he had been moved to from Incirlik, on twenty-four hour permanent call. One of the few men Bolan trusted without hesitation, Jack Grimaldi was ready to burn his way to the pickup zone in his pride and joy, *Dragon Slayer.*

A call from the President to Turkey's leader, asking for permission to base Grimaldi at the Turkish air base had been granted. It had been a diplomatic success for the U.S. President. He had spoken on a secure link, explaining to his Turkish counterpart the sensitive nature of the mission and had made it clear what was at stake. Turkey, a longtime ally of the U.S., would be close to any outbreak of hostilities in the region if they escalated. The mention of nuclear proliferation added weight to the argument. Diyarbakir had been used by the U.S. on a number of occasions in the Gulf wars and was an ideal staging point for *Dragon Slayer.*

Using a pair of compact, powerful binoculars Bolan studied the layout of the sprawling residence perched in isolation on the mountain slope, overlooking the wide panorama of the Caspian, some twenty miles to the north of its position. In his free hand Bolan had a satellite image of the house and grounds, taken by the U.S.A.'s orbiting Zero Station. The ultrasecret station, capable of defensive and offensive strikes, also maintained high-spec digital satellite imagery and Stony Man was able to call on it for assists whenever needed. Bolan's request for intel on Razihra's residence had produced a selection of detailed images that had been encased in plastic sheets. The images confirmed what Bolan saw through his binoculars.

Razihra kept his house and estate under guard. Bolan had been observing the estate for more than an hour after getting in close. He had already monitored the number of guards and their routes. There were garages beneath the lower terraces of the house, and a number of vehicles were parked near the doors. At the rear of the house was a large concrete helipad. A white Bell 206B-3 JetRanger III stood on the pad.

Bolan had scanned the target area a number of times. He repeated his check again, wanting to be sure he had covered everything. He wasn't going to have the luxury of time once he made his move, so the more he covered now, the less chance of error. He wasn't naive enough to believe that he could eliminate all risks. Absolute guarantees of success didn't exist because as long as there was opposition, there was always the chance of the unexpected. The most detailed and planned operations had been blown because of human deviation. It took only one man, changing his routine for whatever reason and at the inopportune moment, to destroy what had been meticulously worked out beforehand.

He finished his scan and leaned back against the oak tree. Lowering his binoculars, he took out the photo images again and checked them through. Nothing appeared to have changed much since the images had been taken twelve hours earlier. Bolan thumbed through the half-dozen images before putting then back inside his combat vest. He took a looked at his watch; a half hour before noon.

Time to move out.

This was going to have to be a daylight strike. Bolan had decided he couldn't sit around and wait until dark. The forested mountain terrain would be treacherous once the light faded. It was difficult enough maneuvering around now while he could see where he was walking. In darkness it would be tantamount to pure recklessness. He wouldn't be much use to McCarter and Fayed if he broke a leg stumbling around in the darkness. Or got himself trapped by falling into some unseen ravine.

There was a soft rumbling coming from the cloud-heavy sky over the peaks behind Bolan. Torrents of rain swept down off the higher peaks, slashing across the verdant slopes. Visibility lessened, and he saw this as his opportunity to get closer to the house and grounds. What restricted his vision would also do the same for Razihra's guards.

He took out the cell phone and used the speed-dial. The Tri-Band phone relayed his call to the satellite receiver and redirected it to Grimaldi. The Stony Man pilot picked up immediately.

"Sarge?"

"Warm her up, Jack, I'm going in. Come get me."

There was a momentary silence as Grimaldi phased Bolan's signal into *Dragon Slayer*'s computer navigation system. "Locked in on your signal, Sarge. Just make sure you keep that phone switched on."

"Will do, Jack. Make it a fast run."

"No expense spared, I'm on my way." Grimaldi paused. "Watch your back, buddy."

Bolan cut the connection, left the cell phone activated, secured it in the padded slip pocket, then eased into the dense undergrowth and began his approach to the target area.

HE CROUCHED IN THE HEAVY foliage with the main residence no more than a few hundred yards in front of him. Bolan had worked his way to the rear of the place, heading for the helipad. He needed to disable the aircraft to prevent any last minute escapes. A single guard patroled the area, armed with an AK-47 and wearing a long waterproof coat against the continuing downpour. He was hunched over as he tramped his waterlogged path, head down to prevent the slanting rain from stinging his face.

Bolan discarded his poncho. The rain soaked him in seconds, but he needed the freedom to move that the protective cape had restricted. He secured the Uzi by its webbing strap and slid the Tanto combat knife from its sheath. He had been watching the guard for the past twenty minutes and knew the man's route step-by-step. He would make his move on the next circuit. Bolan saw the man reach the limit of his patrol area and take a look around. The heavy rain would prevent him seeing very far. It was coming down hard enough now to bounce when it hit the ground.

As the guard turned and started back on the path that would take him by the American's location, Bolan eased forward. He let the guy reach his position and walk past, then rose silently, a tall-black clad figure dripping rain, the combat knife already curving around to seek its unsuspecting target.

Bolan's left hand dislodged the guard's cap, allowing his fingers to get a grip of the man's thick hair. The Executioner yanked the his head back, pulling the flesh tight across his neck. The chill caress of the Tanto steel was all the guard felt before blood began to pump from the gaping neck wound, spurting from the severed carotid artery. It spilled down the rain-slick coat, washing away in the downpour.

Moving his left hand down, Bolan clamped it over the guard's mouth, hugging him close and backed into the under-growth. He went in far enough for full concealment and man-handled the dying guard to the wet ground. The man was already losing consciousness, his spasms lessening. Bolan took the AK, checking the magazine and making sure the weapon was ready to fire. He saw there was a reversed second magazine taped to the first for a fast reload. Using the AK would preserve his Uzi loads.

The soldier exited the foliage and moved to the helipad. He crouched beneath the JetRanger and took one of the explosive packs from his satchel. He wedged it in between a couple of landing struts and flicked the small activation switch.

During his observation of the house and grounds, Bolan

had picked out the separate structure that housed a large generator for power. It lay to the east of his position, close to a stand of trees and foliage. He moved away from the helipad, melting silently into the greenery and made his way around the perimeter until he was behind the stone-built enclosure.

Pressed against the wall he could feel the vibration coming from the generating plant. Sleeving rain from his face, Bolan edged his way around the building and checked the entrance. The door was closed but not secured with anything more than a slide bolt. He opened the bolt, cracked the door, slipped inside and pulled the door shut behind him. The muffled sound of the large generator drowned out the noise of the torrential rain. The air inside was warm, tainted by the unmistakable odor of diesel fuel. The interior of the generator house was spotless. Bolan catfooted across to the base of the generator and crouched to slip another of his explosive packs beneath the front of the unit, where the blast would do most damage to the control functions.

Exiting the building, Bolan closed and bolted the door, moving swiftly to the rear again. His next targets were the vehicles parked outside the row of garages. He spent a couple of minutes checking the area around the vehicles. He would be more exposed than he had been, but he needed to plant his explosives. Blowing the vehicles would add yet more distractions when he made his move for the house.

Bolan watched as two guards made their way down the slope of the terrace that overlooked the garages, coming to a stop atop the stone walkway that overlooked the garage frontage. In their waterproof coats, hats pulled low against the sweeping sheets of rain cascading down from the higher slopes, the guards were in deep discussion over something. Thunder rumbled again over the mountain peaks. In unison the guards turned and walked back toward the house.

Taking his cue from their retreat, Bolan made his run for the line of vehicles, his black figure a silent shadow. He didn't stop until he reached the closest vehicle, a dark-colored Humvee. He rolled under the vehicle, one of the packs in his hand and clamped it to the underside, the magnetic strip secure against the steel chassis. He repeated the maneuver down the line of parked vehicles. When he came to the last in line he sensed the warmth emanating from the exhaust system. The black 4x4 had only recently arrived at Razihra's residence.

Bolan was sliding out from beneath the 4x4 when he saw booted feet moving toward the vehicle. There was no way he could avoid being seen as his body emerged.

A man's voice exclaimed in surprise as Bolan came out from the underside of the 4x4. There was a rattle of weaponry and Bolan saw the muzzle of an AK angling down at him. He didn't pull back, instead continued his forward slide, bringing his right leg around in a sweep that kicked the guy's legs from under him. The man uttered a startled cry as he was left in midair for seconds before slamming to the ground on his back. Breath gusted from his lips and the back of his skull cracked hard against the solid stone. Bolan followed through with the heel of his boot, slamming it down across the guard's exposed throat. The guy gagged once, his torso straining against the assault before he became limp. Bolan pushed to a crouch, bending over the guard. Before he shoved the body beneath the 4x4 he relieved the guard of his AK's double magazine, dropping it into a side pocket of his blacksuit.

If he had been counting numbers, Bolan would have accepted his were dropping quickly. He might not be lucky enough to avoid further confrontations, so he needed to close in on the house as fast as possible now. Luck might stay on his side for a time, but it was fickle and could desert him at any time.

He angled to the west side of the house, staying low, using anything he could for cover. An abundance of green foliage dotted the area, and Bolan used it to conceal his approach until he hugged the west wall of the residence. A number of windows ran the length of the building, but none close enough to betray his presence. The soldier took off the satchel that had held the explosive packs. He had one left and slid it into a pocket. It might come in handy later. From another pocket he took the handheld detonating device and flipped the On switch. The light glowed red. Bolan pressed the button.

The explosions lit up the entire area. The Executioner felt the ground shake under his feet. As he made a visual sweep he saw the helicopter, the generator building and then the line of parked vehicles blow apart in balls of fire. The heavy explosions shattered windows in the house. Smoke coiled up from the burning wreckage. Debris scattered in wide swathes. Flaming gasoline from the wrecked vehicles sprayed the area, burning into the foliage.

Bolan sprinted down the side of the house, heading for the rear, anticipating that everyone's attention would be focused on what had happened out front. As he rounded the far corner of the house he was confronted by a pair of Razihra's armed guards. They saw Bolan as he came into sight and raced forward, bringing up their AKs. The American had his own weapon already online and pulled the trigger first, scything down the pair in a hail of 7.62 mm lead. The savage velocity of the AK's delivery punched through their clothing and cored into their flesh, spinning them off their feet in a mist of red. Bolan followed them down, head shots making sure they wouldn't get up again.

He heard a shout from nearby and saw another armed guard emerged from a door, firing on the run, his AK's muzzle jerking as he moved. Bolan stood his ground and tracked in his own weapon. The AK jacked out a burst that chewed wood from the door frame, then moved on to catch the guard in the side. He stumbled, bouncing off the edge of the door. As he fell into clear view Bolan hit him again, the AK's slugs shredding his throat and rising to take a chunk out of his skull.

Bolan ducked low as he reached the door, stepping through and moving away from the rectangle of light. He heard the rush of booted feet closing in on the open door at the far side of the room. A man called out harsh orders and armed guards crowded the door, weapons up as they raked the room. Bolan had already dropped prone, rolling for the cover of a heavy wooden desk. Wood and plaster splinters showered over him. While the weapons crackled brutally Bolan used the sound to cover his movement to the far end of the desk, where he rose to a crouch and returned fire. His AK's burst caught the men crowding the door, slugs ripping into flesh and dropping one to the floor. A second reeled away, clutching at a shredded arm and shoulder.

Bolan felt the AK lock on an empty magazine. He ejected it, turning it around and clicking a fresh one in place. He worked the bolt, pushing the first round into the breech. Plucking a stun grenade from his harness he pulled the pin and tossed the bomb through the open door, turning away and covering his ears. He heard the sharp detonation. A yell of frustration followed the explosion. Bolan hit the open doorway, his AK seeking targets as he broke through into a wide, open area dotted with furniture and low tables. He greeted the onrushing guards with short, accurate bursts that drove them to the tiled floor. The tumbling bodies stood little chance against Bolan's relentless advance and he cleared the area.

Movement overhead caught his attention. A man leaned over the rail of the second-floor gallery, a pistol in one hand, the muzzle aimed in Bolan's direction. The pistol cracked once and the soldier felt the passing sting of the 9 mm slug as it grazed his right arm. He returned fire, seeing wood splinters explode from the rail into the face of the shooter who stumbled back—but not before Bolan recognized him.

Bolan saw the central stairs that led to the gallery and went for them at a run. He needed to get to the man. If he was here, then he would know where McCarter and Fayed were. Bolan reached the gallery and saw the bullet-scarred rail where his shots had hit. He spotted blood on the floor. More red drops showed which way Rafik had gone. Bolan followed, aware he was moving deeper into Razihra's lair, but his need to find his friends and free them pushed him on.

As he reached the far end of the gallery he heard activity below. Checking it out, he saw a group of guards clustered near the stairs. He was spotted in the same moment and the house rang to the collective power of multiple AKs firing. Bolan had already pulled back from the rail. Before he moved on he snatched an HE grenade from his harness, popped the pin and released the lever. He held it for a heartbeat, then tossed the grenade over the rail, turning to continue his pursuit of Rafik. The blast of the grenade was well behind him as he turned down the only passage Rafik could have taken without Bolan spotting him.

The passage had doors on either side. The soldier's keen eyes detected one swinging shut, on his right. He moved to stand to one side, waited a couple of seconds, then booted the door back against the inner wall.

Rafik was on the far side of the room, struggling to open double doors that led out onto an exterior gallery that circled the outside of the upper floor. Rain was driving in at the glass doors.

"Not yet, Rafik," Bolan said. "You've got something to tell me."

The Iranian threw an anxious glance over his shoulder. Bolan saw that the splinters from the rail had torn the left side of his face. Blood had streaked his flesh, running down to soak his white shirt.

"There is nothing I have to say to you, Cooper."

Bolan strode across the room, his dark-clad figure imposing in its stature and Rafik knew he had made a bad mistake. He tried to avoid Bolan, but the American simply reached out with his left hand and took hold of Rafik's collar. He yanked the man away from the doors and threw him bodily across the room. Rafik collided with a chair and crashed to the floor. He lay stunned until the Executioner reached him again, pulling him upright and slamming him against the wall. Then he hauled off and hammered his fist into Rafik's face, hit him again, driving him to his knees. Rafik groaned as the numbing pain engulfed him, blood dripping from his torn flesh.

Kicking the door shut, Bolan rammed home the bolts. He turned back to Rafik, knowing he was going to have to get what he needed fast. He wasn't sure how many more of Razihra's guards remained.

Bolan caught a handful of Rafik's hair and yanked his head back. The Iranian stared into Bolan's cold blue eyes and saw a vision of Hell on Earth.

"Where are my friends? Make it easy on yourself, Rafik, because one way or another you *are* going to tell me."

Rafik spit blood from his mouth, feeling loose teeth in his gums. He shook his head. "I will not tell you. They are going to die, just as you will when Razihra has you in his hands."

"One thing I know, you won't be there to see it."

"Are you going to kill me, American?"

"Damn right," Bolan growled.

He dragged Rafik to his feet and pushed him against the closed door, jamming the muzzle of the AK into the man's neck. Keeping his weapon in place Bolan moved to Rafik's side, his back to the wall.

"What are you doing?" Rafik asked, a tremor of fear edging into his voice.

"Waiting to see if your buddies knock before they come in."

"If they shoot…"

"They'll save me the job." Bolan pushed the AK's muzzle harder against the Iranian's flesh. "Tricky position you got yourself into. I guess Fayed would approve."

"That…" Rafik didn't finish. He was suddenly very aware of his situation and the fact that the American saw him as having betrayed Fayed and his group.

"I saw what your friends did to Fayed's men. And their own lab workers. I won't forget it, so don't waste my time, Rafik."

The sound of activity on the other side of the door made Rafik squirm. He felt Bolan put more pressure on the AK's muzzle.

"If I tell you?"

"No *if* about it."

"In the east wing there is a secure unit. They are there." His words tumbled out, anxiety at his vulnerable position making him hurry. He could hear raised voices beyond the door. "Let me move. Please. They might…"

Bolan caught his collar and dragged him away from the door. He had heard the click of weapons being readied. As Rafik stumbled across the floor, autoweapons thundered on the other side of the door, splintering the wood panels. Bolan turned his own weapon and stitched the door with a figure-eight pattern that reduced the wood to tatters and found human targets on the other side.

Replacing the spent magazine with one from a blacksuit pocket, Bolan sensed movement behind him. Rafik was back at the gallery doors again. This time he managed to free them, pushing them wide and moving out onto the rain-swept gallery. He turned to show Bolan a triumphant grin on his bloody face as he stepped clear. If he had looked closely he would have spotted the warning in the American's eyes.

Bolan had seen a couple of the guards racing along the gallery, alerted by the gunfire. They had to have mistaken Rafik for the intruder as he ran out through the gallery doors—and directly into their line of fire as they opened up with their assault rifles. Rafik caught the full force of the combined AK bursts. The 7.62 mm slugs ravaged his chest and torso, opening bloody wounds and tearing his ribs apart. Rafik twisted sideways, not even making a sound. He fell against the gallery rail, sliding down it to curl up in a bloody heap.

The guards were congratulating themselves when the real intruder stepped out of the room and onto the gallery. Bolan tracked in with his AK and cut the pair down where they stood, their blood spraying across the gallery and being washed away by the still hammering rain.

Moving past them, Bolan headed for the far end of the gallery, struck once again by the hard force of the downpour. He was heading for the east wing, hoping he was still in time to reach McCarter and Fayed before anything happened to them.

CHAPTER THIRTY

Bolan swung around the end of the gallery and saw stone steps leading down to ground level. Over his shoulder he could see thick smoke still billowing from the wrecked vehicles. The rain was dispersing the smoke before it rose very far into the air. From where he crouched at the head of the steps, concealed by the balustrade, he could see the pair of armed guards positioned at the heavy door of the square-built annex jutting from the side of the house. The one window he could see had a thick metal grille bolted on the outside. The two guards were agitated by what had been happening, but their orders were obviously to remain at their post. They were obeying that order but not the duty.

There was no time for hesitation. Bolan had no idea where or when he might be confronted by more of Razihra's security. If McCarter and Fayed were behind that locked door, he needed to find out now.

He rose to his feet, allowing himself a clear field of fire and raised the AK, flicking the select lever to single shot. He picked his first target and held his aim, easing back on the trigger. The crack of the rifle was followed by the target slumping back against the wall behind him, a 7.62 mm slug having cored in through his skull. As the first guard went down Bolan tracked in on the second, punching out two fast shots. The guard stumbled and went down without a sound. Bolan was moving down the steps before the second man hit the ground.

The heavy door was double-bolted. Bolan racked the bolts back and booted the door open.

"Travis? Fayed?"

The interior was stark. The only light that through the barred windows illuminated bare concrete floor and untreated stone walls. A pair of crude bunks was the only furniture.

McCarter sat on the edge of one bunk. Across from him Fayed, on his feet, had turned at the sound of Bolan's voice. From the badly bruised and bloody condition of their faces it was obvious their stay at Razihra's home had been less than pleasant.

"You going to sit there all day?" Bolan asked.

McCarter's unshaved, battered face turned his way. The Briton managed a weak smile. "Nice of you to drop in."

Bolan noticed then the bloody dressing around McCarter's left thigh. "Bad?"

"Rafik shot him at Wadi Hattat," Fayed said. "Razihra's people cut it out as part of their interrogation. They used a knife and no anesthetic. I would do the same to Rafik if I had the choice."

"He's already paid his dues," Bolan said.

"He is dead?"

Bolan nodded. "Can you help Travis?"

Fayed nodded. He moved to McCarter and helped the man up. McCarter was about to protest but Fayed hauled him over his shoulder, straightened and glanced at Bolan.

"Cooper, get us out of here."

Bolan checked outside. It was still clear. He bent and

snatched up the discarded AKs, handing one to Fayed and the other to McCarter.

"Not one of my most dignified exits," McCarter muttered from where he hung across Fayed's shoulders.

"Just be careful where you place that rifle," Fayed said.

They pressed hard against the wall. Bolan scanned the rain-swept area in front of them.

"We might have company, so keep your eyes open." He pointed to a distant stand of timber on the far side of the area. "That's where we're heading. Fayed, you move out and I'll cover you. Once you start keep moving. Don't stop for anything."

"We walking out of Iran?" McCarter asked conversationally.

"Got a ride coming in, but we'll need to buy some time until he gets here."

"Anyone we know?"

"Jack and his lady. Already on their way."

A distant shout warned them they weren't alone.

"Go. Reach those trees we have a chance to stay under cover."

As Fayed started out, Bolan turned and saw armed guards at the top of the gallery steps. He opened up with the AK, his burst blowing chunks of stone into the faces of the lead guards. He drew his aim down and caught one man in the chest. A second man took a slug in the shoulder and withdrew. Bolan freed a grenade, armed the bomb and tossed it to the head of the steps. The blast showered the area with debris and pushed the guards back. Bolan turned and followed Fayed as he splashed his way across the rain-soaked ground in the direction of the trees. McCarter bounced awkwardly on the man's shoulders.

They were a third of the way across when autofire reached their ears. The falling rain obscured the shooters' vision and the shots fell short, kicking up gouts of sodden earth. Bolan caught up with Fayed and gave a strong arm to support the Iranian and his burden. Despite the indignity of his position, McCarter managed to keep up a grudging banter. Bolan saw that the dressing on his leg had started to bleed, soaking through the rough bandage, and he realized the Briton would have been in considerable pain.

As the three men entered the welcome shelter of the trees the pursuing Iranians maintained their fire. Bullets struck the trunks, scattering bark chips and shredding the undergrowth.

"Keep moving," Bolan said.

He dropped back, resting his AK against a trunk, and took two of his remaining three grenades off his harness. He pulled the pins and eased into the shadows, waiting, listening to the advancing guards. The shooting had died, the Iranians conserving their ammunition until they were able to actually see their quarry. They moved in closer to the timberline, weapons probing ahead, searching the ragged fall of shadow in among the trees. Bolan remained still, watching as the Iranians paused, moving closer as they discussed their strategy. There appeared to be some dissention. One man was waving his arm, pointing in another direction, making a circling motion. Whatever his thoughts, they were ignored by the others, as they all indicated they should go directly into the trees.

Bolan knew he wasn't about to get a better chance. He released the lever on one grenade and threw the bomb in the direction of the grouped guards. It landed shorter than he had hoped, catching the attention of one man who screamed a warning. His cry was lost in the sharp crack of the exploding grenade. Men were hurled to the ground, lost in the confusion of the moment. Bolan repeated the move with the second grenade. He had already turned, snatching up the AK, and was swallowed up in the gloom as the explosion came. He pushed forward, picking up the trail left by Fayed, and caught up with the Iranian and McCarter a few minutes later.

"Fayed, let me take over," he said.

The Iranian offered no resistance as Bolan took McCarter from him. When there was no comment from the Phoenix Force leader, Bolan realized he had passed out. His AK hung from his neck by its strap.

"You go ahead," Fayed said. "I will watch our back trail."

Bolan struck out, checking his watch. He figured at three hours remained before Grimaldi and *Dragon Slayer* put in an appearance. It might even be dark by the time he showed.

Before Grimaldi left Incirlik for Diyarbakir, he and Bolan had pored over maps and satellite photographs provided by the Air Force. Grimaldi had indicated his best flight path, one that would follow the Turkish border with Azerbaijan until it merged with Iran. He would follow it until he hit the coastline of the Caspian Sea before turning south inland and the Alborz Mountains to make his pickup. Bolan's cell phone signal would be locked into *Dragon Slayer*'s computer system, the pinpoint accuracy being monitored by the Zero Platform and constantly updated to keep the combat chopper on course.

"No sweat, Sarge," Grimaldi had said. "I'll be there."

No sweat.

Bolan didn't need confirmation. It wasn't the first time he had placed his life in Grimaldi's hands and he doubted it would be the last. If the Stony Man pilot said he would show up, then he would.

THEY WERE DEEP INTO THE foothills of the Alborz Mountains now. The storm showed no sign of letting up. As they pushed farther into the hills it gained in strength, sweeping down from the higher slopes. The occasional rolls of thunder echoed down from the gray sky.

The sodden ground underfoot made travel difficult, slowing Bolan and Fayed. After an hour they were forced to call a halt, taking refuge in a thick stand of timber overgrown with heavy foliage. Bolan lowered the unconscious McCarter to the ground, checking the crude bandage on his leg. The wound was bleeding again.

Fayed was watching as Bolan did what he could with the bandage. "While they dug out the bullet he remained silent. He said nothing when they questioned him, or when they beat him."

"He wouldn't," Bolan said. "Travis has a stubborn streak that just won't let him quit. The harder he's pushed, the harder he gets."

"You could be describing yourself."

Bolan glanced at the Iranian. "Sometimes we are what we do."

"In your case I sense a difference. A man who battles hard but who can show compassion when needed. That is what separates you from the likes of Razihra. He tells everyone he is doing God's work. That what he desires is for the greater good of our country. But all he does is prepare to drag us into further suffering, with little thought for the hurt he creates. This nuclear thing he wants to thrust upon Iran. What purpose will it serve? It will anger many countries. Frighten others. I know America will frown on it and perhaps use it as an excuse to strike at us. So will the Israelis. You saw what Razihra was planning for them. He wanted to terrify them with his nerve gas. To kill as many as he could. Why? It would achieve nothing. You prevented that. But now the Israelis know his intentions and they will watch us even more, just waiting for the chance to attack us." Fayed held up his hands in a gesture of futility. "Tell me, Cooper, where will it end? Will it ever end, or do we prepare for more years of this senseless aggression between our peoples?"

"Smarter people than me most likely couldn't give you an answer to those questions, Amir. There should be an easier way. Good people are trying to talk to each other. That's important. But as long as the Razihras of this world are around, they have to be faced and dealt with. If they're not they could win by default. Somebody needs to make sure they don't win. I guess that's where we come in."

AYATOLLAH MUHAR RAZIHRA stared out through the side window of the JetRanger helicopter. He was tired and the last thing he needed was this trip back to Tehran. Too much had happened over the past few days. Each operation he commanded had been systematically torn apart, his people killed. His carefully laid plans corrupted. He was still having difficulty coming to terms with the destruction of the facility at Wadi Hattat. So much planning and preparation gone—the gathering of his people to work on the nuclear program, tis satisfaction when Nevski had procured Gregori Malinski to head the project. It had all gone well. The purchase of American technology that would enhance the development. The slow but certain advances as Malinski guided the team at Wadi Hattat through the intricacies of nuclear physics and how to relate them to a viable nuclear device.

But then things had started to fall apart, starting with the discovery of an infiltrator within Nevski's organization. The man had been eliminated, yet further mishaps began to occur, such as the loss of Novak and the man impersonating him getting as far as the secret camp in Jordan. Razihra refused to dwell on what had happened since then. It had culminated in the final indignity of having Wadi Hattat demolished and his lab teams compromised, leading to his decision to have them silenced in order to maintain his security.

The only glimmer of success had been the assassination of

Shahan Baresh, Masood's spokesman. The death of the negotiator had at least brought the planned talks to a halt. Following Baresh's death the conference had been canceled, at least until Baresh's funeral had taken place. Which was why Razihra was on his way back to Tehran. He had been summoned to attend, and to show a respectful face, he could hardly refuse.

It didn't sit well with Razihra. He needed to pursue some kind of recovery program so he could start work again on his nuclear research. His development program was to have been the crowning glory in his campaign to wrest control from Nuri Masood. The military had been depending on the success at Wadi Hattat to strengthen its grip on the country. With the financial backing from the Chinese, money had been no object. Beijing's long-term strategy had been focused on Iran becoming a dominant force in the region, even above Iraq. The American-led invasion of the country had deposed Hussein but had foundered as the warring factions within the country had lost Iraq its initial impetus. With its own nuclear capability Iran could have forged ahead, making the other nations within the Middle East region turn to her, even fall in behind. With the military strength, plus the vast oil reserves she held, Iran's potential could have been realized.

That potential might now become a redundant concept for the near future, until Razihra's dream of nuclear dominance was once again brought to fruition.

With Wadi Hattat in ruins and the progress of the research back at zero, Razihra was having to martial all his resources to begin again. It wasn't impossible, just time-consuming, unless he could find another route that might advance matters swiftly. There were, at least, two factors in his favor.

Anatoly Nevski was eager to offer his services, and the Chinese, in the shape of Fu Chen, still held true to their promises. They were willing to add more money to the pot and offer help in providing technology that would give Razihra's project another kick start.

Razihra's thoughts drifted back to the radio message. It had informed him of the hostile attack on his retreat in the Alborz Mountains. Working back on the time scale, Razihra realized he had only taken off from the retreat an hour prior to the attack. Substantial damage had been done to the house. His security force had been decimated and Rafik, the agent who had infiltrated the group working against him had been killed. The two captives apprehended at Wadi Hattat had been freed and were, at the time of the radio call, still on the run. Razihra's security force was searching for them. The captives, especially the man named Travis, were important pawns in Razihra's game. He hoped his people got them back. He would use them as political blackmail against both the West and also Masood. The Americans would pay dearly to keep their involvement in Iran's internal politics silenced, because Razihra knew without a doubt they were behind the strikes against his people and projects. The CIA mole, who had been instrumental in providing information and access to U.S. technology, had been in touch with Nevski. His report had indicated that the CIA Special Operations director had been in secret negotiations with the American President and from those talks the man calling himself Cooper had dealt himself into the game. Razihra couldn't fail to acknowledge the man's success at thwarting ongoing operations. His fighting skills and his survival techniques were without parallel, which had proved to be unfortunate as far as Razihra was concerned. Although he wasn't named in the radio report, Razihra was convinced that the man called Cooper was behind the attack on the mountain retreat.

How, he wondered, could one man keep turning up at locations so far apart?

The answer was so simple it almost eluded Razihra at first. Then he realized the solution. Cooper had to have moved with the cooperation of the U.S. military or one of its covert agencies. It had to be that. There was no other means by which a single individual could cross such distances using normal of travel. If the U.S. government was helping, then it was a culpable accomplice. If Razihra could gain some definite evidence of that, he could threaten to expose American influence in the affairs of another country.

Razihra reached for the helicopter's satellite phone, quickly tapping in a number he knew by heart.

"Anatoly? Good. Listen to me. We need evidence that the Americans have been involved in orchestrating these strikes against us. This man, Cooper, has been moved around by either military or agency assistance. Get your man to find out how it has been done and get his hands on something, anything, that will confirm this. If we can get such information, it will give us a lever to get the U.S. off our backs. Political embarrassment, especially with presidential elections on the horizon, wouldn't be welcome in America at this time. They already stand accused of unwarranted interference in the internal affairs of too many countries as it is."

"I'll see what can be done." Nevski paused. "Have you considered what we discussed earlier?"

"Yes. Let me get this funeral out of the way and then I will make the trip to discuss future matters with you. Anatoly, I have every confidence in you but…"

"But can we achieve your goal? Yes. Wadi Hattat was a great loss. Now we need to look forward and what I propose will get you where you want to be. You have Anatoly Nevski's word on that, and I *never* let my clients down."

"Thank you, my friend. I will speak with you after tomorrow."

"Arrangements will be in place. I look forward to our meeting."

"THEY ARE CLOSER," FAYED SAID.

Bolan eased to his side, wiping rain from his face. He followed the Iranian's finger and made out the shapes moving upslope. He counted at least four.

"There'll be more," he said. "Flanking us. Check the other side."

Fayed moved away, the rain striking the foliage covering any noise he might have made.

Checking McCarter, Bolan saw the Briton was awake, watching him.

"This wasn't in the game plan," McCarter said. "I was supposed to be watching *your* back."

Bolan had turned so he could monitor the progress of Razihra's men. "You aren't going to start grumbling?"

"I might. A wounded man's allowed to have a moan now and then."

"Just don't make it your life's work," Bolan said, grinning.

"Striker, is Flyboy going to make it?"

"He'd be hurt if he heard you even asking that."

McCarter fell silent. When Bolan turned he saw McCarter had slipped into unconsciousness again. Blood loss was taking its toll. He checked his watch and debated whether he should call Grimaldi. He decided against that. Knowing the man as he did, *Dragon Slayer* would be pushing the limit. When Jack Grimaldi was on a team pickup, nothing mattered except getting there. If necessary he would fight off the Iranian air force if he had to.

The crackle of autofire caught Bolan's attention. It came from the direction Fayed had taken. He heard the Iranian's weapon respond, caught the flicker of muzzle-flashes. The firing alerted the four guards advancing on Bolan's position. They broke apart, increasing their pace as they began to lay down covering fire. A valley of 7.62 mm slugs clipped the foliage around Bolan.

He set his own AK for single shot, bracing his weapon with the sling around his arm, and tracked in on the closest hostile. The guards were well in range now, which lay them open to Bolan's marksmanship. His sniping skills had served him well over the long years of his personal war, and they were ingrained in him now to the point where he didn't need to even think about what he was doing. Bolan had used the Kalashnikov many times. He knew the weapon's potential, range, muzzle velocity. Its killing power. He employed all those qualities now as he brought the leading guard into his sights, allowing for the angle of the slope and the drift of the wind that was slanted the rain across the mountain slopes. His finger eased back on the trigger, held, then completed his pull. The AK cracked once, the sharp sound lost quickly. The guard paused in midstride, head snapping backward as the steel jacket cored into his skull just above his left eye. The force tossed him back and he tumbled down the slope in the loose, formless way the dead assumed.

The moment he fired Bolan tracked in on the next target, acquiring and firing before the man could conceal himself. His shot struck the side of the guard's head, blowing out the top of the skull in a misty spurt of bloody bone and brains.

As the second man went down, his surviving partners opened fire on Bolan's position, wasting ammunition on full-auto. Bolan and McCarter, already flat to the ground, were below the trajectory of the volleys.

The Executioner let the firing cease, still able pinpoint the guards on the slope below him, even after they had dropped to the ground themselves. He had both their positions locked in his mind, able to make out the bulk of their bodies behind the tangled foliage. They were about eight feet apart, maintaining stationary poses. Bolan imagined they would be assessing their chances of getting clear and staying alive now that they had realized how exposed they were. He had no intention of allowing them the opportunity to formulate a plan.

The firing from Fayed's position had leveled out to a sporadic exchange, each side taking an occasional shot. The Iranian would have to hold his own until Bolan dealt with his confrontation.

A sudden heavy gust of wind swept rain across the slope. It temporarily disturbed the foliage around Bolan, exposing him, and one of the guards saw his chance, rising from his own cover and opening fire. His weapon was still on full-auto and he fired in haste, before he had locked on to his target. Autofire at short range could be effective, but lost some of its value over a longer distance. Slugs buried themselves in the sodden earth feet below Bolan's vantage point. He held his position, bringing the AK online and laid a single shot in the shooter's chest, spinning him aside. As the man began to fall, Bolan hit him with a second shot that took him in the side, cleaving a rib bone before it pierced his lung.

Out of the corner of his eye Bolan saw the remaining guard rising, hoping to take advantage of his partner's hasty move. The man's assault rifle was already lining up on Bolan as the black-clad figure rolled aside. The single shot cored into the slope where the soldier had been a second before, raising a spout of sodden earth and grass. The Iranian guard swung his rifle to follow the big American, but lost his target as Bolan rolled again, this time back to where he had been lying before. The move confused the guard, only for an instant, but it was long enough for Bolan to lock on and fire, his finger stroking the trigger three times, each 7.62 mm round lodging in the target's chest.

On his feet, Bolan ran in a low crouch, directing himself to where Fayed was still firing. The driving rain beat against his face, blurring his vision until he wiped his eyes to clear them. He stopped short of the Iranian's location, tight against the trunk of a tree and scanned the slope below Fayed's position. To his right he saw Fayed, secure behind a grassy mound, exchanging shots with a shooter yards downslope. A second guard was keeping Fayed pinned in his defensive position, allowing the first guard to move in closer with each exchange. Bolan saw a third guard, flat on his back to the far right of Fayed.

Snugging the AK against his shoulder, Bolan tracked in on the guard pinning Fayed down. He waited until the man paused to snap in a fresh magazine, the fired. Bolan's shot drove in through the back of the shooter's skull and blew out below his left eye. The man half rose, then pitched face-forward to slide down the wet slope. The remaining guard, seeing his partner go down and realizing he was now outnumbered, backed away, half sliding, half crawling until he dropped into a hollow that hid him completely. Bolan laid a few shots across the rim of the hollow to persuade the man to stay out of sight.

Catching Fayed's eye, Bolan signaled him to move back to their original position.

"I let myself get outflanked," the Iranian said. "Glad you were around."

"I had to do something otherwise I'd have to carry Travis all the way myself."

Fayed took McCarter for the first stretch as they pushed on up the higher slopes, battered by the wind and the rain. Thunder still rumbled in the lofty peaks.

"I won't imagine Iran as all desert ever again," Bolan said.

"This part of the country always surprises people," Fayed said. He jerked his head in the direction of the peaks. "Get beyond those mountains and the climate soon changes to what they expect of Iran." He turned to look at Bolan. "Right now I would welcome some hot sun and warm sand under my feet."

Bolan held up a hand, silencing the Iranian. He was staring down slope, back the way they had come. He appeared to have heard, or seen, something. Fayed was unaware of anything, but he trusted the big American's instincts. He waited, not wanting to break Bolan's concentration. After a time the soldier leaned back.

"Tell me," Fayed said.

"Helicopter coming in."

"Your pickup?"

Bolan shook his head. "Too soon for that. And the engine noise is different. This isn't what we're waiting for. Someone's called in backup. There must be a military base in the area."

"There will be one outside Ramsar."

Bolan took a look around. "We need better cover. We're still exposed here."

They angled across the sloping ground, Bolan pointing Fayed in the direction of a rocky stretch. They broke out of the timber and had to cross open terrain to reach the rocky area. The wind dragged at their clothing, slowing them, and they were still yards from cover when Bolan heard the familiar sound of rotors. He had been hoping they could gain the protection of the rocks before the chopper reached them, but that wasn't going to happen. Bolan turned to see the helicopter swooping down out of the rain, heading directly for them.

"Fayed, keep moving. Get to cover," he yelled above the roar of the helicopter's engine.

He stood between Fayed and the chopper as it dropped lower. The pilot had to juggle the controls as the side wind kept pushing against the fuselage and threatening to nudge it off course. Bolan dropped to one knee and shouldered the AK, angling the muzzle up at the approaching aircraft. He began to pull the trigger, attempting to lay his shots into the Plexiglas canopy. It was more of an attempt to make the pilot ease back rather than an expectation to disable the helicopter. He knew he had scored at least one hit when the chopper pulled back. The pilot opened up with the underslung machine gun, the line of 30 mm shells gouging up chunks of sodden earth to Bolan's left. They were close enough to make him move. He jacked out the last of the magazines rounds, then pushed to his feet and made a run for cover, scrambling around the edge of the rocks where Fayed and McCarter were concealed. The moment he was under cover Bolan ejected the empty mag and retrieved his final one from his side pocket. He watched the helicopter as he clicked the mag in place and cocked the assault rifle.

"He's not going away now," Bolan said. "More likely he'd directing the ground team right to where we're sitting."

"Maybe you can try another shot at him."

"He'll stay out of range now. Just hover and keep us spotted."

Bolan twisted and checked out the rocky area. The jumbled rocks, overgrown in places with thick foliage, marched up the steeper slope behind their position. He scanned the spread of rocks. They covered a wide expanse of the slope.

"What are you thinking, Cooper? That we can work our way out of this place?"

"Right now we don't have many choices. Two in fact. Stay here and wait for the ground team, or try to get clear before they come."

"I never was one for just sitting around."

Bolan hoisted McCarter over his shoulders. He took his AK from Fayed.

"Let's move," he said. "Down that drop and under the foliage. We can follow it up to the next level."

"You will be all right?"

"Ask me in a few minutes."

They worked their way between the rocks, the dense foliage providing cover as they made a slow climb through the tangle of stone and greenery. Bolan was hoping the falling rain would reduce the vision of the helicopter's occupants for long enough. If they could move clear of the original position and reach a higher level of the slope, they might avoid the spotters in the aircraft. The heavy weather might work in their favor in this instance.

Bolan found that the same criteria applied to them, as well. McCarter's solid weight across his shoulders made progress slow. With only one hand free, he found climbing difficult. And though the overgrowth of tangled greenery shielded them from the helicopter, it didn't prevent the torrential rain from spilling through, wetting the ground underfoot and drenching them constantly. Fayed picked up Bolan's problem and moved in close to add his support. Between them they spent an exhausting thirty minutes working their way up the slope, hampered by the conditions and the loose ground under their feet. They stumbled, grazing their hands and faces on the coarse rocks, but there was no other option open to them, and they were committed now to getting clear.

As they took a break, Bolan eased McCarter to the ground and worked his way to where he was able to see through the intertwined foliage. The helicopter was still hovering in the same area, turning back and forth in slow arcs. The pilot had obviously decided that getting too close was only liable to get him shot at again and was staying just out of range. Which at least allowed Bolan and Fayed some leeway. That might change with the arrival of the grounds troops. With that in mind Bolan bent and hoisted McCarter into position.

"You go ahead, Amir. See if you can pick an easy route."

The Iranian pushed by and moved ahead.

Bolan denied the existence of aching, bruised muscles as he fell in behind the man. McCarter stirred restlessly for a time but made no more movement. The foliage reduced daylight, throwing uneven shadows where Bolan was walking and, combined with the loose ground, made it hard to see what was underfoot. Up ahead Fayed missed his way and loose rocks slid in a miniavalanche, helped on their way by the water running down from the higher slopes. Bolan tried to avoid the slide, falling back against the slabs of rock. He kept a grip on McCarter as he regained his footing.

"Cooper?"

"I'm okay."

If Fayed made a response, Bolan failed to hear it as the heavy sound of the helicopter reached them. Bolan looked up through the tangled foliage and made out the dark bulk of the machine as it moved overhead. The crew in the chopper had realized that the silence from their quarry had indicated a change in tactics. Flying over the spot where Bolan and Fayed had taken cover would have confirmed that. Now the crew was on the hunt again, and it wasn't going to take them long to figure out what had happened.

The chopper pulled back, the deafening sound receding. Bolan knew it was temporary. The pilot wanted to get into position for a strike.

"We need to get out of here," Bolan said as Fayed joined him. He indicated a gap in the rocks. "That way. Go, Amir."

The Iranian turned and pushed his way between the rocks, Bolan following. They moved awkwardly over loose stones and slimy mud washed down from the slopes. Bolan was starting to feel the weight of his Stony Man partner. McCarter's bulk added to the difficulty of working his way through the narrow defiles in the rocks. A couple of times Bolan's footing missed solid ground and he went to his knees, struggling to rise again. But he did gain his feet, gripping McCarter tightly, his AK hanging by its sling around his neck. Forcing his way through the rain-slick rocks, his body begging for relief, Bolan kept moving.

The sudden thunder of the aircraft's machine gun drowned even the falling rain. The hot fusillade sent streams of 30 mm shells on target. They ripped through the greenery, shredding everything in their path, scoring the rocks themselves. The pilot eased the helicopter the length of the strip, then curved off and made a wide sweeping return, hovering again.

Bolan caught up with Fayed as they rounded a large outcrop. He slumped against the rough surface, easing McCarter off his shoulders and lowering him to the ground. He dropped to his knees and checked McCarter. The Briton turned his head and eyed Bolan.

"You look worse than me, mate," he said.

"Think so?"

Fayed was watching the stationary helicopter as it moved back and forth. "They will call in the ground team soon."

"We need to reach higher ground," Bolan said. "An open area for our pickup."

"Can't be soon enough for me," McCarter stated.

"Come on, let's keep moving," Bolan said.

"I will take him now," Fayed offered.

"This time I'll walk," McCarter said. "I've been holding you two back long enough."

"You can't…"

McCarter used the rock at his back to push to his feet, freeing the AK around his neck. He checked the magazine and cocked the weapon. "I'm all right."

Bolan knew there was little to be gained by arguing with the stubborn Briton. And he was aware of McCarter's need to be independent. He would have felt the same in McCarter's position. He consoled himself with the fact that if McCarter did keel over, there were two of them around to offer help.

They moved out, Fayed in the lead, with McCarter in the second position and Bolan brining up the rear. They paced themselves to fit with McCarter's slow shuffle. He made an effort, but he was unable to move very fast, his leg hindering his movements.

On the far side of the outcropping, the rocks gave way to timber and lush vegetation. They were also exposed for a stretch, the rain adding to their discomfort. Bolan noticed the buildup of heavy clouds over the distant peaks, moving in their direction. The storm wasn't likely to fade away for some time.

The crackle of autofire interrupted his thoughts. It came from behind them. Bolan turned and saw a number of gunners slogging across the slope to their right, the bulk of the helicopter moving to join them.

"Get to the trees," Bolan yelled.

He turned to face the oncoming hostiles, shouldering his AK and holding his aim as he tracked one of the distant men. He could see the wink of the muzzle-flash as the man fired on the move, heard the sodden chunk as the slugs struck the soft earth. Bolan had his sights on the moving figure, seeing the man slip and stumble on the rain-slick slope. He led his target for a few seconds to lock on, then stroked the trigger. The Kalashnikov snapped out its shot and the target stopped, arms thrown wide before he went facedown the grassy slope. Life ended in that moment, instantly, the man going from existence to nothing in the space of a heartbeat.

Bolan turned and followed the distant figures of Fayed and McCarter. The Briton was struggling to keep up, only his stubborn refusal to quit keeping him on his feet. Fayed, looking back over his shoulder, saw McCarter's slow advance and fell back to cover him. Bolan closed up, and he and Fayed formed a defensive shield behind the man. The crackle of autofire added to the urgency of their withdrawal into the timber. Bullets slapped the trunks, tearing out ragged chunks of bark. As they entered the shadowed closure of the trees, Bolan heard the rapid delivery of the helicopter's machine gun again, the 30 mm slugs thumping into the ground, then the trees.

McCarter, using a substantial oak for cover, dropped to one knee. He brought up the AK and braced himself against the rough trunk. The AK's muzzle rose and he began to fire off single rounds at the rain-blurred outline of the chopper, hot casings jumping from the ejection port as he targeted the attacking aircraft. Leaving McCarter to his task Bolan and Fayed engaged the ground team working its way out from the rock formation and across the open stretch. Fayed made the first hit, his 7.62 mm slug taking the target's leg from under him. The guy went down, clutching his shattered thigh, blood oozing between his fingers from the ragged tear. Bolan spotted a pair of hostiles coming in from their extreme left, making a wide loop that brought them parallel with the ragged tree line. He altered his shooting stance, swinging around and laying down a solid wall of fire that put one man down with bullets in his chest and the surviving man hugging his neck where a steel jacket had clipped his main artery. The other hostiles dropped for cover.

The looming shape of the helicopter began to pull back, veering to left and right before it slipped from sight below the slope.

"You hit him?" Bolan asked.

McCarter scowled at him. "Is it that hard to believe?"

"Not really. I was wondering why it took you so long."

Even McCarter had to smile at that. "Bloody cheek. I think I just cracked his windshield. He's probably just gone to change his undershorts."

"Let's not waste the chance to move on," Bolan said.

They pulled back deeper into the timber, letting the closeness of the trees and the spread of vegetation swallow them. The high canopy reduced the rain's intensity. Within the forested area the air was stifling and smelled of decay. Underfoot the thick layer of mold deadened the sound of their passing.

"WHY HAVE YOU RETREATED?"

"Captain, they almost shot me down."

"Get back up there. If you do not I will have you shot myself. For cowardice."

The helicopter pilot held back from making any further reply. He simply closed down his microphone. "Easy for him to say," he said to his copilot.

"He might think differently if he could see what I'm looking at right now."

He meant the 7.62 mm bullet that was lodged in the Plexiglas windshield of the helicopter.

"If that was a test of my faith, I think I passed."

"Are we going back up there?"

The pilot stared at his companion. "What do you think? I would rather have that bullet fired at me again than defy Captain Shiraz. You did know he is a distant cousin of Ayatollah Razihra? No, obviously not, or you would not have asked such a foolish question."

SHIRAZ PASSED THE HANDSET back to the radio operator. He sat back in the seat of the 4x4, watching rain drive against the windshield. He hated being out in this weather, driving back and forth across the treacherous slopes, watching his men struggle against the elements. He demanded obedience from them, even though he knew they weren't at fault. The sudden storm had caught them all unaware. The weather in this part of the country could change in an instant, from calm, warm days to fierce rain that swept down off the high Alborz peaks. Then there might be weeks when not a drop of rain fell.

He stared up through the haze of rain at the misty heights thinking about the three fugitives his teams were pursuing. Despite the inclement weather, or perhaps because of it, they were making fools of Shiraz's men. And taking a deadly toll of them. Shiraz had taken a tour of Razihra's retreat before he had come into the field. He had been shocked at the damage to the residence and the security force. The lone intruder who had freed Razihra's captives had hit the place hard, taking out a large number of the guards before releasing the prisoners. And since the three of them had been on the run the toll had risen. Enemies of the state they might have been, but Shiraz had to respect their skill and their bravery. Even now, with a stronger force still advancing, they were putting up strong resistance.

Razihra wouldn't see it that way. Over time his bitterness against the West had burned away whatever humanity he might once have possessed. It had turned him sour, with little joy for life left in him. His secular existence allowed him little else. He was overly single-minded, driven by his greed for power and control. That desire had become a fever that consumed him, taking away his ability to even consider compromise when it came to negotiation with the Americans. He saw them as voracious enslavers who wanted to tear apart Iran and squeeze it dry, a nation of murderous people intent on supplicating the people and crushing them beneath their boots.

The Americans and their greedy allies, the Israelis, would divide Iran between them. They would seize the oil and all the other riches of the country, leaving nothing for the Iranians themselves. It was a black-and-white scenario in Razihra's eyes. He refused to consider any other way forward than intimidation and confrontation. It was his way or death.

Shiraz recalled his conversation with Razihra a short while ago. His orders had been explicit, with no allowance for failure. Razihra wanted the three hunted down, captured alive if possible. They could not be allowed to escape the country. It didn't matter how many were sacrificed as long as the fugitives were brought to justice.

A sharp rap on the window snapped Shiraz out of his thoughts. It was his sergeant. Shiraz turned up the collar of his coat as he opened the door and stepped out into the rain.

"The second squad is in position, Captain," the sergeant informed him.

Shiraz nodded. "Let's get this done. Do they have the targets spotted?"

"As well as they can in this weather, sir."

"Don't apologize, sergeant, I'm not that happy with the situation either."

"Do we commence firing?"

Shiraz nodded. The sergeant gave the order to the radio man, who passed the command to the team higher along the slope. Moments later the first mortar round was fired.

CHAPTER THIRTY-ONE

It was more by chance that Bolan saw the smoke as the mortar left the tube.

"Incoming," he yelled, turning to flag down McCarter and Fayed.

They hugged the ground, hearing the soft moan as the mortar round dropped and exploded thirty feet away. The earth heaved, the explosion lifting dirt and shredding timber in a dark burst.

"Fall back," Bolan ordered. "They'll drop a few more and move in under the cover."

They broke from their position and pushed deeper into the timber, hearing additional mortar rounds fall. The explosions rocked the earth under their feet. Bolan counted at least half a dozen detonations. He could imagine the ground teams working their way up to the tree line, weapons ready as they searched for their targets. Pushing on by the smoking craters left by the mortars, searching to see if there were any casualties and reporting back they had found nothing. That would bring the order to continue the pursuit.

It wasn't over yet.

The flat crackle of autofire came minutes later, followed by the vicious sound of bullets tearing at the foliage. More clipped at tree bark, thudded into solid trunks. Distant shouts wafted up the hill as the pursuers came on, guiding each other, searching the moving shadows, falling into an irregular skirmish line.

Bolan checked his AK. He was down to his final magazine. When that was out of ammunition he would change to the Uzi, and he still had his handguns and a single grenade. McCarter and Fayed had only the single magazines that had come with the AKs. He glanced at his watch. At least forty minutes remained before Grimaldi showed up. It was going to be close.

McCarter, limping badly, turned and crouched beside a thick oak. He could see the advancing enemy gunners moving in and out of the gloom. The Briton watched for a few seconds, then raised the assault rifle and picked his fist target. The sharp crack of the AK was followed by the distant target going down hard. McCarter had already pinpointed his next target, arcing the AK's muzzle to the left the moment he fired his first shot. The uniformed figure, seeing his closest companion go down, jerked off to one side, seeking solid cover. He was fast enough and McCarter's second shot caught him in the chest, slamming him to the forest floor.

Pulling back, McCarter caught up with Bolan who was covering him.

"Minus two," the Briton said. "Will I be glad when Jack shows up. I haven't seen so much bloody rain since I was in Manchester last."

Bolan let him move ahead, falling in behind, keeping his eye on the distant gunners. They had hung back briefly after McCarter had taken down two of their number, but were starting to advance again. The occasional shot was fired but had little effect at the distance.

Fayed raised an arm, beckoning Bolan to his side. He indicated the way ahead. The trees were thinning out, showing a series of slopes covered with thick foliage and a scattering of rocks.

"If they are thinking ahead, the helicopter could be waiting for us to come out into the open."

Bolan saw the sense in the Iranian's argument. As long as they remained within the cover of the timber, the chopper crew had little chance of seeing them, but once they emerged it could target them without difficulty.

"We don't have much choice, Amir. Our pickup isn't going to get to us unless we're in the open. And we can't hang around in here with those armed guys on our tail."

Fayed shrugged. "Then we must go."

They covered the final stretch, reaching the edge of the forested area. Bolan scanned the way ahead—thirty feet of exposed ground before they could slip into the cover of the closest rocky section. They crouched and studied the terrain. The big American was the first to notice that the rain was easing off.

"You two go ahead. I'll hold our pursuers back as long as I can."

"Not for *too* long," McCarter advised him.

"Go on, get out of here."

McCarter and Fayed broke cover and headed across the open ground, the Iranian staying close to the Briton, who was still favoring his leg. Bolan dropped to the sodden ground, leveling the AK and peered back through the trees and undergrowth. He saw movement and picked out the uniformed gunners emerging from the gloom. He selected his first target, holding the sight steady, then stroked the trigger, putting the man down with a single shot. Return fire tore at the foliage over his head. The shooters were mistakenly assuming their enemy was firing from an upright position.

Bolan used the distraction to change his position, wriggling around the base of a towering tree, using its solid bulk as cover. Leaning into the trunk, he steadied his rifle, tracking another enemy as the cautious figure pushed out through thick foliage. Bolan shot struck the guy in the chest, knocking him to his knees. Going for a second shot, the soldier realized the AK was out of ammunition. He dropped the empty weapon, rolled to a crouch and pulled the slung Uzi into position. Seeing a number of armed figures coming into view, Bolan took his remaining grenade, pulled the pin and threw the bomb in the direction of the group. The moment it detonated he pushed to his feet, turned and sprinted after McCarter and Fayed.

The echo of the explosion was still audible as Bolan headed for distant cover. Then by the too familiar thrum of helicopter rotors beat the air as the enemy aircraft rose into view above the tops treetops. It angled in toward the running men, the underslung machine gun opening up. A line of heavy-caliber slugs thunked into the sodden earth, kicking up dark spurts of soil. Bolan felt debris strike his legs as he weaved toward the rocks. The thunder of the helicopter filled his ears as it overshot his position, making a tight curve as the pilot tried to make a return run.

Ahead of Bolan, McCarter was leaning against a large rock, his AK raised as he pumped shot after shot at the chopper. As Bolan reached him the Briton lowered his rifle, shaking his head in anger.

"Bloody hell, my eye must be off. I could have sworn I hit that bastard a couple of times. He was low enough for me to count the rivets on his underbelly."

"He'll be back," Bolan said, "so let's move before he shows up again."

McCarter nodded and they worked their way to where Fayed was waiting for them.

"Your man—will he make it?"

"If he doesn't, it means no one could make it," Bolan said.

He took out the cell phone he had been carrying in his combat vest and thumbed the key that would link him to *Dragon Slayer.* He waited as the sat link made its connection and then heard Grimaldi's voice, faint but audible.

"Hey, Sarge, you checking up on me?"

"Buddy, we need you. We're under fire. I have one walking wounded and ammo is running low. Apart from that, we're doing fine."

"Sarge, you still know how to make a guy feel guilty. I have your signal on lock. I'm on the last leg, so hang in there. Stay hard, pal."

Bolan keyed off.

"Incoming chopper," McCarter yelled. "That bugger is starting to piss me off big-time."

The dark outline of the helicopter came in from south of their position, swooping low as it angled across the slope. The rattle of its machine gun added to the general din. Thirty millimeter shells tore at the earth, scored off jutting rocks, the line of fire coming close to their position. The chopper passed over them, banking sharply to make yet another run, and as it cleared the area more firing came from the ground team. It was a coordinated attack, the chopper used as a distraction so the men on foot could launch their strike.

"I think they forgot one thing," McCarter said as he turned to face the advancing opposition. "They have to move across open ground and face an upgrade."

The Briton had gauged the conditions correctly. The enemy might have had more people, but they were committing themselves to a wet, soft slope that hampered their progress and left them exposed to hostile fire.

"Their choice," Bolan said.

"More likely Razihra's choice," Fayed stated. "He would have given the order to their commander. No excuses. No quarter."

Bolan raised the Uzi, his finger easing back on the trigger. The SMG crackled fiercely. Beside him McCarter and Fayed cut loose with their own weapons, and between them they sent a blistering burst of fire that cut into the advancing figures. Men went down, some permanently, others twisting in agony from wounds. The attack was short-lived. Before Razihra's force could establish itself, the gunners were forced back to distant cover, dragging their wounded with them. They had fired off a few rounds before they were driven back.

"If I get my hands on that Razihra bloke, I won't need a bloody gun," McCarter said. "I'll rip his throat out."

"Now you see how Razihra uses everyone," Fayed said. "He doesn't care who gets killed as long as his orders are carried out."

"If we get the chance," Bolan said, "we'll have to make some changes."

CAPTAIN SHIRAZ SNATCHED THE handset from the radio operator. "Sergeant?"

"We took a number of casualties, Captain. They have the advantage of being on higher ground."

"The helicopter? Where is the damned helicopter?"

"About to make another run."

"If they give you enough cover try again."

"Yes, Captain."

"Sergeant, do not sacrifice your men needlessly. And if anyone asks you can say *I* gave you that order."

"Yes, sir."

Shiraz handed back the handset, then turned to his driver. "Get me up there as close as you can."

The driver rolled the 4x4 forward, taking it up the rising slope.

HE'S PERSISTENT," McCARTER SAID, watching the helicopter drop lower. "I just hope he has a good pension plan."

The Briton was flat to the ground, the AK tracking the chopper as it inched forward by degrees. The pilot was taking no chances this time around. He was unable to see his targets, so he was making no risky maneuvers until he could be certain of his position.

Bolan and Fayed had concealed themselves in the dense foliage. McCarter had found himself a hollow in the muddy earth at the base of a slab of stone. Constant exposure, rain and time had eroded the underside of the slab, leaving an overhanging rim that had offered McCarter the ideal location to secrete himself and wait for his opportunity.

Until Grimaldi showed up there was little else they could do. As the heavy rain slackened, offering the attack group a window of opportunity, Bolan and his partners were left with little choice except to defend themselves. Low on ammunition, with nowhere left to run, they had to stay put.

"WE HAVE THEM PINNED DOWN," the helicopter pilot radioed to Captain Shiraz, "on the eastern section of the slopes, less than a quarter mile from your position. Captain, do we take them down?"

"My orders are to take them alive if humanly possible."

"I have feeling they will resist to the end."

"You and me both. Lay down some hard fire around their position. Make it uncomfortable for them."

"I understand. Out."

Shiraz raised his eyes and watched the circling helicop-

ter. It turned and took up a position where it had a clear sight
of the enemy. Moments later the machine gun began to fire.

"Let's get up there," Shiraz ordered his driver.

THE PROLONGED BURSTS OF cannon fire ravaged the area.
Gouts of sodden earth, shredded foliage and stone chips filled
the air. The heavy-caliber shells shrieked down on Bolan and
his partners. There was little they could do but remain under
cover and hope that the intention was to pin them down and
not wipe them out.

Bolan considered making a break, but dismissed the thought
almost immediately. That would be part of the strategy. To get
them to panic and run. Once they did that, exposing themselves
on the open slopes, the chopper's gunner could make his decision on whether to end it there and then or to hold them in his
sights until the ground teams caught up. Either way they were
between a rock and a hard place. Surrender? Bolan didn't even
want to entertain that notion. Razihra wanted his fugitives alive
and under restraint so he could use them for his own advantage. If they were captured, there would be little chance to make
another break. Razihra's people would make sure of that. Allowing them to escape once was bad enough. If they let it happen again they would be in as much trouble as the escapees.

The helicopter flew in closer, the rate of fire maintained.
The earth around Bolan was alive with shell hits. He was
showered with wet earth, his ears ringing from the excessive
fire. He felt the Uzi in his hands and realized that it was useless. The SMG didn't have the power or the range to deal with
a hovering helicopter. The only one capable of offering any
kind of resistance was McCarter.

YARDS AWAY, BURROWED DEEP in the sticky wallow of mud
under the rocky ledge, David McCarter was studying the he-

licopter. He already had his AK in firing position, waiting his chance. The aircraft *was* in range, but taking a killing shot needed more than that. The AK, for all its merits, wasn't a heavy-caliber weapon. The 7.62 mm ammunition had its limits. On one-to-one combat against a human target it was fine. It had proved its worth over decades, on battlefields across the globe, and McCarter had employed it endless times. Here on this windy slope, with the rain still falling, he was contemplating using it against a machine. He accepted he had gained a lucky hit earlier, scoring the Plexiglas canopy, but even that hadn't brought down the machine. He was hoping for a surer hit this time, one that might destroy the helicopter and give them the opportunity to make a break.

Well, David, my son, he thought, you'd better make this one hell of a shot because once you start shooting, that pilot is going to be one pissed-off Iranian and he'll start shooting for effect.

Ignoring the cold, clammy feel of the mud he was lying in, McCarter sighted along the AK, bringing the muzzle into target acquisition. He could see the solid bulk of the aircraft, the orange wink of flame from the machine gun. He saw the aircraft yaw slightly to one side as the pilot brought it around and heard the slam of shells hitting the rock above his head, felt the rain of stone fragments around him. It made him wonder if the pilot could actually see him and was making this personal.

If it isn't for you, chum, it bloody well is for me, McCarter thought.

The Briton slid his finger across the trigger, holding his target. He sucked in a breath and held it, the AK's muzzle rock steady in the moment before he gently squeezed the trigger and felt the rifle kick back as it fired. Out the corner of his eye he saw the shell casing flip from the ejection port and spin over and over as it dropped.

The helicopter erupted in an expanding ball of flame, totally disintegrating before McCarter's stunned gaze. It blew apart, scattering flaming debris across a wide area, dropping to earth with a solid crash. Smoke tailed in after the flame, rising into the gray sky, almost concealing a hovering black shape that began to move in, dropping lower as it pinpointed their position.

It took a moment before McCarter acknowledged he was looking at the Stony Man combat helicopter *Dragon Slayer.*

BOLAN HAD SEEN *Dragon Slayer* a second before Grimaldi's missile took out the helicopter, turning it into a boiling fireball that dropped and spread itself across the mountain slope. He turned to check on the advancing ground teams and saw they were still coming. The destruction of the chopper made them halt, staring up at the incandescent ball of flame that had been their backup. He knew the shock would evaporate quickly and the motionless crew would continue its advance. He pushed to his feet, turning to where McCarter and Fayed lay.

"Let's go," he yelled.

McCarter and Fayed appeared, heading across the open slope in the direction of the matt-black helicopter as Grimaldi swung in to hover a couple of feet off the ground. The side hatch slid open, offering a safe haven. Bolan and Fayed moved up to the limping Briton, grabbing his arms to ease his progress, and for once the Phoenix Force leader didn't object. They manhandled him up to the hatch and pushed him inside without ceremony.

A barrage of autofire flew at them, 7.62 mm slugs striking the ground in their wake. Bolan turned to see a couple of uniformed men haul themselves over the last ridge of the slope, firing as they advanced on *Dragon Slayer.* He brought the Uzi up and triggered a burst that forced the men apart. Moving slightly away from *Dragon Slayer,* Bolan locked on and brought down one of the Iranians, catching the guy in the hip and lower torso. The man dropped to the ground, clutching his riddled body. His partner hesitated, glancing at the wounded man, then angled his AK in Bolan's direction again, only to receive a killing burst from the Uzi that spilled his blood in the rain-sodden earth.

Bolan turned and dived toward the hatch, scrambling inside beside Fayed who was bending over McCarter, his hands clamped over the bleeding leg wound. Bolan hit the button and the hatch slid closed, sealing itself shut.

"Go, Jack, go!" Bolan yelled. "Get us the hell out of here."

He felt *Dragon Slayer* power up as Grimaldi hit the throttles. The deep whine of the powerful turbines pushed the helicopter up and around. The Stony Man pilot had already laid in the return course, the combat chopper's integrated computer system plotting and setting the parameters for the flight back to Turkey.

The urge to just stay where he was, surrounded by *Dragon Slayer*'s safe environment, was almost overwhelming. Bolan was weary, his body begging for time to recover, but he found himself looking at Fayed bending over the muddy, prone figure of McCarter, and concern for his friend pushed his own thoughts to the back of his mind. Bolan moved across the cabin and reached to open one of the fixed lockers. He dragged out a med kit and laid it on the cabin floor. He slid his combat knife from its sheath and passed it to Fayed.

"Get that wound exposed."

Fayed nodded and started to cut away cloth from around the bloody bandage.

Bolan had a hypodermic needle in his hand. It was a sedative dose, already prepared for use. He broke the plastic cap and leaned over to inject the fluid into McCarter's arm after pushing up his sleeve.

"Hey, that hurt."

"It'll hurt you more than it does me," Bolan said.

"I thought that was supposed to be the other way around."

Bolan grinned. "Not this time, pal. I've waited a long time to stick a needle into you."

"Bloody Yanks."

Fayed had exposed the raw wound in McCarter's leg. He began to clean the bloody area. "He needs expert medical attention. Anything we do will only be temporary."

"Once we get to Incirlik they'll get him to the base hospital," Bolan said. "Amir, I need to talk to the pilot. You'll be okay?"

Fayed nodded, then reached out to grasp Bolan's arm. "Thank you, my friend. I owe my life to you. It will not be forgotten."

"No problem. But I have a feeling we still have something left to do."

CAPTAIN SHIRAZ SURVEYED THE wrecked helicopter. His sergeant was advancing across the slope.

"They have gone," he said. "We failed to stop them, Captain."

Shiraz managed a weary smile at the obvious comment. "So we did, Sergeant. They fought a good fight. Recall your men. Arrange for the wounded and the dead to be returned to base. There's nothing else to be done up here."

"You will inform the Ayatollah?"

"In time, Sergeant, in time. Right now I am more concerned about the men. Razihra can wait until I am ready."

"Yes, sir," the sergeant said. "I'm sure he will understand."

The sergeant was never quite sure what he had said that was so amusing. Shiraz was still chuckling as he turned away and returned to his vehicle.

CHAPTER THIRTY-TWO

Stony Man Farm, Virginia

"Anatoly Nevski has been expanding his circle of influential friends," Aaron Kurtzman said. He brought up an image. "This is Lorcan Chernak. The guy is a big player in arms sales. Makes Nevski look smalltime."

"Lorcan?" Bolan asked.

Kurtzman grinned. "His father was Georgian. Mother Irish. Some combination. She was working in New York at the UN and met Gregor Chernak there when he was in the Soviet diplomatic service. A translator. Lorcan was the result of their liaison. Problem was that daddy already had a wife back in Mother Russia, so things were a little difficult. When he was old enough, the boy went to Russia to stay with Gregor and never came back.

"Being bilingual, he was useful to the Soviets. He moved into negotiating military contracts and started to pick up his own clients. After the fall he set up on his own, moving a lot of ordnance because he knew where it was being stored. It seems he'd maintained some helpful contacts and made a load of money in the first year or so. Since then he's expanded and has a global client list. Rumor has it he's even negotiated for some Western agencies. I haven't been able to pin that down, but I get the feeling he's got some protection out there."

"How does Chernak tie in with our mission?"

"Like I told you, Nevski has been running some orders through Chernak. Doing him some favors in return. One of those favors was bringing Razihra along and introducing him as a potential client."

"Okay, Aaron, what's Chernak doing for Razihra?"

"From what I've been dredging up, electronic snooping across Chernak's cell phone and Internet, it looks as if he's arranging a face-to-face meeting. It's amazing how much these people still use cell and landline phones to communicate. Even e-mail. I figure they don't believe their own little call can be picked up from all the stuff being sent."

"Sending an engraved invitation through the mail isn't going to work."

"I guess not. You asked what Chernak might do for Razihra. You recall those supertorpedoes the Iranians were bragging about some while back? The ones they said could scupper any U.S. warship in the Gulf? U.S. intelligence is pretty certain it's based on a Russian design. They call it Shkval. There are stories that the Russians helped Iran with the development. But Chernak's name has also cropped up tied in to supplying the Iranian's with technical data and a number of the actual torpedoes."

"You about to tell me Chernak can supply nukes to Razihra?"

"Striker, you totaled the guy's secret base, wiped out all his research and development. He's back to zilch. But we all know he isn't about to give up. He'll start up again, but as a prevent gap there's nothing to stop him stockpiling a few nukes from the BombsAreUs store. I can't prove it but I'm damn sure Razihra isn't meeting with two arms dealers to top up his hoard of vodka. Chernak's in the business of high-end armament. He's pretty well able to supply anything for a price, and we know Razihra's Chinese buddies will keep his bank balance topped up."

Hal Brognola chose that moment to make his presence known. "Aaron, there's a tie-in with MOSSAD coming through. Put it up on screen. Striker, this should interest you."

Kurtzman tapped into the secure satellite feed and an image, flashed on the big monitor. While Kurtzman fixed the image Bolan and Brognola donned headsets so they could communicate with their Israeli callers. On screen the MOSSAD image showed two figures facing the camera.

"I am pleased we were able to set up this meeting," one of the Israelis said. "My name is Reuben, the section chief. I believe your Mr. Cooper will recognise Agent Sharon." He gestured at the seond man.

"Good to see you, Ben," Bolan acknowledged. "I'm informed you have something I'll be interested in."

"It follows on from what happened in Jordan," Sharon said. "Our intelligence section spent some time going through a large amount of cell phone and Internet chatter between Razihra and his various cells. I'm sure your people have been doing the same."

"They have. Anything specific?"

"Lorcan Chernak. Russian arms dealer. One of the biggest."

"I was filled in with his background just before you called. It looks like he's hosting a get-together for Razihra and Nevski."

"Exactly what we worked out. The way we see it, Razihra has his back to the wall. His big operation has come to nothing. His military backers are going to be disappointed now they've lost the nuclear advantage. Razihra isn't about to sit back and forget that. He wants Iran to have the advantage."

"As long as the Chinese continue to bankroll his efforts Razihra will keep trying," Reuben stated. "One way or another he's determined to come out on top.

"Which is why he's making this trip," Bolan said. "To buy his way back into the game."

"As far as we are concerned, that can't be allowed to happen," Reuben said. "We can't, and won't, let go of what he was going to do to us. If he starts to negotiate for more weaponry, who's to say he isn't going to purchase more nerve gas? Weapons-grade uranium? Maybe even assembled nuclear devices. He's as much of a threat now as he was before you destroyed his previous weapons' cache. Razihra isn't about to give up. Is America?"

"The President is aware of the situation," Brognola said. "The fact Razihra's stolen U.S. technology has been neautralized covers our initial reason for Cooper's mission. We could step back from this now."

"That suggests the possibility you still have an interest."

"More than you might realize."

"I'm listening."

"Razihra is intent on creating friction in the region. His aim is to boost Iran to the top as far as nuclear clout goes. That's reason enough for the U.S. to be concerned because he's well aware we aren't going to stand back and let that happen. So any preemptive action now is to stall future confrontation. President Masood is genuinly trying to keep this kind of scenario from being set up, which is why Cameron Gordeno was instructed to make contact with him and arrange a one-to-one meeting to discuss the matter. Gordeno was to have had his meeting once the funeral of Dr. Shahan Baresh was over. Very few people knew about this. What they still do know is that Cameron Gordeno and his security team were all killed in an ambush shortly after the funeral."

"You suspect Razihra?"

"We know it was," Brognola said. "The CIA director has bagged his informer. One of his own advisers. The man is responsible for aiding Razihra by furnishing him with information regarding nuclear technology and revealing the identity of an undercover agent that subsequently led to that agent being killed. This only happened a short time ago, so I would be grateful if you maintained your silence over the matter for the moment."

Reuben nodded. "Has this individual given any information that might prove useful to out mutual benefit?"

"He is cooperating right now. Once he realized there was no way out, he decided to protect himself by offering us intel," Brognola replied.

"Useful, I hope?"

"He identified the assassin responsible for Marchesse's death. Same guy who took down Gordeno and his detail. He's a UK citizen named Victor Capstone. He used to be SAS but when he left he branched out into assassinations. Pretty good, too, by all accounts. Right now he's on an extended contract for Nevski. Just before he was picked up he heard from Nevski that he and Lorcan Chernek are fixing a meet with Razihra to discuss terms for follow-up sales of hardware. And that might include nuclear material," Brognola stated.

"I'd say that qualifies as useful information," Reuben said.

"The location hadn't been fixed at the time of his apprehension."

"Will that be forthcoming?" Reuben asked.

"We might be able to find out from another source I've just been informed about. If that proves useful we go ahead with the mission."

"You can leave that to me," Bolan said. "It's time we put an end to this for good. These people have run their course."

AFTER THE LINKUP HAD ENDED Bolan found himself sequestered with Brognola in the big Fed's office. As Brognola
closed the door Bolan waited, aware he was going to be told
crucial news.

"Aaron managed to get a photo of Capstone," Brognola
said, passing it to Bolan. "He worked some of his computer
magic and pulled it from the UK's MOD data bank. It's from
Capstone's military years."

Bolan studied the image, noting the penetrating, direct
stare from the man as he looked directly into the camera lens.
It was an expression he wasn't likely to forget.

"There's a plane standing by at Andrews to take you to
Moscow. Commander Seminov has information pertinent
to the mission. He asked for you personally." Brognola
cleared his throat. "Seems you're the only man he really
trusts."

"Hal, what's this all about?"

"I don't know, so you'll have to wait until you have your
face-to-face."

"Just because we're helping out the CIA doesn't mean we
have to play their game."

"From what Seminov implied, I don't think he trusts his
own people. So that's why the clandestine meeting. When you
touch down, he'll meet you. Seminov will take it from there."

"Should I pack for a long visit?"

"I'd say a busy one."

Bolan smiled. "Something warned me you were going to
say that, Hal."

"I'm going to see David later."

"Tell him thanks for the assist and I'll see him when I
get back."

"Make it fast then. He's threatening to hop on a plane for

London first chance he gets. *Hop* being the operative word for the next few weeks."

"Hal, no problems letting Amir partner me on this?"

"It's okay with me."

"He kept his end up in Iran, and he has a big stake in bringing down Razihra."

"Hell, Striker, don't we all. The President's not in a forgiving mood over this whole deal, and he isn't going to sit back and let Razihra start it all up again. Not with Masood showing signs he's considering talks. As long as Razihra's around, he'll keep the pot stirred along with his military cronies. The Israeli head honcho is chafing at the bit over the ZK386 threat. He's all for going into Iran with all guns blazing. The President has had to do some hard talking to hold him off. We need to get his done ASAP, for our own sake as much as anyone else. Last thing we need is another crisis in the Middle East. If Razihra is allowed to keep pushing that's going to happen. And as long as he's courting the help of people like Nevski and Chernak, they'll welcome him with open arms and dollar signs for eyes."

"Until somebody stops them."

"This pair have contacts all over. People in powerful positions. If we could get our hands on their databases that kind of intel could be damn useful for all concerned."

"Okay, Hal, I get the message," Bolan said.

"Sharp as ever."

"Give me time to get my gear together and we'll head for Andrews."

Moscow, Russia

COMMANDER VALENTINE SEMINOV, clad in a heavy overcoat that made his solid bulk even bigger, embraced Mack Bolan as if he were a long lost relative. As far as the Russian was concerned, Bolan *was* family. They had shared difficult times together on previous missions and Seminov had great affection for the American. He opened the rear door of the big black Russian saloon car and they climbed inside. Seminov closed the door.

"So you have come to cause trouble for mutual enemies?"

"I'll try to keep you out of it this time."

Seminov's face lit up in a wide smile. "Always you make jokes. But I know if you are here you are not going to be sitting around singing campfire songs. Am I right?"

"No fooling you, Valentine."

"Your people advised me you wanted my help, and·I am pleased to give it. If we can rid the world of Nevski and Chernak, then a lot of people are going to be happy." Seminov placed a large hand on Bolan's shoulder. "From what your man told me, you are after quite a mix of bad fish."

Bolan nodded. "A real collection."

"You have met with them already I think," Seminov said, indicating the bruises and abrasions on Bolan's face.

"We've locked horns."

"All these bruises, Cooper. Tell me, my friend, are you slowing down?"

Bolan smiled. "Valentine, there are days I believe I'm just standing still."

Seminov's booming laugh filled the car. "That I will never believe. Now, you have a partner with you?"

"Waiting on the plane. He said Russia is too cold for him. Amir Fayed is Iranian. He has a big stake in this. The man known as Ayatollah Razihra is involved in the purchase of stolen technology. He's determined to force through his pronuclear policy in Iran, and he's been dealing in illegally purchased U.S. data and hardware. Up to now we've been able stall his plans and take out his facility in the Iranian desert.

He's going to meet with his arms supplier, Anatoly Nevski, and partner with Lorcan Chernak to broker a deal for merchandise to replace what was destroyed. That may include another consignment of ZK386."

"The bioweapon? I heard about that. The ZK386 should not be on the market for any reason. The stockpiles are down for being destroyed. This damned weapon is so unstable it is not even considered for reassessment."

"Razihra was able to get his hands on a shipment. If it hadn't been located and destroyed in Jordan, Razihra's people were going to use it against Israel. Looks like he hasn't learned his lesson, and he's going for more. And if he could use it against Israeli targets, who might be next?"

Seminov considered the implications of allowing the bioweapon to fall into irresponsible hands. "If ZK386 was ever used by some outside organization, we would stand accused of negligence. These days there is more than enough of that taking place, Cooper, and not all in Russia, eh?"

"The U.S. is aware of its obligations. It's why I was chasing down the stolen technology. It's an old cliché, Valentine, but it still rings true—guilt by association. Razihra wants the easy option, so he buys in his nuclear hardware. The Chinese are in on the deal, offering him unlimited funds in return for future assurances concerning oil and closer ties. Nevski, and now Chernak, are simply supplying the goods."

"The OCD has been running an operation in conjunction with your Justice Department. We are attempting to gain enough evidence on Chernak concerning his human trafficking, though I have to admit nothing solid has been forthcoming. There is interference from high places blocking our efforts. I am embarrassed to admit that even in my department there may be eyes and ears that belong to Chernak."

Bolan nodded. "I spoke with Justice. And it appears you have your old friend working with you again."

"Ah, yes, the beautiful Kira. Only your man, Leo Turrin, and I know about Kira. No one else. We thought it best to keep her presence totally covert."

Kira Tedesko, previously working out of Pristina on the female slave trade, had been caught in a sweep by traffickers and found herself a captive in a lockdown in Kansas. That was until Mack Bolan hit the place as part of his mission to bring down a Russian *Mafiya* organization. Tedesko had teamed up with Bolan to complete the assignment, and when it was all over was recruited by Leo Turrin into his Justice Department task force. Bolan hadn't seen her for some time, or heard from her, and it was evident now why she had been silent. Before her meeting with Bolan and while she was still with the Kosovo Civil Police, Tedesko had traveled to Russia and had worked with Valentine Seminov.

"How long has she been on assignment?" Bolan asked.

"Almost three months now," Seminov said. "And doing very well. She has worked her way into Chernak's mob and is providing me with useful information. Your Justice Department has great interest in Chernak and anything Kira could learn would help their own investigation. Now the investigation has moved up a notch with this Razihra affair, Kira could have more to handle."

"Is she okay?"

Seminov raised his big hands. "As well as anyone can be working undercover. Cooper, she is a very experienced young woman. What else can I say?"

"I'm just thinking about an American undercover agent who got into Nevski's organization. *He* was doing fine until someone betrayed him and he ended up on a London back ally with a pair of bullets in the back of his skull."

"Did you know him?"

Bolan shook his head. "No, but what he managed to pass back before he died started this mission and led us all the way to Razihra and Nevski. It appears there was a CIA rogue agent working for Nevski who tipped them off and got the undercover man assassinated. It isn't only your department with bad apples in the barrel."

Seminov produced a number of photographs and spread them out for Bolan to inspect. "Kira you know. The one with his arm around her waist is Max Lubin, one of Chernak's lieutenants. Lubin is important in the organization. He is an able logistician, responsible for arranging distribution, finding locations and greasing palms. He's also deep in the trafficking business as he appears to have a knack for dealing in people. Strangely though, in his personal life he is a disaster with women. Just look at the man. Not exactly star material. But he is a hopeless romantic and falls for any woman who smiles at him. Kira spent a month at the club in Moscow Lubin frequents and got a job as a dealer at one of the tables and got Lubin interested. Now he can't leave her alone. He fell for her like a schoolboy getting a crush on his teacher. Kira has been playing it very slowly, but over the past few weeks she has been able to send intel that has proved invaluable."

"What about protection for her?"

"I can't get too close in case I am spotted. And before you get mad at me, Cooper, Kira made it clear from the start that the moment she feels compromised she will walk away. That young woman is smart, but she is not suicidal. And without her I might not have gained the location of the meet Chernak has fixed for Nevski and Razihra. Kira told me about it only a few days ago. Lubin will be taking Kira as his guest."

"Valentine, I don't want anything to happen to her, but I understand that right now we can't pull her out. If she disappeared right before a big meeting, Chernak might suspect something."

Bolan had mixed feelings over the matter. He understood the need to maintain Kira's cover. The more she could learn, the harder the evidence would be against Chernak and the rest. He respected her skill and professionalism, while at the same time felt deep concern over her safety. Undercover work was one of the most risky of agency assignments. Against other types of operations it was the one that had the most chances of going wrong. One false move on the part of any undercover agent and his, or her, cover could be blown in seconds. Even the simple act of making a telephone call could expose the agent. And if that did happen, retribution was usually swift and unpleasant. The criminal fraternity didn't look kindly upon those seeking to expose them, and they would strike out without remorse. Bolan had only to think back to the start of this mission and the death of Carl Marchesse. He had been exposed and that exposure led to his untimely death. The thought of that happening to Kira Tedesko did not sit lightly with Mack Bolan.

Seminov picked up the American's feelings and placed a big hand on Bolan's shoulder. "*Tovarich,* we must not let anything bad happen to her. I like that young woman, too. So it will be down to you to make certain she survives whatever you have planned."

Bolan concentrated on the rest of the photographs Seminov had provided. The Russian identified each individual.

"I am sure your people gave you information about these mongrels. The red-haired one is Chernak. Yes? The color comes from his Irish mother. Don't be fooled by his genial looks. Chernak is no fool and is very powerful in his chosen profession. The man will buy and sell anything from guns to people and everything in between. He's got plenty of important contacts. For himself he's charming, able to make himself liked, but underneath he is just another mobster. Violent. Very cruel when he wants to be. He has killed, we know that, and likes to use his hands to beat people. Men or women. He can speak in English and French. Enjoys the materialistic side of the life his wealth brings and is not afraid to show it."

Bolan studied the image, storing it, with the others at the back of his mind. "Where and when is this meet, Valentine?"

"I was wondering when you were going to ask that, Cooper." Seminov dug into his attaché case and produced more material, including maps and more photographs. "From my own files, Cooper. This is Lazos. An island in the Aegean. Very exclusive island. The deep water natural harbor gives way to some spectacular terrain. Chernak has a villa there, looking out over his harbor. It is his private domain. There is a helipad next to the house and at the rear a runway that will accommodate medium-size aircraft."

"Kira has verified the meet will be there?"

Seminov nodded. "Chernak's guests are arriving the day after tomorrow and they will have their talks on board his motorized yacht the *New Enterprise* in the harbor. According to Lubin's pillow talk, Kira learned that Chernak always holds his business meetings on board the vessel."

."Then I'll need to be around when they do," Bolan said. "Getting them together in one place is just what we need."

"That *we* does not include me, I suspect."

"Valentine, I understand your difficulty here. You need to distance yourself from what's going to happen. You said yourself there are too many high connections involved. Chernak has protection, and we all know how it works. If word on this gets out, Chernak will hear about it and the meet will be canceled. We won't get another chance like this. Make yourself high-profile. Be seen in all the right places. You have nothing to do with this. Your investigation is still under way, but not making much headway. Let that stand. The people reporting to Chernak need to see that. It will keep them comfortable. Unsuspecting."

"We hope."

"Cheer up, Valentine, there's always hope."

"I wish I could be there to look out for you. I can't, so I have brought you something that may give you comfort."

"Oh?"

"I knew you would be going after them," Seminov said. "And I also knew that I would not be able to accompany you."

"Valentine, you're making me believe you've got a bunch of flowers behind your back."

Seminov's laughter boomed. He pushed open the car door and gestured for Bolan to follow him. They went to the rear and the Russian opened the trunk. "Better than flowers, my friend." He leaned inside and lifted out a Russian-made RPG rocket launcher and a shoulder-sling that carried half a dozen rockets. "My contribution to the cause. Use them well."

CHAPTER THIRTY-THREE

Bolan and Fayed had made their approach to Lazos from the north side of the island, their insertion aided by a MOSSAD covert unit operating out of the Greek island of Rhodes, where Israeli Intelligence operated the undercover unit for information gathering and observation of activity in the Aegean area. Hal Brognola had liaised with Director Reuben and obtained his cooperation in the mission on the promise that once Bolan had completed his strike, MOSSAD would be allowed to go in and gather what information they could after the American sent them an arranged signal.

"Thanks for including us in this," Sharon had said as he stood beside Bolan on the deck of the motor cruiser. It was predawn, the soft night warm, the Aegean calm. "If we even manage to get only a little intel from any records, it could prove useful."

"Ben, we're all in this together no matter which way the dice roll," Bolan said. "Razihra is going all out to make trouble. Nevski and Chernak don't give a damn as long as they make money. They see Razihra as a long term customer, so they'll do what they can to keep him sweet."

"Not this time, hopefully," Sharon said.

Bolan checked his watch. "I'd better go and run my final check to make sure Fayed and I have everything we need."

Sharon followed him belowdecks. In the main cabin Fayed had laid out their equipment.

"I presumed you would prefer to check your personal weapons yourself," he said.

"Force of habit, Amir."

Bolan's Desert Eagle lay beside the Beretta 93-R. There was a 9 mm Uzi, with an extended magazine, a Cold Steel Tanto combat knife and a selection of fragmentation grenades. The RPG Seminov had contributed lay on the table next to the rocket sling bag. Bolan made his firearms checks quietly and efficiently, working the mechanisms before loading each weapon. The Desert Eagle was holstered on his hip, the 93-R in a leather shoulder holster. He slid the combat knife into a sheath on his right thigh. Pulling a combat vest over his blacksuit, Bolan added additional loaded magazines for his weapons. He clipped grenades to the vest, then swung the sling bag holding the RPG rockets over his shoulder.

In addition to his Uzi, Fayed carried a Glock 17 pistol. He had accepted a combat knife from Bolan. Grenades hung from his combat vest.

Sharon handed out sturdy transceiver units they could attach to their belts.

"You can talk to each other, and when you want us in just hit the yellow button."

"You'll be hearing from us," Bolan promised.

The intercom buzzed. Sharon answered, acknowledging the message. "Time to go," he told Bolan.

On deck the MOSSAD crew had readied the black rubber boat Bolan and Fayed would be using for the insertion. It was large enough for two. There was no power unit. Paddles would be used to keep noise down.

"Should take you a couple of hours to hike across to the south side of the island," Sharon said. "Then you'll have plenty of time to get into position and wait for Chernak's guests to show up."

The boat was lowered into the water. Bolan and Fayed climbed in, pushed off and began to direct the small boat toward the still shadowed island.

"Good luck," Sharon called.

Bolan had time for a quick wave before the Israeli vessel faded into the gloom. Then he and Fayed were alone with only the slap of water against the sides of the boat breaking the silence.

CHERNAK'S SHOWPIECE, THE *New Enterprise,* had been bought with the money he'd made through his numerous business ventures. The 340-foot, diesel-turbine-powered seagoing vessel, capable of 18 knots, was where Chernak made his deals. Entertaining his guests with a lavish style, he provided for their every whim while on board the ship. The three decks housed luxurious cabins, each equipped with king-size beds and en suite bathrooms. Large-screen HD television fed from satellite stations and DVD players were installed in each cabin to provide twenty-four-hour entertainment, and guests were able to choose DVDs from an extensive library that catered for every taste. Computer stations occupied a place in each cabin, with up-to-the-minute facilities that included e-mail and satellite communications. Chernak's dedicated crew, handpicked, ran the ship and also provided security protection. Able to house up to fifty guests, the *New Enterprise* boasted an excellent dining experience in the upper deck saloon. There was an expansive choice of wines and drinks to be enjoyed from the bars situated on each deck.

Chernak's sleek office suite, situated on the middle deck area, had a conference room next door. Satellite communications, for phones and computers, meant that clients, there to do business with Chernak, were able to send and receive details of agreements, and to initiate bank transfers, without moving from their luxurious leather conference chairs, while Chernak's staff provided tea or coffee of the highest quality during negotiations. He had a simple rule for the conference room. Under no circumstances were alcoholic drinks served when deals were being made. Chernak wanted minds and reflexes at their best, refusing to allow alcohol to take the edge off hard decisions.

The aft deck was fitted with a helipad that could accomodate Chernak's personal white-and-gold Bell JetRanger. A pair of twenty-foot, outboard motor-powered launches hung from electric davits at the stern. Smaller lifeboats were held in davits along either side of the lower deck. The vessel's bridge was an electronic buff's dream come true. Navigation was state-of-the-art, with computer-controlled functions and digital readouts. On-board radar scanned the horizon.

The ship established Chernak's reputation as a successful businessman. It showed his clients they were in the presence of a master of his trade, one not to be trifled with. Lorcan Chernak could be whatever he wanted—wealthy, powerful, with wide-reaching influence and the ear of many important people on both sides of the law. He was untouchable.

Or so he thought.

Anatoly Nevski completed his tour of the *New Enterprise,* returning to the main lounge and his host.

"Lorcan, I am very impressed. This is a beautiful vessel." He sank into one of the plush leather window seats. "Tell me, have I turned a bright shade of green?"

Chernak grinned. "Are you that envious?"

"Yes, I am."

"If we pull off this deal with Razihra, you'll be well on your way to affording something like this yourself."

"Seeing this and the rest makes me realize I have a long way to go in this business."

"You'll get there, Anatoly. We are in a growth industry, you and I. All aspects. Whether it is the trafficking, drugs, armament. They are expanding. Look how much they have grown in the past few years. You opened up a new venture yourself when you started providing people like Gregori Malinski to your clients. An astute move on your part. Very well thought out."

"It's not something I would want to put in my résumé at the moment."

"Unfortunate that he decided to jump ship. But these things happen. One thing we cannot determine is a change in someone's character. Even I would have missed that one."

"I don't like failing. It affects client confidence."

"But Razihra is still here. He needs what you and I can offer, which is why you will ride out this setback. Give Razihra what he wants, and he'll be eating out of your hand. Believe me, Anatoly, I know how these people think."

Nevski leaned forward. "So, Lorcan, can you tell what I'm thinking right now?"

"I would say you've been considering how nice it would be if you got rid of me and took over my businesses. Owned this boat and stepped up to be top man in the business."

Nevski's eyes gleamed with amusement. "Which is why I would never even take it any further. I'd have to be a rare kind of moron to think I could take you down. I'd rather learn from you and do business with you."

"Then we can benefit from each other. I have a contact in Uzbekistan who can provide us with nuclear materials from a storage site. Low yield, but it could be used in the construction of a radiological bomb."

"I have heard about those. A nuclear layer with a conventional high-explosive core. Not a complete nuclear weapon, but one that would spread contamination over a small area."

"Terror weapons ideally suited to Razihra's current way of thinking. While he proceeds with his nuclear capability, something like that would satisfy his needs. The uranium enrichment process for his main missile program is going to take longer than he realized." Chernak crossed to the bar and helped himself to a drink. He poured one for Nevski. "The procurement of nuclear warheads is another matter to consider. My contact in Uzbekistan may be able to locate some of those."

A crew member entered the lounge to inform Chernak his guests had arrived on the island. Chernak placed his drink aside. He picked up one of the telephones and contacted the bridge.

"Hakim, I am going ashore to greet our guests. Bring the ship to the jetty. We will come aboard a little later and you can take us on a pleasant excursion around the island." Chernak finished his call and beckoned to Nevski. "Come, Anatoly, it's time we went to welcome our friends."

ON THE HIGHER GROUND overlooking the villa, Mack Bolan and Amir Fayed studied the arrivals through powerful binoculars. They had seen the Learjet set down on the runway behind the villa and had checked out the arrivals, identifying the principal players. Yusef Khammere followed Ayatollah Razihra, who was in deep in conversation with Fu Chen. The Chinese was closely flanked by a pair of sober bodyguards in dark suits. Chen himself sported a pale cream linen suit and a white fedora. From the ID images provided by Seminov,

Bolan was able to recognize Max Lubin. The man was of average height, balding and with a thin face and sallow complexion. Bolan didn't allow himself to be influenced by that. What went on in a man's brain had little to do with his external looks, and from what Seminov had told him about the man, In addition to his logistic skills, Lubin had a flair for the trafficking business. In-depth reading of the man's file had revealed Lubin to be one of the key players behind the ongoing success of Chernak's white slavery trade; to some that might have seemed a lurid reference to what the man did, but it pinned it down exactly. Lubin dealt in selling other humans for money. The unfortunates were traded as little more than livestock. They were passed from hand to hand after being snatched from their home, taken for thousands of miles and then bartered over and ending up as unregistered labor, or worse as prostitutes, sold to sexual deviates, or helpless pawns in the pornography industry. In the twenty-first Century, with all the advances in technology, the market for this debasing trade was growing. It was a sad indictment in Bolan's mind that man still defiled his fellow humans for nothing more monetary gain. It saddened him, but also turned his attention on the soulless creatures who actually involved themselves in the vile trade and reaped the profits.

Men like Anatoly Nevski and Lorcan Chernak.

They were like addicts, high on the runaway success of their ventures, wanting more and more. Guns, drugs, flesh peddling—and their current obsession with the needs of Razihra, a man determined to continue his ambition of becoming all-powerful in his own country by placing Iran on the nuclear slide to confrontation and international posturing.

He lay and studied these men, his mind already ticking them off as needing the cleansing flame of the Executioner. The hell he was about to bring down on these men might not stop their collective crimes against humanity, but at least it would send out a warning to others that government and agency dithering aside, someone was willing to walk that extra mile and deal out some kind of justice.

Bolan moved his glasses and focused on the slim, dark-haired beauty on Lubin's arm. Dressed in expensive designer clothes that flattered her stunning figure, smiling and devoting all her attention to the man beside her, she looked the part.

Kira Tedesko.

The ex-undercover cop, now working out of Leo Turrin's Justice Department organization as Max Lubin's arm candy. Tedesko's glossy hair, now grown long, swung as she turned her head from side to side, and if he hadn't known better Bolan could have believed she had looked his way deliberately, those striking eyes and generous mouth beckoning him. He pushed the thought aside, aware that she had no idea he was now also targeting Lorcan Chernak. There had been no way Seminov could have contacted her. All he had done was to offer Bolan the information she had sent to him about the location of the special meet that was taking place here on Lazos. The woman would have no idea what Seminov might do with the information she had transmitted. With the Russian unable to even acknowledge her, Tedesko would be in the dark as to any follow-up. It was in the nature of undercover work that an operative might sometimes have to continue playing the role, hoping for a break and maybe praying that someone was about to step in and bring the game to a successful close. Bolan tried not to think back to the start of this mission, brought about because another undercover agent, shortly after sending vital information, had been killed because of another's treachery. Thinking about Carl Marchesse, Bolan focused in on Tedesko again, and made a personal vow he wouldn't let the same thing happen to her.

Times were when allies and friends, sometimes simply good people who had done the right thing, ended up hurt, or dead. Bolan had his own internal roster of those faces and names. They came to him in the night, unexpectedly, reminding Bolan of their sacrifices, of the deaths that might not have been if they had simply turned aside, denying that standing up to the savages was anything to do with them. Those friendly ghosts served as reminders to Bolan that despite the legions of Evil, there were still those willing to fight back. They were the silent masses. The ones who wanted little more than to be allowed to live *their* lives in safety, but all too ready to accept the times when turning the other cheek did nothing except feed the fires of brutality and violence. They refused to turn aside. They resisted. They fought back and often they paid with their own lives. But every one of them became a part of Mack Bolan, giving him the glimmer of hope in the darkness. When they drifted into his dreams he welcomed them as fellow warriors, grateful for the reminder that he wasn't completely alone in his struggle. They were with him now, as they had been right from the start of his War Everlasting, and he drew from their strength, even as he mourned their passing.

"Hang in there, Kira, I'm with you now," Bolan whispered softly.

BESIDE HIM AMIR FAYED was watching one of the *New Enterprise*'s boats heading toward the jetty. He focused in and identified the passengers in the boat.

Anatoly Nevski. Lem Kirov. At the front of the power launch stood Lorcan Chernak, an easy smile on his face, red hair blowing in the breeze.

"Cooper, they are being very obliging. All coming together for us," Fayed said.

"Pity we weren't sent an invitation," Bolan replied. "Amir, it looks like we're going to have to crash the party."

"IF YOU CAN DRAW THEM to the front of the house, I can try to get the domestic staff out through the rear," Fayed said.

"Okay. I'll wait for your call, then make some noise."

"Good luck."

"Amir, if you spot Kira Tedesko, do what you can to get her out of the fire zone."

"All that I can do if I find her."

Fayed turned and vanished in the thick shrubbery, leaving Bolan alone, to wait, and to hope they did get to Kira before anything put her in danger. She was going to be as surprised as any of Chernak's visitors when the strike was launched, and it was easy for problems to arise in the heat of a rolling battle.

FAYED WAS CLOSING IN ON the rear of the villa when he heard a rustle of sound to one side and, turning, faced an armed security guard. The man's autorifle was slung from his shoulder. He didn't make an attempt to go for it because he was too close to Fayed. His immediate reaction was to lunge for the Iranian, hands clawing for intruder's throat. As the two men came together, each struggling to gain the advantage, Fayed hooked his right foot behind the other's and kicked the guard off balance. They went down hard, still clawing for control over the other, landing telling blows that tore skin and drew blood.

Pushing hard, Fayed got his assailant to roll aside. The Iranian followed through, launching a savage punch that slammed against the man's jaw. The guard's face turned bloody. He drove a hard knee into Fayed's side, over the ribs, drawing a gasp of pain. Before Fayed could steady himself the guard kicked out again, the force of the blow toppling Fayed facedown in the dust. He sensed the guard pushing upright and knew he had to end this now. Cooper was waiting for his signal so he could launch his attack, and he couldn't let the American down.

Shaking his head against the pain, Fayed pushed up off the ground as he heard the thump of boots. The guard was coming for him again. He struggled to come up with any move that might save him from attack, knowing he couldn't use his handgun because of the sound alerting Chernak's people too soon, and at the last moment he remembered the Tanto combat knife on his belt. He reached for it, slid the keen blade free, and as the guard loomed over him Fayed swept the blade around in a brutal arc. It cut the guard across his right front thigh, the blade slicing through the his pants and making a deep cut in his flesh. As blood welled up and soaked the cloth, the guard let go a wail of pain.

Fayed pushed up on his knees, coming to eye level with the guard, bent almost double over his wound. Fayed's hand moved again, the glittering cold blade flashing in the clean air. This time it cut across the guard's throat, then back as Fayed reversed his strike. The blade opened the guard's left cheek, a large flap of bloody flesh drooping from the gaping wound, blood surging out in a flood. The guard went to the ground in a shuddering, bloody heap, his moans fading as quickly as his pumping blood soaked into the earth.

Fayed put away the knife, wiping blood from his hands across his blacksuit. He checked his weapons, then moved on quickly, reaching for the transceiver to call Cooper.

BOLAN ACKNOWLEDGED FAYED'S call. The Iranian was in position at the rear of the villa. Now it was down to him. He had moved in closer to the jetty and had climbed on top of a metal water storage tank where he had a clear sighting of the *New Enterprise*.

The soldier crouched by a large inlet valve on the top of the tank, staying on the side away from the water. He eased one of the RPG rockets from the sling around his shoulders and fed it into the launcher. With the weapon primed and ready, he checked the vessel's position. The ship was closing in on jetty, sliding silently and gracefully through the calm water. He let the vessel reach within fifty feet of the jetty before he raised the RPG and leveled it at the JetRanger on the aft helipad.

"Score one for the good guys," Bolan said quietly, and launched the missile. He watched the smoke trail as the rocket soared across the water and impacted against the helicopter. The JetRanger vanished in a boil of fire, debris scattering across the rear deck, the explosion breaking the comparative calm of the island. Burning fuel spilled across the ship. Loading a second rocket, Bolan hit the ship just below the waterline. The detonation tore a ragged hole in the side of the ship, water starting to pour in. Even as alarms sounded Bolan punched a third, fourth and fifth rocket into the lower hull, seeing the *New Enterprise* start to tilt as the ingress of water took away its balance. The ship was still moving forward, uncontrolled now and closing in on the jetty. Bolan backed off from his place of concealment and ran toward a neat stack of large fuel drums, moving past them until he was a safe distance away. He slid his final rocket into the launcher, sighted down and hit the fuel drums. They blew with a massive explosion, throwing blazing liquid over the area. The jetty began to burn as the spilled fuel soaked into the wood. Bolan dropped the empty RPG and pulled off the sling that had held the missiles. He unlimbered his Uzi, turned and cut into the bushes that edged the now blazing jetty. Behind him the ship plowed into the jetty, thick wood beams splintering under the deadweight of the drifting vessel.

Armed men raced out of the security hut on the approach to the jetty, casting around as they searched for whoever was responsible for the destruction, their anger at being attacked showing clearly on their faces.

One of the sharp-eyed guards spotted Bolan as he made his break from cover and headed for the villa. The spotter opened up with his SMG, a line of 9 mm rounds chewing up the ground in Bolan's wake. He kept moving, aiming for the next piece of cover, a low stone wall. The Executioner rolled over the top of the wall, coming quickly to his knees and turning the Uzi on the advancing security guards. They were all well-armed with AK-74s, the assault rifles in pristine condition. His first, short burst, slapped the lead guy down as the 9 mm slugs ripped his left side open. The man went down screaming, hugging his bloody torso as his fellow guards ran by. They moved forward with caution and took the full fury of Bolan's assault. The Executioner watched the three of them falter and go down as his autoweapon dealt them fiery death. Then he was moving again, using every piece of cover he could as he worked his way toward the villa.

The screech of tires on concrete reached his ears. Bolan turned and saw an open Jeep swerving around the perimeter of the docking area. The moment the two armed passengers saw Bolan they opened fire, the hastily shot bullets falling wide of the mark. The soldier moved sideways, causing the Jeep to overshoot and by the time the driver hit the brakes to slow the vehicle, Bolan had taken up his new position. He cut loose with the Uzi, catching the closer of the two shooters. The guy tumbled from the rear of the Jeep, slamming hard to the ground. The second man rose to his feet, angling his AK over the rear of his seat.

In a crouch Bolan punched out a short burst that ripped through the seat backrest and into the shooter. The guy flopped back, one arm catching the driver across the back of the head. The driver stalled the Jeep, tried to start again, then thought better of it and snatched his handgun from its hip holster. He dived from the seat, landing awkwardly and rolled, trying to regain control of his tumbling body. Bolan tracked him and laid a short burst into the guy's back. The 9 mm slugs cored their way through flesh and he slid into a still pose. Moving up to the Jeep, Bolan took cover. He pulled one of the grenades from his harness and yanked the pin. Checking out the area, he saw that it was temporary clear. He dropped the grenade into the Jeep's foot well and moved away, diving to cover behind a rise of stone steps that led toward the villa. The Jeep was obscured by the grenade's explosion, smoke and debris raining down. The vehicle became engulfed in flame, its blackened carcass fragmented and twisted from the blast.

The security force seemed fewer in number than Bolan might have anticipated. He reasoned that Chernak, successful as he was, considered his personal island a safe haven, a place that was beyond the reach of anyone who might be termed a threat. It was a vain attitude. One that someone like Chernak and, to a lesser degree, Anatoly Nevski, might ascribe. They dealt with clients of good standing and basked in the shade of protection from their more high-profile customers. It was in the nature of individuals like Chernak to place themselves on a higher plane than those around them. Impervious to challenge and believing their own publicity, they became careless as their immense wealth grew.

AMIR FAYED HEARD THE start of the explosions as rockets hit the ship. He picked up the other blasts and the following gunfire as he broke cover and made for the rear of the villa. The strike, he saw, appeared to be having the effect Cooper had predicted, drawing Chernak's security force to the front of the building, allowing Fayed a relatively clear approach. He flattened against the rear wall, seeking the fastest way into the building. He was drawn toward the open door of the kitchen block. The cooking odors emanating from it confirmed its use. Fayed eased around the door and peered inside. A number of white-clad figures milled about, listening to the gunfire. He slipped inside, flattening against the inner wall, taking in the preparation tables, the ranges and the cooking implements. There were five staff members in the kitchen, three men and two young women.

"If you don't want to become involved, get out now," Fayed yelled in English.

The kitchen staff turned at the sound of his voice, faces registering alarm at the sight of a heavily armed man dressed in combat gear.

"Who are you?" one of the men asked. His English was slow and accented.

"We're not here for you. Get out while it's safe. Tell the others. Stay and you could get hurt."

The man translated for the rest of the staff. They began to move to the door.

"Are there more staff in the house?" Fayed asked.

"A few."

"Can you warn them?"

The man indicated a wall phone. "I can use that."

"Do it. Tell them to come to the kitchen and to do it quickly before the shooting reaches the house."

The man punched in a number. His call was answered after a long pause and he spoke quickly to whoever had picked up.

"They are coming as quickly as they can."

Fayed gestured for the staff to move out the door. "Tell them to get as far away from the house as they can. Advise them not to do anything that might endanger themselves. Do it. Get them out of here."

The kitchen staff filed through the door and moved away from the house in the direction of the far side of the island. The man who spoke English stood waiting until the other staff began to appear. He gave them the same instructions. No one offered any resistance.

"All of them?"

"Yes."

"Good. Now go yourself."

As soon as he was alone, Fayed closed the kitchen door. He locked it and slid the security bolts home. Only then did he key the transceiver clipped to his combat vest.

"The house staff has all gone, Cooper. We are clear."

Bolan's reply was short and precise.

"You know what has to be done."

Cleansing was as good a word as any. The villa and its remaining occupants were the ones Bolan and Fayed had come for. They had to be rooted out and given the justice they deserved.

THE DISTANT RATTLE OF AUTOFIRE had penetrated the room where Razihra and Fu Chen were waiting to be joined by Nevski and Chernak.

Of the two it was Razihra who reacted strongly. With everything that had gone wrong over recent days, he was nervous. He maintained an outer calm but inside his confidence was wearing thin, and the sudden explosions and gunfire did little to ease his condition. He moved to one of the panoramic windows overlooking the harbor and saw the *New Enterprise* trailing smoke and listing as she drifted toward the jetty. Razihra felt a touch of panic. He forced himself remain calm as he sensed Fu Chen at his side. The Chinese observed the damaged ship, then turned to his two bodyguards and spoke to them quietly. One of the men left the room.

"I suggest we move away from the window," Fu Chen advised. "If a stray bullet comes this way, I doubt the glass would stop it."

He took his own advice and resumed his seat at the conference table, his bodyguard following and standing close by.

"I believe Fu Chen is correct," Khammere said to Razihra. "Remaining at the window could prove to be a mistake."

Razihra glanced at the man, nodding absently, and took his place at the table again. "How long are they going to keep us waiting?"

"Under the present circumstances I would say a little delay is inevitable," Fu Chen said.

"I was assured this island was safe."

"Define *safe*, Razihra, and perhaps we will have something to work with. If not, you will have to accept my word there is nowhere in this world that can be called entirely safe."

"Only an Oriental could make such a profound statement."

"Not profound, Muhar, simply an observance of a simple fact."

Fu Chen's bodyguard returned. He bent close and spoke to his superior. Fu Chen nodded and took a little time to consider what he had been told before he addressed Razihra.

"I am leaving," he stated simply. "Nothing profound there, Muhar. My aide tells me there has been a hostile incursion. As we saw, the ship has been attacked and a number of Chernak's security men have already been killed. At the moment no one knows exactly how many are in the attacking force. It would be prudent to leave, and I am going to do that."

"Fu Chen, we have business to discuss," Razihra said, his tone holding a stinging rebuke.

The Chinese smiled gently and stood.

"There comes a time when discretion overrides other considerations," Fu Chen said. "It appears, Muhar, that our association has run its course."

Razihra's face hardened at Fu Chen's words. "You will walk out now? Desert me? I refuse to accept that."

Fu Chen showed his amusement. "*You* will not allow? Have you forgotten who I am, Muhar? Fu Chen, a godless Chinese, who does not come under your authority. Nor do I fall in supplication to your deity. My position as a representative of the People's Republic bestows on me the final say in how our alliances proceed. Listen to the sound of battle out there, Muhar. Our Russian hosts appear to be struggling to maintain the status quo. Even to my unsophisticated mind any and all negotiations have been put on hold."

"Then we will make further arrangements…"

"I regret having to say this, Muhar, and have resisted until now, but your rhetoric is becoming tiresome. As is your continuing ability to stay in control. I have witnessed all your current schemes fall apart. Your people have failed to preserve your bases, and now your Russian contacts are under siege. The 'phrase diplomatic' withdrawal comes to mind."

"You *must* listen, Chen. I am Ayatollah Muhar Razihra, my authority sanctioned by God, and my—"

"Your mission has been reduced to rubble, Ayatollah. It is time to retreat. Accept defeat and walk away. Given time, perhaps Beijing will look upon you with favor again. But we have many other options open to us, and I see no profit in spending time on a lost cause."

Fu Chen spoke to his bodyguards. They followed him from the room, leaving Razihra alone, except for the silent Khammere. Razihra's advisor decided to stay that way, unsure how the Ayatollah was going to react to Fu Chen's about-face. He was familiar with Razihra's moods and did not want to be responsible for adding to the current state of affairs.

Razihra crossed to stand at the window overlooking the harbor. Smoke was still rising from the *New Enterprise,* staining the sharp blue of the sky. The bow of the vessel was buried in the wreckage of the wooden jetty. Crew members were fleeing the damaged vessel even as Razihra watched. There was a certain irony in the name of the ship, now marred by the damage inflicted by the attack. A parallel with the way his affairs were being affected. And like the vessel, his own projects were going up in smoke.

At that moment in time Razihra wished he was blessed with a sense of humor so he might view everything philosophically. He had not. His life had maintained its somber course, from his early years, up until the present. He viewed life as a constant struggle, both physically and mentally. He had no time for what he termed the inconsequentials of life. The problem with retaining a limited outlook was what happened when it was damaged. Losses had the greater impact when there was little, or nothing, to replace them. Razihra reluctantly accepted that his time here on Chernak's island was over. It was time he returned to Tehran and regrouped. He was a man of great resourcefulness. He was certain he could find another backer to facilitate his operations. The driving force behind him, pushing his vision of becoming an important figure in his country's future, would not allow him to fade into the shadows.

"We will leave," he said to Khammere. "If these people cannot help us any longer, then we have no further use for them."

Khammere nodded, turning toward the door. He had taken only a single step when the double doors were kicked open and an armed man stood framed in the opening.

"I see all your friends have deserted you, Razihra," Amir Fayed said.

Razihra stared at the combat-suited figure. Fayed was disheveled, bloody, but the hard gleam in his eyes was steady as he moved into the room and stood with his back to the wall.

"Do you know who I am?" Razihra asked in a tone that suggested he was speaking down to Fayed.

Fayed's expression showed the scorn he felt for the man in front of him. "Yes, Razihra, I know who you are, and I know what you have done. I could list all your dishonor, but murderer, betrayer of Iran, fanatic who would drag us into chaos would be enough to decide your guilt."

"My guilt is of one who wants to make his nation powerful. To let us stand against our enemies. If we allow Masood to lead, he will simply reduce Iran to a second-rate nation with no say in anything. The Americans will dominate the region and we will have nothing to defy them with."

"Ha. You believe that threatening them with nuclear weapons will force them to stand down? Razihra, you have so much blind hate, you see nothing. What would have come from killing Israelis with that bio-weapon? Nothing but more bloodshed and years of conflict. Have you learned nothing except how to destroy and alienate? I see a man who trades in deceit and treachery, with little regard to his faith."

Khammere, sensing that Fayed's attention was fully fixed on Razihra, went for the gun inside his jacket. He yanked out the pistol and brought it around to track in on Fayed.

The muzzle of the AK in Fayed's hands moved faster, his finger stroking the trigger and sending a lethal burst of 7.62 mm slugs into Khammere. The front of the adviser's shirt was shredded as the steel jackets punched in, savaging flesh and bone, then creating damage to vital organs. Khammere was kicked back by the burst, stumbling and falling to the floor. He lay facedown, blood spreading out from beneath his prone body.

At the sight of Khammere falling Razihra turned and sprinted for the other end of the room, where a single door offered a vague hope of escape. He heard the harsh crackle of fire from Fayed's weapon and felt the stunning impact as the slugs hammered into his back. The force turned him sideways and he slammed against the wall, clawing at his chest in a vain effort to stem the rising pain. For a moment he locked eyes with the advancing figure of Fayed, thrusting on hand in his direction, finger pointing accusingly, and then the AK crackled again, jacking out the rest of the magazine's contents. Razihra released a desperate scream as the bullets were driven into his body. He felt the light around him darken as he fell to the floor, his ravaged system collapsing. Blood dribbled from his slack mouth as he curled up at the base of the wall, his body shuddering in the final moments of life.

Amir Fayed ejected the spent magazine and snapped in a fresh one as he crossed the room to stand over the bloody corpse. He lowered the AK's muzzle and fired another burst into Razihra's body before he turned and walked out.

FU CHEN FOLLOWED HIS bodyguards through the villa, taking a route that had been mapped out the moment they had arrived. Their way took them to the rear of the sprawling building and out a small side door. They moved quickly, away from the building in the direction of the landing strip where the Learjet that had brought them to the island had been turned and sat waiting at the end of the runway. This was standard practice for the aircraft and its crew, acting under orders from Lorcan Chernak. He had the plane always ready for departure in case of emergencies, which favored Fu Chen's plans.

Behind the Chinese trio the gunfire increased. It didn't involve them, so Fu Chen and his bodyguards ignored it. They reached the plane. The boarding steps were down. One of the

Chinese bodyguards went up the steps and inside the jet, Fu Chen following, the second bodyguard close behind. Fu Chen went directly to the flight deck where his bodyguard was holding a pistol on the flight crew.

Fu Chen heard the sound of the steps being retracted and the hatch being closed. He smiled at the flight crew.

"We can go now. Prepare to leave."

The copilot protested angrily. "No one uses this plane without Mr. Chernak's express approval."

Fu Chen glanced at the pilot, with an embarrassed expression on his face. "Can I ask something? Is it possible for you to fly this aircraft on your own?"

The pilot nodded. "Of course."

Fu Chen said something to his bodyguard. The Chinese turned his gun on the copilot and fired a single 9 mm round into the man's skull. The pilot stared as his companion went to the floor, his head a bloody mess.

"Back to my original request?" Fu Chen asked.

The pilot nodded and took his seat at the controls. The bodyguard sat in the copilot's seat, his pistol held on the pilot as he began his start-up procedure. The second bodyguard dragged the dead man away. As the Lear's engines began to power up, Fu Chen nodded in satisfaction.

"What course do I set?" the pilot asked.

"Return us to Athens," Fu Chen said. He turned and left the flight deck. He settled in one of the comfortable leather seats, his second bodyguard sitting across from him. "As soon as we are in the air, Teng, you may bring me a drink. I see no reason not to enjoy the flight."

CHAPTER THIRTY-FOUR

Bolan's objectives were clear in his mind. Make contact with and eliminate the ongoing threat that Nevski and Chernak presented. As long as they were willing to locate and supply WMDs to individuals or organizations capable of using them, the arms dealers were as guilty as the perpetrators. They shared the guilt of death and suffering with every bullet they sold. Nevski had willingly sold canisters of ZK386 to Razihra with little conscious thought as to the consequences. His prime motivation had been hard cash. The Russian's lack of conscience marked him for Bolan-style retribution. Nevski's blooming partnership with Lorcan Chernak, with the pair willing and intent to supply Razihra with nuclear materials, did little to enhance their reputations as far as Bolan was concerned. The Russians were seeing a future golden with opportunity. That wasn't what Bolan had in mind for the pair. No lesser in its vileness was the other side of their business—the trafficking in human lives. Bolan hadn't forgotten that, nor was he likely to when he considered the young woman working undercover within Chernak's mob.

Kira Tedesko was in the middle of Chernak's mob. Willing, maybe, but that didn't put her above being hurt—or worse. If her deception was exposed, she was dead.

He let his train of thought drift away as he crossed to the front of the villa, catching sight of a gunner edging around a partway open French window. Sunlight glinted on the barrel of an SMG. Bolan turned aside, his Uzi racking up into the firing position as the hardman leaned out to lock on his elusive target. Bolan triggered the Uzi, feeling the Israeli assault weapon jerk in his hands as it jacked out a hard burst of 9 mm slugs. The leading edge of the French window blew apart in a haze of splintered wood and shards of glass. The gunner stumbled into view, the right side of his torso and chest punctured by the slugs. Bolan hit him with a second burst, the force spinning the guy half around, blood welling from the bullet wounds and spurting from a severed artery in his neck. He fell forward, his weapon spilling from his hands. The Executioner moved forward, kicking the splintered French window aside and ducking as he entered the room. An autoweapon opened up from the far side of what turned out to be an enclosed swimming pool. The spray of shots hammered the wall inches from Bolan as he went inside. He dropped, firing from the hip, his aim true as he picked up on the figure opposite. The moving gunman was hit in the hip and lower body. The impact tipped him off his feet and he crashed onto the gleaming tiles that bordered the pool, blood spidering out from beneath him. His SMG clattered nosily on the tiles.

Bolan saw the opening on the far side of the pool that led into the villa proper and ran around the perimeter. The man he had just put down raised himself on one arm, clawing for a handgun holstered beneath his expensively tailored blazer. He dragged out a heavy-caliber revolver and swung it in Bolan's direction. The soldier might have cut him some slack if the guy had stayed down, but he had dealt himself back into the game, unfortunately with a bad hand. The Uzi crackled briefly, the sound echoing around the pool area with a harsh edge to it. The fatally hit guy arched over, his head punched open by Bolan's final volley. Dripping blood, he missed his balance and slid over the edge of the pool and into the still water. He made barely a splash as he hit the surface and sank.

Reaching the far side of the pool, Bolan approached the arched exit, which brought him into a wide room dotted with plants and chaise longues. The ceiling was a curve of toughed glass that let in the heat of the sun, turning the air warm and heavy with the scent of the lush flowers mingled in with the green foliage. Bolan saw stairs across from him that led into the main body of the villa. He sprinted across and mounted the stairs. As he stepped onto the upper level he saw a team of gunners materialize from the passage ahead. Beyond the gunmen he saw a tight group moving away—one of them a woman with long dark hair.

Kira.

Bolan had no intention of losing sight of her. He snatched a grenade from his combat vest and pulled the pin. He took a short count then lobbed the grenade in the direction of the armed guards, quickly stepping back into the cover of a plaster alcove. The guards scattered as the grenade bounced along the floor. Then it was in among them. The blast tossed the men like limp rag dolls, the shrapnel tearing into vulnerable flesh. The moment the fragmentation load had stopped flying Bolan moved out, skirting the dead and the dying, and trailed the retreating group.

The soldier rounded a corner of the wide passage. The group he was closing in on had reached a short rise of wide marble steps leading to a pair of high carved doors. He had no difficulty recognizing his quarry: Nevski and his close aide, Lem Kirov. Chernak's red hair marked him clearly. A few steps behind was Max Lubin, his left hand wrapped protectively around the waist of a dark-haired female as he hurried her away from the perceived threat.

Lorcan Chernak pushed to the front, reaching out to tap in a code number on the keypad. The high doors began to swing open.

Lem Kirov, his face set in an angry scowl, turned to check behind and saw Bolan. He called out something that made the whole group follow his gaze, and dragged a gleaming pistol from beneath his jacket, firing in Bolan's direction. The single shot came close. The soldier dropped to one knee, leveling his Uzi. He triggered a short burst that caught Kirov in the chest, spinning him, the pistol flying from his fingers. The spread of the burst sent a couple of 9 mm slugs off target. They caught Anatoly Nevski in the right upper arm, tearing at soft flesh and spraying cloth shreds and bloody flesh into the air. Nevski gave a startled yell, breaking his stride. He fumbled for the weapon he carried on his hip, managing to get the pistol free from the holster. He started to turn, then fell back under the heavy burst of Uzi fire that came from another direction. Bolan threw a quick glance and saw Amir Fayed standing in an open doorway, his Uzi jacking out the 9 mm slugs coring into Nevski.

As the Russian went down, spitting blood, Chernak stepped through the high doors and out of sight. Bolan moved to follow, his attention diverted as Max Lubin crouched and snatched up the weapon Kirov had dropped. He angled the muzzle up and fired in Fayed's direction. The Iranian slumped against the door frame, his left side bloody. Bolan swung his Uzi in Lubin's direction, staying his finger as he realized Lubin was too close to Kira for a safe shot. Whatever Bolan had been considering became redundant when the woman made her own move, catching Lubin unaware. Gone was the sweet, attentive young woman who hung on his every word.

In her place was a fast-moving spitfire who launched a crippling blow that snapped his head back, shattering teeth and turning his mouth into a bloody mush. Lubin missed his footing and fell, his dazed senses trying to comprehend what had just happened. He still had the pistol in his hand and turned it on Tedesko. It was the worst thing he could have done. Her right foot lashed out, kicking the weapon from his hand, breaking fingers in the process. She leaned forward and dug her fingers into his hair, yanked his head back and drove her knee into his face. Lubin's features were reduced to a bloody mask and he fell back, sprawling across the marble steps. He twisted onto his stomach, trying to push himself upright. He didn't even hear the single shot that drove a 9 mm slug into the back of his skull and laid him back down onto the marble steps.

"Cooper," Tedesko said. "I might have known it was you when everything started exploding out there."

Bolan joined her. "Valentine said I might need to keep you out of trouble."

"Did he now. Looks like you were both wrong."

Bolan reached Fayed. "Amir?"

"I am all right. Razihra is dead. Cooper, don't let Chernak get clear. Go."

Bolan had realized the Uzi was empty. He didn't waste time reloading. Dropping the SMG, he took out the Beretta, flicked the selector for 3-round bursts, then headed for the door that had let Chernak slip away.

Bolan turned to go, catching Tedesko's eye as he passed her.

"Be careful," she said.

Bolan stood at the high doors. Over his shoulder he said, "Amir, hit that yellow button now."

LORCAN CHERNAK ENTERED INTO the low-ceilinged room that housed his data bank and communications center. The air-conditioned room was dominated by the curving bank of computers and peripherals. The soft hum of the equipment normally soothed him, but at this moment Chernak was in a state of mental confusion. From the moment the first explosion had heralded the demise of his prized vessel and the *New Enterprise* had listed, crabbing her way in toward the jetty with smoke and fire rising from the sleek hull, Chernak had envisaged a sudden downturn in his fortunes. His ordered world of business, his great wealth and the protection he had around him, all faded into nothingness under the crackle of autofire. He had no idea who was behind the attack.

Rivals?

He had rivals, but for the most part they were people he worked with rather than enemies. Bartering went on between the dealers when one was able to provide an item someone else required for a client. There was always a middle ground to be reached where everyone was satisfied, and Chernak had never had more than the odd disagreement with his business rivals.

If not rival dealers, who else would launch a strike against him, on his own island? He had an understanding with the Greeks. He paid the area customs officials a high gratuity to be left alone, and as long as he doled out the money he was allowed his privacy. He discounted any form of military intervention from the Greek military. Chernak had solid contacts there and had done business with them in the past. Of course there was always a government policy shift that might have rescinded any earlier agreement, but he felt that was doubtful. Any regime needed its covert means of acquiring arms, for whatever reason. Chernak had a policy of never asking questions, no matter what a client wanted. Probing suggested he might disapprove. Whether he did or not he wouldn't show that disapproval. Money was money, after all, and it didn't matter to Chernak where it came from, who it came from, or the possible use of the purchase.

So the nagging doubt still plagued him—until the tall man in black entered the room, pistol in his hand, his eyes fixed on Chernak. From descriptions he had received via Nevski and Kirov, and earlier conversations with Razihra the man confronting him was the American Cooper, the man who had created so much chaos with Razihra's plans. Chernak was curious about the man, and now that he found himself face-to-face he could understand why he had been able to hand out such widespread destruction. Just looking at the man Chernak felt the powerful presence, the commanding aura that surrounded him. The blue eyes scrutinizing Chernak were ice chips. They gave little away except to make Chernak realize he would receive little sympathy from Cooper. He had been targeted. Set on his course and undeterred, Cooper wouldn't stop until his mission was accomplished.

Chernak became aware of the silence that had fallen beyond the com room. Behind Cooper the high doors were almost closed and there was no visible movement. It made Chernak nervous. Despite the cool air in the room he felt sweat beading his face.

"Do I get a chance to walk away?"

"About the same as those you kill."

"I have never taken a human life."

"The weapons you trade for cash? They kill. Your finger is on every trigger."

Chernak managed a choked laugh. "You can't use a tenuous link like that to judge me."

"I can and I do. But let's talk about your other business. The human trafficking. Deny you're involved in that. The young women you take off the streets and ship across the world. Remember them, Chernak? You treat them like animals. Sell them to be abused and destroyed. Go ahead, tell me I have that wrong, too."

"He can't," a quiet voice said.

Chernak looked beyond Bolan and saw the young woman who had been with Lubin for the past several weeks.

"You bitch…"

"If I am, it's being close to your kind that made me one."

Chernak felt the room close in on him. He looked around and realized there was no way out. Cooper and the woman stood between him and the door.

"We could make a deal," he said, and realized immediately the hollow desperation in his words. But he found he was unable to stop. The pleas tumbled from his lips. Right then he would have offered anything to stay his execution.

He failed to realize his vast wealth, his possessions, meant nothing. The decision had already been made. His guile deserted him. His threats to bring in his high-priced lawyers had no effect. He backed away and came up against the edge of the desk that held his data banks. The contacts high and low. Telephone numbers and Internet profiles. The global network that held together his supply and demand details. It had become useless. All that carefully collated and stored information was going to get him nothing.

If only he could have…

His final thought failed to materialize. Lorcan Chernak was still scrambling to unholster his Walther PPK when the triburst from Bolan's 93-R delivered the final verdict and blew his head apart.

I am not their judge.

I am their judgment.

I am their executioner.

"YOU NEEDN'T HAVE GONE to all this trouble," Tedesko said. "If you wanted to see me, all you had to do was call."

"I'll remember next time."

"My intel got through to Seminov? That's why you're here?"

"Partly. I was on another mission and yours overlapped. Same people, different reason."

She came to stand beside him, scanning the computer setup. "I expect you were after his arms contacts."

"And the Iranian. Razihra. Long story, Kira. I'll bring you up to speed later."

"Are you going to download all this to your people?"

Bolan nodded. "Leo will be able to access what he needs."

"What about your Iranian friend?"

"Fayed? He got what he came for. Razihra."

"I sense a *but* in there somewhere."

"We won this battle but the war isn't over."

Tedesko smiled. "When is it ever over, Cooper?"

Bolan didn't answer that. He didn't need to. The war, his War Everlasting, defined itself. It went on. He followed and he would keep following, because it was what he did. What he *had* to do.

Ben Sharon's team arrived to find a strange calm over Lazos. No resistance. The few survivors from Chernak's security force were huddled together watching the still burning ship wedged into the wrecked jetty. Sharon made sure the area was secured, then made his way inside the silent villa, making a cursory examination of the dead before he went to locate Matt Cooper. He found him in Chernak's data room, talking over a satellite phone to his people in the States. Bolan raised a hand in recognition when he saw the MOSSAD agent. There was a dark-haired young woman with Bolan. Sharon knew she would be the undercover operative Kira Tedesko. After completing his call Bolan joined Sharon.

"Left anything for us?" Sharon asked.

Bolan indicated the computer setup. "It's all in there, Ben. My people have already downloaded the data for their own use. You can do the same for MOSSAD."

"Will we be pleased?"

. Bolan grinned. "I have a feeling you will."

"Anyone missing from the lineup?"

"Only Capstone, the hitter who took down Baresh and

Gordeno. I figure him to be the one behind the killing of undercover CIA agent Carl Marchesse."

"He was the one who brought you into this, wasn't he?"

Bolan nodded. "Capstone won't be forgotten. His day's coming."

"That sounds personal."

"Sometimes it is, Ben."

HE STOOD IN SEMIDARKNESS, only a small light on the desk illuminating the images laid out in front of him. They were not the clearest or sharpest pictures, but they showed the face in enough detail for Victor Capstone to be able to identify the man. They had been rescued from a surveillance tape, one of a number installed in Ayatollah Razihra's villa in Iran. Transferred to photo images, the pictures had been forwarded to Razihra, then to Anatoly Nevski. The Russian had sent the images to Capstone, along with a note informing him the appropriate fee had already been deposited to Capstone's private account. Another assignment. One with a degree of personal attachment from Razihra and Nevski. They wanted this man dead very badly. The twist was that both Razihra and Nevski were dead themselves now, along with Chernak. It made no difference to Capstone. He had accepted the contract and he would honor it. No matter how long it took. He studied the image of the man in black, armed and dangerous. He realized that he had a challenge ahead. Here was someone worthy of his talents. Stalking his quarry this time would be extremely interesting.

"Start looking over your shoulder, Cooper," he said. "I'm coming after you."

TAKE 'EM FREE

2 action-packed novels plus a mystery bonus

NO RISK

NO OBLIGATION TO BUY

GE07

JAKE STRAIT

TWIST OF CAIN

BY FRANK RICH

Jake Strait has been
hired by one of the rich
and powerful to find an
elusive serial killer, who
is handy with a nail gun
and is a collector of
body parts. Except
Jake Strait has been
set up from the start.

**Available in October
wherever books
are sold.**